I0760945

Valkyrie

THE RELUCTANT QUEEN

VALKYRIE: ASCENSION OF THE NINE REALMS BOOK ONE

MELISSA A. CRAVEN

The Reluctant Queen

Valkyrie: Ascension of the Nine Realms Book 1

Copyright © May 2, 2022

By: Melissa A. Craven

Midnight Hour Studio INC

Atlanta, Georgia

All rights reserved. Printed in the United States of America. No part of this book may be used or reproduced in any manner whatsoever without written permission except in the case of brief quotations embodied in critical articles or reviews.

This book is a work of fiction. Names, characters, businesses, organizations, places, events and incidents either are the product of the author's imagination or are used fictitiously. Any resemblance to actual persons, living or dead, events, or locales is entirely coincidental.

For more information contact: **Hello@Melissaacraven.com** or visit the author's website at Melissaacraven.com

Cover design by: Seventh Star

Edited by: Carrie Harris and Chase Night

Proofreading by: Caitlin Haines

Interior design by: BooklyStyle

ISBN: 9798815407794

First edition for print May 2, 2022

Printed in the United States of America

To my Family
For realizing I would have made
a terrible adulty-adult

NORTHERN KINGDOMS

VALSGARD
Home Of The Valkyries

MANAHEIM
Home Of The Druids

ÚLFAHEIM
Home Of The Berserkers

VÖSTLAND
Home Of The Warders

JÖTNALAND
Home Of The Jötnar

THE NINE REALMS

JÖTNALAND

ÚLFAHEIM

VÖSTLAND

Southern Kingdoms

Northern Kingdoms

The Fjords

Byrn Bay

Eyja Island

The Restless S

Armur Mountains

Citadel

VALSGARD

Vahland Reach

Queen's Bay

Broken Isles

Dyre Forest

The Skye Sea

MANAHEIM

Andmur

Druid Temple

CHAPTER 1

"It's not going to kill you." Morgana fussed with the yards of fabric threatening to choke me to death.

"You don't know that." I glared at my best friend.

"It's just a dress, Thea." She rolled her eyes.

"You know perfectly well what this dress represents." I sank to my knees on the aged wooden floor of my bedroom, the elaborate ball gown fanning out around me. I'd spent most of the morning wondering if tonight's events might actually kill me.

Pasha, the white skýja leopard I raised from a cub, sniffed at the sea of fabric separating us. With a low growl, the big cat turned up her nose at the dress and leaped onto the window seat, preferring to bathe herself in the warm sunshine rather than bother figuring out what had her Lady so distressed.

Today was a special day for me—Princess Alithea, Queen Heir of Valsgard. My First Ascension would take place tonight, a ceremony that would mark my sixteenth year and officially set me on the path of becoming Queen of the Valkyries … someday. It would also see me betrothed to a stranger before the evening was over.

"You're ready for this, Thea." Princess Morgana moved to place a silver winged tiara on my brow. The black sapphires glittered against my dark hair in the fading sunlight streaming through the windows.

"I will never be ready for this." I accepted Morgana's outstretched hand and stood, smoothing a hand over the skirt of my ball gown. "Not even a little bit." I admired the dress in the tall mirror occupying the corner of my room. I was not a fancy dress kind of princess—I was a leather-wearing, training-with-my-shield-maidens kind of princess. But this dress was a spectacular work of art. Yards of black and silver silk flowed gracefully to my feet, where a train of fine silver feathers brushed the floor. Layers of intricate silver lace and beadwork covered the bodice, and floor length sleeves fell in a cascade from my elbows.

"I know we've dreaded this day since we were kids." Morgana paused to give me a reassuring smile. "But you look beautiful." The Druid princess stood behind me, her tawny skin painted with golden Druidic symbols was a stark contrast to my pale, unadorned complexion.

"You are still a kid." I elbowed her playfully. Despite the three-year age difference between us, thirteen-year-old Morgana had been my best friend since she was an infant and there was no one I trusted more—except perhaps my elder sister, Sylvanna.

"You *will* get through this." Morgana leaned against me, admiring our reflection in the mirror.

"I never thought this day would actually happen." I turned toward my best friend with tears in my eyes. "I always thought Mother would eventually hear me—that she would see it doesn't have to be this way. But she's so traditional." My hands fluttered up to my tiara, fussing with the weight of it on my brow. For a moment I couldn't catch my breath.

"Relax, Thea." Morgana squeezed my hands, forcing me to breathe deeply and exhale with her. "Today is nothing more than your First Ascension." Her eyes shone brightly with tears, but she smiled through them. "It's a happy day to mark your sixteenth year. Don't even think about the betrothal. That's not important today. You won't have to marry this boy for at least two more years. You have time still."

"For what?" I turned to pace the length of my room, twisting my hands together. "To get to know him before I'm forced to marry the boy my mother's council has chosen for me? I'll never be okay with that, Morgana."

"I know. But you have two years to show your mother how much you oppose this marriage *after* you prove to her you've tried to meet her halfway. She's always said you'll feel differently once you meet him."

I whirled around to face my life-long friend. "You know that's not what this is about!"

"Of course, *I* know," Morgana soothed, wrapping her arm around my waist. "But your mother needs to see you try first. Let's just get through today and then you can spend the next two years showing her that nothing has changed. Maybe then she'll finally understand just how opposed you are to this archaic tradition. The Chosen Sons might have been necessary a thousand years ago when your numbers were few, but Valsgard is stronger than it has ever been."

I nodded, biting my bottom lip. "But what if she never understands?" Even Morgana didn't grasp that this went far beyond my aversion to the betrothal traditions. It wasn't that I didn't want to marry a stranger—I didn't want to be queen. Period.

A soft knock came at the door. "Thea?" A little blond girl poked her head into my bedroom. "Oh, Princess." She bobbed a quick curtsy. "You look like a vision of the Mother herself."

"Anika, you don't have to call me Princess." I bent to talk to the ten-year-old shield maiden in training. "You know we're like family." We *were* family. It was the secret everyone knew but no one acknowledged: Nika was my cousin.

"I know, but you look just like the Mother Valkyrie from the story books." Nika fingered the feathers adorning my ball gown. "You think I'll ever get to wear a dress so fine?"

I smiled at the little girl, envying her more than she would ever realize. Nika would have so many choices I would never have. "Did they send you to find me?" I took the girl's hand.

"Oh yes! They're ready for you, Thea."

"Here we go." Morgana took my free hand. "Time to meet the dozen boys raised to become your perfect consort."

I stood at the threshold of the palace ballroom with the loyal Pasha purring at my side. Sinking my hands into her thick fur, I drew strength from her calm spirit. Part of me—a huge part—wanted to run and never look back. But a smaller part knew I owed this to my mother. My queen. It was my duty to our people, and I was raised, above all else, to do my duty.

"Don't let me fall, girl." I scratched between Pasha's ears, and I swore the cat understood me. She had a way of looking at me sometimes, a depth of wisdom shining through her icy blue eyes.

"Ready, Princess?" A handsome young gentleman offered his arm. "I am to escort you, your Majesty." He gave a curt bow.

I stared into the fathomless golden eyes of a predator, at a loss for words. He was slightly taller than me, with a lean muscular build and long brown hair swept back at the temples in fresh braids, his angular face expressionless. He was a Berserker—an enemy of the Valkyries—making his presence here more than unusual. The Berserkers and Valkyries had a long history of bad blood between them. They were fierce in battle, but perilously unpredictable. For those with the Berserker nature, there was nothing more dangerous than a man or woman lost to the spirit-beast inside. To have one here—escorting the princess on the night of her First Ascension—was nothing more than a well-timed political move on Mother's part. Everyone was a pawn in the queen's court. Even her sisters and daughters.

I took his arm, bare to the shoulder in his Berserker's attire of leather vest and tight breeches of the finest linen. Handsome though he was, there was something menacing about his presence, as though he disliked me on sight.

"Your name?" I turned to face the grand double doors of the ballroom, kicking the hem of my dress as I moved. Two attendants scurried behind me to straighten the train.

"Does it matter, Princess?" His gruff voice set me on edge. "You have much on your mind, no doubt." He turned defiant eyes on me. "It's not every day one gets to ruin the lives of eleven young men with a single choice."

Anger surged through my body at his insolence. "That may be, but you must remember, sir, it is not *my* choice." I studied the man beside me. His sun-browned arm was like stone under my hand.

"What brings a Berserker to the Valkyrie court on such an auspicious night?"

"I suppose you do, your Majesty. You are the reason we're all here."

Perplexed, I noted the sneer he couldn't seem to hide. The man clearly despised me, yet I was certain I'd never laid eyes on him.

"Would that I could have it otherwise." I turned my attention to one of my silent attendants, who gave a nod. It was time.

"Announcing Her Royal Highness, Princess Alithea Viktory Skuld Ahlstrom. She Who is Becoming. Queen Heir of Valkyries." The court herald struck a gong just before the double doors opened, allowing the crowd below their first look at their next royal vessel in all her finery. Gazing across the sea of strange faces, I forgot all about the surly man at my side. I suddenly felt more self-conscious than I ever had. I was accustomed to the Valkyrie courtiers, but tonight there were nobles from all the Northern Kingdoms in attendance. Druids, Warders, enormous Jötnar, and even a few more Berserkers had come together to celebrate my First Ascension.

Gasps rang out across the ballroom as I made my way down the white marble stairs on the Berserker's arm, praying to the blessed Mother of all Valkyries I wouldn't fall and break my neck in this stupid dress. Pasha padded along beside me, showing me up with her graceful stride.

Pausing at the bottom of the stairs, I stepped away from my escort—his job was complete for the evening—and dipped into a curtsy, properly greeting my guests. I knew my role and played it well, but I wanted to scream at everyone present that it was all a farce. I'd spent my life pretending to be a good princess, but that was just it. I was pretending—I wasn't truly fit for this job. Deep in my soul I knew I'd make a terrible queen. But no one ever listened to my protests. The power of the gods had chosen me as Queen Heir when I was just a child and I had lost any semblance of power I may have had to choose my own destiny.

My heart was like a stone in my chest as I approached my mother's throne at the apex of the ballroom. Sweeping into a low bow this time, I murmured my greeting. "Good evening, Mother. Thank you for organizing such a fine celebration." Pasha sat back on her haunches, eyeing the queen with her startling blue eyes.

"Nothing is too good for my daughters," Queen Brenhilde

Ahlstrom said. She stood, tall and imposing, with her golden blond hair falling to her waist. "Rise and join me, my darling. You too, Pasha," the queen added in amusement. She guided me to the empty throne placed beside hers for this occasion. Pasha made herself comfortable on the black velvet pillow between us.

I had never sat on a throne before, and I felt silly now as I slid back into the uncomfortable seat that left my legs dangling several inches above the floor. It reminded me of a moment from my childhood: I was seven and Morgana was four, and we were playing dress up in the queen's closet. My small feet had disappeared in Mother's shoes. Growing up, I could never quite get that image out of my head. I had impossible shoes to fill. For most of my life, ascending was a vague something I would have to do someday. Becoming Queen Heir when I was twelve was the first big step toward that destiny. But today was *someday*.

"Please return to your dancing," the queen announced, taking her place on her throne.

The quartet started up again and the ladies and gentlemen of the court swept around the ballroom. Their laughter reached my ears as I watched them dancing, light on their feet and without a care in the world. None of them had to sacrifice their lives for the crown. At sixteen, I didn't really know what I wanted out of life. I only knew without a doubt that I wanted the freedom to make my own choices. Unfortunately, for a Queen Heir of Valsgard, most of my choices had been made before I was born.

"Relax, Alithea. This isn't your funeral." The queen cast a disapproving look at me.

"Cut the child some slack, Brenna," Grandmother Agertha said from her place among the female royals, seated just behind our thrones. "It's a big day for our girl; she's allowed to be nervous. I seem to recall on the day of your First Ascension you couldn't string together a decent sentence until it was over."

"That's because you used your healing magic to calm me down. A little too well, I might add." Mother chuckled at the memory.

"I could offer you the same, Thea." Grandmother cocked her head, a mischievous smile lighting her eyes.

"Thank you, Gram." I smiled over my shoulder at my feisty grandmother. But my problem wasn't just nerves. Underneath it all I felt … betrayed. Those closest to me knew how I felt about the betrothal to one of the Chosen Sons—and becoming queen—yet here we were. I was facing my worst nightmare simply because it was tradition for the strongest of the queen's daughters to marry the most powerful and virile young man across all the realms.

I watched my older sister Sylvanna dancing with Princess Morgana and the other young nobles of the court. I envied their carefree laughter. In so many ways, Sylvi was the perfect princess. Mother's eldest child had the wisdom and poise to rule, but like most of the court, the power of the gods overlooked my bright sister, choosing me instead as the vessel that would funnel the power to all the Nine Realms once I ascended. Without a strong vessel, what was left of our broken world would wither and die, like it should have at the final battle of the last age.

Drums sounded from the palace grounds, echoing through the open doors to the fragrant gardens. I tried to swallow, but with the beating of the drums, my heart seemed to have seized in my chest. It was time.

"Breathe, my darling," Mother whispered, gently squeezing my hand. "They will bring the young men to greet you first before my council announces who they've chosen for you. Just remember, today is about meeting the one. The others don't matter."

My mouth went dry as I nodded, unable to find the words to tell my mother just how much this crushed me. Of course they all mattered. None of them had been given a choice either.

Just as they had when my sister was born, sixteen years ago the queen's council selected thirty-six young boys and infants from the noble families across Valsgard and the kingdoms beyond—all prized princes, dukes, lords, and first sons. Sylvi's Chosen Sons were either dismissed or selected for me when I was named Queen Heir. My potential consorts had spent their lives training in a secret mountain fortress of Vahland Reach for the chance to become the perfect husband and companion to the future ruler of Valsgard and High Queen of the Nine Realms. To anticipate my every need and desire. Over time, the council had whittled their numbers down to twelve, dismissing those deemed unfit to stand at my side.

A wizened old Valkyrie in royal blue robes made his way across the crowded ballroom, his unsteady gait matching the beat of the drums that announced his arrival. A line of strong young men followed. Heights and features varied—particularly among the few Jötnar Sons who were broader and taller than any other men of the Nine Realms. All were handsome and fit. Each was dressed in black trousers and a fine brocade vest of blue and gold.

They lined up in front of me, beaming at me with identical expressions of adoration I hadn't earned. They didn't even know me, yet they were chosen to serve me and give up whatever titles they might have inherited otherwise. I imagined how they must hate me behind those perfect smiles. Their torsos were bare aside from the open vests, boldly displaying the brands that marked them as consorts in training. Most wore the brand on shoulder or chest. A black circle the size of my palm enclosed the symbol for the house of Ahlstrom: a winged helmet encircled with a ring of power and the initials AVSA across the helm. My initials.

Bile rose in my throat and someone slipped a cool glass of wine into my hand. I took a fortifying sip, but it tasted like vinegar in my mouth. I knew the boys had all been marked in some way when they were chosen, but I never realized they were branded like cattle. And with my initials. It was barbaric and shame welled within me at what had been done to them in my name.

As the old master gave a speech and introduced each of my prospects by name, I failed to hear any of it. "What happens to the others?" I quietly demanded of my mother.

"Others?" The queen smiled absently. "The ones not selected?"

"Yes, what happens to them?"

"They leave, darling. Most of them will go into the military or return to their kingdoms to pursue other lives."

"But they have an everlasting mark to remind them and their future wives of this insanity?"

"Wives? No, Thea. The prospects not chosen will never marry. How could they when they've been passed over by the Queen Heir?"

"Passed over? You make it sound like I've personally discarded them as trash, careless of ruining their chances at happiness, when you know very well how opposed I am to this archaic nonsense." My voice rose above the drone of the old man who had trained these boys since they were children.

"We shall talk of this later. You are making a scene."

I wondered what the queen would do if I really did make a scene, telling the whole court just what I thought of this practice.

I couldn't bring myself to meet their eyes. Eleven lives would essentially end tonight and there was nothing I could do about it.

As the master finished his speech, the prospects knelt before the queen's throne, bowing their heads in silence. They were like puppets on a string, and I wondered what it would be like to spend my life with someone trained to give in to my every need. It would drive me mad.

"Relax, Thea," my cheeky grandmother whispered behind me. "Think of them as handsome young stallions to father your future daughters. You can fall in love with whomever you please once you've given the realm a few heirs." She waggled her dark eyebrows for emphasis, returning to her bottomless glass of wine.

Gram was right, in her own weird way. But I would never erase the image of that brand from my mind, knowing so many lives were ruined because of me.

"We beg of the council: please reveal whom you have chosen as a worthy consort for our Queen Heir," Mother intoned in her perfect, queenly voice.

Elder Leda Vollan approached the throne, dipping into a low bow. "Thank you, your Majesties. It pleases me to announce the chosen consort who will be betrothed to Princess Alithea this very evening at the stroke of midnight."

I was either going to pass out or vomit. Maybe both. After years of begging to be heard, this was really happening, and I was powerless to stop it. Nervous laughter escaped my throat and I slapped a hand over my mouth, much to the amusement of the anxious court. I was Queen Heir, for crying out loud! One day I would be Queen of Valsgard and High Queen of all the Nine Realms. How could I be so powerless?

The echoing vibration of a gong jerked me from my thoughts, shaking me to my core.

"Fiske Rylund," Elder Leda announced in a clear, firm voice that was a death knell for me.

Those not selected were quickly whisked away, vanishing from the ballroom as if they'd never existed. The handsome young man who approached me now was familiar. I'd grown up with him in the Citadel with the other noble children of the court—before he went away to school. And then I only saw him on his brief visits home. Fiske Ryland was the son of Elder Sonje Rylund, head of the Queen's council. And I loathed him.

Fiske bent his tall, lithe frame and knelt before me, bowing his sandy blond head. "It will be my life's greatest honor to serve as your husband and loyal companion. Together we will give birth to a new generation of queens to carry on the Ahlstrom dynasty for ages to come."

I stared, aghast, at the boy before me. He still had the gangly appearance of youth, not yet grown into the man he would one day become. This had to be some kind of joke. Fiske Rylund was the most spineless weakling I'd ever met. How could Mother's council have chosen him? How could this ... sycophant be the strongest young man in all the Nine Realms?

"Thea, darling," Mother prodded me to respond.

"Th-thank you, Lord Fiske," I stuttered, glancing around the ballroom for help, but I was alone in this. "Er, you can stop bowing now."

Fiske stood in a fluid, graceful motion. an indulgent smile illuminating his handsome face. Kind blue eyes begged me to accept this, to accept him. "May I have this dance, your Royal Highness?" He held a hand out to me and I had no choice but to take it, symbolically accepting not only the dance but the stifling life of duty that simple gesture represented.

CHAPTER 2

My footsteps thundered across the Vahland bridge to the Citadel, my dark skirts billowing behind me like a storm cloud I couldn't outrun. Pasha's growls chased away anyone who dared try to stop me, but it wasn't like I could actually escape.

The crash of turbulent waves in the Queens Bay sounded far below as I rushed through the gates of the mountain fortress, knowing full well the guards would betray me the moment the queen sent someone looking for me. I didn't have much time.

"Alithea Ahlstrom, where do you think you're going?"

Crap. I slid to a halt on the stone steps leading up to the Citadel entrance, Pasha coming to rest on her haunches beside me. "Aunt Astrid, uh … hi." I should have known the Queen of the Citadel would be on duty tonight. It was my aunt's job to protect the city of Vahland Reach and their high queen. While everyone else celebrated, Astrid and her shield maidens kept watch over the city.

"Hi, yourself." Astrid made her way down the steps and draped an arm over my shoulders. "You're here now. I suppose they won't miss you for a few minutes longer." She guided me up to the entrance hall. "You wouldn't be trying to escape your own ball, would you?" She studied me with clear blue eyes that seemed to see right through me, down to the thoughts that plagued me this night.

"No. Not exactly." I sighed. "I just needed a quiet minute to think."

"I can understand that." Astrid moved to sit on an elaborate iron bench in the grand hall, patting the indigo and gold cushion beside her. "Come, niece, there is room enough here for you and your beautiful dress."

Where the palace was warm and inviting, the Citadel was cold and dark, but I'd spent the happiest days of my childhood behind the protection of the Citadel walls. To me, it was home in a way the palace never had been.

With an irritable sigh, I sat beside my aunt, tucking my voluminous skirts under the bench. Pasha sank to the cool floor, rolling onto her back to scratch against the rough stones.

"Tell Aunt Astrid what's bothering you. Though I can hazard a guess." She nudged me playfully.

I leaned forward, bracing my elbows against my knees like I would had I dressed in my usual leathers. I got a face full of silk. Shoving it aside, I let my guard down. "I just always thought if I really had to do this, I could find a way to like the person I was betrothed to."

"Thea, you can't have given the boy ten minutes yet. How do you know you will never like him?"

"It's Fiske Ryland." I wrinkled my nose in disgust. All I could remember of the boy I'd grown up with was a lot of whining and complaining about the games I used to play with the other noble children in the Citadel gardens. He would kiss up to me and Sylvi one moment and the next he would instruct us on what proper princesses should and shouldn't do.

"Ah. I can see how that might be a bit of a disappointment for you, but it's been years since you've seen each other. He's not a child anymore, Thea—and neither are you. You'll need to get to know each other all over again."

"It's not fair, Aunt Astrid." I leapt to my feet, clenching my fists as I paced across the dark entrance hall.

"That's one way to look at it." Astrid stood, her simple white robes fluttering around her boot-clad feet. "Or you could try to make the best of it. Talk to your betrothed and tell him how you feel."

"He's not my betrothed yet." I flung my hands down at my sides.

"He will be within the hour. You need to figure out how to get on the same page with him and move forward as a united front, with the same interests, for the good of the people you serve. Whether those interests are romantic or more political in nature doesn't matter. You must find a way to work together."

"I know. You're right." My shoulders slumped. It all sounded so logical and cold. Not at all the future I once imagined as a little girl dreaming of becoming a queen just like my mother with a handsome king consort. Like the father I adored, who died when I was just a child.

"I will leave you to your thoughts." Astrid took my hands in hers. "Trust your instincts, Thea. You will make the right choices for yourself." She left to make her way up the stairs, joining her shield maidens as they watched over Vahland Reach from the battlements.

I stood alone in the grand hall, feeling like the cold stone walls might swallow me whole. Staring up at the vaulted ceiling, I almost wished they would.

Trust your instincts. My aunt's words echoed in my mind. I was running again before I made a conscious decision to do so. Pasha, my ever-present shadow, followed.

The more I thought about the kind of life I would have with Fiske, the harder I ran through the familiar halls of the Citadel. I could see it so clearly—a lifetime of suffocating under the weight of a loveless marriage and a life of duty where protocol would dictate my every waking moment. But tonight I still had my whole life before me and I wanted to be the author of my own destiny. I wanted to choose my path, make mistakes, and learn from them.

"What am I doing?" My hands balled into fists as I came to a halt in the queen's chamber, deep within the mountain of the Citadel. I didn't know what had led me here of all places. The torchlight bounced off the rough stone walls, casting shadows across the ancient hall. The only sound was the rustling of my ball gown and my labored breath rasping in and out of my lungs.

I should be back in the ballroom, celebrating with my family, regal and confident in the future that would be set in stone with the completion of my First Ascension ceremony at midnight when my betrothal to Fiske would be official. The clock was ticking and I was mere minutes from the future I'd spent my life running from. They were probably already looking for me.

"Why couldn't I be Astrid's heir?" I gazed around the empty chamber, looking for answers I wouldn't find among the colorful mosaics that adorned the floors and domed ceiling, depicting the rich history of the Nine Realms.

I'd asked myself that same question for years. Ever since it became clear to the court and more importantly, to the queen's council, that the power of the gods had chosen me. It was such a subtle shift in power among my female relatives who were also vessels for the power. As they grew infinitesimally weaker, I grew stronger. I didn't understand it then, but it had sealed my fate.

My heart thundered against my ribs as I paced across the chamber, stopping each time my toes touched the golden medallion marking the center of the room.

"I can do this. I can begin my ascension. It doesn't mean I have to become the queen yet." Nausea made my stomach heave at the thought of marrying Fiske in two years' time. "Mother is stronger than she has ever been. It could be years and years before I actually have to rule. It's all just ceremony now."

So why was I here? I glanced down at my feet, just brushing the edge of the golden medallion. It was engraved with the image of the first Valkyrie queen from the last age. Brenhilde Ahlstrom I, my many-times-great-grandmother, stared at me in disapproval along with the first kings and queens of the Northern Kingdoms. The Berserker king with his black stallion kindred. The Druid queen with vines clinging to her. The beautiful giantess of the Jötnar clans standing head and shoulders above the rest. And the great Warder king veiled in snow and ice among the mists of Hel. Each ruler seemed to cast judgment on me, finding me severely lacking.

"I'm sorry," my words rushed out in an anguished breath. "I'm not worthy to follow in your footsteps." I couldn't force myself to take the next step. Would it really take something this drastic to finally get through to Mother?

Behind me lay a life that would never be mine.

Ahead lay a life of infinite possibilities, but it would mean leaving everything I'd ever known. If I was brave enough to take the last step.

"You can't go dressed like that." Sylvanna's voice echoed across the cold chamber.

I closed my eyes with a sigh, grateful my sister was the first to find me. It was kind of hard to hide from Sylvi when she was a gifted seer.

"What are you talking about, Syl?" I turned to face my sister. "I have to get back to the party and prance around like this is the happiest night of my life."

Sylvi dropped a bag at my feet. "Cut the pretending. We both know today is not the happiest day of your life, but it is the day you stop being so gray all the time."

I reached out to grab my sister and pulled her into a hug. All day I had struggled with those who didn't understand, but Sylvi always got it. "I'm so scared, Syl."

"Of course you are. You're positively blue with fear and your aura is murky with indecision."

Most people thought the queen's eldest daughter was more than a little odd, but my sister saw the world in colors and light, with powerful auras and numbers only she could see and interpret. She was a seer like no other. Intelligent and far more capable of ruling as queen than I would ever be. She had always been the logical choice, and it was only a matter of time before the queen's council—and the power of the gods—would see it too. They'd all made a mistake overlooking Sylvi for her strange behavior and setting their sights on me instead.

Staring into my sister's eyes, I could see it so clearly, even if no one else could. Sylvi was the future of Valsgard, and I was the only thing standing in her way.

I lifted my hands to my throbbing head. "What do I do, Sylvi? How can I make such an impossible decision?"

"You know the right choice for you, Thea. One of these days you will find your way. You'll find balance and confidence too, but you're only sixteen. You're allowed to be turquoise for a little while." Sylvi handed me a smooth, polished lump of turquoise.

I examined the cool stone in my palm. If the rest of the Valkyrie court took the time to learn what Sylvi's colors meant, they would understand her a great deal more.

"Turquoise is the color of idealism, right?" I wrapped my fist around the stone, shaking my head. "I'm the Queen Heir. I don't get to be idealistic and frivolous. I have a duty." I heaved a great sigh of regret. I didn't want the burden of the crown; I wanted to be young and reckless.

"Everyone should have a time of freedom to figure out what color they're going to be. A future queen especially deserves that much." She took the stone from my hand and bent to tuck it into the bag she'd brought with her, which still lay at my feet.

"I don't think it's in the cards for me, sister." I ran my hands up and down my bare arms, turning back toward the palace and my imminent betrothal.

Sylvi's face fell. "You can't marry Fiske. It will destroy you."

"I don't see how I have much choice." I shivered at the memory of the brand he wore so proudly over his heart. I couldn't imagine how much that must have hurt for a child.

"He's a sweet boy, but he is not your intended." Sylvi squared her shoulders. "No matter what Mother's council has decided. For you, Fiske lacks magenta and his aura is far too purple and his spirit too yellow for the station he's been given. Besides, you've already made your decision, Thea. I'm just here to give you my blessing and a few supplies you'll need. You'll be back. And when you return, you'll find yourself settled somewhere between magenta and gold with a decidedly red aura."

"Between balance and success, with a … passionate aura?" I frowned, trying to follow my sister's language of colors.

Sylvi shrugged. Passionate maybe, but ambitious as well." She held me at arm's length. "If only Mother's council understood me as well as you do." Sylvi turned me around and began to unbutton my dress. "You can't travel in this thing."

"Where am I going?" My throat went dry. Of course, I'd thought about it. That was why I found myself in the queen's chamber now. But I couldn't actually do it. Could I? "What about Pasha?" I glanced at my childhood companion, nervously prowling the edge of the room.

"I will take care of Pasha." Sylvi helped me shed my gown's many layers, tossing me a pair of doeskin leggings and my favorite tunic. "Hurry, we don't have much time." She glanced over her shoulder, her eyes flashing opaque for a moment before they cleared to their normal ice blue. "They're coming."

I scrambled into the warm clothes, shoving my feet into my best boots as my heart raced in anticipation of what I was considering. "This is insane. Mother will kill me."

"In time she will understand." Sylvi turned me toward the medallion in the floor. "I've always said you are three, Thea. Fiske is not part of that equation. Go find your three."

I dug my heels into the floor, bracing against my sister's push. "Wait. I'm not ready, Sylvi. I can't do this." The heavy footsteps of guards sounded on the stairs. I had only seconds to decide.

"Of course you can. The Druids do it. Why not you?" Sylvi nudged me forward. "Cross the bridge, Thea. Go see all the colors and then, when you're ready, come home and tell me all about it. I'll be waiting right here when you return."

"Mother help me, am I really doing this?" I turned panicked eyes on my sister. She gazed back at me steadily, her gentle spirit and calm determination settling me.

"I love you, little sister. But this path you're on right now is not the right one. Don't let them catch you."

"I love you too, Syl," I whispered as I took the bag and heavy cloak Sylvi shoved into my hands. With a deep breath, I stepped across the medallion, leaving everything I knew behind.

CHAPTER 3

Three years later

The dead guy was hot.

Not that he was actually dead yet. But he would be in a few hours.

I kept my head down as I pulled a draft beer. Angling the frosted mug to reduce the foam, I suppressed the urge to meet his gaze. That would only freak him out and I didn't need a bar full of panicked people.

"Come on, gorgeous." He leaned over the counter. "My friends are drunken losers tonight and I could use some intelligent conversation. What time are you off?"

"It's been a long shift already." I slid the frosted mug to one of the many customers vying for my attention. "Can I get you a drink?" I tried to steer the conversation back to bartending.

"I'm DD for the night." He nodded toward his group of idiot friends, currently raising a ruckus at the pool tables.

"Poor you." I smiled, pouring a row of tequila shots for a table of giggling sorority types.

Next place can't be a college town. I moved to the end of the bar to wait on a few new arrivals. College kids wouldn't know what a decent tip was if it hit them in the face.

It had only been a few weeks since I arrived in the sleepy little Carolina beach town, but I was already scouting my next move farther up the coast, away from Wilmington. I was always on the move, never settling down in one place for long. It was the way it had to be. I liked the smaller coastal towns, especially in the off-season. A person could easily disappear in the outer banks of the Carolinas.

"How about a drink after work?" The hot-dead-guy was back again and I wanted nothing more than to lose myself in his friendly banter. But his death called to me, begging me to meet his gaze.

I closed my eyes, absently pinching the bridge of my nose to quell the tension brought on by his arrival. "Like I said, it's been a long night. I'm diving into bed face first for some serious sleep as soon as I leave here." I tried to give him a friendly but distant smile while keeping my eyes cast down at the sink full of dishes I should be washing before Kelly arrived for her shift.

"How about tomorrow? Or your next day off?" he persisted, attempting to capture my gaze. It was only natural he was drawn to me in his last hours.

I winced. He wouldn't have a tomorrow, and the last thing he needed to be doing right now was wasting what little time he had left on a total stranger. A stranger who didn't have the power to save him. No one could—when your number was up, you were out of time.

I cast a wary glance around as the strain from resisting my natural impulses threatened to me. My throat tightened and my palms itched, while sweat pooled at my back. I wouldn't be able to hold off much longer. "Why don't you go back to your friends and try to enjoy the rest of your evening?" My mesmerizing voice came out in a low, grating rasp.

He nodded slowly, blinking. "Good idea."

The boy gave me one last glassy-eyed stare before turning toward his friends. The tension in my shoulders immediately subsided. He would obey the one who had seen his death. The one who would guide his soul to the afterlife in Andlang, a place I could never enter. There was a time when my ancestors could come and go from the beyond as they pleased, but that was before the last age. The afterlife was different now.

"What's up, Thea?" Kelly ducked behind the counter, tying on an apron. "You don't look so good, girl. You've got some wicked dark circles under your eyes. When's the last time you slept?"

I swiped a palm across my face, schooling my features. I couldn't let my co-worker see too much. "Thank God you're here. Would you mind if I head out early? I have a raging headache."

A headache I wouldn't be able to shake until the dead guy met his end. I had a job to do and now that I'd seen his violent death looming on the horizon, I wouldn't be able to rest easily until my work was done.

"Sure, get some sleep, girl," Kelly said. "I've got this."

"Thanks." I cast a last glance over my shoulder at the nice guy who didn't deserve what was coming for him tonight. He was laughing with his frat-boy friends. He still had time, but I was already running out of it. I rushed to the back of the bar and out the alley exit.

The rows of historic southern downtown buildings were punctuated with creepy dark alleys lined with shady back doors and leaky dumpsters. I darted toward the alley entrance, hoping I could make it down the block to the public parking lot, but the familiar cramping of my shoulders and tightening of my eyes told me I would have to risk doing this here.

I glanced behind me, spotting a rusted old fire escape, and sprinted straight for it. With a carefully aimed jump, I latched onto the ladder to pull it down, but it didn't budge. *Even better.* No one could follow me now. I pulled myself up and quickly scaled the ladder to the rooftop. I scouted this rooftop when I first took the job at Harkers Tavern. It was the tallest structure around and it would do in a pinch.

I headed for the shadows at the back of the building, kicking off my shoes and shedding my black t-shirt along the way, grateful for the human invention of racerback sports bras. They were perfect for nights like this. I flung my hair clip to the ground, letting my long dark hair cascade down my back. As the white-hot pain of transformation cleaved my skull in two, I suppressed a shriek and collapsed, hunching over as my body buckled and my skin split from shoulder to waist.

I groaned as bones cracked and reformed and my hands and feet bent in an unnatural way. Blunt fingernails curved into sharp talons. My legs ached as the bones lengthened and hollowed, leaving me taller, lighter, and more agile. Feathers sprouted from the gashes in my back, unfurling and stretching like limbs seldom used. As my wings expanded, so did my shoulders and ribcage, lighting my body on fire. My entire being raged with the heat of my natural form. Every inch of me hurt as blood rushed through my veins and my heart threatened to burst. My breath came in great ragged gasps. It had been far too long this time.

I lay on the blacktop roof, spent, but I felt more alive than I had in months. Climbing to my feet, I trembled with the suddenness of my change. Valkyries took on their natural forms only when they had a duty to perform, a battle to fight, or for training purposes. Since coming to the human realm I'd had little need for my Valkyrie.

I rotated my head from side to side until my vision began to clear. Avian vision. It was always an adjustment. Rubbing the palm of a taloned hand over my face, I could feel the sharp angles of my cheekbones in my otherwise human face. I took a step forward on bare feet, my curved toenails clicking on the surface of the roof. The enormous weight of my wings tugged at my shoulders as I walked, raven black and silver feathers dragging behind me like a cloak.

The momentary fatigue passed as Valkyrie strength flooded my system. I flexed my wings, all six of them. My primary wings arched high over my head, unfurling with black and pewter feathers. Secondary wings moved in perfect sync with my primaries. Silver and pewter feathers stretched wide to a span of double my height. My tertiary wings pointed to the ground, falling behind me with feathers of silver and white. Retracting my massive wings, I stepped up to the edge of the building, away from the lights of the nearby boardwalk.

My dark hair fell nearly to my waist, threaded with fine black and silver feathers that blended with my wings. Among the shadows, one might think I was a human girl with incredibly long hair, so fine were my feathers. But I was not human. I was Valkyrie. And death walked in my shadow.

His soul called to me as I ran from rooftop to rooftop, barely pausing to leap the gaps between buildings. I could fly, of course, but I couldn't risk being seen in this world. Humans no longer believed in the old gods or the creatures they created to outlive them.

I was close. I could hear the steady thump of his heart and the bass beat of the music from his car down on the street. He waited at a deserted intersection for the light to turn green, his drunken buddies in the backseat still acting like fools.

After a lifetime of this, I still felt the urge to intervene, an intense desire to save him from the violent death awaiting him once he crossed into the intersection. But I also knew from experience that death would have his due. Even now I could feel him breathing down my neck from the shadows.

"Patience," I murmured into the void. If I intervened, death would get more creative and the next time it would be far worse than a quick end by car accident.

I stood at the edge of an old building, the talons of my bare feet gripping the red brick facade. I could see the large truck speeding toward the intersection, oblivious to the light changing from green to yellow. This driver was drunk, having neglected to elect a designated driver the way my charge and his friends had. Yet the sober driver would pay the ultimate price for the other driver's hubris.

My breath caught in my throat as one light turned red and another green. The gods had been cruel when they created the first Valkyries to collect the fallen from battle, sentencing me and my kind to a lifetime of service to death. Like carrion birds on a battlefield, my ancestors once had the honor of selecting the bravest of the fallen to send to the afterlife where only the greatest warriors were taken. But that was before the gods nearly destroyed my world. More than a thousand years later, the Valkyries ruled in place of the gods, yet we were still chained to death. Only now our charges weren't limited to war heroes, but included victims of violence and cruel ends as well.

The blare of horns and the crunch of metal and shattered glass brought me back to the present. I wouldn't leave the boy to die alone. His friends would live, but only I could help him now.

As I crouched to swoop down, I heard the unmistakable sound of massive wings spreading in the darkness. My blood ran cold and my spine went rigid. I didn't pause long enough to see the other Valkyrie. I turned and fled the way I'd come, leaving the boy's soul for the other to claim.

My heart raced as I flew over Harkers Sound toward Gloucester and the mainland. There was only one way off of Harkers Island by car and I couldn't risk it. I flew high enough so anyone who spotted me would think I was a bird of prey out for a late-night hunt. I couldn't go home. There was only one course of action now that Mother's bounty hunters had caught up to me … again.

I had to leave. Tonight.

I couldn't fathom how they'd found me so fast this time. I should have had a few more weeks before there was any danger of discovery. But they were getting more daring and vicious in their pursuit.

I flew until the cool ocean breeze calmed me and cleared my mind. *Mother's bounty hunters will never drag me home before I'm ready.* My life belonged to me. Not to my mother or my people. I would return to Valsgard one day—on my own terms.

CHAPTER 4

I circled the abandoned barn, searching for any sign I was followed before landing. The forest around me went silent, acknowledging the predator in its midst. I originally chose this spot for its privacy and location far from the main roads—the chance of discovery was slim.

My wings dragged over the uneven ground as I opened the huge barn door. Mounds of dry hay bales stood unmoved along the back wall where I stacked them a few weeks ago when I first arrived in the area. I went to work, moving them to the other side of the barn to reveal the car carefully concealed beneath a heavy gray tarp. She was my pride and joy. I smiled as I pulled the tarp free, eager to get behind the wheel again.

The classic black convertible was the only luxury I allowed myself to keep from one place to the next. I drove a beater car to work, one I could afford to lose if I had to abandon it on nights like this one. But Josie here was my girl. Driving her fast down deserted roads took me back home to pleasant times flying over hills and valleys, racing Pasha below.

I kept the convertible's trunk stocked with everything I would need to start over. Clothes, money, my perfectly legal-looking identification documents I'd paid a fortune for, even a supply of food, water, and camping gear.

I wiped at the sweat beading my brow. Time to get moving. I could sense the boy's soul was at peace now, but I was still too anxious to change back to my human form. I caught sight of myself in the driver's side mirror, my dark wide eyes in a panic. Tonight had been close. Too close.

"Get a grip, girl." I took a deep breath, running my fingers through the fine feathers cascading down my back and plucking bits of hay from my wings. For nearly three years, I had avoided my Valkyrie form as much as possible. I couldn't risk the chance of being seen and ending up on some supermarket tabloid. While I enjoyed my simple human life, I missed my Valkyrie.

I stared into the mirror, concentrating on steadying my breath —in and out—and slowing my heart rate. With my mind focused, I watched the black void around my eyes begin to recede and my cheeks return to their fullness. The swirling darkness of my eyes faded back to their natural green, sparkling in the moonlight. I arched my back as my wings withdrew and my shoulders returned to their normal state.

Dragging in a ragged breath, I threw my telltale feathered hair back into a messy bun and pulled a fresh t-shirt over my head. I checked my reflection once more and slammed the trunk closed before I slipped into the front seat. Easing out of the barn, I headed for the dirt road that would lead me along the back coastal roads that crisscrossed up the east coast. I'd have to drive most of the night, following the plan I'd mapped out weeks ago, but it was safer than the highways. I would head north to Cedar Island and find a new hideout, making a new life along the islands of Pamlico Sound. I could disappear there for at least a year, moving slowly up the coastline to Virginia Beach.

"Mother's bounty hunters will not catch me. Not this time." I gripped the steering wheel, wondering if I could ever think of Mother without also thinking of the way her bounty hunters came after me with ruthless persistence.

With the top down and the wind in my hair, I began to relax as I wound along the rural roads—not too fast and not too slow. Nothing to attract unwanted attention.

At almost two a.m., I was the only one on the road. I wouldn't be getting any sleep tonight or the next. I had to move quickly and with stealth. Maybe I could find a little island among the nature reserves and make camp until the bounty hunters lost my trail.

I slammed on the brakes just as something darted in front of me. The unmistakable jet-black wings had me hitting the gas a second later, swerving around the woman in the road. Checking my rearview mirror, I looked for signs of the others. There were always four. And they were vicious. The price on my head was a fortune few bounty hunters could resist.

"Wait!" I heard a desperate cry over my own frantic gasps.

I felt the flutter of wingtips as they passed over my head to land on the hood of the car. Dark wings framed his fine features, pale skin, and short dark hair.

He was a Valkyrie. The kind that shouldn't exist. I hit the brakes again as I met his gaze, certain I was about to die.

Panicking, I bolted from the car and ran down the deserted road, my boots pounding against the pavement as I searched for a way out. I cursed myself for transforming back to my human form. I wouldn't be able to manage the change again for at least a day. I was so out of practice, the shift from one form to another left me exhausted.

"Stop, please?" the male Valkyrie begged as he circled above me. "I won't hurt you."

It was silly, the way I ran. I could never outrun a Valkyrie in flight, but I also couldn't seem to make my body respond to that bit of knowledge.

He landed in front of me and I skidded to a halt. His black-as-night wings lowered behind him as he took a tentative step toward me, his hand outstretched as if to gentle a scared pet.

"I just wanted to meet you," he said.

My eyes darted all around, my mind a chaos of panic. I was going to die right here and I'd never see my sister again. I always thought I would return once things at home had settled down. It hadn't occurred to me that I'd never get a chance to make things right with Mother.

"I've never met another angel before. I'm sorry if I scared you." He raised his hands to show me he was unarmed.

Angel? I turned to face him, and my eyes widened in shock. In the darkness and my blind terror, I hadn't realized he carried three sets of wings, just like mine. He had first generation Valkyrie blood. The mark of high royalty.

"You're a seraph, right?" He took another hesitant step forward. "Like me."

"What?" I shook my head in confusion, trying to figure out where this male, *foresworn* Valkyrie had come from. And why he didn't seem to have a clue what he was.

He's faking it.

"Seraph?" He wasn't making any sense. My heart nearly stopped as he approached.

"An angel of death. I'm sorry if I stole your thunder back there. I couldn't let him die alone like that, and I didn't realize he was yours. I didn't know there were others like me." He gave a nervous laugh. "I'm Ben." He lifted his hand toward me like he wanted us to shake hands and be friends.

"Ben?" I asked softly. "Is this some kind of joke? Some pathetic attempt of my mother's to get close to me?"

"Joke? No." Ben cocked his head, frowning. "You have a mother?"

"Are you for real?" I finally took a breath.

He shrugged. "I thought I was alone."

"You are. You shouldn't exist," I said flatly. "And if you had any sense at all, you would leave right now and forget you ever saw me."

"Shouldn't exist? There are Angels of all kinds, aren't there?" His face twisted in disgust.

I let an incredulous smile curve my lips. "You really expect me to believe you don't know what you are? Does my mother think I'm that stupid?"

"Listen, I don't know who your mother is, and honestly, I don't know much of anything else either. I've lived my entire life on instinct alone. All I know is what I've been able to find out through a lot of research and assumptions."

"You think you're an angel?" I felt a pang of sympathy. If he really didn't know what he was... Had some distant royal dumped him here in the human realm because she couldn't face her duty?

Ben rubbed the back of his head in frustration. "What other creature has six wings? What guides dead souls to heaven?"

"Heaven? You've been researching the wrong histories," I said with a frown.

Maybe this guy was for real and he truly didn't know what he was, but that was a risk I couldn't afford to take. All male Valkyries were born grounded in their human form except for a rare few scattered throughout history who were born with a female's ability to transform. Those unfortunate children grew into terrible men, known as foresworn Valkyries, who could not contain the power of their Valkyrie form. Ages ago my ancestors had ruled that a foresworn Valkyrie male could not be allowed to live—particularly a royal who could serve as a vessel of the gods. Ben should have been executed at birth. Except Ben's mother had obviously tried to save him, secreting her son away in the human realm to give him a chance at life. She would die for that betrayal.

"What can you tell me?" Ben asked. "You're the first I've ever met like me. Whatever that means, I need to know."

"You are Valkyrie," I whispered. "A dangerous one."

"Valkyrie?" Ben tested the word. "I've never even considered it."

"Well, now you know." I turned back toward my car.

"Wait." Ben followed. "I have a million questions."

"I bet you do," I said, picking up my pace. "But I'm not the one to answer them. Sorry. I travel alone." I reached for the door handle.

"At least tell me your name?" Ben pleaded.

"Jessica Jones," I said without missing a beat. "Have a good life."

I sank back into the driver's seat and buckled my seatbelt. I had a long night of driving ahead of me, but as I pulled away, I glanced back. Ben stood in the center of the road, watching me leave. A weird urge to protect him came over me. Or maybe it was just guilt. If I left him without a warning, bounty hunters would find him and execute him on sight. It was my duty to let that happen.

I gripped the steering wheel, fighting the instinct that told me to leave him as a distraction to throw pursuers off my trail. But as I watched him in the rearview mirror, I felt like I'd just abandoned a puppy on the side of the road. A puppy who could tear my world apart if given the opportunity. Still…

With a deep sigh of regret, I hit the brakes.

CHAPTER 5

I woke up in the backseat of my car after a fitful few hours' rest. After dropping Ben off at a crappy motel last night, he'd made me promise to meet him for breakfast. I knew he had questions, and he deserved answers, but I was having second thoughts about seeing him again. I climbed over the front seat to sit behind the wheel and stared blankly ahead, torn with indecision. Why had I stayed when every instinct told me to run? In the clear light of day, I saw him for exactly what he was.

Ben was bait. And I'd fallen for it.

It was just too convenient that I happened to run into him. Mother's bounty hunters had to be behind this.

It was time to go, right now before I wasted another minute. I cranked the engine and headed north toward Cedar Island like I'd planned. But with every mile, I felt more and more like a heartless jerk.

What if he wasn't a trap meant to distract me? What if he really was just an innocent bystander? Then I was leaving him to face Mother's bounty hunters on his own, knowing they would follow my trail and eventually find poor, unsuspecting Ben. They would execute him on the spot, and he'd never see it coming.

"Whatever, Thea, it's not your responsibility." I spoke aloud in a vain attempt to convince myself I wasn't being cruel and ruthless just to save my own neck.

Twenty miles outside of Beaufort, I swerved into a gas station for a quick break.

I stared at my reflection in the bathroom mirror as I busied myself with brushing my teeth and washing my face. After changing into fresh clothes, I ran a brush through my hair and popped into the store for a supply of Diet Dr. Pepper and an assortment of gummies, my favorite travel snacks.

The simple task of gassing up for a road trip made me feel more in control of the situation. I slipped my sunglasses back on and leaned against my car while I filled the tank. I loved to drive. It was my favorite thing about the human realm. I liked nothing more than climbing behind the wheel of my own car, heading out for parts unknown with the wind in my hair—answerable to no one but myself. It was almost as good as flying. The sense of freedom I felt on the open road was exactly what I needed now.

Forget Ben. Let him take care of himself.

I returned the hose to the gas pump and turned around to slip into the front seat, but someone was already there. I jumped back, immediately chastising myself for not paying attention to my surroundings.

"Where're we going?" Ben glanced over the rim of his dark sunglasses. "You promised me breakfast, Jessica ... or whatever your name is." His smile was disarming, and he was much less intimidating in his human form, even with his tattoo sleeves and nose piercing.

"It's Thea," I muttered. "How did you find me?" I leaned over the driver's side door, refusing to get in the car until we got a few things straight.

"You're funny." He grinned, tilting his head back against the headrest. "You think I stayed at that fleabag motel? I've been following you since last night, and I'm going to keep following you until you answer my questions, so you might as well take me along for the ride. Or do as you promised and head over to that pancake house across the street and feed me."

I wasn't going to shake him like this. "Fine." I yanked the door open and shoved him into the passenger seat. "Where's your car?"

"Car?" Ben shook his head. "Why drive when we can fly?"

"You flew here? In daylight?" I stared at him with my hand frozen on the key in the ignition. "Are you insane?"

"Maybe, but I know how to avoid being seen."

"You're going to get yourself killed."

"You underestimate me, Thea. Now, are you going to answer my questions or are you going to keep drilling me about nonsense?"

"You're annoying." I started the engine. "I'll answer your questions, but you have to answer mine too."

"Deal." He winked, reaching to shake my hand.

"Just until breakfast is over and then I'm leaving." I accepted his handshake, ignoring his transparent attempts to charm me.

"We'll see about that. I can be very persuasive." Ben slapped the dashboard and pointed across the street. "Let's eat; I'm starving."

"With humans, I have no doubt you always get your way, but a Valkyrie won't fall for such tricks." I pulled away from the gas pump. If Ben truly didn't know what he was, I had a lot to teach him over breakfast. But that was all the time I was going to give him.

"That answers one question, then," he muttered. "We're not human?"

"Not anymore." I sighed. "Valkyries have a form similar to humans because our ancestors were once human."

His brow furrowed. "I used to think I must have died at some point and came back as an angel with no memory of my former life." He snorted at himself. "So how did we become Valkyries?"

"My turn for a question." I pulled into a parking spot at the diner. "Where did you come from?"

"No idea." Ben gave me a look. "I grew up in the foster care system."

"What does that mean?" I had spent the last three years in the human realm, but my knowledge of their ways was limited to what kind of drinks they liked and how their world revolved around earning and spending money. I also liked Netflix. A lot.

"Nu-uh. My turn. How did we become Valkyries?"

"The old gods made the first generation of Valkyries to do their bidding on the battlefield. We were strong and fierce warriors, but our job was to collect the souls of the fallen and escort them to the hall of the gods in the beyond."

Ben took a breath to ask another volley of questions, but my stomach growled. "My turn." I hopped out of the car and headed for the diner.

Once seated in a booth at the back of the restaurant, I gave him a careful look. "What's foster care?"

"I grew up a ward of the state. No parents. No history. No nothing. When I could no longer hide what I am, I ran away and I've lived on my own ever since." He shrugged. "My turn. You say our job *was* to collect the souls of the fallen, back when the gods were in charge. What does that mean now?"

"The gods all died ages ago. They nearly destroyed our world with their final war. Those Valkyries who survived the war rebuilt a new world from the ashes of the old one. What was left of it." I glanced up as the waitress approached. "You really don't know any of this?"

Ben shook his head. "Nothing."

"What can I get you two?" The waitress peered over her glasses at us.

"Pancakes," Ben said. "Tall stack for me with scrambled eggs and bacon.

"Same," I said, "but with cheesy scrambled eggs and sausage."

"And coffee," Ben added.

"Lots of it." I closed the menu and handed it back to the waitress. "And plenty of cream."

"Warm syrup?" she asked, taking our menus.

"Lots of it," Ben and I said at the same time.

The waitress poured our coffee and left us with the fresh pot before bustling away. I watched her disappear into the kitchen and then turned back to Ben.

"Okay, I'll give you a quick history lesson and then I get three questions," I bargained.

"Deal." Ben sat back against the worn pleather booth seat.

"Right. So." I took a deep breath, glancing around the noisy café. I hoped I could explain this in a way that would make sense to him. "Thousands of years ago the old gods met their end on the final battlefield. It was supposed to be the end of our world. All the seers agreed on that. There was no way to avoid it. When their twilight came, the power of the gods would die with them, and with their power gone from our world—a world they created—nothing would survive." I took a sip of coffee. I hadn't thought about any of this in such a long time, but all my childhood lessons with Elder Leda came rushing back.

"The Valkyries fought bravely alongside the gods against their greatest enemies—er..." He was going to think I was insane if I said giants, which was the human word for the Jötnar clans, but something was lost in the translation. The Jötnar were large people, but they weren't what humans thought of as giants. "Um, other creatures of our world," I said in a rush. "It was our sworn duty to serve the gods until the end. When the father of the gods fell, most of the Nine Realms were hanging by a thread—"

"Nine Realms?" Ben interrupted. "You're losing me." His brow furrowed in confusion.

"Our world was once made up of nine separate realms, including the human realm. After the final battle, most of the worlds were destroyed, leaving only one fragment of the place the gods once called home—and the human world which the Allfather protected ages and ages ago. Now all of us coexist in that one fragment of our world as peacefully as we can."

"And these people of the Nine Realms are all different ... creatures? Like Valkyries?"

"Something like that," I sighed, not wanting to make this more difficult than necessary. It wasn't like Ben could ever go there. It wasn't safe for him. "The father of the gods was the only thing holding it all together," I continued. "At the last moment, when he took his final breath, the first queen of the Valkyries stood with him, poised to take him to the afterlife.

"Some say it was an accident and some say it was a final gift, but when the father died, the power of the gods fell to the Mother of all Valkyries. She became the first vessel for the power, allowing what was left of our world to survive. Our ancestors picked up the pieces to rebuild a world where the gods no longer reigned. Instead, the Valkyrie queens rule over all that remains, holding the power of the gods for all those of the Nine Realms who need it to survive.

"Now, many generations later, the Valkyries have built a powerful empire. Our queen rules over the Valkyrie nation known as Valsgard, and also serves as High Queen over all of the Nine Realms. Each realm holds a seat on the high council and together they rule our world. Every generation, a new queen ascends as the power of the gods chooses a Queen Heir from among the noble daughters of the queen's blood. The power always chooses the strongest and wisest ruler to be the next vessel. She alone is strong enough to hold the power of the gods in her capable hands, though she is unable to wield it once she ascends to the throne."

I eyed our waitress as she headed our way with the stacks of pancakes, feeling only a little guilty at how much of our history I'd neglected to tell him.

"Can I get you anything else?" the waitress asked, setting a small cup of warm syrup in front of each of us.

"Oh, I'm going to need a bunch of these," Ben said.

"Can we get, like, a pitcher?" I asked.

"Each?" Ben added.

"Of syrup?" The waitress blinked at us.

"Yes."

"Warmed," Ben added.

"Um, okay." The waitress gave us a skeptical, slightly disgusted look and turned on her heel.

"So that's it?" Ben asked. "We survived a war and then took over for the gods and carried on from there?"

"That's the gist of it, yes." I took a huge bite of cheesy eggs.

"But somehow I ended up here without a family." He gave a deep sigh of longing. "Can you show me how to get back?"

"I get three questions now," I reminded him, snatching the small bottle of syrup just as the waitress set it on the table. She'd only brought one.

"You going to leave me any?" Ben stared at the steady drizzle of syrup I poured over my pancakes, eggs, and sausage.

"Sorry." I finished and handed him what was left of the little pitcher. "I'm obsessed. We don't have anything like this in Valsgard, and I'm a sucker for anything sweet."

"I usually gross people out when I pour syrup on everything," Ben said, filling his plate with the sticky sweet goo. "But syrup on cheesy eggs is a new one, even for me."

"Don't knock it till you try it."

"Oh, I'm going to try it next time." Ben smiled, refilling both of our coffee cups.

"First question," I said. "How did you manage to keep yourself hidden from humans when you were younger?"

"It wasn't always easy," Ben said. "I was adopted once. But when they realized my hair was full of feathers, they freaked out and sent me back into foster care. I've kept my hair short since then, not letting it get long enough for the feathers to show. But then when I was twelve..." He swallowed and glanced down. "Well, let's just say sprouting wings doesn't make puberty any easier so I had to learn to control it. Quickly."

"Wow, that's rather impressive," I admitted, though I struggled to believe anyone could control their Valkyrie so well. "It takes a great deal of focus and will to avoid the change once it is triggered by imminent death." Maybe it was his self-control that made him seem so ... normal.

Ben shrugged as he stuffed a huge bite of pancakes into his mouth. "I guess. I ran away from my last foster home, and I've been on the move ever since. I try not to stay in one place too long so no one gets too close, you know."

I offered him a sympathetic smile. "I do." I knew exactly what that life was like. Ben was just as lonely as I was. Probably even more so—the poor guy had thought he was an *angel* all this time. I reached for his hand across the table without even thinking about it. "Now you know."

"You get two more questions," he said, giving my hand a gentle squeeze.

"Do you ever lose control? Of your temper especially?" I asked carefully. Despite all the horror stories I'd heard about male Valkyries like Ben, he didn't seem to fit the mold. At all.

"Sometimes. But no worse than most people, really. Why?"

"I get one more question." I chewed nervously on my lip. "How did you find me and what do you want with me?"

"That's two questions." He pointed his fork at me. "But I'll allow it. I think I must have sensed you somehow. Is that a thing? I don't know how else to describe it, but for the last several weeks I've felt this … dire need to head up the coast. Like a beacon humming in the distance. I just had to find out what it was. Turns out it was you." He shrugged, turning his attention back to his pancakes. "To answer your other question, I don't really want anything from you. You're the only Valkyrie I've ever met. Naturally, I have questions. A desire to connect."

"Connect... Like how?" I frowned. Legends of the male Valkyrie read like a horror story of war, blood, death, and rape. But I just wasn't getting that vibe from Ben. He was genuinely nice. I liked him and it felt so good to talk to another of my kind. But I wasn't looking to… connect. If I wanted that, I'd go back to Valsgard.

"Like the normal way." Ben laughed. "Haven't you ever had a friend, Thea?"

"Yes," I said, my heart clenching painfully at the thought of Morgana and my sister. I missed them both so much it hurt. "But I've been on my own here for a long time now. And I like it that way," I added firmly. Just in case he got the wrong idea.

Ben was hot with his bad boy vibe, dark features, and beautiful honey-colored eyes that made him seem like a lost puppy. But I wasn't going there. For many reasons, not the least of which was that he shouldn't exist. In my world, males were grounded—born without the ability to transform. They were also subservient to the women in their lives, a custom that had made living in the patriarchy of the human realm a huge culture shock.

“Don’t worry,” Ben said with an easy shrug. He leaned forward and winked. “You’re not my type anyway.”

“Oh?” I rolled my eyes at myself for taking the bait. “And what exactly is your type?”

"I like tall, smart women." Ben gave a devilish smile.

"And I like scruffy, strong men with backbone." I made to stab him with my fork.

"Hey, now." He dodged my playful strike. "I like smart blonds who have their act together, you know. Dean’s list, career types with five-year plans, pink cardigans with pearls, just itching to date the guy from the wrong side of the tracks. I'm the kind of guy who needs direction in my life. And I don't know you very well, but you strike me as the type to hunt and maim my type."

"You'd be right about that." I laughed, but it held a note of bitterness. "I'm the sort who needs direction too."

"Cut from the same cloth, you and I." He eyed my leather jacket, silver rings, dark eyeliner, and the metal studs in my ears.

Mother would freak if she could see me now in ripped jeans, grungy tanks, and clunky boots. Sylvi was the sweet, blond, put-together type, perfect with her books and the kind of talents I would never possess. I missed Sylvi, but knew she was finally thriving in her role as Queen Heir. Now that I was out of the way.

I licked the syrup off my fork and split the last of the coffee between us.

"So, what are you going to do now?" I asked. "Now that you know what you are?"

"Same as always, I guess. Unless you care to answer my question now?"

"What question?" I hedged.

"Can you show me how to get back to our realm?"

I swallowed my coffee and sat back against the booth. I could not allow Ben anywhere near Valsgard.

"I'm afraid we're stuck here," I lied, casting my eyes down at my plate. "The bridge to this realm was damaged in the final war, and a few years ago what was left of it was destroyed. Now there's no way back."

Ben's face fell in disappointment. "Are there others like us? Here in the human realm?"

"Don't know." I shrugged. "I imagine there are some."

"For one tiny moment there I thought I might have a chance to find my family." He breathed a resigned sigh. "I guess I'll never know what happened to my parents or why they left me here to fend for myself. Who does that?" He fumbled with an empty sugar packet.

"Children are greatly revered in our world, especially among the Valkyries," I said.

It was true. Partially anyway. Daughters were greatly revered. Sons were as well, to a certain extent, but not sons like Ben. His mother had failed in her duty to execute him at birth and suffered a Valkyrie boy to live. She had undoubtedly thought abandoning him to the human realm was her son's only chance at life.

I wished I could tell him just how much he was loved. No Valkyrie would have such love for a son—a dangerous son who would climb over the backs of his willfully slaughtered family to gain power—or so the legends of his kind claimed. Now, I wasn't so sure those legends held as much truth as I'd once thought.

"If your mother brought you here as a child, she was probably trying to protect you." I offered him the vague half-truth.

"I guess I'll never know," Ben said sadly.

And if he was lucky, he never would.

CHAPTER 6

"I need a wingman," Ben said with all the seriousness of a nineteen-year-old guy on the prowl.

"Is that a really bad pun or are you trying to actually ask me something?" I set a pitcher of peach margaritas on the counter for one of my waitresses. I was back to work at Harkers Tavern, but it was a slow afternoon.

"See that blond over there?" He turned, leaning against the bar, and waved at the perfectly tanned, bikini-clad girl sitting on the front deck with her friends. The girl giggled and waved back. "Help me get her away from the herd?"

"The herd? You are a disgusting little man-child, aren't you?" I shoved him as I picked up my book and settled back on the stool behind the counter.

"You know what I mean, Thea." He moaned. "You're my wingman. Go build me up to her and her friends, make me look good, and I'll swoop in for the kill."

"The kill? You really are a misogynist pig. I am not helping you get laid. You don't need any help in that department, anyway." I tried to return to my book. Ever since I agreed to let Ben stay with me, he went for a different girl each night and was usually successful. Which meant I got peaceful nights at home alone, and someone to hang out with on my days off. It was kind of a win-win for me.

"Seriously. She's a pre-med student at Duke University and she's only here for the weekend. She's so smart. Totally out of my league and totally my type. Go find out if she likes bad boys." He tried to push me off my stool and toward the deck.

"Bad boys?" I let out a ringing, hysterical laugh, which just made him scowl at me. "Oh, Ben." I wiped my eyes. "You're like one of those Peter Pan boys who refuse to grow up. Having more tattoos than sense and wearing a leather jacket at the beach does not make you a bad boy. Seriously, if you put the kind of effort into getting a job that you do in getting laid, I could quit my job and let *you* support *me* for a while."

"Then let's go to New Orleans and I can get my old job back."

"What's in New Orleans?" I hopped up to clean off a vacant table and retrieve my lousy tip.

"It's my favorite place in the world." Ben's face lit up with his disarming smile as he followed me, gathering up the empty beer bottles while I wiped the table.

"And you had an actual job there?" I arched a brow at him. Ben wasn't the type to keep a steady job.

"Yes." He rolled his eyes. "I worked in a voodoo shop in the quarter. My friend Daria runs it. She's mostly deaf, but that's never slowed her down. She's amazing, and the closest thing to family I've ever had, like a big sister."

"It sounds … interesting." I sighed. It could be a good place to hide out for a while. It might even throw Mother's bounty hunters off my trail if I randomly broke my pattern and moved halfway across the country. I ducked back behind the bar and restocked the cooler for the coming afternoon rush.

"You'd make a lot more working in the Quarter than you do in these little beach towns." Ben slid back onto the stool at the counter.

"If you love it so much, why did you leave?"

"There was a bit of a misunderstanding with the local authorities." Ben waved it off like it was a nonissue. "I headed down to Florida for a while before I came to find you. But that was months ago. You'll love it there, Thea. The jazz music and the culture. And the food is incredible."

"All right." I surprised myself by saying yes, but the more he spoke, the more it seemed like a good idea. And I really needed to put as much distance between Ben and those who pursued me as possible. "You pay for the trip and my motel room till I get a job there and we'll go."

"Ugh." He flopped back down on his stool at the bar. "Maybe I can get Daria to wire me some cash."

"You're like a tick, you know." I rapped him on the back of the head as I walked past him to deliver a second round of beer to my sole customers inside the bar. "You latch on and don't let go no matter how hard I try to shake you off." I smirked at his indignant look.

"Hey, that's mean."

"Get. A. J.O.B."

"I'll do some odd work to get the cash for NOLA and then we're going." He stood up and leaned over the counter. "Spot me a few beers, will ya?"

"Go!" I laughed. "Hook up with your girl. You can be her problem tonight."

"I'll be home later. We'll get Thai takeout and watch *Jessica Jones* on Netflix. My treat." He shoved off the bar and sauntered out to the deck.

"No doubt dinner will be on the blond." I shook my head.

As the sun began to set, customers headed inside in droves, seeking respite from the heat and a refreshing drink before the dinner rush sent them all to the nearby restaurants.

"Your boy Ben sure has a type," Kelly commented as she lined up a row of tequila shots.

"He's more trouble than he's worth. Want him?" I joked. “I warn you, though, he’s like a barnacle.”

"I'm considering dying my hair blond, if that answers your question." Kelly laughed, heading out to deliver her shots while I took care of the customers at the bar.

Ben was keeping the guests on the deck entertained, ordering copious amounts of margaritas for the patrons there. He wasn't paying, but he was definitely earning his keep tonight. The tips and orders were rolling in. *Maybe we should hire him as some sort of entertainment.* I tucked a roll of bills into my apron and took the next order.

My shift would be over after the happy hour rush and I was looking forward to a quiet night alone to think about my next moves. I couldn’t believe I was actually contemplating going to New Orleans with Ben. But I’d gotten used to having him around these past weeks, and it made me sad to think of him leaving. It was nice having a real friend. One who knew what I was. Well ... mostly what I was.

“What are you doing now?” I paused the documentary I was watching on Netflix. It was my night off after a long week at the bar and Ben was driving me insane.

"I'm bored." He climbed onto the bed beside me, dropping his head in my lap with a sigh.

"There's this other documentary we could watch on conspiracies."

"You and your documentaries need to get a life." He stared up at me like he thought I might be kind of pathetic.

"What? It's a great way to learn about humans. Don't you find them fascinating?"

"No. Not even a little bit. *We* are fascinating, but you never want to talk about Valkyries. You never even shift. Not since that first night."

"I haven't needed to."

"Need? Thea, you get to shift whenever you want. You can freaking fly, but you'd rather spend your nights eating popcorn and drinking cheap wine, watching documentaries about humans rather than going out there and hunting them."

"Hunting?" A chill swept down my spine as it always did when Ben said something that might indicate he wasn't as harmless as he seemed. A lifetime of hearing murderous, bloodthirsty stories about his kind left me constantly wary, even as I grew fonder of him.

"Wow, Thea. Not literally." He rolled his eyes. "I mean hunting those who will need our help."

I stared at him, my jaw dropping. "Are you saying you go out of your way to find humans who are about to die?"

"It's a rush, helping them to the other side. I don't know." He shrugged. "It gives me purpose."

"You don't … dread it?" I couldn't imagine finding enjoyment in our sacred duty.

"For a long time I did. It really sucks when they realize they're dead, but I like seeing their faces when they see the other side for the first time. They go from being heartbroken that their lives are over to euphoric when they see heaven and know it's only the beginning of something new."

"Andlang," I corrected, absently running my fingers through his short hair.

"What?" Ben frowned up at me.

"The other side is called Andlang."

"Andlang? Not Valhalla?"

"Andlang is the only part of the other side that survived the final battle. Just like our home realm, it's a fragment of what once was. All souls go to Andlang now."

"Oh. Well. It's beautiful. I never get tired of visiting when I take someone there. Not that the souls there ever bother to acknowledge me in their midst."

My hand stilled in his hair. *He can enter Andlang?* The original Valkyries used to travel to the other side at will, but since the final battle, Andlang had been closed to us. We could guide the fallen to the gates, but could no longer enter. It was heartbreaking. To be so close to such untold beauty and promise, left with only a glimpse of the afterlife through the gates.

"What's wrong? Did I do it again?"

"Do what?" I shoved my thoughts aside. Ben would never return to our realm, so it didn't matter what he could do that others of our kind couldn't. As long as he kept his Valkyrie under control.

"Say something that totally freaked you out, but you're going to pretend like it's all okay and change the subject."

I smiled. He knew me far too well for someone I'd only met a few months ago. "The first Valkyries used to be able to visit the afterlife whenever they wanted."

"Sometimes I wish I didn't have to leave, but they get mad if I stay too long." Ben sighed, the skin around his eyes darkening. He wanted to shift, and he wanted me to shift with him.

"It's not safe, Ben. We could be seen." I frowned down at him, wondering if he was too daring for his own good.

"I didn't say anything."

"But you were thinking it."

"Fine." Ben sat up to face me. "So I want to shift and spend the night flying out over the ocean. What's so bad about that? No one will see us."

"Trust me, Ben. It's just not safe."

"Is this the part where you avoid telling me what you're running from? Because that's getting a little old, Thea."

"I'm not running." I fiddled with the remote control, refusing to meet his gaze.

"Then let's go back to our world where we don't have to hide."

"I told you, we can never go back. The bridge to Valsgard was destroyed."

"So, what was all that the night we met when you were convinced your mother sent me to find you? Where did you think she'd sent me from?"

I winced. I hadn't done a very good job covering up my lies.

"She lives here too." I blurted the first thing that came to mind.

"You're such a bad liar. I have a sense for these things. I know when someone is lying, and you spend a lot of time with your pants on fire." Ben stood up, shoving his feet into his boots by the bed.

I glanced down at my lap, confused. But that was my general state of existence around Ben. "My pants are not on fire."

"Not literally. It's just a rhyme humans say when someone's lying. Liar, liar, pants on fire."

"I'm sorry, Ben. I—"

"It's okay, Thea. You're allowed to have your secrets. I just wish you'd tell me about the ones that involve me."

"You're right." I scrambled off the bed. "Let's … let's get out of here. Go someplace quiet and I'll tell you what I know."

"What you know about what?"

"You." I didn't bother grabbing my shoes or purse. I wouldn't need them where we were going. "Coming?" I grabbed my car keys and opened the motel room door.

"Yeah." Ben scrambled to follow me, locking the room behind him.

"Hop in." I slid into the front seat of my car.

"We don't need to drive, Thea. We can just duck around the corner in an alley."

"If we're doing this, we're doing it my way. Get in."

I drove out of town along the back roads until I was sure no one would see us creeping down a dirt road toward the sound.

"Valkyries only shift when it's necessary," I said, keeping one eye on the road and one on the rearview mirror. "We believe our Valkyrie form is sacred and we only call upon it when bound to do our duty to those lost souls we meet along our journey. We also shift when a battle is at hand, or when training, but in our daily lives, we don't call upon our Valkyrie on a whim. At least not often," I conceded with a half smile.

"Sounds like a missed opportunity to me." Ben shrugged out of his jacket as the car rolled to a stop. The planes of his face were already changing.

"Once you shift, fly straight up as fast as you can into the cloud cover." I scanned the area uneasily.

"I've done this before, you know?" Ben rolled his eyes.

"You want to stay somewhere around fifteen-thousand feet. High enough that anyone watching will think we're hawks or raptors out for a hunt, but low enough that any air traffic might look down and think the same."

"Yes, Mother." Ben toed his boots off and left them in the car along with his jacket and shirt.

My Valkyrie wanted out just as badly as Ben's. I hadn't transformed in weeks and my wings were itching for a long overdue stretch. Ben's raven black wings exploded out of his back as he ran along the dirt road, taking to the sky like he was born in flight. I followed him, a lightness in my chest I hadn't felt in ages. I shot straight up into the sky, soaring past Ben until I reached the concealing clouds.

He streaked after me as I led us out past the sound and over the open waters of the ocean—the only place I felt safe enough to fly. Out here I could see for miles and nothing could sneak up on me.

Ben flew just below me, and I was reminded of all the hours of flying lessons with Aunt Astrid, learning battle tactics and flight maneuvers while Pasha ran through the woods, bounding up rocky slopes to keep up with me.

Without another thought, I dropped onto Ben's back and sank my claws in, not enough to hurt him but to get his attention.

"Cheater." His laughter reached my ears as he rolled, shaking me off his back before he dove and disappeared among the clouds. I raced after him, but he caught me around the middle, his body slamming into me and sending me plummeting toward the ocean. I caught myself and shot after him again. We were like two young falcons, playing along the air currents and attempting to knock each other out of the sky.

We flew up and down the Carolina coast all night, until my wings ached. Reluctantly I landed on a remote cliffside. Ben was right; I had to get out more. But I also had to warn him of the dangers lurking in the shadows. He needed to know what he was up against.

"That was just what I needed." Ben collapsed in the grass beside me.

"We have to talk." I sat up, letting my wings drape around me and shield me from the cool breeze.

"Oh no, she has her serious face back on." Ben lay on his side, propping himself up on his elbow.

"This is serious. I should have told you weeks ago, but I didn't want to scare you."

"All right. I'm listening." Ben gave me his undivided attention.

"One of these days I will have to go home." I glanced down at my hands folded in my lap.

He was silent for a moment. "So, that whole 'the bridge is out' thing was a lie?"

"Sort of. The bridge *was* destroyed back in the final battle, but there are still ways to navigate it. It's a dangerous journey. One I don't relish making again."

"Let's do it, Thea." Ben scrambled onto his knees, facing me. "I want to know where I came from. I want to find my family. I need to know what happened and how I ended up on my own here."

"You can never go back, Ben. It's not safe for you." I swallowed my doubts and fears and told him everything. He deserved to know that an executioner's block waited for him should he attempt to enter the Nine Realms.

"So, I'm it?" He frowned down at the grass and wound his fingers through it, pulling up a clump. "I'm the only … flighted male?"

My heart twisted at the forlorn sound of his voice. "You're a foresworn Valkyrie. To most of us living now, you're a legend come to life. You have to be the first foresworn in generations."

"And every single one born like me went bad?" Ben lifted his gaze to mine, his eyes filled with a sadness I couldn't comprehend. "No chance the regular Joes just didn't end up in the history books?"

"According to our histories, every single male like you," my voice dropped to a whisper, "ultimately turned into a blood-thirsty, power-hungry … beast, hell-bent on taking over our world. There was a dark period of our history a few generations after the final battle. We know very little of what happened then, but we do know that was a time when Valkyrie sons ruled the skies over Valsgard. It's called the Reign of Terror."

"And if I go back, they'll shoot first and ask questions later." Ben swallowed, his eyes fixed on the clump of grass still clutched in his hand.

"Yes. You can't risk it, Ben. It's not safe." I tried to reach for his hand but he pulled away.

So, I'm stuck here." He lay back in the grass, interlacing his fingers behind his head. "Forever. While you actually chose to leave, and can go back anytime you want, my world is closed off to me."

"It's why your mother brought you here, Ben. I mean, it must have been. She loved you enough to save you. And if it helps, I'm so glad she did. We haven't known each other long, but you're like my own family, and even when I have to return one day, I'll never forget you. That will have to be enough. You can't ever go back. They will kill you."

Ben nodded. "I get it." He stood. "I'll see you at home. I need some time to think."

He dropped off the edge of the cliff, and I watched him soar into the clouds, wishing I could give him the pretty words he wanted to hear.

CHAPTER 7

The truck was definitely following me. I glanced in the rearview mirror again. Stepping on the gas, I picked up my speed. *Tiny increments*, I reminded myself. I couldn't let whoever was behind me realize I'd noticed.

After leaving my very last shift at Harkers Tavern this afternoon, I made a few stops before heading back to the motel. I allowed myself to be distracted with thoughts of everything I needed for the big move to New Orleans with Ben. We were leaving tomorrow and I was so excited, though I still couldn't believe Ben had managed to talk me into it. The boy was certainly persuasive.

We had plans to get an apartment and there would be plenty of opportunity for jobs in my line of work. Maybe I could even open my own bar one of these days—if I decided to make the human realm my permanent home. I wasn't sure when it happened, but Ben had crept his way into my life and my heart like the lovable little brother I'd always wanted and never had. He was my best friend here, and I couldn't stand the thought of leaving him all alone. I had to return to Valsgard someday, but that didn't mean I had to stay there. The longer I lived among humans the more I could see a life for myself here. It was easier. No one expected anything from me. A simple life without the pressure of royal obligations was a tempting possibility.

After leaving the grocery store, I felt the telltale signs that someone was following me. My ice cream dinner was melting in the backseat, but I kept driving, moving farther from town. And Ben. I had to protect him at all costs. The truck still followed, far enough behind to avoid drawing notice—but I lived my life watching my back.

I cursed myself for staying in one place too long. I should have left Harkers Island with Ben weeks ago like I'd planned when it was just me. Mother's bounty hunters were predictable, and I had always stayed two steps ahead of them … until I grew complacent. Now they were going to catch up with me and Ben would pay the price for my mistake. Unless I could lead them away.

"How long have they been watching me?" Icy dread slid down my spine as I watched the truck with the darkened windows. It wasn't just me they would be after. They could already know about Ben. They could be going after him this very minute.

Regret stabbed at my heart as I tapped on the gas again. I had to get back to the barn. It was time to go and it looked like I was going to have to leave Ben behind. At least I'd prepared him for this, but he never took my warnings seriously enough.

I grabbed my phone to call him. My heart hammered in my chest as I listened to the ringing. I breathed a sigh of relief when he picked up.

Hey, this is Ben. I haven't listened to voicemail since the turn of the century. If you actually want to talk to me send a text, otherwise, don't bother calling back.

"Ben, you have to get out of Harkers Island. Now!" I tossed my phone in the passenger seat and smashed my fist against the steering wheel. "Stupid humans and their stupid technology! I knew what I had to do, but I didn't know if I could bring myself to leave Ben and save myself.

Take him with you.

My foot pressed down on the gas. I had to try. But if we were going to run, I needed my things—my beautiful convertible and all my important documents, not to mention the money I had stashed in the barn for just this reason. I kept driving, leading my pursuers on a merry chase just to buy myself more time to think. A desperate plan formed in the back of my mind. It was reckless and risky, but it was our only shot.

"How did I get so careless?" I muttered to myself, heading for the side road on the outskirts of town where the train tracks flowed into an old rusty bridge. The kind where the road just barely dipped below the tracks in an opening big enough for most cars. But not for large, overcompensating trucks. I could lose them there, cutting through the old junkyard to ditch my car. Once I was in the air, I'd lose them long enough to stop by the barn and figure out where to meet Ben.

The truck was gaining on me. They knew I was onto them by now, but I had the advantage. Once I was on the other side of the bridge just ahead, I was home free. My body was already humming with the onset of my transformation. My skin prickled, responding to the adrenaline coursing through my veins. I just needed a brief window of opportunity to get ahead of my pursuers and I would be in the air. No matter how talented Mother's bounty hunters were, they would never be as fast as a royal in flight.

The hum of two motors sent my gaze back to the rearview

mirror, but the truck was the only vehicle behind me on the long, dark road. Darting a glance in each direction, I saw them ahead. Motorcycles. They'd come from behind, racing around me. They were going to cut me off at the bridge.

I screeched to a stop in the middle of the road just a few yards from the bridge that would have saved me. I was cornered, but not about to give up.

The familiar tightening of my shoulders had me out of the car before anyone from the truck could make the first move. The junkyard just beyond the tracks would give me the cover I needed to transform.

Legs pumping and lungs burning, I ran. I would not lose after all this time. They would not drag me back home. Not without a fight. Whenever *I* decided to go home, it would be on *my* terms and no one else's.

"Princess Alithea, wait!" A familiar voice carried on the wind, but I didn't hesitate. This was do or die and I wasn't falling for a dirty trick.

"Amara, Vendela, follow her!" a harsh voice barked out orders.

The motorcycle engines ripped through the night, but they didn't approach me as I ran up the embankment and across the tracks. My hands and feet lengthened, making my boots tight and painful. I stumbled as my eyesight shifted from human to Valkyrie.

"Your Majesty! Please?" the familiar voice sounded closer. My pursuer was on foot behind me, his long legs eating up the ground to catch up with me.

Fiske? What was he doing here? He was the very last person Mother would send to bring me home. Was this some kind of joke? I fell to my knees; the excruciating pain of too large feet stuffed into my leather boots was too much.

"Go home, Fiske." My voice grated with the stress of my transformation and the ring of my authority over him. "Tell Mother to give up. I'm not returning. Not yet." I managed to kick my boots off and scrambled down the other side of the tracks.

"Alithea, we are not your mother's bounty hunters," said a big brute of a man. "Stop running like a child and face the consequences of your actions." Like a Viking from the old legends, he stood at the top of the tracks, a disapproving, hulking shadow in the flood of headlights.

Who did this guy think he was? I whirled around in a rage, my back ripping open to release my wings. I crouched, about to shoot up into the sky where they would never find me.

"No, Alithea!" Fiske shouted. "Sylvi sent us."

My wings fluttered in agitation and my fists clenched, ready for a fight. "She wouldn't send bounty hunters after me. My sister respected my decision to leave."

"She's desperate." Fiske took a hesitant step forward into the light. "I have a message from her."

"What?" the big man in charge demanded. "The princess entrusted a message to *you*?" He took a menacing step toward Fiske and I flung myself in front of him. I hated everything he represented, but I wasn't about to let this brute harm the boy I was once meant to marry.

"Don't come any closer." I took a step back, forcing Fiske backward behind the wall of my wings.

The bounty hunter ignored my warning and stepped toward us. I could see his face in the light now. His Berserker eyes heated with the rage of the beast inside him. Like all of his kind, he had the eyes of a predator, and more muscle than brains. I knew better than to trust a Berserker with their animalistic natures and disdain for powerful women. Valsgard and Úlfaheim were mortal enemies. Why would Sylvi send someone like this to find me?

If I were smart, I'd be in the clouds by now, but Fiske's words anchored my feet to the ground. Sylvi wouldn't send bounty hunters after me without good reason.

I turned in a circle, keeping Fiske safely behind me. I was surrounded. A blond Berserker woman dressed in furs stood with a pair of daggers in her hands, and another dangerous, dark-looking young woman I couldn't place closed in on me.

I still held the upper hand as the only one with the ability to fly. That was indeed a telling clue here. In recent years Mother sent female Valkyrie bounty hunters. Vicious ones who would make escape difficult in this instance.

This ragtag team didn't make any sense—and that alone felt like Sylvi was trying to tell me something. The ferocious Berserker man and woman—and Fiske, of all people—waited impatiently for me to make the next move. But it was the quiet, regal-looking young woman I couldn't take my eyes off of that gave me the most concern. Her slitted green eyes flashed in the headlights and her long dark hair fell in a tumble of wild braids down her back. Her flawless ebony face held a fathomless expression. Dressed in leathers and with a feral glint in her eye, she was by far the most dangerous, I realized with a start. Dragons were rare, and they only associated with those they were completely loyal to. I didn't want to cross this woman.

And Fiske. Poor, unsuspecting, boring Fiske. He'd grown into his lanky height, a handsome young man now, but what kind of insanity had he gotten himself into with this group? And how had he made it across the bridge in one piece?

"I just want to give you the message," Fiske said, shoving back the fall of sandy blond hair from his face as he stepped in front of me. "That's the only reason I'm here. Sylvi knew you'd pause long enough to wonder why I came." He held out a folded piece of parchment with a shaking hand. "She really needs you, Alithea. We all do. We're desperate."

"Give it here." I held my hand out, keeping an eye on the male Berserker. He was the one in charge here. Sylvi might have sent them, but that one couldn't be trusted.

I snatched the rumpled parchment from Fiske and stepped back, running my thumb over the indigo wax seal. Glancing at the silver ring on my index finger, I confirmed it was a twin of the one that had made this imprint. Sylvi's ring. I broke the seal and scanned the contents. It made zero sense—or it wouldn't to anyone who didn't know my sister as well as I did.

"What does it mean?" Fiske asked.

"You've seen this?" I demanded, turning my accusing stare on him.

"No!" He took a step back. "Of course not. I just know Princess Sylvi, so it probably doesn't make much sense."

"It doesn't. Unless you're me..." I took a step toward the headlights.

Sister,

I know you aren't three yet, but I need you to be purple. Come where the diamonds are in shadow and do not ever forget that you are half of a whole. Our house is no longer gold and indigo. I can't do this without you.

The Druid is not your foe. He would have the world see him as the color of midnight, though he is really a warm brown and lovely shade of azure.

Sylvi

Classic Sylvi. I understood what she was asking behind all of the seer waffle, but to anyone else it was pure and utter nonsense. She was begging for help, asking me to be brave enough to return home before I was ready. But the gold and indigo bit had me worried. Those were the colors of the Ahlstrom dynasty—my family. I didn't want to consider what it might mean if our house was no longer under the gold and indigo banner of the Ahlstrom Queens.

"Why is your Queen Heir asking for my help?" I folded the paper and stuffed it in my pocket.

"If you come with us, I will brief you," the Berserker said, taking another step toward me.

I threw my hand up. "I'm not talking to you, Berserker."

"You may call me Druan, Princess." His white teeth flashed in the headlights.

Ignoring him, I turned toward Fiske. "Answer me."

After a moment's hesitation he responded. "Sylvi isn't your mother's heir."

"Of course she is. That's why I left." I walked away from that role three years ago. The instant I left the Nine Realms and the power of the gods, the role would have fallen to my more suitable sister—there was no other vessel strong enough to take my place.

"In your absence, … we've been at war," Fiske said. "Your Majesty, please, you must come home. We need you. Your mother won't last much longer."

CHAPTER 8

"Okay, we're here, so tell me now. What do you mean my mother won't last long?" I demanded as I charged into my motel room, kicking Ben's dirty clothes into the corner. The bounty hunters had insisted I return home to pack before they would tell me anything. I would be moving on tonight no matter what happened in the next few minutes; I just prayed Ben was busy with one of his girls.

"The queen is dying," Druan said, looking around my room with disdain. "She needs the rightful heir to stop throwing a temper tantrum and return to Valsgard to do her job." There was an odd musical quality to the way he spoke that made his harsh words sound almost pleasant.

"She can't be." It had to be a trick. My mother was the strongest woman I knew. She had a lifetime still ahead of her to rule over all of Valsgard and the Nine Realms.

"Your mother isn't well, Majesty." Fiske took a hesitant step toward me. The other Berserker bounty hunter filed silently into the room behind her leader, taking a seat on the lumpy old couch where Ben slept most nights. The woman I suspected was a dragon took up guarding the door, peering out into the night through the window.

"What's wrong with her? Is Aunt Astrid ruling while she is ill?" I sank onto the bed behind me. "That must be why Sylvi hasn't taken on the role of Queen Heir. She would lead the Citadel while Astrid cares for Mother."

"The Queen of the Citadel and Princess Sylvi are trapped inside the Citadel along with most of our loyal people," Fiske said.

"Then if Mother is unwell, who is ruling Valsgard?" My hands clenched into fists, itching to wrap around his throat if he didn't start giving me answers that made sense.

Fiske quailed at my anger, shrinking back against the dresser.

Druan moved to stretch out his legs on my bed, his long dark hair brushing his shoulders. He wore the top half swept back from his face in a series of messy braids tied back in a leather thong. In the modern human setting, he looked out of place, like a figure from history, even in jeans and t-shirt.

Druan scowled at me as he spoke. "Three years ago, when you ran away, the council and your mother sent her bounty hunters to bring you home, but you evaded them. When it became clear that you would not be returning, the council expected the power of the gods to turn to your elder sister as a suitable replacement."

"Sylvanna is strong enough." I lifted my chin in defiance. "It should have been her from the beginning. It is her right as princess to follow in our mother's footsteps."

"But she wasn't the only potential Queen Heir," Druan said. "Your cousin, Princess Neela, is far stronger than your sister."

"*Neela*?" I frowned at the absurdity of the idea. "She's a Warder." I hadn't seen my cousin since we were small children.

"She is a powerful woman—a power-hungry one at that—but her mother, your eldest aunt, was a Valkyrie royal. Neela has been siphoning the power of the gods from your family and your people since the moment you left Valsgard. She's grown stronger with each passing moon."

"No." I shook my head, standing from my perch on the edge of the bed to pace restlessly across the room. "A Warder can't be a vessel *of* the power. They siphon *from* the vessel to fuel their Warder magic. That's how they rule over Vöstland with such an iron grip." The Warder nobility presided over the harshest wastelands where the other Nine Realms sent their prisoners. A Warder such as Neela would have charge of a unit of prisoners. Those prisoners were bound to her. Their prison wasn't made of walls or wilderness. *She* was the prison with the power to construct the most brutal and barbaric prison worlds she could cast them into at will. She could also bind them to her, forcing them to serve. These prisoners did what she said, went wherever she went, with never a moment of free will. But Warders weren't allowed to use their magic outside of Vöstland. It was forbidden.

It's just not possible," Thea insisted.

"Neela's mother is a Valkyrie Princess—your own mother's sister—and her father is the Warder king." Druan followed my pacing with his raptor's gaze. "She *is* a royal and as much a Valkyrie as you are. The very fact that you so easily dismissed her for her Warder blood is the very reason she has usurped your throne right out from under your nose." Druan's disdain for me was evident in his sneer. "She's siphoned your mother to within an inch of her life and taken your people as her prisoners."

"No, it can't be." The blood drained from my face. "Sylvi and Astrid would never let that happen." A Warder at the helm of Valsgard was the stuff of nightmares. If Neela was as powerful as Druan claimed, she could use her Warder magic to imprison the minds of everyone who called the Nine Realms home. They would be her puppets. It would shake the very foundation of the High Council of the Nine Realms. *If* she were strong enough to control them all. But she was just a Warder—and only a half Warder—it wasn't possible for her to be a vessel too.

"Princess Sylvi has done the best she can, but she needs help." Fiske's hand trembled as he reached out, as if to take mine in a comforting gesture. At the look on my face he thought better of it and his hand dropped to his lap.

"She has siphoned from Sylvi and Astrid too," Druan said. "None of your blood can stand against your cousin so they are in hiding to protect what power they still hold. You are the only one strong enough to stop her. Your people are prisoners, Thea, and their Warder doesn't need prisons made of walls and cells to hold them captive. Neela is Valkyrie. But she is also a Warder, a dangerous combination. Only those trapped inside the Citadel are safe from her influence."

I stopped pacing and raked a hand through my sweaty hair. "Trapped? How? How did this happen?"

"More than two years ago, Neela and her mother, Princess Svana, arrived for an amicable family visit—six months after you ran away." Druan crossed his ankles, looking perfectly comfortable on my bed with his big muddy boots tracking dirt all over my blanket. "Neela was already siphoning the power of the gods and building her army of mind slaves, though no one realized it until it was too late. In a single bloody battle, she seized control of your mother's throne. A few of your mother's council managed to get Sylvi inside the Citadel and behind Astrid's protection. They've been under siege ever since. It's only a matter of time before she wears Astrid down. The power of the Citadel Queen and those of your mother's council inside her walls weakens every day."

"And the bounty hunters?" I turned my back on Druan and the

others, unable to face them. "They've been ruthless in their pursuit."

"The bounty hunters you've been running from the last two years aren't your mother's. They are Neela's creatures, their minds enslaved by her Warder magic. If they take you, you're as good as dead. Neela knows she cannot gain the full power of the gods until she kills you. It's the only reason she hasn't killed your mother yet. Queen Brenna is the only bargaining chip she has and she's not afraid to use her."

"So what now?" My shoulders slumped in defeat and I sank back down on the edge of the bed, unable to stand. I thought my absence was the answer to everything, but I left a disaster in my wake.

"You return with us immediately," Druan's tone brooked no argument. "We will get you inside the Citadel to your sister and aunt. Then it will be up to you to defeat your cousin. The remaining loyal council members still believe you to be the rightful heir. The power of the gods will begin to shift back to you once you return to Valsgard. Your people—all the people of the Nine Realms—have been clinging to you as their only hope all this time. While you've been here in the human realm, tending bar and living a pathetic life of solitude. It ends now. You're leaving with us if I have to carry you home kicking and screaming." His wide chocolate brown eyes burned with some emotion I couldn't understand. Anger and possibly a fierce hatred that made little sense between perfect strangers.

"You forget who I am, Berserker." My own anger coiled inside me. No one spoke to me that way. "You know nothing of my choices or the difficult decisions I have made that have taken me away from my home—my family, whom I love more than you could ever know." My Valkyrie form shivered beneath my skin as I leaned toward him, my eyes darkening with fury and the threat of my words. "I will do my duty and return to set things right, but it is not for you to judge me."

"Let's take a breather, shall we?" The young Berserker woman hopped up from the couch and seated herself beside me. Where Druan's Berserker heritage was more obvious, hers was subtle. The eyes gave it away, though. One silver and one green—the eyes of a wolf. She was a voluptuous beauty, but behind that facade lay the heart and mind of a beast that couldn't be trusted. Berserkers and Valkyries had a long history of war and strife that kept their people at odds. For Sylvi to send two Berserker escorts, she must be in dire straits indeed.

"Vendela is right," Druan said. "Enough talk. Alithea, pack your things. We'll leave at first light." He made himself more comfortable on the bed, like he intended to sleep there.

"We leave now." I stood, glancing at the clock. If even half of what Druan said was true, I had to return home as soon as possible. But I also had to think about Ben's safety. These hunters were only concerned about bringing me home. Ben wasn't even on their radar. The best thing I could do for him now was disappear from his life without a trace.

"There is no way we're entering the bridge at night," Druan said. "It's not safe. We spend the night here and leave at dawn."

"I'm leaving now." I crossed the room to sift through my closet with trembling hands, shoving my essential belongings into a backpack. "You know as well as I do the closest entrance to the bridge is hours from here and none of you can fly—except maybe the Dragon standing watch at my door. And I doubt she intends to give anyone a lift." Dragons were fiercely proud and wise beings, but it astounded me that this one deigned to travel under Druan's authority.

"Amara is a valued member of this team. You will refer to her by her given name." Druan seemed determined to throw acid on my open wounds.

"Fine. But you—" I stuffed my favorite and most ironic Marvel t-shirt into my bag, "—will remember that I am the daughter of a queen. Whether I want to be or not, my position demands respect."

"Well, you're not my queen, sweetheart." Druan crossed his powerful arms over his chest with a scowl. "And that rust bucket you're driving isn't going to make it to the bridge."

"You will drive that monstrosity of a truck. Amara and I will ride in the back." I cast a glance at the young Dragon still guarding the door. She gave a curt nod in reply. I was fairly certain the hours ahead would be quiet ones. Legend said most dragons who took on human form were mute, refusing to speak anything other than their own tongue, though it was believed that their voices were so captivating that was the real reason they chose not to speak.

The drive northwest into the Appalachian Mountains would give me time to think. I shrugged into my leather jacket and snatched up my pack. I would need to figure out a way to deal with my cousin. Once I was home, I would have to right everything that had gone wrong in my absence. The only thing I knew for certain in this moment was that I had screwed over everyone I'd ever professed to love. And I was about to do the same thing to Ben.

"Give me a moment. I'll meet you at the truck." My voice thinned to a whisper.

"I will wait with you." Druan waved the others from the room.

I ignored him and stepped into the bathroom where I scribbled hasty directions to the barn on the toilet paper wrapper and left my keys and all my cash on the back of the toilet. No explanations. No goodbyes.

It was better this way.

CHAPTER 9

The cool mountain breeze flowed across my skin, leaving a pleasant chill in its wake. I embraced the darkness of the beautiful night, casting a glance at my silent companion. Amara seemed comfortable in the open air. Both of us were creatures of the sky, content traveling in the back of the truck.

A hazy warm glow radiated from Amara, like a fire burned deep within her body. She smelled of charred things and a lovely woodsy smoke that reminded me of warm winter nights by the fireplace in Mother's bedchamber. Thoughts of Mother sent my heart sinking like a stone. *What has she been through because of me?*

But I couldn't think about home just yet. I needed a clear head to focus on the perilous journey in front of me. I'd traversed the bridge between the realms only once before, and it had nearly killed me.

A relic from before the ancient war that nearly destroyed my world, the bridge was once a beautiful structure, connecting each of the Nine Realms in a network of magical highways. Now only a fraction of it remained, a fragile, treacherous labyrinth linking the human world with what was left of the Nine Realms.

Once on the bridge, we would head north toward my home in Vahland Reach and never deviate from that course, no matter what lay along the path. To step in any other direction would spell imminent death to those brave—or foolish—enough to attempt the journey. In the centuries after the war, the bridge had taken on a life of its own, driven by the madness of those who died there. Now it was home to a fathomless, angry void that would do whatever it took to lead travelers astray.

Last time, my desperation drove me; this time, an overwhelming sense of failure would see me to the other side. I always believed I made a great sacrifice when I fled to the human world. I thought I was leaving my people in more capable hands. Instead, I'd left them to suffer, to believe I cared more about myself than my duty to them. That thought gutted me.

I glanced at the nearly full moon hanging just above the horizon. Dawn was only an hour away. Upon sunrise, we would have one day and a night to cross the bridge. Should we linger any longer in that dying place between the realms, the bridge would take us. The madness would slowly consume us until we wandered into the most dangerous parts of the bridge, never to be seen again.

Druan slowed the truck as we rambled down a winding road through the rural mountains along the Appalachian Trail. We were nearly to the entrance. I met Amara's gaze in the dim light as the truck rolled to a stop on the side of the road.

"We're on foot from here," Druan announced as he slid out of the truck. Overgrown brush and vines nearly covered the dirt path that led forward. I climbed down from the truck bed and joined the others, trying not to let my nerves get the best of me.

No one was looking forward to this journey, and a still quiet settled over us as we hiked up the narrow path that led deeper into the mountains. The cave entrance was just ahead, one of many such places in the human world. A sense of wrongness vibrated in my bones with every step I took. The bridge had a way of warning off any who wandered too close. Even now, I fought the urge to backtrack to the main trail.

But I wasn't human, and I wasn't from this world. As I neared the cave, I felt it. Closing my eyes and tilting my head back, I let the pull of home wash over me. The power was strong here and it called to my Valkyrie, rippling just beneath my skin. Despite the tug, I still wasn't ready to leave this world behind. I loved my life here; as boring as some might think it was, it was mine. The life that waited for me at the other end of this journey was not one I had ever, or would ever, choose for myself.

"We're nearly there," Druan announced in the unnatural silence of the forest.

"We should wait until the sun has fully risen before we cross over." Vendela cast a wary glance behind us. "Our time on the bridge will begin at full sunrise. We must wait until then."

Druan nodded, continuing on the rocky path forward.

The cave entrance loomed overhead like the maw of some formidable creature waiting to consume everything that crossed its path. I hesitated. It would be ungodly cold on the bridge and I wasn't prepared for it. Glancing down at my ripped jeans, boots, and the "I Got This" t-shirt from Goodwill, I decided I definitely did not have this. Even with my worn leather jacket, I wasn't going to make it to the other side without freezing to death.

"Don't worry, Princess," Druan said, his voice taking on his usual mocking, musical tone. "We have furs and supplies waiting for us at the gates."

I nodded, picking up the pace. Now that we were here, I was

ready to get this over with. Dawn was fast approaching, and I didn't want to waste a minute of the time we had to make the perilous journey.

"Pick up the pace," Druan barked orders. "The clock is ticking." He was the first to enter the cave, shining a flashlight into the darkness ahead. Vendela, ever his shadow, followed directly behind. Fiske stuck close to my side, but I didn't want—couldn't—have him clinging to me the whole way. I jogged ahead to walk with Amara, letting Fiske fall behind.

I cast one final glance at the human world I'd grown to love. Despite my years of solitude, I had enjoyed my time here and the freedom it gave me, but I always knew an expiration date loomed over me.

Goodbye, Ben. Did you even know how much your friendship meant to me? You saved me in so many ways. I fought the threat of tears that burned my eyes. Leaving Ben behind killed something inside me. I let one tear fall as I thought about how badly he wanted to see Valsgard, and the loneliness he would suffer as the only one of his kind in a world that would never fully accept him.

"Dry your eyes, Princess." Druan's insults were grating on my nerves. "Vacation is over. It's time to grow up and face your duty."

I clenched my fists, dying to throw something at his arrogant face. "I get it, Druan, you think I'm a spoiled princess. But you don't know me." I wanted to shove him into a hole and leave him behind. "You don't know the sacrifices I've made or how much this is killing me to leave, knowing what a mess I've made when all I ever wanted was to do the right thing. You can think whatever you want about me, but keep it to yourself." I stomped past him and Vendela, grateful for Amara's quiet strength as she kept pace with me.

"*Sacrifice*?" Druan snorted as though I had said something that truly offended him.

"Leave it, Druan," Vendela warned, pulling him back.

As we ventured farther into the rocky cave, the walls closed in around us, funneling us toward the gate at the heart of the mountain. The temperature dropped dramatically, each step colder than the last until I shivered in the darkness.

"Stay close, everyone," Druan said. "The gate is just ahead."

A spark of light illuminated the cave, growing brighter as we approached. Supplies lay stacked along the cave wall, including a pile of furs they'd discarded on their journey here. I was grateful for the fur-lined cloak Fiske draped around my shoulders and the pack of provisions Vendela pressed into my hands.

"We all know the rules of the bridge, but let's review them for Thea's benefit in case she's forgotten." Druan couldn't seem to resist hurling his thinly veiled insults my way whenever possible.

"I haven't forgotten." My whispered words came out in a white, vaporous cloud. No one who had made this journey could ever forget.

"Vendela will lead the way. Thea, you will travel with me. Amara and Fiske will bring up the rear."

Great. I would rather travel with Amara, but the Berserker seemed to take a special interest in reminding me just how much of a failure I was.

"Those of you who can fly, shouldn't bother trying it. The laws of nature inside the void do not allow flight. The air is too heavy and you will fall to your death if you're lucky, or the void will take you if you aren't. As soon as we enter, the darkness will engulf us, and the only thing that will keep us from peril is the pathway itself. Flashlights and torch light is of little use inside so don't expect help of that sort because the shadows won't tolerate light in their world.

"Keep a foot or handhold on the pathway whenever possible. It will anchor you. The creatures of the darkness will whisper to you, attempting to lure you off the northward trail. Don't listen to the voices; they will drive you mad until you join them. If you stray, we will not come after you." He gave Fiske a scathing look. "If you do get separated from the group, continue north no matter what lies in your way, and you will make it through, eventually. Keep walking no matter what. No sleeping. Stay warm and hydrated. Eat whenever you can, you will need the sustenance to keep your strength. You have water and dried meat in your packs, but you need to manage your resources to last. Any questions?"

I shook my head along with the others. The thirst and hunger I could handle. The fear, I would manage. But the pressure of that unholy darkness ... it would test the boundaries of my sanity.

CHAPTER 10

I shivered in the growing darkness as Amara and I climbed the three stone steps up to the dark archway so black it could have been made of solid shadow. Adorned with ancient runes and symbols that no longer held meaning, this remnant of the bridge gave off some strong *go away* vibes.

The air was so cold it seemed to freeze in my lungs but it would only grow colder once we stepped through that arch and into the void. Cold and dark, save for the dim blue light of the pathway. I still had nightmares about the first time I crossed the bridge as a scared kid. Those were the two most frightening days of my life and I was about to do it all over again.

"It's okay, your Majesty." Fiske hovered right behind me. "We'll get you there safely. It won't be so bad together." He reached for my hand, but I stepped away, putting some distance between myself and the boy I was probably still betrothed to. Three years hadn't changed the way I felt about that situation. Though I was impressed that Fiske had braved the bridge to deliver a message from Sylvi. Maybe he wasn't the sniveling, cowardly sycophant I remembered. Maybe he'd grown into a man in my absence.

I still wasn't going to marry him.

I sighed, my breath coming out in a thick white cloud as my nose hairs shriveled in the Arctic air. Three years hadn't changed anything. I might be returning to a world in turmoil—but that world still needed me to be the Queen Heir. Like it or not, the safety and future of the Nine Realms rested on my inadequate shoulders. I would be expected to pick up right where I left off with my betrothal and First Ascension duties. I would have to learn to accept that because my people mattered more than my own happiness. They always had, but I couldn't think about Fiske, marriage, or the mess I'd made of everything. I would figure those out later.

I moved up to the top step, putting myself between Vendela and Druan, leaving Fiske to navigate the horrors of the bridge with the dragon at his side. Fiske was a decent guy. He just wasn't my guy. And he never would be.

"This is it," Druan announced unnecessarily. He cast a glance at me. "Once we take the next step, there's no turning back." This archway only went one way, and that was forward.

Vendela was the first one to disappear into the darkness. One moment she was there and then the black shadows swallowed her whole.

"Let's do this." I squared my shoulders and followed the Berserker woman, Druan right on my heels.

Icy darkness engulfed me in a silent tomb from one moment to the next. There was no turning back now; the only way out was through the other side. The void quickly closed in on us as the others followed. Moving silently in single file, I could no longer make out Vendela's form just in front of me, though I could sense she was there. Fiske's muffled gasps sounded tinny and distant behind Druan, whose presence I could feel at my back. The dragon was silent as ever, but I could feel the wispy touches of her heat just behind Druan.

The frigid air seized in my lungs and I struggled to exhale as the pathway began to glow in a familiar, dim blue light. I stretched my hands out to either side, just short of touching the bridge. That wasn't something I was prepared to do unless I had to. The bridge didn't like to be touched. The stone beneath my feet cast an iridescent blue glow, my only guide for the next day and night.

Fiske cried out behind us, but fell silent with a murmur of distress. "Is he okay?" My voice took on a curt tone. With Druan right behind me, the others faded into the darkness, leaving me to travel with this man alone. The man who seemed to truly despise me.

"Why does the boy irritate you?" In the heavy atmosphere of the void, Druan's lilting voice sounded like an intimate whisper in my ear.

"He doesn't irritate me." I carefully placed my footsteps, dividing my focus between the slick walls closing in on me and what little of the pathway I could see before me. It was like walking a tightrope without a net, but rather than falling to my death, it was the taint of the shadows in this world I had to contend with. I could feel them swirling all around me, whispering and waiting for me to make a mistake so they could pounce.

"I can practically hear your eyes rolling in your head every time he speaks. Indulge me. We have nothing better to do with our time here." Druan followed closely behind me, his chest nearly pressing against my back. "What was it about him specifically that sent you running to another world to escape your betrothal ceremony?"

"It was never about Fiske as a person. He's a fine young man. A tribute to his training."

"But you have this 'young man' who was bred like a prized piece of horseflesh, branded, trained, and chosen just for you. What Valkyrie woman wouldn't want such a man at her beck and call?"

I wished there was enough light so he could see the glare I threw in his direction. "It wasn't what I wanted." I could say a great deal more on the matter, but I didn't owe this man an explanation.

"Just toss him back when you get home. From what I hear there's a whole pool of others just like him. All raised to anticipate your every need. Pick the one who suits you most."

"I wouldn't expect you to understand. You believe I abandoned my family and friends, my people and my duty, all because I didn't like the boy the queen's council chose for me? If you must know, I ran because I didn't want to be queen. I ran because I knew in my heart I wasn't the right person to lead my people and the First Ascension Ceremony—that happened to include my betrothal—was just the first step toward a duty I wholly believe is not rightfully mine."

Druan's only response was a grunt.

We walked on in the deafening silence, the pressure of the atmosphere making it difficult to breathe. It felt like we'd traveled for hours already, but it could have been mere minutes. Time could get away from you on the bridge.

As the last of the cave walls fell away and the pathway descended in a downward spiral, the hair on the back of my neck raised with awareness of the unnatural beings that occupied the bridge. They were stirring in the darkness, growing more aware of our presence. I could feel their eyes on me, hear their ethereal voices beckoning in soft whispers, begging me to join them. Ghostly fingertips brushed at my skin in the barest of cold touches, but whatever remnant of protection the bridge had left kept them at bay. Goosebumps stood out on my arms and hot, putrid breath stirred my hair in the suffocating darkness.

One step in the wrong direction and the beasts would drag me into the void, making me one of them.

"You feel him?" Druan whispered, glancing up into the abyss as he stepped closer, refusing to allow the darkness to separate us the way it had the others.

"I feel a lot of things," I murmured. "Lots of eyes." I pulled my fur cloak tighter around me.

"It's the ancient one," Druan said. "The old dragon serpent, as old as the Nine Realms. Older even than Yggdrasil."

"Pretty sure Jörmungandr is the one breathing down my neck." I knew the Berserker must be feeling just as vulnerable as I did in this wretched place.

"He is Amara's many times great-grandfather." Druan shuffled his foot forward, searching for the pathway.

"Perhaps he will give us his blessing and let us pass without incident."

"Somehow I doubt that," Druan said grimly. "I think he's angry we have disturbed him."

"All the more reason to move quickly." For the first time I felt grateful he was here.

"Druan? Are you there?" Vendela called from farther down the path. She sounded frightened.

"I'm here. Keep moving, Dela; we will catch up." He pushed us forward and I quickened my pace to keep up with Vendela, praying to the blessed Mother that Fiske and Amara wouldn't lose us.

Hours blurred into each other and the cold seeped into my bones. From time to time I glanced over my shoulder. I thought I heard footsteps, as though the shadowy creatures followed, just waiting for one of us to stray off the path.

"What is it?" Druan followed my gaze to see what had caught my attention. I could just make out Fiske and Amara right behind us, but nothing beyond. It was such a strange sensation to be so close, yet I couldn't hear them, so heavy was the silence in this realm.

"Nothing." I turned back, peering at the compass dangling from my pack to make sure we were still heading north. The pathway could be deceptive, but as long as the needle pointed north, we would make it to the other side in time. The slightest deviation could send us off chasing shadows and phantoms before we even realized it.

The pathway continued to narrow, the suffocating void pressing in on us from all sides. It forced Duran to follow me, his arms stretched out like guardrails as if he could protect me from the void.

Finally I could sense Vendela just an arm's length ahead of me, though she might as well have been a hundred yards away. I felt bad for leaving her to take the lead by herself.

"Will she be okay?" I shifted my backpack, the weight of it seemingly heavier than when I packed it. Even the weight of the fur mantle I wore felt heavier than it should.

"Dela is never truly alone. She will be fine." Druan pressed us forward.

The cold monotony of the bridge threatened to drive me crazy. Something was bound to throw us off course, and that knowledge kept us all on edge.

I saw a brighter light ahead and the pressure began to lessen slightly as the pathway widened. Sheer cliffs of iridescent stone rose on either side of us creating a narrow passage heading northward. It wasn't as cold here. I breathed a sigh of relief, taking several deep breaths for the first time in hours.

“Can we take a rest here?” Fiske’s disembodied voice echoed behind me.

“Quiet!” Vendela whisper-shouted.

A loud crack sounded above, making my heart skip a beat.

“Time to run.” Druan grabbed my hand and jerked me forward as falling rock rained down. A deafening earthquake punctuated his words and the ground shook beneath my feet.

I gripped his hand, feeling the Berserker’s pulse quicken under my thumb.

“Stay together,” Druan called as he shoved me into the tight passage.

I reached blindly for Vendela's hand but couldn’t find her. Druan pushed me along the crumbling path until we were running, but as the left cliff fell away, the ground began to shift and slide beneath our feet.

"Backs against the wall," Druan ordered. I slid my pack in front of me and pressed my back against the remaining cliffside. Slimy creatures clawed at the iridescent stone wall at my back, trying to get to me. Their voices grew loud in my ears, morphing from ethereal whispers to shrieking wails.

My heart pounding painfully and my hands grew clammy with cold sweat. I slid my foot along the narrow ledge, all that remained of the pathway, and inched along in small steps.

“We have to keep moving.” Druan’s hand clutched mine like a lifeline. I could feel the steady thrum of his heartbeat.

“Dela?” He called out for his friend, a note of panic in his voice.

“I’m okay, Dru. Keep moving.” Her ghostly voice drifted back to us.

But Druan wasn’t moving. He was plastered against the wall.

“Hey Fiske?” I called out softly. “You back there, buddy?”

“Yes, your Majesty, thank you for your concern.”

I rolled my eyes. "The Mother save me; I can't live with that for the rest of my life."

Druan snorted, finally sliding his feet along the ledge. "I thought all you Valkyrie women liked the bootlicker sort."

"You're disgusting." I watched as he inched slowly along, his breath coming in shallow gasps. He was trying to keep his panic in check and arguing with me seemed to be the distraction he needed. "Don't believe everything your people say about mine. Not every Valkyrie of our matriarchy is a man-hating shrew."

"You should take your own advice, Princess. Not every Berserker of the patriarchy is a brutish caveman either."

I grunted but kept my hand locked around his, moving forward and setting an even pace. The ledge we stood on was barely a foot wide. For a man as big as Druan, it was no wonder he was having trouble finding his footing.

"Let go of my hand, Princess," he hissed.

"No, I don't think I will." I gripped him tighter.

"If I fall, I'll pull you into the void with me."

"Then don't fall." This man had done nothing but bark orders at me from the moment he came into my life, but in this particular moment, I was the one in control and I needed to take charge if we had any hope of making it off of this bridge alive. "Vendela, are you still in front of me?" I peered into the oppressive darkness.

"I'm just ahead of you, Alithea. Keep going."

My skin crawled, and not just from the deathly cold hands trying to claw through the stone cliff to get to me. Druan's hand trembled in mine and I knew how he and Vendela must be feeling. Berserker rage tended to come to the surface at the worst times. I squeezed his hand gently. "My Valkyrie wants out," I whispered. "She wants to fly us all out of here to safety."

"Don't you dare," Druan growled, taking another painful step in the right direction. "You'll sink like a stone here in this dead air."

He was right, but the urge was strong. I fought with my Valkyrie shivering beneath my skin, resisting the instincts that screamed at me to transform.

"Of course not. I just meant . . . you must feel a similar sensation with your . . . familiar." Berserker warriors often bonded with an animal they felt a special kinship with. With her wolf-like eyes there was no doubt Vendela held a bond with a fearsome wolf, but I suspected Druan's familiar was a big beast of a bear.

"My kindred," he corrected me. "I had to leave Sam behind. She will join me when we return. And I imagine it's quite different. I don't turn into a beast; I'm just aligned with one."

"Yes, but don't you essentially become them when your Berserker rage takes over?"

"I do not dominate Sam or take her over. She allows me to see through her eyes and lends me her strength and senses. You've been listening to too many stories."

"So what you're saying is, it's not the same thing at all and I've just been listening to old Valkyries talking nonsense about Berserkers." With nothing anchoring me but his hand, I pressed my free hand flat against the wall, praying to the Mother I wouldn't lose my balance and tumble off the side of this mountain.

Druan's feet moved as long as I kept talking. He froze like a statue whenever I stopped. As the ledge continued to narrow, I could smell his sweat and fear. The big, strong Berserker was terrified and for some reason that made him seem almost human.

"Exactly," Druan said. "There is much our peoples have embellished about the other over the centuries."

"Perhaps our generation will be the one to end that nonsense." I could hope, but after centuries of rivalry between the two nations, it would take more than my generation to wipe out the bad blood between us.

"How are we doing, Thea? Tell me we're almost through this rough patch?"

It was the first time he'd used my preferred name, and without the mocking tone. "One step at a time, Dru. We'll get there eventually."

I placed my foot in a precarious position, my heels throbbing from supporting all my weight. My back pressed so tightly against the stone wall my bones and muscles ached with the slightest movement. I was exhausted from the tension and stress of our predicament. If we didn't reach the end of this ledge soon, we were going to fail.

I slid my foot forward, searching for purchase, but the two-hundred-pound man-child behind me had stopped moving. His fear was beginning to win, and I did not have time for a Berserker meltdown. I looped my arm around his and tugged.

"Come on, tough guy. You don't want to miss out on all the gloating when you hand me over to my sister. That'll be a big payday for you, won't it?"

"There *is* a hefty price on your head," he managed, his deep voice a rasp. "Though I never dreamed it was such a big head." He was a jerk, but the jerk was moving again and that was all that mattered.

"Did you just say I have a fat head?"

"Lots of hair," he murmured. "And feathers."

"Most people like my feathers," I muttered. "Humans think I pay a lot of money to make my hair look like this."

"Humans are odd creatures. Are we even headed north now?" He pressed his head back against the wall, his chest moving too rapidly with his breath.

"Let's hope so, but I'm not checking again until we get off this ledge."

"Druan?" Vendela's voice rang out in the darkness ahead. She sounded closer this time.

"I'm here," he called back.

"Follow my voice. You're almost here."

Druan seemed to respond to the confidence in his friend's voice. He picked up the pace, and I breathed a sigh of relief when the ledge began to widen under my feet. After hours of inching our way along the face of a sheer cliff, we reached the other side.

I took several clumsy steps forward and when I was finally able to turn away from the wall my back was drenched with sweat under my fur mantle. My legs felt like jelly, but the first big hurdle was behind us, though we'd barely begun.

"Come, the pathway widens ahead." Vendela's voice guided us forward until the iridescent light of the bridge finally illuminated her form. She sat slumped on the ground, her head resting against her knees. I slid to the ground beside her, my legs giving out now that we were safe. The unquenchable thirst hit me hard and I fumbled for my canteen. Taking a few deep sips, I forced myself to save the rest for later. I would need it. My empty stomach gurgled and I searched through the pack of provisions for a strip of dried beef.

Right now, I wanted to curl up and sleep, but one did not sleep on the bridge and expect to reach the other side alive.

"We have to keep going." Druan dropped down beside Vendela, pulling her into a tight embrace. The commanding tone had returned to his voice.

"In a minute." Vendela cradled her head in her hands.

The shimmering pathway glowed with a bright turquoise light here, but it turned into a sharp upward hairpin curve that loomed overhead, like a road through treacherous mountains twisting back on itself.

I stared into the void, just able to make out the pathway as it twisted and turned above us like an ancient snake. I could see all the different branches that had once led to other realms. In ancient days this area must have been a main thoroughfare. I had trouble imagining what that must have been like.

Fiske and Amara stumbled onto the path in a burst of activity. Fiske was shaking like a leaf and Amara seemed only mildly alarmed. I watched as they both scrambled for their canteens, desperate for a drink that would never slake their thirst. I was responsible for these people. They were here risking their lives because of me.

I cleared my throat, staring down at my lap as I clutched my backpack to my chest. "Thank you all for working so hard to bring me home." My voice sounded harsh to my ears as it echoed off the crumbling walls. "I only apologize you had to come get me in the first place." I looked around in the eerie light, meeting each of their gazes. "Had I known what my actions might cause when I left, I never would have. I hope you all understand that."

Druan gave a disgusted snort, but Amara nodded her regal head, the light of understanding burning bright in her green eyes.

I climbed to my feet, tugging my cloak close as I lifted my backpack onto my back. "Have we lost north?"

"No," Vendela said, "we are still headed true north, but we must go forward, not up. She pointed to the sheer cliff facing us.

"Can't we follow the winding path?" Fiske gestured to the faint blue light marking the road twisting and turning above.

"That way leads northeast. True north is straight ahead, and we must follow it."

I tilted my head back to look up at the rocky mountain standing in our way. Pieces of the path dotted the cliffside, casting a ghostly blue glow. I couldn't even see where the northward path became whole again. It didn't matter—this was north and we had to keep going no matter what lay in our path.

"Wait!" A desperate voice called behind us.

For one moment we all stared at each other, checking to see who was missing.

"It's a trick," Vendela whispered.

"No." I shook my head, horrified. *He wouldn't.* Taking two steps back the way we'd come, I heard the frightened voice again. "It's Ben." Fear lanced through me. I couldn't send him back now. The only way out was through. If my people didn't kill him, I would.

"Ben? Who's Ben?" Druan stepped between me and the darkness.

"My friend." I shoved past the stubborn man. "Ben?" I ran back a few more steps, heart in my throat as I searched the shadows for his stupid face, half hoping I was just hearing things. "Follow my voice if you can hear me."

I waited, unable to breathe as I stared into the void we'd just traversed.

A cold, clammy body slammed into me, almost knocking me to the ground.

"Thea, I'm so sorry. I can't do this alone. I know you didn't want me to come, but I followed you and I … what *is* this freak show place?" His heart hammered against mine as he clung to me, trembling from the cold.

I wrapped my arms around him and anxiously scanned his face. His dark eyes stared back at mine, lit with a thousand questions. "It's okay." I brushed my hand over his cheek. This was the worst thing that could happen for him, but I was overjoyed to see him again.

"I'm sorry. I'm so sorry," he whispered, pressing a kiss to my forehead. "I've never been so happy to see your grumpy face."

"Don't be sorry," I answered, shifting until my lips almost touched his ear. "Say nothing of what you are," I murmured as softly as I could, hoping the others wouldn't hear the warning.

"You're not going to kick my butt for following you?"

"There's nothing to be done about it now. You can't go back." I took his frozen hand and turned back to the others.

"What is this human doing here?" Druan pulled Ben away from me, peering down at him like he was considering tossing him into the void.

"He isn't human," I blurted, anxious to keep Ben from ruining his chances of surviving their world before he even arrived. I cast about for a reasonable lie and offered the first thing that came to mind. "His father was a Berserker." Ben had a bit of the look of a Berserker with his dark eyes and careless manner. Druan would buy it. "He just didn't know what he was until we met. It's a long story, but I trust him with my life. He comes with us."

"Your Majesty, are you sure?" Fiske eyed Ben with a sneer of distaste.

"Did he just … Your *Majesty?*" Ben's eyebrows shot up in surprise. "Your Majesty?" His laughter rang out, echoing like a gunshot, and he quickly slapped a hand over his mouth. "You? Thea? Come on." He gave me a skeptical look.

"We have better things to do than mock me." I shoved him ahead.

"Are you like a queen or something?" He walked backwards a few paces.

"Alithea is Princess of Valsgard and will be Queen Heir when we return." Fiske managed to puff himself up like an angry chicken.

"Princess?" Ben cocked his head and squinted at me in the darkness. "I'm sorry, I just can't see it." Humor laced his tone.

"You'd do well to try, boy," Fiske hissed.

"What's this guy's problem? Is he like your boyfriend or something?"

"I am her betrothed," Fiske answered regally at the same time I said, "No."

"*Betrothed?*" Ben mouthed the word. "Oh, this is too much. It's like I've fallen into a Black Mirror episode." He shoved his hands into his pockets, shuddering, and that was when I realized he had to be half frozen by now. "Can we leave this place? I'm freezing and there're some creepy voices out there whispering in the dark."

"We'll share my cloak." I tried to slip out of my fur.

"Enough." Druan raised a hand. "Alithea, keep your cloak. Ben will travel with Amara; she will keep him warm. Fiske, move ahead with Vendela. I'll bring up the rear with the princess."

"Warm? Which one is Amara?" Ben turned to face Vendela and the dragon. Amara snorted a puff of smoke at him. "Whoa, what was that?" He took a step toward her. "Ooh, you are warm." He sidled up next to her. "Can I hug you? I'm freezing."

Amara gave a low growl but allowed him to stay close.

"Is he always so chatty?" Druan asked.

"Unfortunately." I forced a smile to mask my fear. Ben was going to regret ever meeting me, but for the moment, I was desperately happy to see him. I could keep him safe. I *would* keep him safe. With whatever waited for me at home, I needed a friend I could trust. One who could remind me not to take everything so seriously.

"Can he climb?" Druan asked.

"He has a name, and it's Ben." Ben swept into an elaborate bow. "And yes, I can climb, among many other talents."

"All right everyone, we don't have enough climbing gear for six," Druan announced. "You come with me, Princess; we'll double up." He tossed a set of gear to Ben. "Dela and Fiske will lead the way with Amara and Ben in the middle. Let's make this quick, we have a lot of time to make up."

I wasn't comforted by the thought of climbing such a long way with someone who was clearly afraid of heights. But I followed him anyway, waiting for the others to begin their ascent. Druan pulled the climbing gear from his pack and set to work strapping me into the double harness that would hold both of us.

"We will have to take turns climbing," he said. "This is going to be a long night. Have you ever done this before?"

"Yes." I nodded, trying not to recall the memories. "On my way to the human realm—and without climbing gear." I took his answering grunt as one of begrudging respect.

Druan worked quickly, securing our lines to the sheer cliffside. He moved with expert precision, sinking anchors into the wall and looping lines from one safety to the next as we began our way up to the northward path.

Once again, we faded into a cocoon of darkness, just the two of us. The hissing voices called to us, but I ignored them. Druan seemed remarkably more in control now than he had on the ledge. His body language showed no trace of fear. He was quiet, concentrating on each movement.

We developed a system as we went. I took over sinking the anchors into the wall and he looped our safety lines. We worked together to pull our combined weight up a few feet at a time.

Druan reached for the next handhold and I anchored another clip, on and on without an end in sight. My arms screamed in agony after the first hour, but we had to keep moving at a steady pace. We'd already lost so much time.

"My grandfather taught me how to hunt," Druan said softly, breaking the silence. "When I was just a boy."

"Isn't that some kind of a Berserker rite of passage?" I frowned, not sure what brought on this conversation.

"Berserker fathers teach their sons how to hunt, but my father ... was never overly involved in my life." Druan's forearms bulged as he pulled on a cord. "So my grandfather taught me our ways as much as he could. "When I was seven or eight." He reached for the next handhold, looping our safety lines before lifting us up a few more feet. "I was on a hunting party with the other boys who grew up on my father's lands. Though I was the Jarl's son, and they served my father, I did not grow up with them and didn't fit in. So, I wandered off on my own. I thought I could outsmart the hunting party and reach the destination before everyone else." Druan's muscles strained with each movement, yet his single-minded focus was obviously on our conversation.

"I climbed high up into the mountains and worked my way along a ledge until there was nothing in front of me or behind. I was stuck."

"I see." The fear of the last hours made more sense now. He must have relived every moment of that harrowing experience from his childhood.

"I stayed there all night, frozen in place. I didn't think I would ever make it out. My grandfather had to come find me."

"How did your people react when they discovered your struggle?"

"They didn't find out." Druan smiled. "My sneaky grandfather guided me back to the trail and told me how to reach the top of the mountain—a significant rite of passage for Berserker boys. It earned me some level of respect among my peers that day. My grandfather never told anyone that when he found me, I was a sobbing, sniveling coward of a mess." He chuckled at the memory.

There was something so mesmerizing about his voice. I could listen to him recite the lawbooks of the Nine Realms and find it interesting—so as long as he wasn't insulting me.

"Stuck on a mountain ledge all night with nowhere to go?" I could imagine how horrible that must have been for a seven-year-old. "The few hours we spent back there were enough to make me never want to go hiking again."

"I much prefer climbing with gear," Druan said dryly. "This way I can control my journey." He reached up for the next ledge. "I can select my own path, allowing me to have a say in my own destiny. Inching along a ledge just waiting for the path to run out leaves too much up to fate for my taste." His breath had become labored and a sheen of sweat covered his brow.

"Want me to take over for a little while?" I gazed up at the towering cliffside stretching into the abyss. If we didn't get off this mountain soon, we weren't going to make it.

"Are you sure you can manage it? I'm kind of heavy."

"My Valkyrie can, but I'll have to partially shift first. Can you hold us steady for a moment?"

"I've got you," Druan responded.

As we hung there, I reached for my inner Valkyrie. I couldn't fully transform—that would be disastrous with my heavy wings—but I could definitely use the strength and stamina of my other form right about now.

My hands elongated and my bones lightened. I felt Druan shift imperceptibly beside me as my weight changed. My eyes tightened and my shoulders clenched as my Valkyrie tried to flood my system.

"Easy," I murmured, warning her she couldn't come out fully. She calmed and the transformation stopped.

"Take a rest while you can." I took up the lines and set a steady pace.

I climbed as long as I could and when I tired, Druan took over again.

"How did you do this alone, Princess?" Druan suddenly asked. "And at such a young age? You must have been terrified."

"The first time? I was fueled by desperation and at the end of my rope," I said. "I was facing things that were far more terrifying to me than anything I might have come across here. My only way out was forward, so I just kept moving."

"And now?" he asked.

"Same thing." I gave another yank. "I never wanted to be queen, especially when I believed there was someone much better for the job, but now it doesn't look like I have much choice. My people need me, and I won't let them down again."

CHAPTER 11

I took a deep breath and sank to my knees on the solid ground beneath me. My body ached and my arms burned from the exertion of the last day. We finally reached the mountain peak and stumbled onto a healthy section of the bridge. The pathway here glowed with a vibrancy we had yet to see. Only a few of these sections still existed and this one seemed like it had remained untouched since the great war. I was almost mesmerized by the swirling rainbow iridescence of the stone.

"Five minutes, everyone," Druan said. "That's all we can risk."

Ben collapsed next to me, stretching out on his back and flinging an arm over his eyes. He looked exhausted. I patted his shoulder in sympathy. "You okay?"

"I don't think so. No." He turned to face me. "This place freaks me out. I can hardly breathe here." He tried to take a deep breath that sent him into a coughing fit.

"It's the pressure of the void." I rolled onto my side toward him, sharing a corner of my cloak with him. "Just take shallow, even breaths and you'll be okay."

Ben latched onto my hand. "Don't hate me for following you."

"I don't." I squeezed his hand. "But you're going to have to be careful. They won't hesitate to kill you if they find out."

"You told them I'm a Berserker. I don't even know what that is." Ben's voice was barely a frightened whisper in my ear.

"They're pretty much human but they have a special bond with what they call kindreds—usually a wolf or a bear. For now, just be yourself—just maybe not so extra—and keep your Valkyrie in check, no matter what happens."

Ben nodded, shivering in the absence of Amara's heat. "My traveling companion doesn't talk. Like at all. She has no words."

I let out a laugh that echoed in the silence. "That must be killing you." Ben loved to talk more than anyone I'd ever known.

"At least she's hot—in more ways than one." Ben sat up and glanced over his shoulder at Amara resting beside Vendela. "I may have a new type."

"That dragon will cook and eat you before she'll give you the time of day."

"Dragon?" He arched a brow at me. "That's … intense." He gazed at Amara with renewed interest.

"You're hopeless." I shoved him.

"You love me, you know it."

"I tolerate you at best."

"Whatever, I'm your favorite person." He flashed an arrogant smirk.

"I'm afraid for you, Ben." I bit down on my bottom lip to keep from saying too much. "But I am glad to have you with me." I stood and stepped up onto a boulder to survey our surroundings. The rocky mountaintop was wide, like a ridge, stretching out far into the distance. I could see clearly here in the brighter gleam of the stone. The blue iridescence of the path blazed like a beacon through the mountains, but I had a bad feeling this branch of the bridge wouldn't lead us to Vahland Reach.

"Which way is north?" Vendela stepped up beside me.

I glanced down at my compass and turned in a circle, my shoulders drooping as I stopped when the needle pointed north. Walking to the far edge of the summit where Druan stood, I peered into the darkness below.

Vendela joined us, her face grim. "We will have to scale down to the pathway below to continue north," she said.

"So we've only climbed over an obstacle in the road?" My voice came out higher than normal in my shock. "We haven't made any real progress?"

"Afraid not," Druan said.

I gazed down into the depths of the darkness to see the dim light of the north road far below.

"It suppose it could be worse." I sighed as I turned back to face the group. "But we need to move if we're going to make up for the time we've lost."

"Climbing down will be easier," Druan said. "But we're going to have to push to make up time once we get down there."

Vendela passed around a meal of beef jerky and dried fruit. I took several great gulps from my canteen, my mouth dry as sandpaper. It was as if the void had sucked the moisture and nutrients from my body, like it wanted to drain my life force as much as I wanted to drain the contents of my canteen.

Once again, I found myself in close quarters with Druan as we scaled down the northern cliffside. It was a quick descent. When we reached the bottom, the pathway shimmered with an indigo light and loomed wide, but there were no boundaries. The path dropped off into the void on either side. We would have to be careful not to stray too close to the edge.

"We should run, for a while at least." Vendela said, her tone apprehensive. "As long as the trail is wide enough."

"Agreed." Druan gathered up his things and took a final sip from his canteen. "Keep to the middle of the road where it's safest."

Vendela led the way, setting out with an even jog. As we settled into a rhythm, she picked up the pace. Before long, my legs burned and my lower back cramped from the effort to keep up. I was out of shape and it showed, but Ben ran as though he did this every day.

I cast a glance over my shoulder, unable to make out the enormous mountain we'd just climbed over. Anger welled up inside me, anger at the gods for nearly destroying our world. This was once a beautiful place of safe passage, and now it was a ruin—a relic of an ancient world I wasn't sure I would ever understand.

"Come on, *Majesty*, you can do better than this," Ben taunted as he ran beside me. "You've spent too many nights alone with Netflix and the couch."

Icy sweat trickled down my back despite the freezing temperatures. My arms pumped as I ran, keeping pace with Vendela and Amara as they led the way.

"Shut your face. Unless you want to end up tossed into the void." My breath came out ragged and my words nearly unintelligible.

"Yeah, you think you could catch me, Princess?" He held his arms out wide as if challenging me to try.

"I will do the honors if you two don't shut up." Druan jogged just behind me like a demon on my tail, pressing me to run faster.

After running as fast as I could manage for more than an hour, I was spent. My steps faltered and my legs trembled. The others slowed around me until we were all walking and panting. I felt like barfing up a lung or two.

The path suddenly widened into a flat plain, casting an other-worldly glow in the darkness. For the first time since we left the mountaintop, I could clearly see the others and our surroundings. My breath came out in a white fog as I gazed around the strange clearing. The void was still there, an ever-present pressure crushing in on us from all sides.

"Take a break," Druan announced. "Eat, drink, catch your breath and then we move out."

I nodded, sinking to my knees where I stood. The ground was slick and cold like ice, but it was heaven to be off my feet and I intended to enjoy every second of such luxury. Ben slumped to the ground beside Amara, his head bobbing toward his chin as he promptly fell asleep.

"How are you feeling, your Majesty?" Fiske crouched beside me with concern-filled eyes that creeped me out. "Can I get you anything?" He fussed over me like my childhood maid.

He was too nice to strangle, but I wanted to shake him until the impulse to anticipate my every need died a slow and painful death. Not that Fiske could help the way he was raised any more than he could help the brand on his shoulder. The one that marked him as mine.

"My name is Thea, Fiske," I said kindly. "You know I don't expect formality from my friends."

"Friends?" Fiske beamed as he fumbled through his pack, producing a bag of trail mix. The kind I loved, with bits of chocolate and dried pineberries. "I seem to recall a lot of death threats when we were kids, but not much friendship." He handed me the bag. We'd spent our summers together in the Citadel when Fiske and the other children of the nobility were home from school. I just never realized Fiske attended the fortress school for the Chosen Sons.

"Maybe I've changed." I snatched the bag and tried to ignore the way he stared at me in awe. "But marriage is still off the table." I gave a shudder I hoped he would blame on the cold. "I cannot marry anyone who was raised the way you were. I want … a choice. And I want the person I marry to have a choice too."

"I do understand that." Fiske nodded with a rueful smile, helping himself to some trail mix. "But I don't think you ever realized—I made my choice. I've always loved you, Thea." His warm gaze met mine, begging me to understand his point of view.

"You loved the idea of me. You were raised to adore me. To anticipate my every want and desire and never even look at another woman. They *branded* you and the others with *my* name because the Chosen Sons had the right pedigree and potential to become what they deemed a Queen Heir's consort should be."

"And in the end, the council chose me," Fiske said, a spark of life glinting in his eyes. "I fought for that honor. For years." He dropped to the ground to sit beside me. "You have no idea what I went through to win your hand, but you didn't want me." He hung his head in shame like he'd somehow failed in his life's goal. "What's happened since your absence is all my fault. I wasn't enough for you. I failed our people."

"First, I am no one's prize to be won. And second, you get those thoughts of failure out of your head right now, Fiske Ryland. You did nothing wrong. I'm just the stubborn princess who doesn't like to be told what to do. You weren't the one I'd choose, but that doesn't mean I left because of you."

"You ran away from our betrothal ceremony." His shoulders slumped. "What was I supposed to think? What were our people supposed to think?"

My stomach dropped as I realized for the first time what a

mess I'd made of his life. "I'm so sorry about that. I was a scared kid and my world was closing in on me. It was never about you and the betrothal; it was about the life those things represented. I want a life where I get to make decisions for myself. At sixteen, no one listened to me and I didn't see another way out."

"It's okay, your Majesty. I've only ever wanted you to be happy."

I sighed, wondering if his training would ever fade enough for him to make a life for himself that didn't include me.

"Time to move out," Druan called to our tired group. "I'm going to scout ahead; follow when you're ready." He turned toward the open plain and I felt an urge to follow him and put some distance between me and Fiske.

"Do you have enough water, your Majesty—I mean Thea?" Fiske's Adam's Apple bobbed anxiously in his throat. "I've been conserving my water, so I have extra for you if you need it."

The dry rasp of my throat begged me to accept his offer, but I couldn't. "I have plenty, Fiske. Please don't sacrifice your comfort for mine. It's not your job."

"You might not see it that way, but I do. Our people do." He fumbled with his canteen.

My hands balled into fists at my side. "I don't want to be some-one's job."

Fiske looked down at his feet, unable to meet my gaze. "I know. It's just … I have no other use, your Majesty. This is what I was born for. What I was chosen by our people to do with my life. I can't just turn that off."

I climbed to my feet, refusing his help. "How about we meet somewhere in the middle of this mess, then?"

"What do you mean?" Fiske's eyes widened.

"You've spent your life learning how to please me. It would please me for you to speak your mind and be a trusted friend and advisor. I need all the friends I can get, but what I don't need right now is a husband."

"I can do that." Fiske stood taller, as if he suddenly had a purpose that made sense to him.

"But hear me now." I placed my hands on his shoulders, forcing him to look at me. "If there is ever a chance for you to be happy pursuing another path, a future with someone you really love, then I want you to grab hold of that person and never let go." I turned toward the pathway to join Druan, leaving Fiske gaping behind me.

The pathway was slick with a thick layer of ice. I moved carefully, slipping and sliding before Ben glided up beside me and grabbed my hand. We both almost went down and it would have been comical anywhere else.

"Don't pull me down with you!" I clutched his waist.

"Who's the barnacle now?" Ben locked his arm around me.

"You two need to stop clowning around and get over here." Druan's unamused voice drifted through the darkness from up ahead.

"We can't have another delay," I groaned, trying to find my footing so we could move quickly.

The ground trembled beneath my feet and a noise like shattering glass rent the silence.

"Dru!" Vendela screamed.

I jerked my head toward the spot where Druan had stood only a moment ago. A gaping hole lay there now.

"Vendela, no! It's an ice shelf!" I ran after the Berserker woman. "Get down now or you'll fall through." I flung myself onto my stomach, sliding toward the hole in the pathway. "Stop." I shot my hand up to halt Vendela's approach. "We don't need two of you down there."

Vendela scooted carefully to the edge of the hole, mimicking my movements to distribute her weight evenly. "What's down there?" Her wolfish eyes flashed silver.

It was a long drop into the darkness below. But I could just make out the splash of water.

"It's a lake," I gasped, relieved he'd simply fallen to a lower level of the path and not directly into the void.

"He's going to freeze to death." Vendela looked like she was about to dive in after him, but I laid a firm hand on her shoulder to stop her.

I didn't think about it as I shed my cloak and cumbersome bag. My Valkyrie took over the moment I lunged through the opening in the ice, plummeting through the darkness. My wings ripped out of my back, but they were useless in the dead air. Screaming, I fell toward the inky black lake.

Tucking my wings around me, I crashed through the surface feet first, the frigid water biting my skin like a thousand tiny daggers. I spread my wings to slow my descent and looked for Druan. He floated into the black depths of the lake, swirling with ghostly shadows I didn't relish having a close encounter with. His arms hung suspended in front of him and his hair fanned out around him. If he went in headfirst, the impact at the surface had probably knocked him out and his waterlogged cloak was pulling him down. My Valkyrie was strong, but I'd never tried swimming with my wings out. I was about to now.

Diving deeper, I hugged my wings close to my body, using my arms to slice through the water. I reached for Druan, wrapping my tertiary wings around his waist. I kicked toward the surface but made little headway. My waterlogged wings were too heavy. Just as my lungs started to burn, I flapped my wings, beating against the current that dragged us down. I felt something pop and a wave of agony spread like fire down my left side.

I managed to break through the icy surface, hauling Druan's

head above water. I needed him to wake up. My sodden wings would pull us back under and I didn't have the strength to do this again.

"Wake up, Dru." I slapped his face as I struggled to keep us above water. My left side burned with every movement, but I kept us afloat with my right wing.

"Thea?" His eyes fluttered open. "What happened? What did you do?" He groaned.

"I saved your neck, but I'm afraid I'm going to need you to return the favor, sooner rather than later. We're either going to drown or freeze to death if we don't get out of here."

"Can you shift back?"

"Not yet and definitely not with a broken wing." I gasped from the pain and cold, spewing icy water from my mouth.

"You can let me go. I'm awake now."

"If I do, I'll sink like a stone. My wings are too heavy."

Druan's frozen hands wrapped around my waist as he searched in every direction, looking for solid ground. "You can stop trying to save me now and climb on my back, you blasted stubborn Valkyrie." He guided us through the water.

"Stubborn?" My voice shook despite my best efforts. I needed to get out now. "I just saved you, and you're giving me crap for it?"

"You should have left me." Druan's lips trembled as I gripped his shoulders, my good wings fanning out behind us.

"I'm not the type to leave anyone behind. Even ill-mannered bullies who don't have sense enough to say thank you when they've been rescued."

"You call this a rescue?" Druan struggled through the murky water, making for the rocky cliff just visible in the low light.

"You're breathing, aren't you?" I gritted my teeth through the pain. If it hurt this much when I was almost completely numb from the cold, I would be in big trouble once I was warm again.

"For the record, I'd choose a good drowning over freezing to death any day."

"You're just grumpy because a woman saved your hide." All I got in response was a typical Berserker grunt of disapproval.

Bright white light erupted overhead.

"Druan?" Vendela shouted over the roar of dragon fire. "You better not be dead."

"No such luck, Dela. The princess broke her wing."

"You say that like I did it on purpose," I snapped.

"You know better than anyone that you can't fly here."

"It was instinct." I kicked toward the rocky shore, eager to get away from him and assess the damage to my wing. A Valkyrie and a broken wing were never a good combination. I prayed to the Mother it was a clean break.

Amara's white-hot flames melted a wide hole through the thick ice directly above us.

"You okay, Thea?" Ben peered anxiously through the hole. "I'm coming down there to get you."

"Stay there, Ben. I'll be fine." Sucked in a breath, bracing for the pain as I pulled myself out of the water and onto a boulder. The last thing I needed was Ben playing the hero and doing something he shouldn't be able to do.

"Can you climb?" Vendela asked, tossing the climbing gear down so we could scale the sheer cliff up to the opening Amara made through the ice.

"I'll need help with the Valkyrie."

"I have two perfectly good arms," I reminded him.

"Your wings are too heavy. You'll injure yourself worse if you try to climb up on your own."

I opened my mouth to press my argument, but Amara landed beside me in a crouch. Smoke puffed from her nostrils and her eyes blazed with the heat of her dragon fire, yet she held onto her human form. Still, she burned hot like a brazier. We both huddled close to her warmth as the dragon silently examined my wing.

"It's bad, isn't it?" I bit my lip, glancing down at the unnatural angle of my primary wing as it dangled at my side.

Amara only nodded, making a sympathetic sound in her throat as she met my gaze with her intense dragon eyes, the narrowed black pupils surrounded by a sea of green as wild as the Druid forests of Manaheim. So much wisdom rested behind those eyes that looked at me with warm sympathy now.

With a nod, I agreed to Amara's silent assessment. "It must be done." I braced for the pain headed my way.

"What?" Druan glanced between us. "What is she doing? We don't have time for this," he protested as Amara helped me lie down on the big boulder. Druan moved to toss me over his shoulder, but Amara stepped between us, sending a stream of fire toward him, a clear warning to back off.

"Fine. Bind her wing and let's go. The clock is ticking, and we still have a long way to go."

"It's not broken." I eyed Amara's movement, accepting the leather belt she'd removed from her waist. "I almost wish it was." My natural power accelerated my healing. I would make a full recovery from a clean break in a matter of days. But this wasn't a simple break.

"It's dislocated?" Druan's voice dropped in sympathy. "What can I do?" He knelt beside me, looking to Amara for instruction.

The dragon pressed against my shoulders, indicating he should hold me down.

"Yep, this is going to hurt." I wedged the leather belt between my teeth and searched for something to hold on to.

Druan crouched above me, resting his hands against my shoulders. "Grab my forearms and squeeze as hard as you need to, but try not to break anything."

"I'll do my best not to crush your delicate bones," I mumbled around the belt.

Druan snorted and Amara rolled her eyes.

"I'm ready." I took a deep breath. "Just try not to cripple me … please." I locked eyes with Amara.

The dragon gave me a regal nod. If I had to dislocate a wing, having a dragon on hand to slip it back into place was the best possible scenario. Amara understood the gravity of the situation like no other. A dislocated wing joint could permanently ground a creature of flight. I couldn't imagine a world where I could no longer fly.

Amara carefully arranged my injured wing, draping it across the rocky terrain and forcing the limb back to its natural position. With another nod, she straddled the wing, placing her foot at the juncture of the joint. Lifting the lower half, she held it steady as Druan counted to three. At three, Amara threw her weight back, pulling my lower wing with all her might.

I screamed as fire shot down the length of my body, the bones popping and sliding into place. Immediate relief washed over me like a cool blanket. Druan held me tight as my breath shuddered and I struggled to take in the air I needed.

"Majesty!" Fiske called down to her. "What's happened?"

"Thea!" Ben shoved him aside. "Talk to me. What's going on down there?"

"I'm okay, Ben. I'm okay," I muttered as Amara massaged the joint, coaxing it to stay in place. For a Valkyrie, once dislocated, a wing joint was susceptible to dislocating again and again. I would need to be careful over the coming weeks until I regained strength in my limb. And traversing the bridge was not high on the list of acceptable activities for an injured Valkyrie.

"Can she shift back now?" Druan asked.

With a shake of her head and snort of disapproval, Amara

refused to allow it.

"I think it would dislocate again if I tried to shift," I said. Amara nodded, miming the importance of me taking it slow.

"Slow?" Druan shot to his feet, running a frustrated hand through the wet hair at his nape. "We were already behind schedule." He glowered at me.

Amara silently pointed at the shattered ice where Druan fell through, as if to remind him he was the reason we were even further behind schedule now.

"Fine, help me get her out of here." Druan and Amara guided me back to my feet. The weight of my sodden wings pulled on my injury.

Amara shook her head, making an annoyed sound with her tongue. She moved my wing carefully, folding it against my side. It felt better in that position, with less stress on the joint. Amara snapped her fingers at Druan and wrapped her belt around my waist, binding my wing to my side.

"I think she wants your belt," I said.

"Right." Druan sighed, slipping it off his waist. "Hurry this along." He tossed the belt at Amara.

"She's just trying to make sure I'll be able to fly again," I muttered. "Don't rush her."

"You can't fly in the void, Thea."

"Not here. She's trying to make sure I'll be able to fly again … ever. This is a serious injury for our kind. I'm grateful Amara is here to help me." I grasped the dragon's hand as she finished immobilizing my wing. "That feels much better."

Amara nodded, though worry lines creased her brow.

I dropped her hand and straightened my shoulders. "You've done the best you can in these circumstances. I trust you."

Amara lowered her head slightly, the closest a dragon would ever come to bowing before any king or queen.

CHAPTER 12

"I'm so sorry, your Majesty." Fiske fluttered around me, trying to make himself useful as he helped me back into my dry cloak. "Are you warm enough? Once we get back to the Citadel, we'll get you to the healers. They'll take care of your wing."

"Dude, she's going to scratch your face off if you don't stop fussing over her." Ben inserted himself between Fiske and me. "Knock it off, Bro."

"Your Majesty, who does this boy think he is?" Fiske did his best to mimic Ben's trash talk.

"*Boy*?" Ben took a menacing step toward Fiske, who ducked behind me for protection.

"Blessed Mother Sigrún, save me from these idiots." I sighed. "Amara took care of me just as well as any of our healers, Fiske. I'll be fine. Ben, he's just worried, leave him be."

"You really want me to leave you alone with super creep here?" Ben jabbed a thumb over his shoulder.

"Well, I didn't say that," I hissed. "Just don't be a prick."

"We don't have time for childish love triangles." Druan shoved Ben toward Amara and sent Fiske back to Vendela. "Stay together and move fast, but be vigilant. We can't afford any more delays."

"Love triangle?" Ben and I shared a sneer. "He has met us, right?" he whispered. "We'd kill each other."

Druan let out a feral sound I couldn't place, but it shut Ben up.

Ben looked at me in horror. "That sound he just made … that's not natural."

"We have a few hours left," Vendela said, looking as weary and stressed as I felt. "It can't be much farther now."

"It's *not* a love triangle." I pushed past Druan, following Vendela and Fiske, my good wings dragging heavily behind me.

"Could have fooled me." Druan fell in step with me, casting a wary eye on my injured wing strapped to my side with his belt.

I ignored him, focusing on my breathing. Soon, the only sounds that reached my ears were the huffing and puffing of my companions and the soft whispers from the void. Everyone was feeling the pressure. If we didn't make it out soon, the madness would begin to set in.

Cold sweat trickled down my back as the shadowy voices grew louder, trickling into my mind, trying to convince me it might not be so bad to sit down and rest for a while.

I focused on the pain. The pain was something real.

The voices and paranoia were not.

My breath had grown shallow, and my lungs were ready to explode, but I kept moving silently at Druan's side, keeping my eyes trained on my feet as the incline of the pathway spiraled up into oblivion. The voices morphed into phantoms that swirled around me, telling me lies I fought to resist.

Your mother is dead and it's all your fault.

Stay here with us. It's a just punishment for your selfish acts.

You don't deserve to rule.

Part of me wanted to step off the pathway and let the void take me, but my people needed me. I might fail. I might make it worse, but I had to try to fix the damage I'd caused. Resisting the voices, I focused on thoughts of home. I needed a plan—I was not prepared for my return.

"Is it getting warmer?" Vendela's voice cut through the phantom whispering. Her red-rimmed eyes seemed sunken into a ghastly face, like she was becoming a creature of the void. I blinked and her normal features came back into sharp focus. The paranoia told me I couldn't trust her, that I should push her back into the abyss where she came from, but the logical side of my brain was still active enough to tell me that was ludicrous.

"I thought it was just me." I pulled my t-shirt away from my sticky skin, scanning my surroundings for familiar landmarks. The blue iridescence of the pathway dimmed behind us, but the light had grown brighter—hotter. Just ahead, the sunlight of my homeland and the sizzling hot boundary where Valsgard borders met the bridge shone like a beacon to welcome us home. Here the stone walls didn't glow or whisper unsettling things. Here, the walls were just stone.

The others grew excited, eager to leave the oppressive world behind, but I slowed my steps. I had a decision to make before I could do this next part.

Druan's steps quickened, reaching back for my arm. I refused. Meeting the Berserker's fathomless eyes, I shook my head. "Not yet," I whispered, and then called out, "everyone stop."

They all turned to me with slumped shoulders and travel-weary faces. Already the paranoia was fading.

"I know you're anxious for this journey to end, but the moment I step through the boundary, Neela will know I've returned. If we stand a chance against her, we need the element of surprise on our side … and an army loyal to me. We can't return to the Citadel. Not yet."

The bounty hunters stood in a circle, looking to Druan for direction.

"What are you suggesting?" Druan stared down at me, his arms hanging like dead weight beside him. "How can she know you've returned?"

I backed away from the group, angling myself toward the craggy stone walls. "The moment I set foot into the Nine Realms, the power of the gods will greet me, as well as my own magic. If I still have their blessing, that is. She will feel it. I can't allow that."

"So you're saying, what? You won't go back?" Druan's face twisted in disgust.

I pulled my shoulders back and stood tall, lifting my chin in defiance as I took another step away from the group. "I will not back down from a fight. But I will do this on my terms. We are nearly at our destination. Up ahead, the bridge branches off into three paths—"

"There is only one way out, Princess," the Berserker corrected me. "And it leads straight into the Citadel where your aunt and sister await your return, and that's exactly where we're all going right now."

"There are three pathways. Trust me—" I felt for the stone wall at my back.

"I've traveled this bridge more than anyone here," Druan argued. "You're mistaken. The pathway does not branch off anywhere."

"Blessed Mother save me, will you give it a rest?" I flexed my hands, itching to sink my talons into his flesh. "Just stop browbeating me for two seconds and let me finish." I gave him my best glare. "The main path leads across the border and directly into the tunnels under the Citadel and Queen Astrid's protection." I pointed to the obvious path that led to a stone archway just visible ahead.

"To the left of the archway lies a treacherous path across the Broken Isles and into Manaheim—to the Druids, our fiercest allies. The Broken Isles are a remnant of the bridge that did not fall into the void in the last age. Though the way is difficult, it is not like the scary place we've just traversed.

"Only a Valkyrie can access those tunnels. But there is a third way through the queen's chamber that bypasses the boundary. That is where I must go now, but I must go alone. Fiske, I need you to open the gateway to the Broken Isles for them." I looked at the others. "He will show you the way to Manaheim. There is a campsite just a few hours in where you can rest comfortably tonight. I will meet you on the border of the Dýre Forest in a few days. Ben, I want you to stay with Fiske no matter what."

"Uh, no." Ben came to stand beside me. "I'm going with you."

"No." Druan dismissed us both. "We will all return to the Citadel as planned. There we can regroup, and Thea can meet with her superiors to discuss the Neela problem." He met my gaze. "There, I listened, happy now?" His sing-song cadence almost made me smile. It came out strongest when he was either teasing or irritated.

"Has anyone ever told you you're impossible to reason with?" I just managed to stop myself from stomping my foot.

"Frequently," Vendela quipped and Druan turned his death glare on her.

"Stay with Fiske," I mouthed to Ben. Drawing a knife from my backpack, I sliced open my palm.

"What do you think you're doing?" Druan grabbed my wrist.

"What I must. This doesn't concern you." I tried to shake him off.

"Let her go, you big bully." Ben kicked him in the shin, but it didn't faze him.

Druan let out a menacing growl. "I promised your sister and your people I would see you returned and I mean to get the job done." He held my arm in a bruising grip.

I glanced down at his fingers encircling my arm. "You would do well to remember I am the Queen Heir, not only of Valsgard, but of the Nine Realms, which means however much I may not want it, I will be your High Queen one day. Release me. Now."

"You aren't anyone's queen yet," he snarled back at me. "I will drag you off of this bridge by your hair before I allow you to shirk your duty one more minute." His eyes narrowed to slits and he made one of those odd screeching noises in his throat.

"You do not know me or my intentions." I wrenched my arm out of his grasp. "I'm well aware of my duty and it would be a lot easier if you could stop bossing me around long enough to let me do it. I will not leave this bridge with you. I will not return to Valsgard in a way that will alert Neela to my presence when I am at my weakest. I must go through the queen's chamber where you cannot follow." I turned, pressing my bloodied hand against a rudimentary emblem carved into the stone wall. "Only those with the blood of a queen coursing through their veins can enter the Northern Kingdoms this way." I melted into the stone, leaving the gaping Berserker behind.

Diamonds sparkled in the sunlight behind me. They weren't really diamonds, but Sylvi always thought they were. She'd been so disappointed to learn they were only crystals. The thought of seeing her soon sent a chill down my spine. I turned to gaze across the chamber. Only a few more steps and I would return full circle.

But my journey wasn't over yet.

I trembled as I approached the mosaic tiled floor spreading out in a circle to engulf the room. A golden medallion occupied the center of the floor, depicting the rulers of my people. Not just the Valkyries, but all of the Nine Realms—what was left of them anyway. The boundary blazed like a hotwire across the room—except where the medallion swept it aside like a curtain entrance into the queen's chamber. I studied it for a moment, bracing myself for the return of magic. Magic I had lived without for three years.

With a deep breath, I stepped onto the golden medallion, waiting for lightning to strike.

My own magic hit me first, like a wrecking ball to my chest, stealing my breath. Then the power of the gods raged through me, a punishment for daring to give up what they bestowed upon my family during the last age. Throwing my head back, I screamed, bracing for the agony that would rip me to shreds before I could put myself back together. But it didn't come. The vessel within me didn't fill as much as I expected it would. Instead a trickle of the power began to collect within me. Slow and tormenting.

Gasping, I stumbled forward, my palms and knees crashing into the rough floor. My body quaked as I grappled with my magic for control. Bright spots of light interrupted my vision and nausea sent my head spinning just before a surge of filthy, shadowy darkness engulfed me and I slumped to the floor.

"Thea. Wake up." Calloused hands slapped my face and I jerked awake, gasping for breath.

"Something's wrong." I forced the words out, my throat raw

from screaming. For years, I'd dreaded this part. I expected a tidal wave of the power of the gods to wreak havoc on my body—I got a weaker version of that, but something dark had accompanied the return of my magic. A rush of tainted fury washed over me, leaving me violently ill and full of shame.

"Where does it hurt? What's happening?" Druan's rough hands searched me for injury. "Talk to me, Thea."

"It's my Valkyrie magic …" I gasped, shaking my head. "It's all wrong." My body shook and my eyes rolled back into my head. "The pain … should be worse. So much worse."

"Worse than this?" He pulled me back against his chest, sitting with me on the cold tiled floor.

I sucked in a deep breath. A feverish sweat left my hair and wings limp and damp. I was going to puke any minute. "The pain from the return of my magic should have come faster, harder and blessedly quick. It's not as intense, but it should be a memory by now."

"We need to get you to the healers." Druan tried to help me up, but I refused to move.

"No. We have to get moving." I sat up, putting a little distance between us. "How are you here?" My brow furrowed in confusion. "This is the queen's chamber."

"Well, you didn't say it had to be any specific sort of queen, so I took a chance my mother's blood would get me inside."

"That doesn't make sense. You'd have to be … the child of a queen." I frowned up at him, searching his Berserker eyes for answers. "And Berserkers don't have queens."

"What about nephews of queens? My mother is the Druid high priestess, identical twin sister to Queen Orlagh of Manaheim. I figured her blood would be close enough."

"But your father is…?"

"A Berserker Jarl hardly worth mentioning." He swept a hand

through my damp hair, smoothing it away from my face. "Are you okay?"

"No." I wanted to have a good cry and then curl into a ball to sleep for a week. "Not at all. Something went wrong." My hands shook and I didn't have the strength to sit up. But the pain was finally abating.

"This chamber is like a back door into the Nine Realms?" Druan glanced around the room.

I nodded. "If I crossed the boundary directly, the power of the gods would return to me in full, alerting not only Neela of my return, but my people as well. We're all connected by the power. The high queen and her heir are vessels that funnel that power to those that need it to survive. It is because of us that you are able to bond with your kindred and tap into your Berserker magic. Without a proper vessel, we would all lose our magic."

"And right now, as much as we might not like it, Neela is that vessel." Druan nodded in understanding.

"And I am not ready to announce my return. Entering through the chamber gives me access to the power so I can begin to siphon again—to refill the vessel within me," I added at his look of confusion. "It also gives me access to my own Valkyrie magic, which I need to become reacquainted with if I'm going to fight Neela anytime soon. Right now, I need a little time, and a lot of information before I can act. For the moment, everyone inside the Citadel is safe and no one will know I am here. But my people all across Valsgard are hurting; I must help them first."

"You don't look so good, Thea. I think you need to help yourself right now." His voice was softer and his eyes filled with worry. His hard edge seemed to have temporarily vanished. I expected it would return with my strength.

"My own magic has returned, but it feels strange. Diminished somehow." I sat up awkwardly and climbed to my feet with

Druan's help. For a moment, I swayed like a tower of bricks about to topple over.

Druan kept a hand on my back to steady me.

"It feels tainted by her touch." I shivered, stumbling across the room, looking for the stone panel that would take us to the Broken Isles from this side of the boundary. "Maybe because for the first time ever, my magic is being fueled by another vessel and not my own."

"What is your plan?" Druan followed me, keeping a wary eye on me lest I fall apart again.

"Oh gosh, you're asking? I'm so used to you charging like a bull through everyone else's plans. I'm not sure my little lady brain can handle making a decision."

Druan's lips pressed into a thin line. "You're not funny, Valkyrie."

I winced at his tone. "And I take it you're more Druid than Berserker?" I dropped my head, feeling like the worst sort of judgmental person. "I'm sorry I made assumptions. The Berserkers and Valkyries have so much bad blood, but I shouldn't have taken that out on you. Clearly my sister trusts you and that should be all that matters."

"My Druid half pleases you?" Druan shook his head in confusion.

"It does because the Druids and Valkyries are allies. And any cousin of my best friend is okay in my book."

"You mean little Morgana? She's several years younger than you, isn't she?"

"The Druid princess was my best friend growing up despite our age difference, and I imagine she's not so little anymore. There is no one I trust more in all the realms other than my own sister. I need to speak with Morgana as soon as possible." I hoped he would see the sense in my plan. I didn't need his approval, but it would be so much easier if he stopped working against me.

"If I know Morgana, she'll already know we're coming."

"That's what I'm counting on." I ran my knife over my thumb and slapped my bloodied hand against the wall to reveal the icy tunnels to the Broken Isles.

CHAPTER 13

"I always wondered, why are they called the Broken Isles?" Druan held a torch, illuminating the tunnel we followed under the mountains of the Citadel.

I was grateful to be away from the pressure of the bridge that didn't allow for such luxuries as torchlight, but it would be far colder once we reached the Isles.

"The city of Vahland Reach lies on an island in Queens Bay." The words rolled off my tongue like a long-forgotten geography lesson. "The Citadel keep was built into the Armur Mountains just across the bay. Those mountains wrap around Vahland Reach like a protective embrace. The Armur Mountains once gave way to the bridge between realms but the Broken Islands are all that remains of the bridge. They connect the arm of the Armur range to Manaheim."

"So the islands are relics of the bridge but they aren't tainted?" Druan followed my weary steps.

"Right. Wait until you see the tunnels that run through the islands. They're magnificent ruins of the old world that still shine with the rainbow iridescence the bridge was known for—but not in the creepy way. These ruins are like the halls of the gods themselves." I both dreaded and longed to see the halls again. I remembered visiting them with my father when I was just a young girl.

"But?" Druan pressed.

I let out a tired sigh. "It's a treacherous path on foot. Nothing like what we just traversed, but it's a cavernous place. Cold and dark with only intermittent patches of sunlight. Even flying, there is no direct path through the halls. The way is littered with boulders and rubble, and there are places that are likely flooded or caved in. We will have to make our way carefully from island to island."

"Are there are bridges between these islands?"

"Of a sort. Enough to get across, at least."

"So not an issue for one who can fly, but for those on foot and with injured wings—"

"It's really going to suck." I peered ahead in the torchlight, eager to catch up with the others and find Morgana. I could trust her to fill me in on everything I needed to know before I faced my cousin. Things she was privy to that my sister's bounty hunters were not. Things Astrid and Sylvi wouldn't know after two years of siege had left them trapped inside the Citadel.

The rough stone tunnel grew icy as we left the safety of the Armur Mountains. The dirt path gave way to smooth, tiled floors and the white iridescent walls shimmered in the torchlight. Huge icicles hung from the cavernous, vaulted ceilings that merged with an oculus, allowing the fading sunlight to flood the hall.

"It's beautiful." Druan took several steps ahead, gazing in awe at the relic of a long-dead era.

"It must have been the grand entrance to the bridge." I turned in a circle, admiring the ancient beauty all around us.

"Where is the camp you mentioned?" Druan pulled me back to our present dire circumstances.

"Just a few miles from here, but I'm hoping we can catch the others before dark."

"We'll never catch them."

"Are you always so negative? They can't be more than a few hours ahead of us."

"I'm not being negative, Princess. It's impossible, you were—"

"Why are you so determined to disagree with me?" I glared at him. I'd had enough of his constant doom and gloom. I had too many other things on my mind.

"I'm not disagreeing with you, I'm just trying to tell you, you're wrong, but if you'll let me finish a sentence, I'll tell you why you're wrong."

"Fine." I put a hand on my hip and cocked my head impatiently.

"They are a full day ahead of us." His toothy smile reminded me of a bear and I shivered under my cloak.

"How is that possible?" I turned toward the fading sunlight shining from the oculus. "It's only late afternoon."

"You spent yesterday afternoon and all night unconscious and thrashing on the floor of the queen's chamber. I couldn't wake you. I thought you were dying. If I'd known how to leave the chamber I would have taken you to the Citadel."

"I was out all night?" I stared at him. "It felt like minutes."

"Most of the morning too. Vendela would have had them up and out by first light. They're nearly to the Manaheim border by now."

"Then we'll have to travel through the night. I don't want to leave them alone in a strange land too long."

"And by them, you mean Ben?"

"Yes, I mean Ben. He's practically human." And a dead man walking if anyone found out he wasn't part Berserker like I claimed.

"Right now you need to rest. We both do or we'll be no good to anyone—and it would be beneficial to everyone if you'd just stop arguing with me."

"Look, I get that you're not my biggest fan." My raised voice bounced around the hall. "You've made that crystal clear, but can we just try to get along—at least until we meet up with our people again? Then you can go back to hating me."

"I don't *hate* you." Druan's voice filled with amusement. "I'm just not overly fond of you."

The campsite was a small chamber off the main hall. It wasn't luxurious by any means, but it looked like an oasis to me. After nearly three days with little rest, I was ready to collapse, even if it was cold enough to freeze the blood in my veins.

"I've never been so cold in my life." Druan clutched his thick fur mantle, drawing it tightly around himself.

"We can get a fire going soon." I stepped down into the dark chamber and took the torch from Druan to light the torches in sconces along the walls.

"Looks like they made camp here last night." Druan inspected the cold embers in the fire pit at the center of the room.

"Looks like your girlfriend left you a note." I crouched beside a series of Berserker runes drawn in soot on the cave floor.

"My girlfriend?" Snorting a laugh, Druan crouched down beside me. "Vendela? She'd get a kick out of that. We are friends. Not lovers."

Lovers? Such a grown-up word. I peered up at the man beside me. He wasn't much older than me, maybe early to mid-twenties. But his manner made me feel inferior and I didn't care for it.

"Well, what's it say?"

"You never learned runes?" Druan frowned at me. He did that a lot.

"That would require remembering lessons I was never very good at. My sister was the scholar. I excelled more at the lessons that put a weapon in my hand."

"I can relate to that." Druan studied the runes on the ground. "It says they left here nearly a full day ago. She must have only let them sleep for a few hours. I imagine she's had enough of tunnels, freezing temperatures, and darkness." With a stretch of creaking bones he rose from his crouch. "She'll want her kindred back with her as soon as possible." He peered up at the dark ceiling as if searching for something.

"We should follow her lead—rest a few hours and be on our way." I was eager to catch up with Ben. He was so reckless, I couldn't help but worry he'd let his secret slip. I crossed the circular chamber to the dwindling stack of firewood against the wall. I gathered kindling and a few small logs, wondering if my magic was strong enough yet to start a fire.

"I can do that." Druan took the logs from me.

I rolled my eyes.

"Not because I'm the man," he said dryly. "Everyone knows about the Queen Heir and her burning magic, but you have a serious injury that could leave you permanently grounded if you aren't careful. You need to rest and not push yourself to test your magic so soon."

"You seem to know more about my injury now than you did when it happened."

"I asked Fiske. He was very worried about you."

So was I, but I didn't have time to consider what might happen if I didn't heal properly.

"I can take you to my mother's temple for healing." Druan crouched over the firepit to arrange the logs and kindling.

"I need to find Morgana first and then decide what my next moves will be."

"The temples aren't too far out of the way."

"The Druid temples are across the Skye Sea in Andmur."

"Which could be on the way if we travel by boat, which would give you time to rest while we travel. Then we circle back to the Dýre Forest just up the river from Andmur."

I shook my head. "I don't' have time to travel in circles. It's only a matter of time before Neela knows I'm back."

"Let's just get some sleep. See how you're doing once we arrive in Manaheim and then we can decide."

"*We*?" I wrapped my arms around my middle, eager for the fire Druan was taking his sweet time building.

"We. Believe it or not, we are on the same side, Thea. Neela has brought much heartache to my mother's people as well as the Valkyrie nation. I will see her deposed, whether that's by your hand or someone else's."

"You have so little faith in me." I rummaged through my bag for my remaining supplies. I was running dangerously low on water. "It makes it difficult to have the confidence I need to face Neela. I have to make it right." I hung my head, too tired for this conversation. "But when others doubt me, it's far too easy to doubt myself."

"Until a few days ago I thought of you as a spoiled princess who chose to run away rather than face her duty to the realm she was born to serve."

"I was sixteen and desperate."

He sat beside me as the flames finally took hold, licking at the dry wood. "I can understand your fears. Perhaps I was too hasty to judge you, but you took one look at me and saw an enemy in my Berserker features and you refused to see anything else." He turned and his dark predator gaze pierced right through me.

"Touché." My face flushed with shame and I scooted closer to the growing fire, stacking another log on. "I will do better. I apologize for judging you."

Druan seemed to be at a loss for words.

I picked up a stick and poked at the fire, shoving more kindling into the flames. "I was trapped inside my tiny little world of the palace and Citadel. Traditions dictated my life long before I was born. I just couldn't make the kind of lifelong commitment they demanded of me when I still didn't know if I was even capable of wearing the crown. It is a heavy burden I feared would crush me."

"I see that now." Druan took the stick from my hands, dropping it into the fire. "It took guts to remove yourself from the line of succession when you felt like you weren't being heard. I can't blame you for that."

"I hear a 'but.'" I held my hands out to the fire, relishing the heat.

"But your choices brought untold consequences to your people."

"And I will make it up to them. Or die trying. And if I ever do become queen, I will devote my life to them." I reached for my canteen, draining the last bit of liquid inside.

"You have more substance than I thought." Druan stared into the flames.

"Is that some kind of backhanded compliment?" I screwed the lid back on my canteen.

A smile tugged at the corners of his mouth. "It is the highest of compliments, considering I thought I was sent to find a princess living out her days in the luxuries of the human world, shirking her duties."

I laughed at that. "Hardly. My mother would die of the irony if she knew her Valkyrie daughter spent her days serving mead to men."

Druan chuckled a deep throaty laugh I found I liked almost as much as his musical voice. "I still say you're a little bit spoiled. You are a princess, after all."

I threw my empty canteen at him. "I will prove to everyone how unspoiled and unselfish I can be."

"Prove it to yourself, Thea. That's all that matters." Druan handed me his canteen. "Drink up. Vendela left us a few pails of snow we can boil for tomorrow. If we don't freeze to death in the night." He rubbed his hands together, tossing another log onto the fire.

"The wood is so dry it's burning up as soon as we put it on." I watched how quickly the flames started to consume the newest logs.

"I will keep the fire going. You can rest."

"There's no sense in that. You're just as tired as I am." I munched on the last of my dried meat, saving the remainder of the trail mix for breakfast.

"What do you suggest?"

"I can keep us warm if you don't mind getting a little cozy." I hoped my face didn't flush as red as the fire.

Druan's eyes widened.

"My wings, I mean. I can insulate us under them, like a tent. We won't even need the fire."

"You have an injured wing."

"I also have five good ones that make the warmest feather-lined tent you could imagine." I didn't relish sleeping so close to a man I hardly knew and wasn't sure I even liked, but there was a strong chance we could freeze to death in the night otherwise.

"Won't your wings get cold?"

"That's what the feathers are for." I laid my cloak over the fir branches the others had left for us near the fire pit.

"You should keep your cloak on, Thea."

"Kinda hard to use my wings when they're under a cloak."

"Right." Druan built up the fire with a few more logs. It wouldn't last long, but it would keep us warm until our combined body heat took over. "How do we do this?" Druan stood over me, gazing down uncomfortably as I lay down on my side.

Laughing, I patted the makeshift bed beside me. "Lie down beside me on my wings. We'll use your cloak as a blanket. I'll be the big spoon."

"Spoon?" He scratched his head uncertainly.

"Never mind. Just lie down on your side, facing away from me."

"Won't I crush your wings?"

"No, just don't bump the injured one." I gestured at my left primary wing still strapped to my body with his belt. The secondary and tertiary wings on that side were fine.

"If you say so." He gingerly lowered himself and spread his cloak over both of us, then lay next to me, his movements awkward and uncertain.

"Big baby," I muttered as I spread my right wings around us, creating a cocoon of warmth and downy feathers. The fire warmed my wings and our living tent was soon heated.

Druan let out a grunt of approval. "This is the warmest I've been in days. Thank you."

"You're welcome." I stared up at the wall of dark feathers and the thin membranes of my wings. Pale firelight shone through in places, illuminating us in lavender light. I wondered how Ben was tonight. If he'd made it to the Dýre Forest with the others yet.

"You make a lovely tent, Princess." Finally relaxing, Druan rolled onto his back and closed his eyes with a smile.

"Thanks, I think."

"If you happen to wake up and see me sleeping with my eyes open, I'm not dead. It's a Druid thing."

"That's impressive for a half-Druid." The Druids had mystical powers they drew from the land, but only the strongest and most highborn of their kind possessed genuine Druid magic.

"You have a way with backhanded compliments as well, Princess."

"Sorry, that was rather rude. I just meant it's impressive for any Druid to attain that level of power."

"Much less a half-breed."

Horrified, I quickly added, "I didn't mean it like that."

"Doesn't make it any less true."

"I've lived my whole life under the watchful eyes of the elite Valkyrie nobles and royals. What I know of the people of the Nine Realms comes from books and other people's opinions. It's not an excuse for my ignorance. I will do whatever it takes to be better than those who taught me. I will learn to be better."

"If all the future leaders of our world can follow your lead in that regard, then we will have a bright future indeed."

"I can't imagine how difficult it must be to live like that, caught between two such opposing worlds. How in the world did your mother ever meet your father?"

"Go to sleep, Thea."

I was so weary, right down to my bones. I was nearly asleep the moment my eyelids drooped closed. It was so wonderfully warm and cozy under my wings, with the fresh scent of the fir boughs under us. I could be content to sleep here for days if I weren't so anxious about Ben.

An outraged, earth-shattering screech rent the air and I shot upright, my pulse racing. "Holy Mother Sigrún, what was that?"

"Sameerah." Druan laughed. "She's mad because she senses me and can't find me."

“Your spirit animal … person?” I lay back down uneasily. “She sounds like she’s ready to tear the mountains apart.”

“She’ll find us soon enough,” Druan muttered. “I’ve told her to shut up so we can sleep.”

”You can talk to her?” I didn’t relish the idea of an angry bear or cougar—or whatever that was that made that noise—finding us alone in the night. “Make sure she knows my wings are delicate and I’m not holding you hostage under here.”

“Go to sleep, Princess.”

"Will we make it out of here today?" Druan asked as we made our way across the cavernous ruin of an ancient hall.

"I hope so. I'm starving." My trail mix had run out hours ago and I didn't relish spending another night inside the Broken Isles. And I was still so worried about Ben. I didn't like leaving him with the others. "We should reach the first bridge soon. Then it won't be far. It just depends on how long it takes us to get across."

"Why would a bridge slow us down?"

"You're about to see."

"What's that noise?" Druan peered ahead.

"The roughest waters of the Queen's Bay."

Druan came to a halt just around the bend. Ice cold, salty sea air greeted us along with the roar of the raging waters below.

"That is not a bridge; that is a deathtrap."

I examined the hanging rope bridge through his eyes. "To be fair, most of our kind can fly so these things aren't as important."

"Your men don't fly," he reminded me.

"Despite what you may think of Valkyrie men, they are strong and brave. Most of them, anyway."

"Your soldiers are. I'll grant you that. But your civilian men are… very Fiske-like."

"I know." I stepped from the tunnel to the edge of an icy cliff. "I've never understood why our matriarchal society insists on putting men down in order to build women up. In my perfect world, we'd all be equals."

I gazed down into the depths of the churning glacial waters below. This wouldn't be easy. The bridge across barely qualified as a rope scattered with bits of driftwood. I needed to change that. Soldiers routinely patrolled the Broken Isles and they needed safe passage through these tunnels.

"You up for this?" I turned to find Druan still inside the tunnel.

"I suppose."

"How about a pact? If I fall, you have to rescue me. If you fall, I have to rescue you." I extended my hand.

"Deal." He grasped my hand, staring at the wide spaces between planks of driftwood. "Think it'll hold my weight?"

"Only one way to find out." I took the first step, releasing his hand to place a death grip on the rope railing. "Don't take a step forward unless you have a good grip on the rope because that's the only thing that will save you if you slip." I wished I could shift back to my human form. My heavy wings dragged behind me, snagging on rusted nails.

"Typical Valkyrie cluelessness," Druan muttered. "Forgetting those of us who can't fly."

"Agreed." I kept moving forward, one precarious step at a time. I refused to look past the plank in front of me. "You still with me?"

I called over my shoulder when we were more than halfway across.

"Right behind you and eager to get off this rock."

A loud shriek echoed above us.

"Sameerah is laughing at me. She thinks it's hilarious that I'm trying to fly with my useless human wings."

I glanced up, nearly losing my grip on the rope bridge at the sight of the giant gyrfalcon soaring above us. "She's a falcon?" My jaw dropped.

"What did you think she was, shrieking like that all night?"

I shrugged. "I was dead asleep and didn't hear her after the first time, but I did expect something enormous and toothy."

"It's highly unusual, I know. My father was humiliated when I bonded with Sam. Most Berserkers bond with fierce predators like wolves, panthers, or bears. But Sam is as fierce a predator among the skies. I trust her with my life. Although she thinks I'm helpless without her. She was not amused when I left her to travel to the human realm."

"She's beautiful. And I'm down with her sense of humor."

"She does not like you, by the way. I wouldn't approach her any time soon."

"I'm a perfectly lovely person; why wouldn't she like me?"

"She blames you for my leaving."

"And what did you tell her about me?" I chanced a glance over my shoulder.

"Let's just say I'll have to do some damage control."

"You do that." I took the last few steps quickly, grateful for the distraction Sameerah brought.

"Here she comes." Druan joined me in the crumbling ruins of the cavernous tunnel on the other side. "And it looks like she went hunting for us." Druan grinned at the pair of rabbits clutched in her talons. The great white gyrfalcon dropped one at his feet and swooped to the other side of the tunnel with the other.

"Sameerah." Druan growled at his kindred. "You just ate. That rabbit is for Thea."

Sam snapped her beak and tore into the rabbit with her talons.

"Sam." Druan gathered a pile of broken branches for a fire. "I'm sure the three of us can share two rabbits."

"Of course." My stomach growled at the thought of roasted rabbit for lunch. I was all too willing to share with the bird.

Reluctantly, Sameerah brought the second rabbit to Druan, nipping at his ankles to voice her irritation.

"You can have the guts. That's your favorite part anyway." He made quick work of the fire while I looked for longer branches to serve as a spit for the rabbits. I chuckled softly as I listened to the grown man argue with the sassy bird.

"She is not useless, Sam. She has an injured wing. You know what that's like."

Sameerah tossed her head back with a testy huff.

"No, I do not think she's prettier than you, you crazy bird. She's just hungrier than you."

I walked back toward the fire, but Sameerah stood between me and Druan and she looked like she was ready for a fight, spreading her wings and fluffing her feathers. The gyrfalcon was huge. Her wingspan had to be at least five feet.

"I can play that game too, you know." I spread my uninjured wings, fluffing my feathers in response.

Sameerah let out one of her signature shrieks, and I thought about doing the same.

"Stop it, you two. You're both sufficiently impressed with the other." Druan finished cleaning the rabbits and tossed the offal to Sam.

I carefully stepped around the falcon, never turning my back on her out of respect. Crouching next to the fire, I speared the meat on the sticks and handed one to Druan. "Thank you for providing us with a meal, Sameerah." I bowed my head to the proud gyrfalcon.

"You've done this before." Druan settled his rabbit close to the flames to cook.

"My kind share many characteristics with her kind. We appreciate respect when it is earned."

"You should know she's insanely jealous of my attention."

After her hasty meal of the offal, Sameerah left us to our meal and to our journey.

"She'll find Vendela and lead us to her when we get off these godforsaken islands."

"We're more than halfway there now. We might make it out before nightfall."

"How many more bridges will we have to cross?"

"At least one more. Hopefully two."

"Hopefully?"

"The last one will be the worst. I'm told it floods frequently. If it's under water, we will have to swim."

"Valkyries," he muttered under his breath like a curse.

"That is not a bridge." Druan stood with his hands on his hips, shaking his head.

"You said that the last two times. Oh good, it's still here." I came up behind him. The roar of the rocky waters below drowned out my sarcasm.

"Thea, it doesn't even go all the way across." Druan turned toward me, an exasperated look on his face.

"You're kind of funny when you're not trying to be."

"That's a ledge."

I peered over the edge of the cliff at the churning waters below. The next island lay just a few steps from the ledge, though I wasn't any happier than he was about the state of the non-bridge. "We can make that jump."

"And then how far is it?"

"Once we make the jump, we're on your turf, Druid." I slapped his shoulder and turned back into the tunnel to get a running start. I didn't relish doing this with my wing bound, but I knew I could make the leap. Charging across the narrow ledge that reached out over the rough seas far below, I lunged toward the other side, tucking in my injured side to protect it. I tumbled head over heels and landed on my right side, the breath whooshed out of me on impact. Druan landed on his feet right next to me a moment later.

"Show off." I grumbled, accepting his offered hand to pull myself up.

"It's about time you two showed up." A Druid woman stood among the rocky shoals, her golden spear planted firmly on the ground beside her. Dressed in leathers and fur, she blended with the natural world around her. The golden paint along her cheeks and around her eyes marked her as royalty—as did the crown of twisted antlers she wore in her dark brown hair. Her tawny-brown skin shone like moonlight in the fading dusk.

"Morgana?" I rushed toward my friend with open arms. The threat of tears burned my throat as I hugged her like my life depended on it. "You're so grown up."

"I've missed you, friend." Morgana held me tight. "It's been too long."

"I knew you'd see me coming." She had the gift of sight. Not in the way Sylvi did. Morgana's Druid magic allowed her to see important events surrounding those closest to her. Sylvi's gift as a seer allowed her to read the signs of the future and interpret them

—and she was an exceptional seer. But the two princesses were as different as night and day in their methods.

"I met your friends here yesterday. We have to talk about that boy."

"I'm not marrying Fiske. Not if I can help it." I looped my arm around Morgana, knowing full well she meant Ben. He wouldn't be able to hide his secrets from Morgana for very long.

"The High Priestess sent healers from her temples for your wing. You'll be as good as new by morning."

"The Mother bless you both, Morgana. I wouldn't know what to do without you."

"You'll never have to know."

Sameerah screeched from the skies, circling overhead and announcing her presence.

"That crow of yours is an irritable pest without you, cousin." Morgana nodded in Druan's direction.

"It's good to see you too, Mor." Druan tugged her into his arms and whirled her around before setting her back on her feet. "Just don't call Sam a crow in front of her if you want to keep your eyes where they are."

"How did I not know you two were so close?" I shook my head at them.

Druan shrugged. "This little nuisance has made it her life's goal to irritate me and Sam."

"And this *brute* has chased all the boys away from me my whole life. He was determined I would know what it was like having a big brother. And that bird of his is a demon in the skies."

"She doesn't like me either." I forced a laugh. I'd known Morgana since she was a little girl, but she'd always visited me in the Citadel. On the rare occasions I visited her in Manaheim, it was for a special celebration. That she'd never before mentioned her cousin made me second guess my half of our friendship. How could I not know about the cousin who was as close to her as a brother? Maybe I was the spoiled, self-centered princess Druan accused me of being.

"She doesn't like any woman who takes Druan's attention away from her."

My smile slid off my face. "I need you to tell me everything you know, Mor. How did any of this happen?"

"We will talk tonight after the healers work their magic." Morgana nodded. "And then I will take you to my army camp in the morning."

"You have an army?" The Druids were fierce people when they needed to be, but they were great respecters of life and peace. They did not engage in battle unless they had no other choice. They were also unquestionably human. Descendants of the humans trapped on this side of the bridge during the final battle. Any magic they now possessed had come to them through generations of marriage to those who could tap into the power of the gods.

"Times must be desperate indeed."

"I'm afraid so. But my army is your army, my friend."

CHAPTER 15

I woke in a strange tent with that horrible feeling of not knowing where I was. It was still dark outside, but I could hear the unmistakable sounds of a war camp moving quietly around me and it all came back in a rush.

I'd slept in Princess Morgana's tent after our arrival at the Druid camp the night before. It was the most restful sleep I'd had since this nightmare journey began. Thank the Mother my wing was perfectly healed now, and I was finally able to shift back to my human form before falling asleep last night. The Druid healers claimed I would likely suffer no lasting damage to my wing because Amara had the presence of mind to bind it tightly. I just wasn't supposed to shift again for the time being.

Lying in the comfort of a warm cot with thick blankets, I contemplated my next moves. With the Druid army's support, I could lead an attack against Neela's army, but Neela was a Warder. A powerful one as the daughter of the Warder King. How much of her army was made up of people held in bondage by her magic, mind slaves compelled to do her bidding or fall subject to the worst nightmare worlds her kind could construct.

"I can hear you thinking over there," Morgana murmured drowsily.

"I have much to think about."

"You are right to worry for your people. Neela has forced thousands to serve in her army of mercenaries, leaving their families behind to starve." Morgana wasn't a mind reader; she just had a knack for guessing what I was thinking about.

"Can I free them from her magic without alerting her to my presence?" I rolled onto my side to face my friend in the dim light of dawn.

"No, but maybe we can work around that."

"How?"

"Come with me." Morgana tossed her blankets aside, exchanging them for a fur mantle.

I groaned as I followed, my shoulders and back aching from my injury. It was far too cold to leave the comfort and warmth of my bed, but we had work to do. I shrugged into one of Morgana's fur wraps and stuffed my feet into warm doeskin slippers.

I found Morgana in the war room of her large tent, filling the cold braziers with coal. I could see my breath and I rubbed my hands together to call on my magic for the first time since my return.

"Allow me?" I stepped beside Morgana and gathered up several briquets of coal. Holding them tightly in my hand, I let my magic trickle into the coal, heating it until it began to burn in my hand. I held them for a moment longer, stoking the fire in my hands with my magic, marveling at how my skin didn't burn. "It's been a long time," I murmured, watching the tendrils of magic weave around the coals. I could see magic in a physical way. To my knowledge I was the only one who could do that.

"You've still got the Burn I see." Morgana gave a hum of satisfaction as I placed the burning coals into the braziers to spread the warmth. "What does it look like?"

"Golden threads of light weaving around the coals in intricate patterns and knots, lifting them away from my skin so I don't burn. It's beautiful." But that last bit was a lie. The magic I held in my hands was ugly. Darkness seemed to squelch the beautiful golden light I remembered from my childhood. I forced a smile as I watched the tainted threads of my magic dissipate as the surrounding coals began to burn in the natural way.

Dusting my hands off, relieved my burning magic still worked, I stepped up to the large table occupying the center of the room. A map of the Northern Kingdoms lay spread across the table. I frowned at the markers on the map representing Neela's army camps and naval ships surrounding Vahland Reach. "She's split her army? Why?"

"You see it as a grave mistake too?" Morgana came up behind me with a warm mug of tea for each of us.

"There has to be a purpose we aren't seeing." I studied Neela's various positions, trying to make sense of it. I could not underestimate my cousin again, but from the looks of her military camps, she did not have the same kind of battle strategy training I'd had.

"She's sent her main army to the north of Vahland Reach to guard Eyja Island and the Fjords." Morgana pointed to the largest camp on the map.

"She's waiting for me to come home," I whispered. "She doesn't know about the bridgeway that leads directly into the Citadel. She means to catch me on my way back into Valsgard through the main entrance on Eyja Island."

"That's why she's parked her ships in Bryn Bay." Morgana's eyes widened. "So you can't get into the Citadel by water. That decision just might be her downfall." Her voice rose in excitement. "The smaller portion of her army stands between the Ivory Forest and Vahland Reach, blocking our way to the Tower Bridge and the palace. She intends to keep the allies apart and she's done a good job keeping us out of the loop. We have no idea what's going on in the palace or the Citadel. We only know a siege is keeping Sylvi and Astrid in the Citadel where Neela can't reach them. We have no idea what's become of the queen, but we do know she is not dead."

My heart nearly burst at the possibility that my mother could be dead. "Druan says she is a prisoner in the palace dungeon."

"Queen Brenna is strong, Thea. She will make it through this. We all will."

I swallowed and bowed my head, unable to find the words to tell her how grateful I was for all she'd done.

"I have to get into the Citadel. But before I do that, I need to free my people from Neela's Warder magic. At least those serving in her army and guarding the way into Vahland Reach. I need to see if they will even follow me after all I've done."

"Your people may never understand why you left, but they will flock to your side when they see you've returned ready to fight for them."

"Am I though?" The threat of tears burned my eyes and I blinked them back. "I'm in no shape to lead anyone."

"You can do this." Morgana took both of my hands in hers. "Imagine for a moment that you're a Druid princess. You've gone into the human realm for your traditional furlough. It's a natural part of our way of life. I will be expected to take my own furlough in the coming years after this unrest is settled. And when I return after a few months or even years of sowing my wild oats and living life on my terms, I'll come home, ready to do my duty."

"But that's the Druid way." I gave her a watery smile and wiped at an errant tear. "My people will never see it like that."

"They don't have to. But you can. If I can do it and come back ready to lead my people, why can't you?" She pulled me into a side hug and I leaned on her.

"You can't free them all," Morgana added softly. "She's bound your entire nation with her magic, but maybe we can help you release some of them from her influence."

I swallowed back my tears of shame. "I will fix this." I gave a decisive nod, trying to convince myself I *could* do this. "But I have to start with the soldiers here." I pointed to the smaller army camp on the map. The one closest to our current location. "And I'll need your help to do it. Once they're free of her bondage, hopefully they'll be willing to help me free the rest of our people, but I won't force them." I would beg if I had to, but I wouldn't ask them to trade one master for another.

"My army is your army." Morgana laid her hand on my shoulder in a gesture of solidarity.

"Still, I would ask them for their help." I sipped my cooling tea, wondering if I really had the knowledge and wisdom it took to lead an army. My young friend had it in spades. Leading came naturally to her and I was glad I had her in my corner.

"What about the mercenaries?" The army camp we were about to attack was made up of paid mercenaries and Neela's Valkyrie prisoners. If I freed my people, I would have to drive the mercenaries away—or kill them.

"We'll send them running for their next payday somewhere else." Morgana moved to add more coal to the braziers. "She pays them well so they will likely retreat to the northern camps around Eyja Island."

"We can deal with the troops north of here later." I studied the map. They wouldn't be able to move into Vahland Reach quickly enough from their position north of the Armur Mountains. "I just have to do all of this without calling attention to myself."

"All of what?" Druan stepped into the tent, closing the flaps behind him to keep the cold out.

"My plan of attack." My eyes were still trained on the map in front of me. If I could pull off a win at the smaller army camp and gather some troops to my side, I needed to know my next steps. Vahland Reach was an island city protected by the massive Armur mountain range from the west, the rough waters of the Restless Sea to the east, and the Broken Isles to the south. From where I stood right now, the only way to get an army into the city was through Neela's army. Beyond them lay the Tower Bridge, the only entrance into Vahland Reach.

"Tell me what you're thinking, Thea." Druan moved to stand beside me.

I took a moment to catch him up to speed.

"I don't want to put my people inside the city through another bloody battle; they've been through enough."

"Then don't." Druan studied Vahland Reach on the map. "Inside the city, Neela only has the palace guard. We can easily take them with Morgana's troops and whatever Valkyrie soldiers you recover from the camp."

"The ones willing to fight, yes, but what happens when Neela's larger army leaves Eyja Island and follows us into the city? It would be a bloodbath. I can't do that."

"You said yourself that the Tower Bridge is the only way into the city." Druan tapped the sketch of the massive bridge on the map.

"Right." Morgana nodded, returning to stand at the table between us. "We take our troops into the city and then we destroy the bridge behind us, sealing off the mountain pass with a carefully planned avalanche and the debris from the bridge."

"I like it." I stared at the map, wondering if it could be that easy. "If we pull it off then the only way Neela's army can reach us will be over the Armur Mountains from the north and across Queen's Bay, which would take weeks."

You'll be back in the palace by then." Morgana set her empty mug on the table.

"It's brilliant." I smiled. This could work. "The Tower Bridge is over a thousand years old. I hate to destroy it." I sucked in a breath, hesitant to commit to such an undertaking.

"It's just bricks and stone, Thea." Druan laid a hand on my shoulder. "It's a beautiful piece of your history, but it's not your future."

"He's right." Morgana nodded. "It's a solid, strategic plan your mother would approve."

A knot of anxiety took up residence in my stomach. "It's the only plan we've got." I inhaled deeply, still trying to convince myself. Part of me felt like they got the wrong person for this job. Yes, I was the princess. Yes, I caused this whole mess and it was my responsibility to fix it. But I was not the capable one here. That was Morgana—I felt like an imposter. But imposter or not, I had a job to do. "We will rebuild when this is all over. When can we leave?"

"You should rest another day," Morgana urged.

"I can rest when this is over. I think we should leave today. But first I need to find Ben and then I have to ask your troops for their help." I retreated to Morgana's room to change into warm clothes, though as the day progressed it wouldn't be nearly as cold as the temperatures we suffered through on our journey here.

Ducking my head through the tent flaps, I stepped out into a beautiful morning.

"Thea!"

My head snapped toward the familiar voice and some of my

anxiety vanished. “Ben! Are you all right?” I rushed across the grassy clearing of the Druid camp, checking him over for signs of distress.

“This place is amazing.” He wrapped his arms around me and dropped a kiss on top of my head. “But I’m so glad to see you. And really glad this place has sun and green grass and no snow. I was beginning to think your world was some kind of perpetually frozen ice world and I was going to kill you for bringing me here.”

“Bringing you?” I shrugged out of his arms and took a swat at him. He dodged my aim, taunting me with a big goofy grin. It seemed nothing could get him down.

“Wait, I brought you breakfast.” He fished through his bag and handed me a few fresh rounds of flatbread still hot from the fire. “I’ve got a couple of smoked sausages in here too.” He pulled three huge links from his bag and gave me one, stuffing the other two back inside.

“Thanks.” I wasted no time ripping into the coarse bread, my stomach rumbling in anticipation. “Has Amara been taking care of you?” I walked beside him along the meandering path through the tents. It was good to stretch my legs.

“Yeah, she’s cool. I’m teaching her sign language.”

“How do you know sign language?” I paused to see if he was joking.

“Remember I told you about Daria, my best friend in New Orleans?”

“Oh right, she’s deaf.”

“Not completely but she taught me sign language. I’m actually pretty fluent.”

“Don’t get too attached to Amara. Dragons are solitary creatures.”

“So she keeps telling me.” Ben stole one of my flatbreads and stuffed half of it in his mouth.

"Look, I'm really sorry about all of this." My words felt empty and hollow, but I owed him an apology. "Getting here was a nightmare and I kind of left you with strangers."

"You've clearly got a lot going on and that Druan guy wasn't letting you out of his sight. We're good, Thea. Just do whatever you have to do and don't worry about me."

"Well, that's impossible." I tilted my head to the side. "You're mine to worry about and I don't intend to lose sight of you now that we're here."

"Can you give me a super-fast lesson on how a half-Berserker half-human hybrid should behave?"

"Just be you. Only … the non-feathered version of you. I'll get whatever you need to keep your hair short. And if anyone asks, just tell them you've only recently found out about your Berserker father, and you haven't yet found your kindred."

"What does that mean?"

I gave him a quick lesson in what it meant to be connected with a predator, though I wasn't the best teacher as I didn't fully understand it myself. I was beginning to suspect it was one of those things only Berserkers could understand. Like me trying to explain flying to a fish.

"I'm used to keeping a low profile and hiding in plain sight. I won't screw this up, promise."

"Your life—and probably mine too—depends on it." I changed course, leading the way to the training grounds. It was time to see if Morgana's troops were as willing as she claimed they were.

More than a thousand Druid soldiers, both men and women, milled about the training grounds and the areas around it. Morgana was already among them, calling them to attention. They moved like a hive in unison, lining up in neat rows and blocks of magic wielders and warriors of the spear to hear the Valkyrie princess speak.

They would be prepared to march before noon, but unlike Neela's mercenary troops and their machines of war, the Druids relied on their own two feet to get where they were going. They spent their lives learning to fight with spears and shields, as well as with their magic. They were fierce warriors I would be proud to have stand with me.

Morgana waved me forward to join her at the platform at the front of the training grounds. Panic seized my chest as I left Ben to cross the field on my own. I had no idea what I was going to say.

"Just be you and they'll respect you." Morgan squeezed my hand and stepped behind me. Druan and Vendela also joined us to show their support.

Staring out at the sea of faces, I sucked in a breath and prayed to the Mother for the right words. The words my mother would have said if she were here now.

"Truth." My voice echoed in the silence. I cleared my throat as thousands of eyes stared blankly back at me, some skeptical, some openly hostile, and some simply wary.

"That's all I have for you today. The truth. Three years ago I left Valsgard and the Nine Realms thinking I could abdicate my position as Queen Heir to my much more capable sister. I've only recently discovered it was the worst mistake of my life that has resulted in the suffering of too many. I will spend the rest of my days making this up to you and to the people of the Nine Realms, but I can't do it alone. I need your help. Today, I ask you to march with me into the Armur Mountains where we will attack the usurper's army and free my people from bondage."

Hushed murmuring swept through the crowd. "I will not ask you to do anything I am not willing to do myself. I will fight with you and you can count on the Valkyries—your sisters and brothers—to forever come to the aid of the nation of Manaheim whenever it is needed."

Deathly silence stretched out for the longest minute, and I thought I had lost even before my fight began.

The roar of approval took me by surprise. I watched as the Druid army raised their spears and shields in a battle cry that would make our enemies weep in fear. Emotion threatened to strangle my voice, but I pushed through it, letting the tears come.

"You are our fiercest allies!" I took a step down from the platform, raising a fist over my head. "I have but one question. Will you fight with me? Will you fight for your freedom and the freedom of your neighbors to the north? Will you suffer a usurper to sit upon *any* throne of the Nine Realms?"

The soldiers shouted their support, beating their spears against the ground. Cries of "We fight!" filled my ears and pride swelled in my soul. Not for me, but for my Druid friends.

Morgana came to stand beside me and I could feel her own pride radiating from her. "We march in one hour!"

I shouted over the din. "You, Queen Orlagh and her daughter, Princess Morgana, have my deepest respect and gratitude." I lifted my fist to the sky as the Druids met my battle cry with one of their own.

My heart raced as I watched each unit march from the field to retrieve their gear and prepare for a battle my enemy would never see coming.

CHAPTER 16

"You're making me nervous." Morgana's forehead creased in annoyance as she strapped armored plates to my wings. Thin and lightweight, the metal would still weigh me down, but I didn't dare go without the protection.

"I'm about to go into a real battle for the first time. I'm petrified. And I haven't flown in full battle gear since Aunt Astrid's training classes ages ago. I forgot how heavy armor is."

"You'd better get used to it quickly, Thea. You're going to be a target the instant Neela's soldiers realize who you are and what you're doing."

"I know. Sameerah will fly with me. She'll give Druan her eyes and ears in the air, while he's on the ground. He'll see everything in the air and on the ground so he can give your commanders accurate information."

"And don't forget Amara. Not many princesses can say they've gone to war with a dragon on their side."

"Thank the Mother for her." I sighed in relief. Every time I remembered Amara would be at my side in her terrifying dragon form, I breathed a little easier.

"Remember what our scouts said. Most of Neela's mercenaries are from the Southern Kingdoms. They're going to soil themselves when they see a dragon in the flesh."

"I can't imagine Neela pays them enough to willingly face a dragon, much less a legion of Druid soldiers and magic wielders."

"Some will try to run."

"I know. We can't let them." I didn't like the idea of killing anyone who wanted to flee, but at the same time I couldn't risk soldiers returning to Neela with news of the battle. She'd find out soon enough. The best I could offer them was a chance to shift their loyalty to me.

"You really think you can free your people?" Morgana donned her own armor of golden chainmail that matched the shimmering lines of paint adorning her face.

I nodded. "I think I know what to do now that I've seen them from a distance. But I won't know for sure until I try to break the bonds. I need to get a closer look."

Druan and Vendela had taken me on a scouting mission last night. I hadn't known what to expect of Neela's army, but I was pleased to discover I could clearly see the bonds tying my people to Neela with her Warder magic. If I could see it, I could destroy it —I just had to figure out how to do that in the middle of a battle.

"Let's do this, already." Ben ducked his head into the tent.

"Morgan, can you give us a minute?" I asked.

"I am leaving to join my troops. See you on the other side, sister." Morgana swept toward the door, giving Ben a once over in his battle gear. "You know it's too dangerous for him to be here, right?"

"Of course." I waited until Morgana left before I spoke.

"She knows about me?" Ben asked.

"She's a Druid princess with the gift of sight. The magic is strong within her and there isn't much she doesn't see." I turned toward my friend. I loved Ben like family and I couldn't risk losing him. "I'm afraid you're going to have to stay here."

"No way. You know I can fight, Thea. I've been fighting my whole life, this is nothing new for me."

"Yes, it is. It's not the battle I'm worried about. I know you can hold your own. But this is war. There will be other Valkyries in the air besides myself and you're going to want to join me. And after the battle there will be blood. The fields will be littered with men and women dying violent deaths. You will not be able to hold your Valkyrie in. He will do what he was made to do, and you won't be able to stop him."

"You think I've never had to do that? I control my Valkyrie, no matter what. End of story. I've had no choice but to keep my secret from the world. I can handle it."

"Have you ever walked a battlefield? I haven't. And I have control of my Valkyrie too, but I know there are times when she will come no matter how hard I try to hold her. You cannot risk it."

"You let me worry about that."

"No. Like it or not, in this world I am your Queen Heir and I am ordering you to stay. It's for your own good."

I left him scowling at my back.

"Dawn is an hour away, the enemy camp will begin to stir soon," Vendela said the moment I left the tent. "We've taken their sentries and the troops are in place. We must move while we still have the element of surprise."

A huge white wolf paced at her side, while a soft gray fox sat patiently on her haunches at Vendela's feet. Vendela's eyes shone with a feral glint. She'd merged with both her kindred and was ready for battle.

"Let's do this." I nodded.

Everyone knew their roles. Neela's army was camped in a valley several miles to the east. The mammoth mountains that surrounded Vahland Reach hemmed in the valley on one side, protecting the camp from the wind. But those same mountains would become their prison. I took my place beside Vendela, leading the remaining troops toward the valley where Morgana waited for the first strike.

I was woefully unprepared for this and everyone around me knew it.

A week ago my biggest concern was rationing out my tips to pay for food, gas, and the cheap motel Ben and I lived in. Now I was back in Valsgard, headed into a battle I wasn't sure I'd survive.

"The soldiers can see your doubt, Princess." Vendela spoke without meeting my gaze. "You would do well to school your features. They need you to be the warrior you were trained to be."

"It's been a long time since I was that girl." I took a steadying breath and from somewhere deep inside myself, I pulled out the Queen Heir mask I'd worn all my life. I could and would doubt myself, but the soldiers fighting for Valsgard this day needed me to be better.

"That'll do." Vendela's voice held a hint of amusement as we marched across the snow-covered trail, my wings trailing behind me like an armored cloak and her kindred prowling along behind us.

"It'll have to. The humans have a saying: Fake it till you make it."

"Wise words." Vendela's voice took on a throaty growl as she merged fully with her kindred.

We would box Neela's army inside the valley before they even knew what hit them. By then, it would be too late. Even now, Druid warriors and magic wielders waited at strategic points around the camp, prepared to create an avalanche to stop any who might try to flee over the mountains.

I tried not to let my fear show when I caught my first look at Amara in her dragon form. It was hard to imagine how the small but fierce woman contained such a formidable creature inside her human form. Scarlet scales glinted against the snow in the torch light. She looked like the physical embodiment of fire itself. Ancient wisdom pulsed around her like an aura. The Druid soldiers kept their distance, but Amara would be my partner in the skies today. As I approached, I nodded with respect. If I were anyone else, I would bow before such a mighty creature, but I was a royal vessel and bowed to no one.

As big as a house, Amara towered over me, fire brewing deep in her chest. Her great talons put mine to shame. Burgundy-black spikes ran down the length of her back and down her great tail. She dipped her head at my approach, wrapping her tail around the area where I stood and lowering her head beside mine as if to say we were equals. Next to her, I felt insignificant and small.

"Don't forget, we will be with you the whole way." Druan came to stand beside me with Sameerah perched on his shoulder. "Anything you say to Sam, I will hear."

The gyrfalcon ruffled her feathers, somehow making herself even more intimidating than the dragon.

"Sam," Druan warned. "We're all on the same team."

I inclined my head in Sam's direction. "I am grateful for your assistance."

"Sorry, she's a bit grumpy today." Druan's eyes danced with amusement. "You're terrified, aren't you?" He chuckled at the look on my face.

"Maybe a little. But I have a dragon on my side so…" I trailed off as Druan leaned forward.

"And a Druid-Berserker half-breed with a cranky falcon for a kindred. We can't all be as flashy as the red dragon." His smile calmed me and I was surprised how much his words set me at ease.

A moment later, Druan's eyes shifted and grew dark like Sameerah's. A rim of gold lined his eyelids, like the feathers around Sameerah's eyes.

I didn't give myself time to think. Without another word, I took to the skies. Amara quickly shot ahead of me, but Sameerah stayed close to my side. With Druan in control, I trusted the bird of prey much more and found her a welcome presence.

Flying low across the treetops, I marveled at the sheer span of Amara's blood-red wings. Studded with dark red spikes and two enormous talons at her wing joint, her wings were remarkably similar to my primary wings in shape and function, but that was where any similarities ended.

"Here goes nothing." I angled into a dive toward the unsuspecting, sleeping camp, circling low over the tents housing sleeping soldiers. Amara followed, giving a great roar and a blast of dragon fire. The battle had begun.

As soldiers scrambled out of their tents, I called on the power of my Valkyrie to give me strength and speed. Amara's dragon fire illuminated the skies, and her mere presence sent Neela's army into a panic.

Mercenaries took up their bows, firing arrows into the sky, but the element of surprise worked in our favor. I dipped low as I circled, taking in the snarl of magic only I could see. An arrow glanced off my armor and Amara dropped in front of me to shield me from further harm.

Weaves of Warder magic hung thick in the air like smoke. This was magic unlike any I'd ever seen. I couldn't make sense of it now, but I was determined to free those caught in Neela's web.

Morgana's troops surrounded the camp, making quick work of the chaos as they trapped the enemy soldiers inside the valley.

The ground shook with the first avalanche happening higher up in the mountains. The Druid Magic wielders would come down closer to the battle for the second one. I had until then to finish my one task.

Swords and shields clanged below and the scent of blood and gore soon filled my senses. As soldiers fought, I studied the spider's web of magic I needed to destroy. It was why we were here. I could see the tightly woven threads forcing my people to take up arms against me. They moved like marionettes on strings, their actions stilted and unnatural.

My own magic welled up inside me and I trembled with the effort to take hold of the slick, oily shadows that were never there before. Something wasn't right and I fought against a surge of panic. "What is wrong with me?"

I banked to the far side of the valley where a rocky cliffside gave me the perfect view of the battle. I needed a moment to collect myself. Landing in a crouch under the weight of my armor, I dragged a deep breath into my lungs. Sameerah squawked above me, circling, her eyes—Druan's eyes—watching for possible threats.

As my fellow Valkyrie sisters took to the skies against me, I watched the bond of Neela's Warder magic flowing behind them like silken threads. I could see it in their faces—they were haunted by the things their Warder made them do. If I succeeded at nothing else today, I had to sever those bonds.

Forcing my way through the taint my instincts told me I should fear, I embraced my magic, letting it fill me as it had when I was a young Queen Heir. But this time, I took in the darkness as well. I didn't have a choice. I needed to figure out what was wrong with my Valkyrie magic, but right now I had to help my sisters.

I leapt from the boulder and took flight, following the Valkyrie closest to me. Reaching out, I grasped several threads of the bond trailing behind her. Heat surged from my fingertips and I gave a hesitant tug, pulling on the wispy strands I'd captured. I met with resistance, but refused to let go. The Valkyrie shrieked as if in pain and her wings beat against the air as she tried to escape my snare. But I had hold of her with my magic now.

I followed her closely as the heat of my magic intensified and the strands of the bond I held began to burn. I gained on her and she hesitated long enough for me to gather the remaining weaves of Warder magic that bound her. Like before, my magic heated and the bond began to burn.

Sameerah and Amara flanked us, shielding us from the volley of arrows from the ground while I tried to free the first of many.

The Valkyrie cried out in pain, but she no longer resisted me. I flew beside her now, murmuring words of encouragement as I burned weave after weave of Warder magic until only one solid cord remained. The core of the bond was made of shadows and vile things I couldn't name. The thicker cord wouldn't burn and as I hesitated the weaves of magic began to reform.

"No." The Valkyrie's harsh voice grated in her throat. "Please don't stop." She slowed her flight, giving me time to think of another way to destroy the final element of Neela's bond.

Gripping the cord tightly in my hand, I lashed out with my talons, raking through the shadows like warm flesh. The final cord fell into ribbons of dark smoke and disappeared with the wind. The bond was gone.

"Princess Alithea?" The Valkyrie stumbled on the wind, flinging out her wings to steady her flight. "You released me." Several emotions flashed across her face, from betrayal and disappointment to joy. "It is my honor to fly with you, Princess." She gave a respectful nod and took up her station at my left, protecting my back as I searched for our closest sister in flight.

"There, Majesty." She gestured to a woman raining down bolts of magic on the Druids below.

As before, I followed her, gathering up the silken threads of the bond imprisoning the Valkyrie before me. Once again, I burned through the weaves of Warder magic to expose the shadowy bond, except this time I didn't hesitate when I clawed my way through the core of shadows. Slick residue coated my talons like warm blood.

Sameerah flew with me, helping me free as many of my sisters as I could reach. She clawed with her talons wherever I pointed and sometimes her talons came away dripping with the black darkness like so much blood, until it too faded in the wind.

"It's Princess Alithea." Astonished cries reached my ears from the foot soldiers below. "She's come to save us!" A contingent of shield maidens flew with me now and together we worked to free the soldiers on the ground, My sisters cleared the way for me to help those in the most dire need.

As the foot soldiers began to realize they were released from Neela's yoke, they changed sides just as I had hoped they would. It touched something deep inside me that I didn't even have to ask them to fight with me. They'd only needed me to show up.

Sameerah screeched and Amara roared as they circled the valley, watching as the battle changed from a sneak attack to an all-out slaughter. I would do right by the fallen men and women of the Nine Realms who chose to fight against me. After. When we escorted them to Andlang.

"Sameerah!" Druan's voice caught my attention. I saw the bolt sailing through the air. My eyes locked with Sameerah's and I only had an instant to wonder what might happen to Druan if he lost his kindred while they were merged in battle. I reached her just in time to pluck the bolt from the sky a moment before it would have killed her.

The gyrfalcon followed me back to the rocky cliffside where Druan and Vendela waited for us. Both looked battle-crazed in the way their kind was known for. Amara slammed into the cliff, perching just above us. Her great wings arched high overhead, shielding us from arrows that bounced off her thick, impenetrable scales. Her enormous tail wrapped around the rocky ledge, embracing us, daring those below to strike against her a second time.

"It never hurts to have a dragon on your side." I reached out to pat Amara's smooth scales but thought better of it. Instead, I waited as she lowered her head to my level. To show my undying gratitude and deepest respect for the noble dragon, I dipped my head, keeping eye contact with Amara. "Thank you, my friend. It has been an honor to share the skies with you."

With a final roar and a blast of dragon fire, Amara chased the remaining mercenaries into the mountains where they would be greeted by the second avalanche of the morning.

Just as quickly as it began, the battle was over.

"Princess Alithea!" Hundreds of Valkyrie soldiers chanted my name. They were mostly men, but more than a dozen females flew around my perch above the valley, giving Amara a wide berth.

I wanted nothing more than to join my sisters in the sky, but I had betrayed them. I couldn't be sure of their loyalty yet. I had to earn it back and that would take more than a single battle.

I walked down the mountainside with Vendela and Druan, their kindred following. Neither was ready to fully return to themselves yet. I could see it in their eyes; they were more beast than human after the frenzy of battle.

The Druid army stood with Princess Morgana. I felt a surge of relief as I saw my dear friend moving through their ranks unscathed.

The Valkyrie men stood quietly, their dripping swords and blood-smeared faces an eerie sight to behold in the silence.

Without a word, I sank to my knees, my wings dragging in the blood-stained snow behind me. "Forgive me. I did not know how my people suffered in my absence." My back curved in penitence as I pressed my forehead to the ground, showing them how deeply I regretted my actions.

A whisper of sound met my ears and when I looked up, my people were also on their knees, their heads likewise bowed.

"Your Majesty." A man I didn't recognize approached me, reaching to help me up. "You're here now and you've freed us from bondage. That's all that matters to us."

"What is your name, Sir?"

"Soren Ness, Princess. I was a captain in your mother's army."

"Do you trust these men and women, Soren?"

"With my life."

I nodded. "I owed you your freedom." My voice rose in the silence. "You owe me nothing in return. Please stand. I am not your queen. Your queen is a prisoner in her own palace." I paced before them, searching for the words my mother would have given them.

"What you do next is your choice, my brothers and sisters. You may go home to your families. You may seek refuge among the Druids or any of our allied nations. Or you can stay with me and help me rid Valsgard of the usurper who dares to call herself your queen."

Cheers rose around me as the men beat their fists against their shields and the women took to the skies, calling my name.

I raised my hand to quiet them. "I am young and stupid."

Startled chuckles scattered across the crowd.

"It's true." I managed a wry grin. "Who isn't foolish at nineteen? I'm no different from any of you. We are all the same. We are Valkyrie." I lifted my chin. "I may make mistakes—I'll probably make a lot. I will fight for you with everything I've got. I will fight for our queen. But I will need your help to free her as I have freed you.

"We march for Vahland Reach tomorrow. I will meet with Captain Ness, our shield maidens, and Princess Morgana to plan our strategies. But first we must see to our dead—all of them. These men and women are not our enemies. Many were career soldiers from the southern kingdoms caught up in a war far from their homes. At the end of the day we are all people of the Nine Realms, and we must escort these warriors to their afterlife."

CHAPTER 17

Weary from battle and the aftermath of ferrying souls to Andlang, I trudged back to camp for a quick rest before heading back out again. I stopped dead in my tracks when I saw Ben working with Vendela and Druan to organize the camp, accommodating those who had switched sides today. "What is he doing here?" I gasped as I turned to Morgana, terror for my friend rooting me to the spot.

"Clearly he doesn't know how to listen to good sense," Morgana said, showing none of the concern I was feeling. "He joined the battle once everyone was distracted. I wouldn't have pegged him for a warrior, but the boy held his own."

"He never shifted?" I would never have imagined the cocky, lazy boy could possess that kind of self-control. *I* didn't possess that level of control.

"Never." Morgana left me to join her troops who were burning the bodies of the fallen.

"I know that look." Ben approached me. "That's your 'Ben has pushed my buttons again' expression."

"You risk too much." I was so angry with him I wanted to shake him, but at the same time I was impressed.

"I felt like the world's biggest coward staying behind." He shrugged. "I had to do my part. And you were amazing." He threw his arm around me, steering me back to the tent I shared with Morgana. "Who knew my prickly friend could inspire an entire army?"

"How are you in control right now?" He seemed so cool and calm. With a sea of fallen warriors still awaiting their final reward, no Valkyrie I'd ever known could hold back their natural form.

"Thea, to survive as long as I have without ending up on the news, in a grocery store tabloid, or in some science lab getting poked and prodded, perfect control was my only choice. I just couldn't stick around the battlefield for the trip to Andlang so I came back to camp to hang with Amara and help where I can." With that he left me at my tent and walked away, never showing the faintest sign that he might shift at any moment.

Maybe he can survive this world after all.

After a light meal and a short rest, I returned to the battlefield where the other Valkyries were back at work as well. Carrion birds circled overhead and I was eager to drive them away.

Giving in to my nature, I set aside any thoughts of leadership and did what I was made for, taking to the skies. Scanning the bloody field, I looked for my people first, but my sisters had already seen to our fallen.

Landing beside a young man from the southern isles, I reached for his stiffening fingers. He was my age, maybe even younger. His life was cut far too short fighting someone else's battle. That was why I'd insisted on caring for all the dead today. For this soldier, today's battle was just about earning a paycheck he probably desperately needed for his family's survival.

Empty eyes stared back at me as I coaxed his soul from his body. Death in battle was violent and confusing. Most of these souls didn't yet realize they were dead. But as ghostly eyes met mine, he knew. It was a frightening thing, seeing the reality of your death burning in the eyes of a Valkyrie—or so I'd always heard.

"It's okay," I whispered. "A far greater life awaits you in Andlang." I helped him to his feet, leaving his bloodied corpse behind. "Don't look." I draped my wings around him, guiding him away from the grisly sight of his final resting place.

"I was just going to serve for a few years. General Fallon paid his mercenaries well, so I could serve less time." His bewildered gaze was one I had seen all too many times. They always haunted me in the weeks after. Tonight I would ferry hundreds of souls to Andlang, and I would remember each by name.

"What is your name?"

"Ari, your Majesty." I wasn't his queen, but he recognized me as the daughter of the High Queen of the Nine Realms.

"I'm Thea, Ari. Tell me about your plans for after you finished your time in the army?" I gathered him in my arms and took flight.

"I was going to buy a ship and become a merchant sailor."

"Maybe you can still do that in Andlang." I flew toward a bright light in the atmosphere where the sky parted to let us through.

"What's it like there?"

"I don't know, Ari. My sisters and I are not allowed into Andlang like we once were. But I have peered through the gates, and it is the most beautiful place you will ever see."

"I'm scared, your Majesty."

"Call me Thea. You are no longer bound by the customs of our lands. Your new life awaits you here." I landed on the other side of the veil where a small island floated among the clouds. I'd visited this island countless times and it still took my breath away.

Gold, silver, bronze, and dozens of other metals I couldn't recognize twisted together to form the tall gates that stood at the center of the green island. Set in an iridescent stone wall, the gates began to open for Ari.

He gasped as he got his first glimpse inside and stepped back into the safety and comfort of my wings.

"You have nothing to fear and a whole new life to gain when you step through those gates. Think of it as a new adventure."

"It's so beautiful." Ari began to move away from me toward the gates where the most stunning, peaceful light shone along rolling green hills, with a sparkling sea in the distance. I could just make out the sound of angelic voices raised in a song of welcome.

A smile lit Ari's face as he took another step, and then another. He paused, turning toward me one last time. Bathed in the pure lights of Andlang, he whispered, "Thank you, Thea."

And then he was gone, and it was time to return to the world of the living to escort another lost soul home.

After the last souls found their way into Andlang, Morgana and I parted ways. She would lead the Valkyrie and Druid armies on the short trek across the mountain pass to the Tower Bridge at the entrance to Vahland Reach. There, they would destroy the bridge and any possibility of Neela's army pursuing us. They would make camp in the fertile valley just outside the city to await my arrival. With the Citadel on one side and our troops on the other, we were about to turn this siege on its head before Neela even knew I was back.

By the time the news of the battle reached Neela, I would be inside the Citadel with my bounty hunters. We just needed to reach the queen's chamber as soon as possible. To do that, we had to cross the rough waters of the Broken Isles by ship. Not something I would advise anyone to do, but we didn't have time for the long trek back through the cold interior of the island tunnels. The ship would get us there in half the time, and time was of the essence.

"I've hired a ship to take us," Druan said when he returned from the docks at the remote fishing village a day's ride south from the Tower Bridge. We arrived there late last night, but I stayed behind at our campsite just outside the village. This close to Valsgard, I was easily recognizable. What with my face on several of our coins.

"When do we leave?" I stood from my seat by the fire, anxious to return home now that we were so close. I was both terrified and excited to see my sister again. And I had a lot of questions only she could answer.

"We leave with the evening tide in just a few hours." He sat down with a groan, drawing his furs around him. "The captain says the trip will be smoother sailing at night."

"Does he know about me?" I crouched down, throwing a few more logs onto the fire.

"Yes, and he's been paid a king's ransom to keep that knowledge to himself. He seems to be a loyal supporter of your mother's at least, though he's not very impressed with you. He says it will be better for you if we board before the fishermen come in for the evening. Neela has supporters among the townsfolk. Despite keeping them in bondage, she's brought new commerce to the town by purchasing food supplies for her army. They have fared much better than the farming villages."

"Fine, we'll leave for the village in an hour." I knew I had many difficult years ahead of me to win back the loyalty of my people—

or find someone strong enough to rule in my stead. If that wasn't my sister—obviously it couldn't be Neela—perhaps there was someone else. And if there wasn't, I would just have to do the best I could and maybe my people would forgive me in time.

"This is smooth sailing?" Ben looked like he was about to puke again.

"I never said it was smooth sailing." Druan closed his eyes as the ship dipped and rolled with the waves. "The Queen's Bay is always rough, but I'm told it's far worse during the day."

Vendela paced the length of our small quarters below deck. She and her fox, Aska, were the only ones who could stay upright on this voyage from Hel. Even her white wolf, Petra, lay beside Druan, clearly miserable. Sameerah chose to fly rather than subject herself to such slow human inventions.

I envied the snobby bird. I'd give anything to make the flight to the queen's chambers on my own, but with my wings so easily identifiable, I couldn't risk being seen. So I sat on the uncomfortable bench, trying not to look out the porthole as the flat-bottomed ship bobbed and rolled across the rocky seas.

After a week of traveling, a battle, and its aftermath, I was more exhausted than ever before. I needed rest and relative safety for a few days before I could decide what to do next. A meeting with the queen's council loomed in my near future and I had to decide how I wanted to approach them: as a child come home to be reprimanded, or a queen returned from a successful battle to guide her council forward. Either way, I wasn't looking forward to it.

"This is awful." Ben collapsed on the bench beside me, looking a little green. "Why is the sea so angry? What did we ever do to it?"

"There's a reason it's called the Restless Sea beyond Queen's

Bay. Be thankful we aren't traversing the open waters. Drink some water." I handed him my wineskin filled with fresh cool water that should help settle his stomach.

"Seriously." He wiped his mouth after several gulps. "Why is it so rough?"

"Most of Valsgard is wild country, nothing like the cities you're used to. To the south and east lie the Broken Isles, full of rocky shores and hidden shoals just beneath the surface. To the north lies Vahland Reach, the island fortress city of the Valkyrie nation. It is surrounded on all sides by the rough waters of Queen's Bay. Just north and west of Vahland Reach are the Armur Mountains. They're nearly impassable. And beyond them lies the Restless Sea."

"So you're saying your city is well guarded by scary terrain most people wouldn't think to travel through." He nodded, taking another sip from the wineskin. "Got it." He huddled closer to my side. "But does it have to be so cold?"

"We come from Vikings, Ben. Ice is in our blood."

"I come from a town called Vegas. It's hot there." He leaned into me with a groan as the ship lurched and rolled onto its side.

"We're going to die." Ben held on to me with a death grip until the ship righted itself.

"You'd think the boy has never sailed before." Druan said calmly from his seat on the floor of the hold.

"You'd be right," Ben's voice shook with anxiety. "I don't mind flying, but floating in a boat was never my idea of fun."

"Flying?" Druan gave Ben a questioning look.

I sucked in a sharp breath, realizing what he'd said. "Oh, what Ben means is—"

"We have planes, Dude. Like ships that sail through the air." Ben mimed a plane soaring with his hand, giving me a nudge that said I needed to chill out. I'd forgotten about humans and their planes.

"Right." I sat back, clutching the bench with a white-knuckled grip. If I wasn't careful, I was going to be the one to out Ben.

The trip was mercifully short but brutal. I could barely walk a straight line when my feet hit solid ground again.

The captain left us on the shores of the Armur Mountains, right back where we started more than a week ago when we first exited the bridge. We approached the hidden entrance among the boulders and rocky terrain, entering the Armur Mountains by way of a narrow tunnel.

From here we could take the right passage and cross the Broken Isles by foot, as we had on our journey to Manaheim, go back across the bridge to the human realm, or we could take the left path and enter the Citadel through the tunnels—the way Druan had proposed from the beginning. But to reach the caves beneath the Citadel we would have to cross the boundary again. And I still couldn't do that.

I turned to face our small group. "Here we are again. Druan and I must go through the Queen's Chamber as we did before. The rest of you will have to cross the boundary here and go through the tunnels to reach the safety of the Citadel. Someone will meet you there. Tell them you are with me and they'll let you in." At least I hoped they would. "We will see you soon." I stood beside Druan and we turned toward the crumbling wall with the odd symbols carved into the stone.

"Allow me." Druan pulled a knife from his belt and slit his hand, pressing his palm against the ancient emblem. Together, we melted through the stone, arriving once more in the queen's chamber.

"Are you going to have to go through that whole … episode again with your power?"

I shrugged. "I don't think so. The power of the gods already knows I'm here and I don't think it has much more to say to me now." I approached the medallion in the floor, hesitating for a moment before I stepped forward, bracing myself.

This time, the rush of power simply knocked me off my feet, like a wave of inky darkness swallowed me whole and spit me back out. I landed hard on my back across the chamber.

"You okay?" Druan rushed to kneel beside me.

"Yeah," I gasped for breath. "I don't think the power is too happy with me right now." I took Druan's offered hand and pulled myself up. The room started spinning and I leaned into him.

"Are you sure, Thea?" He studied my face in concern. "You're awfully pale."

I nodded. "Just a little weak." I did a mental check, making sure I really was sound. The vessel within me had filled during the time we spent among the Druids, but not by much. Upon entering the queen's chamber for a second time, the well had filled a little more. As if the gods wished to test me as a potential vessel they weren't yet certain was strong enough.

"Was it any different? More familiar?"

"Not really. It still feels foreign." I took a tentative step without his support.

"What does it mean?" Druan followed, letting me find my footing on my own.

"It means after all these years, your aura is still gray." Sylvi's voice echoed across the silent chamber as she descended the stone steps, her strange silvery eyes never leaving my face.

I dropped my head, embarrassed to face my elder sister. She was the very essence of nobility itself, strong and certain. She should be Queen Heir now, but the power had not chosen Sylvi.

"Is that her way of saying you're … out of balance?" Druan asked.

I stared at him for a moment. "Yes, that's exactly what she said. Sylvi sees people and the spiritual world around her in colors and auras. Gray means I have fallen out of balance. My time away was supposed to have fixed that little problem."

Sylvi nodded. "Your head no longer listens to your heart. But I believe you still have the power to save us." Her dark skirts whispered as she stepped toward me, taking my hands. "Your aura is bleak, sister. Indecisive and detached. But it doesn't have to stay that way."

"I'm so sorry, Sylvi." I threw myself into her arms. "I'm so ashamed. I thought I was doing the right thing…" My voice failed me as my sister embraced me, running a hand over my hair.

"It was the right path for you, my dear sister." Sylvi held me tightly. "Or I wouldn't have helped you go." She pulled back to search my face. "I'm only sorry I didn't see the red one coming."

"Who's the red one?" Druan asked.

"She means Neela." I hugged my sister again.

"Well, you're back now and we will figure out what to do on this new path. You've done well, the red one will not suspect your arrival. That is a good thing." She gently pushed against my shoulders, stepping back. "This way we have the element of surprise on our side."

"Sort of." I hung my head again. "At least for a few more days."

"What do you mean?"

"I've been home for more than a week."

"And you've been busy making plans. Good, you can catch us all up to speed soon enough." Sylvi guided us up the steep stone steps to the queen's entrance.

"The short version is Morgana will have her boxed in soon."

"I knew it, Thea. You're going to save us all." Sylvi's brilliant smile lit her face. "I am pleased to see you've returned, Druan." She didn't bother to look at him over her shoulder. "I assume the others will join us later?"

"Yes, Princess, and we are all weary from battle."

"Battle?" Sylvi glanced at me, a pleased smile on her face. "You *have* been busy, little sister."

"And eager for a hot meal and a warm bed." I leaned my head on her shoulder as we reached the top of the stairs.

"I know you're exhausted from your journey, but I want to study your aura after you've rested. You are horribly gray, but I believe you have also taken a great lesson from living among the humans. Your time there was not in vain. I think I see a little blue in you."

I frowned, out of practice in speaking Sylvi. "So you're saying I'm gray with a bit of blue? Out of balance ... but at peace with it?"

"No." Druan snorted a laugh. "She's saying you are out of balance as a whole, but you are on your way to finding stability."

"Isn't that what I said?" Sylvi tilted her head at me, her lovely face as serene and angelic as I remembered.

I smiled, tucking my arm through hers. "I missed you, Syl." My sister was rarely wrong in her interpretations. It was comforting to know she didn't blame me for my long absence. I just wasn't sure our mother or Aunt Astrid would be as understanding.

Sylvi led us through a large carved wooden door. "You are two now. It won't be long before you are three, just as I always said you should be. You have learned much these last years. You are wiser now." She nodded to Druan. "And you have strong allies."

"I don't know about being wiser, and I still don't know how I'm supposed to be three." I gripped my sister's hand. I'd missed her nonsense so much it hurt. "But how is Mother? Do you have any news of her?"

Sylvi's eyes filled with tears. "I haven't seen or heard from our mother in more than two years. I'm afraid she is beyond our reach now."

CHAPTER 18

I woke in my childhood room in the Citadel royal residence. My surroundings were so familiar, it was as though the last three years hadn't happened and it was the morning of my First Ascension ceremony. I'd grown up here with the other noble daughters of the Northern Kingdoms, only visiting the palace on special occasions. For a moment, I closed my eyes and it all felt like a horrible dream, as though Morgana would walk in any moment to help me prepare for the celebration.

But deep in my bones, I felt every single moment of the last few years. My body ached as if I were a thousand years older, but none the wiser.

A fierce growl had me sitting upright, blinking the sleep from my eyes as a giant white cat leapt onto my bed.

"Pasha? Is that you?" I threw my arms around the huge white leopard giving me the stink eye. "I missed you, girl." I scratched her behind the ears. "Don't look at me like that, I couldn't very well take you with me to the human realm. You would have scared everyone." But the cat didn't bother to hide her disdain for my excuses. "You got even bigger while I was away." It hit me with a pang that she was no longer a young cat. "You've become quite the lady, haven't you?"

Pasha bumped her shoulder against mine, finally releasing the purrs she'd held back. I could still see the feisty kit lurking in her eyes. My father had given me the rare white skýja leopard when I was fourteen, not long before he died. She was a tiny cub that had recently lost her mother. Skýja leopards lived far longer than most big cats. When I'd left at sixteen, she was two years old, graceful, and beautiful to be sure, but basically an overgrown kitten with a mischievous streak a mile wide.

"You know you're not supposed to be on the furniture." I pointed to the floor and Pasha hissed as she reluctantly obeyed, slinking out of the room to find breakfast.

"Good morning, child." The regal voice sounded so much like Mother's—like home—tears burned my eyes.

"Aunt Astrid." I sat up on the edge of my bed, my back and shoulders throbbing with a bone-deep stiffness I knew wouldn't fade any time soon. With so much traveling, followed by a battle, my injuries and aches had blended together, but they were catching up to me now. The Druid priestess had healed my damaged wing, but it would still be a long time before the soreness eased.

I met Astrid's gaze and saw so much kindness there, shame for my cowardice overwhelmed me. Would I ever be able to look my family or my people in the eye and not feel such guilt?

"I didn't mean for this to happen," I managed in a strangled voice as I dropped my gaze to the floor. My excuses were beginning to sound like empty words even to my own ears.

"Of course you didn't, sweetheart." My aunt came to sit on the bed beside me, her presence warm and comforting.

"I was a coward." I leaned my head against her shoulder.

"You have never been a coward a day in your life, Alithea Viktory Skuld Ahlstrom."

I winced at the sound of all four of my names.

"There is a reason your mother named you after a first-generation Valkyrie." Astrid stroked my back with a loving hand. "Skuld means 'she who is becoming.' Your mother always knew you would be her strong-willed daughter. I was so proud of you for leaving."

I snapped my head up, looking at my aunt with surprise. "Proud? I ran away."

A grim shadow flickered over her lovely face. "I imagine all our circumstances would be much different now if we'd learned to communicate better. You weren't ready and you refused to blindly accept the traditions that sealed your fate before you were even born. We both know Brenna is a traditionalist, but she's your mother, and she was just as proud of you for standing up for yourself as I was. Leaving wasn't cowardice, Thea. It was so very brave. In the days after you left, we realized how little attention we had given your concerns. Darling, we left you no choice but to do something drastic. What came after—no one could have foreseen that, not even Sylvi."

"Aunt Astrid ... I don't know how to fix this." My shoulders slumped. I wanted to crawl back into the comfort of my bed and forget everything.

"From what I've heard, you've done a pretty remarkable job so far."

"Thanks to Morgana," I muttered.

"Yes, I'm sure she's the one who freed all those Valkyrie soldiers ensnared in Neela's Warder magic." Aunt Astrid's biting sarcasm brought a smile to my face.

"You heard?"

"Of course. We all have and it's the only thing anyone can talk about."

Pressure seized my heart like it did when I was a young Queen Heir. The pressure of living up to the expectations of my people. And that was the one thing I didn't want to talk about. "Tell me about Mother, please. Is she safe?"

"She is alive." Astrid stood, avoiding my pleading gaze. "We have much to discuss, but you should eat first." Crossing the room, she retrieved a silver breakfast tray. "I'm afraid it isn't much. Rations are tight these days." She set the tray in front of me.

I stared down at the small bowl of porridge and sliced fruit. A cup of weak tea, piping hot, accompanied the meager breakfast. "Rations? Has it really come to this?"

"We've been under siege for two years, Thea." Astrid sank into the chair beside my bed with a weary sigh. "We've had to make do with what we have. For everything else, we've either gone without or learned how to make or steal it."

I studied the bowl of porridge, losing whatever appetite I might have had.

"Eat, child. Don't let it go to waste. I will fill you in on the details."

I took a bite of the bland porridge, stirred with a hint of honey that was undoubtedly a precious commodity, and forced myself to swallow.

"On the morning after your First Ascension, when it became clear you'd fled to the mortal realm, the queen's council met and our decision was unanimous. In your absence, the role of Queen Heir would naturally fall to Sylvi. Some didn't like it, but we all believed you would return to your duty in time, and if you didn't,

Sylvi would be a fine ruler. Surely the power of the gods would recognize her in time, regardless of what we decided.

"Your mother fought to give you the time we should have offered you in the first place. She forced her council to see that you had every right to make your own decisions, claiming the fact that you'd taken such drastic measures to be heard was a testament to how strongly the council has held on to traditions that your generation no longer believes in."

"She said that? My mother, the traditionalist queen?" I felt a surge of pride for my mother and my queen.

"When Brenhilde was your age, she did everything expected of her. And she was miserable for it. She didn't rebel until she was much older."

"Mother? No." I shook my head. "I can't imagine she would ever have it in her to rebel against the traditional roles of the Valkyrie Queens."

"She defied the system in her own way, but that's a story she'll have to tell you. Eat, Thea. We don't waste food here," Astrid reminded me.

I took another bite of porridge with a slice of yellow fruit. It tasted like ash in my mouth. I wasn't hungry, but I would finish every bite. "What about Mother's bounty hunters?"

"She only wanted them to deliver a message to you." Astrid studied the worn woolen shawl draped around her shoulders. "To let you know she understood and that you could come home whenever you wanted and things would be different."

"I never stuck around long enough to hear that message." I wondered how things might have been if I hadn't run so fiercely from them.

"How did this happen, Aunt Astrid? How has Neela, of all people, managed to take the throne from our queen?" My mother was widely considered one of the strongest queens of our age. She was a powerful vessel, and under her rule the people of Valsgard had thrived. I couldn't fathom a world where the daughter of a Warder could usurp the throne on Mother's watch.

"It took us all by surprise." Astrid shifted uncomfortably in her chair. "For the first few months after you left, everything was fine. It was a scandal, of course, and poor Fiske was beside himself in your absence. We didn't know if we should start the consort process all over for Sylvi or if his betrothal to you should transfer to your sister instead—at least for the time being."

I gasped in surprise. "I never dreamed she would be expected to marry him." My throat grew tight. I was appalled by how much I'd overlooked in my rush to escape my own fate. Had I dumped everything I hated about becoming Queen Heir on my sister without a thought of what she wanted?

"It doesn't matter now. At the time the scandal seemed like an enormous obstacle we'd never overcome. But then your Aunt Svana arrived with Neela. It was a homecoming we hadn't expected, but it lifted everyone's spirits—for a time. I hadn't seen Svana in years and I hardly recognized her daughter. After my sister married King Ulric, she visited only a few times when Neela was a young girl. And they always arrived under heavy Warder escort."

Astrid's eyes filled with sorrow. "I remember Svana when Brenna and I were little girls." She fumbled with the frayed hem of her sleeve. "She was such a strong, vibrant young woman and a fierce shield maiden. She just wasn't a strong enough vessel as Mother needed in an heir."

"I vaguely remember Aunt Svana," I said. But to me she'd always seemed like a meek woman, scared of her own shadow.

"Her marriage changed her."

"Neela was always kind enough when Sylvi and I were just kids," I said. "If a bit standoffish." The distant memory of my older cousin had come to mind often these last few days. Even though she wasn't a Valkyrie, she was still family. As a Warder princess, she didn't enjoy the kind of freedoms she would have had if her mother had married into any other kingdom.

The Warders were an unusual society, and they lived in a harsh land. Their women had few rights and privileges, and it was illegal for them to use their Warder magic without permission. For the first time I wondered how Aunt Svana had ever managed to adapt.

"Neela was a lovely girl when she was a child, but she is a grown woman now, with ambitions that surpass what she could achieve in her own kingdom. Her life among the Warders has hardened her. But we were so happy to welcome her and Svana home. There was even a ball to celebrate the joyous reunion of family." Astrid let out a strangled breath, her gaze dropping to her hands in her lap. "It ended in bloodshed."

"Bloodshed?" I shoved my empty tray aside, the food churning in my stomach.

"In the days leading up to the celebration, it became clear that Neela's power was growing. That the power of the gods strengthened her. At the ball, she arrived wearing a beautiful gown. The garnet beads sparkled under the ballroom lights. It was a traditional royal gown like the Queen Heir would wear. Backless. Her brilliant red wings fanned out behind her like a blood-red cloak—all six of them. The crowd was speechless as Svana and Neela took their places of honor on either side of the queen. The council was furious. Svana never told us her half-Warder daughter was born a Valkyrie royal—a vessel. We all assumed Neela was like her father —more Warder than Valkyrie, as Svana was always weak. We never dreamed a child of hers could ever contend for the throne of Valsgard.

"What happened after her grand entrance?" I asked.

"Neela named herself Queen Heir and directed her men to

seize your mother. The ballroom exploded in a battle to protect our queen, but Neela fought back with her Warder magic, trapping those who resisted her in a prison world of her making, and I imagine most of those poor souls are still there. Others she ensnared under her will, forcing them to serve her. The men she traveled with were prisoners she claimed were Warder guards her father had sent for protection."

"Are you saying Neela is a Warder *and* a Valkyrie? A vessel?" I shivered at the very idea of that kind of power. As a Valkyrie royal, if she were strong enough, and it seemed like she was, she could become a Queen Heir. And like any queen or queen heir, she could siphon the power and hold it for others of the Nine Realms to use. This ability was what held our world together. When a Valkyrie Queen Heir ascended to the throne of the High Queen, she gave up any of her own magic she might have been born with, beyond the ability to shift. That was the only way she could contain the power of the gods. When she took the burden of power onto her shoulders, it burned through her magic.

My own magic allowed me to burn things, and see the magic of others. When … if I ever ascended the throne, I would probably lose that ability. Sylvi was a seer. If she ascended in my place, she would likely lose her sight.

Not many queens could hold onto their own magic while bearing the full brunt of the power of the gods. That Neela could seemingly do both was not a good omen for me.

"She is both, and she is ruthless," Astrid said. "The ball was a bloodbath. Her men slaughtered anyone who stood against her. I remained in the Citadel that night, as my duty requires of me."

"And Sylvi? How did she get away?" I asked.

"The council members closest to her grabbed her and all but dragged her into the Citadel. She was the next in line. They couldn't get to Brenhilde, but they knew they could save Sylvi. The events of the night threw her into a prophetic state and she didn't come quietly. It took her days to recover."

When Sylvi had one of her episodes, her mind went somewhere else and her body was often uncooperative and sometimes violent. It was the main reason the council never saw her as a true contender for the throne—until I gave them no other choice.

"During the chaos, our people fled to the Citadel where they knew they would be safe. As foreign diplomats, neither Neela and her mother nor their soldiers could enter the Citadel without my permission."

The magic of the Citadel Queen wouldn't allow them to step foot inside the fortress.

"We've been here ever since."

"How?" The Citadel was the lifeblood of the city, but I couldn't imagine how they'd survived more than two years trapped inside the mountain.

"We had a few rough seasons, but we've learned to adapt. We have fresh water from the mountain falls that feed our fountains. Our emergency stores lasted us through the first year. We've since learned to grow our own food. We have hunting parties and blockade runners who bring us fresh meat and fish as often as they can. We've acclimated."

"Acclimated?" I held my temper in check, but I wanted to lash out in my frustration with Neela. I knew Astrid and Sylvi had done the best they could, but they should never have been forced into such a situation. Really, I was angry with myself.

"We've been trapped here, Thea. In the early days, we tried to fight back, but we are too few in number. Neela rules through fear and ruthlessness, like a Warder Queen—if ever there was such a thing. Our citizens outside the Citadel's protection are enslaved to her power and have no will of their own."

"What was your plan, Astrid?" I stood to pace the length of my room. The long sleeping gown brushing my ankles felt strange to me after years of sleeping in comfortable t-shirts. I ran a frustrated hand through my hair. "What have you been doing the last two years?"

"Surviving, child. It's taken everything we've had to keep our people fed and clothed. We haven't had the resources to fight a battle we couldn't hope to win. So we've opened the Citadel to all citizens who seek refuge from Neela and her vicious soldiers—whom we don't want to kill because most of them are our people under her influence. Only those loyal to you, Sylvi, and your mother may pass through our gates."

"So you've just been waiting?"

"Yes. Neela sent her bounty hunters after you and at first, we feared she would imprison you too, but you continued to evade her efforts, and we've cheered you on. In time, Sylvi collected her own bounty hunters. People from outside the city. She chose them carefully and sent them out months ago to find you and bring you home."

"For what, Astrid? What am I supposed to do?"

"We've been waiting for you." Astrid leaned toward me, hope shining through the sorrow and weariness in her eyes. "Thea, you are the true Queen Heir. The power will return to you in time, and when the scales tip in your favor, you can beat her. You are the only one who can save us."

"But I'm not the Queen Heir." I turned toward the window, gazing with unseeing eyes at the bright sunlight streaming in through the leaded glass panes. My shoulders slumped. "Not anymore. My magic has changed and my vessel is weak. I'm not as powerful as I once was and there's a darkness there I've never felt before. Something I don't understand. It's like this … shadow has smothered the light of my magic. If you've been waiting for me to come back and save you, that's not going to happen. She's too strong. We may have to face the hard truth that Neela is now Queen Heir and we will have to come to some sort of truce with her."

"You've been gone for three years and you've only been back a few days. We must give it time before we make such assumptions about the strength of your vessel. You left the realm when you were only sixteen. You were still maturing, your power still developing. Perhaps this difference you feel is simply a change you would have experienced as you came of age."

"It feels like … tar tainting my soul. It's not natural."

"Sylvi will look into your aura and see if there's any cause for worry. She's an even more skilled seer now. And it has become clear to us all that she will be my heir. It's why the power of the gods never chose her as your mother's successor. She was already meant to be mine."

"Sylvi will be Queen of the Citadel?" I couldn't wrap my mind around the idea of my sweet, gentle sister as a warrior and shield maiden to the queen. To Neela, if something didn't change soon.

"She is stronger than any of us have ever realized. She is the backbone of the resistance and the reason you are here now. She will be your right hand, Thea. And the two of you will bring the Nine Realms into a bright new future."

"What about our mother?" I didn't want to hear the details of the queen's imprisonment at the hands of our enemy. I feared she might be dead and they were just afraid to tell me. The way Astrid spoke of the future, the queen didn't seem to factor into her vision.

"She is alive. But only just. Neela has kept her enslaved, siphoning the power to within an inch of her life. She will never rise as queen again. If she even lives to see her child on the throne."

My heart sank like a stone in my gut. This was all my fault. If I'd just married Fiske like I was supposed to, none of this would have happened.

"Where is she?" My spine went rigid. I wasn't sure what I could do, but I refused to go down without a fight.

"The palace dungeons. She is far beyond our reach. But I don't believe Neela will kill her. If she planned to, she would have done it by now. I believe she's keeping her alive for Svana's sake. Your mother and Svana were so close when Brenna was young. Svana doted on her baby sisters until Brenna was named Queen Heir and I became heir to the Citadel. Svana was the eldest, but she was the weakest of Mother's children. When she was betrothed to King Ulric, it broke her heart. Mother used her as a diplomatic pawn on a chessboard. Her marriage to the Warder King bought an ally we sorely needed at the time, but Svana was discarded. Married to a man who didn't love her. She should have been a queen, but among the Warders she is less than nothing in a realm that treats their women like slaves. I believe Svana still loves her sisters. But she's had a lifetime of hate that has brought her to this. She is desperate to give her daughter a different life and she might be willing to sacrifice her sister and all our people to give it to her."

The stone in my chest burned like a hot coal, igniting the power inside me. I was always a strong and skilled fighter, but the darkness welled within me now, feeding on my anger. Astrid's voice faded to a din and I saw red.

CHAPTER 19

"Alithea? What's happening?" Aunt Astrid followed me down the winding stone steps into the Citadel proper. Pasha growled softly beside me, a quiet echo of my own righteous anger.

I sensed the growing crowd behind me, but I couldn't hear them through the thick cloud of darkness that housed my rage.

"Come on," Ben urged. "Let's get you back upstairs. You're looking a little rough, particularly around the eyes." He leaned closer, his voice dropping. "Your eyes are all red , Thea. It's freaking everyone out."

"Where do you think you're going?" Druan's calloused voice hissed in my ear. His arms wrapped around me, pulling me back from the Citadel gates, but I fought him. I clawed at his arms with my sharp talons, not realizing my Valkyrie was so close to the surface. "You can't help her, Thea. If you want to help her—or any of us—stay inside where it's safe until you are stronger."

"Hey man, don't force her."

I was vaguely aware of the anger in Ben's voice, but my vision was colored red, like my world was bathed in blood.

"Let her go." Vendela's quiet tone was the only reasonable one among the frantic arguing. "She knows what she's doing."

She and Amara took their places at my side, wordlessly daring the men to stop them from leaving with me.

"It's time we all trust her." Vendela lifted her shield as Druan took a step back, releasing me.

I heard their words, but I was somewhere else—somewhere deep inside myself where the only thing I saw was my proud, regal mother, a captive of a ruthless enemy. "I may not have the power to fight Neela yet, but I will not stand by and let my mother suffer a moment longer." My voice grated in my throat as I stepped through the grand gates of the Citadel, leaving the magic of Astrid's protection behind.

"This is madness." Druan and Ben, along with several other Valkyrie men stepped in front of me. Dragon fire licked at their feet as Amara snorted a warning for them to back off.

"The second she leaves the Citadel, Neela will know she has returned. The princess is not walking in there without protection," Druan snapped back. "Let us go first."

Liquid hot anger boiled inside me. These fools were keeping me from my queen held captive in her own home. I would not stand for it. The slick oily shadow of my magic welled up inside me, feeling unnatural and sickening. This time I didn't care. "If you must."

With Druan's unit marching ahead, I walked along the pathway to the palace. *My* palace. A deceptive calm washed over me, drowning out the soldiers' footsteps. I wore a mask of serenity, concealing the rage surging like a tempest inside me. The darkness of the gods' power had won. It was in control and it only wanted one thing. Neela's head on a pike.

Leaving the protection of the Citadel was like shining a spotlight on my return. Even the power of the gods stood up and took notice. Since my arrival, the power had slowly trickled in to refill the well inside me. Now that trickle became a torrent. I had very little time to act before Neela would respond.

As we crossed the bridge to the palace, Neela's false guards formed up to block me at the gates. Once my mother's men, they were now Neela's prisoners. And just like in the battle, I could see the evidence of Neela's magic that followed these men. Except this time the mark of her magic trailed behind them like streaks of blood.

These men had put up a struggle. I could see it in the violent magic that bound them. I would give them a chance to join me. One chance.

I might not yet be as powerful a vessel as Neela, but I was still a royal daughter of House Ahlstrom and my magic was strong. I wielded the burn like a sword, letting the hot slash of magic arc through the air, clawing through their ties to the enemy.

I barely registered their astonished faces before I was moving again.

"Stand down and let us pass." Vendela's voice rang out. "Your Queen Heir has returned. Join her now and your families will rest easy tonight inside the Citadel. Resist and you will not live to see your rightful queen on her throne."

I stepped toward the palace gates, ignoring the murmurs of my mother's guard. More than half of them lowered their weapons, but Neela's magic began to reform. The trails of blood I'd severed shifted, strengthening the connection.

Once again, I let the burn of my magic fill me and slashed through the bonds holding my people against their will. Acting on instinct alone, I freed them, ignoring the foreign shadowy darkness that tainted my magic further. I feared what would happen when only the darkness remained.

"It's Princess Alithea! She's returned to save us." My mother's guard rejoiced. Joining my entourage, they abandoned their posts. But even in my rage, I took note of the few who slipped away to join the master they chose to serve. I wouldn't forget their faces.

Once inside the palace, courtiers bolted in every direction, screaming in fear as my new soldiers cleared the way for me. They were nothing but a blur of colorful faces, but only a few were tainted by the blood of Neela's magic. The rest were there by choice. I would deal with the traitors later.

"Find her." I issued the order, not caring who carried it out as long as it was done. I was only vaguely aware of the sound of clashing swords behind me and the heat of Amara's fire clearing my path. No one stood in my way as I continued toward the dungeons. I took the winding stairs into the bowels of the castle. Only Druan and Vendela followed.

"It's like she's in some sort of fugue state." Vendela snapped her fingers in front of my face, but I wouldn't let her break my focus. "The red eyes are freaky, but if I didn't know any better, I'd say she was—"

"That is none of our business." Druan's words were a sharp warning.

I turned toward the sound of their voices, but my eyes slid right past them.

"Release the queen," Vendela announced as I approached the deepest part of the dungeon.

"On whose orders?" A man dressed in the white and black livery of a Warder stood at his post in front of the cell door, but I now knew none of them were actual Warders. Just prisoners posing as those who could command prison worlds.

"The Queen Heir has returned," Vendela announced.

"My queen is still in charge. I obey her. Even when I don't particularly want to." He scratched his scraggly beard, taking a stance against us. "You should know better than to face a Warder bound to his queen."

But this man was no Warder and Neela wasn't anyone's queen. He was nothing but a prisoner with no magic to speak of. I could see the strength of the bloody bonds holding him to the false queen he'd served for too many years to count.

"Leave us." My voice sounded strange to my ears.

The man took a step toward me but Vendela darted between us, raising her sword and shield to protect me.

The darkness churned inside me, coating my magic in its slick black oil. The Warder's weapon arced down toward Vendela, but with a flick of my hand a burn seared across his face. His eyes grew bright from the pain.

"I said, leave us." Pasha growled at my side, edging closer to the false Warder. I could see the fear in his eyes. He was just another victim. I severed his bonds, slicing through the years of magic Neela had forced on him.

The man sagged like a puppet with its strings cut. Without a word he left us in a daze, no longer caring about his master.

"How did she do that to a Warder?" Vendela turned wide eyes on me.

"He wasn't a Warder. None of them are." Druan's voice grew incredulous. "Neela is here on her own."

Ignoring their whispered conversation, I pressed my hand against the rough wooden door letting the burn seep into the surface until a wide hole replaced the door. The room was hardly a room at all. More of a closet—the mud walls, slick with moisture, reeked of mildew and filth. A single, worn bench rested in a corner where the queen slumped, chained to the wall. The room was so small, she could put her feet up on the opposite wall, but there wasn't enough room to lie down. My mother had spent more than two years in this cramped cell.

White-hot rage surged anew at the sight of my mother, weak and out of her mind with fear.

"No, please. No more," the queen whispered, her faint pulse visible at her slim throat. Her once golden blond hair was silver now, and shorn close to her scalp in places. Her eyes were hollow and unseeing.

I reached for the shackles binding her to the wall and they blazed like irons in the fire. A moment later they crumbled into dust. I took her hand in mine for a brief moment, but the pain and fear in her eyes was nearly my undoing.

I turned away, unable to look at my mother for the shame that consumed me. I stumbled back out of the cell, the weight of my grief and guilt more than I could bear.

"You can rest now, your Majesty. We're leaving." Druan lifted the queen's frail form and carried her from her cell.

Still, I couldn't see beyond the darkness burning up my soul. The tainted magic pulsed hot within me now as I led the way from the dungeon.

Back in the grand hall of the palace, chaos reigned. Courtiers had vanished and only my soldiers remained. Those who chose Neela over me now lay dead.

"Where is she?" I demanded of the room.

"The usurper, Majesty?" a young soldier asked with a curt bow. "She is in the council chambers. Upon your arrival we barred them inside."

I nodded, gazing around at the aftermath of the fierce battle that had taken place here.

The soldier dropped to his knee, bowing his head. "We took precautions to protect you, my Queen Heir. But the usurper knows of your return by now."

"Well done," I murmured. Offering a brief, appreciative nod, I made my way up the stairs to the council chambers. Pasha padding along beside me. She nudged my hand to get my attention, but though my eyes took in all that had happened around me, my mind was somewhere else.

"Amara, please take my mother to the Citadel," I called over my shoulder, sinking my taloned fingertips into Pasha's fur. I was only vaguely aware that I'd partially shifted.

Druan and Vendela followed me up the stairs as Amara gathered the broken queen in her arms and fled the palace.

A moment later, I heard the flap of leathery wings and knew my mother was finally safe.

"Thea," Druan murmured. "We need to leave if we're going to make it out of here in once piece. We cannot afford to trade your mother for you."

I nodded, but continued my slow march to the third floor of the palace. At my raised arms the burn swept through the wooden barrier the guards had placed and the council chamber doors burst open.

I stepped inside and six stunned faces stared back at me. Just as Neela called on her Warder magic, I lifted my hand and the slick black sludge that weighed on my magic swept across the room, latching onto Neela's arms and binding the bold redheaded woman to her seat. The seat of power she had the audacity to steal for herself.

Neela cried out in pain as she moved, causing her skin to blister and burn around the magical bindings. "Alithea." She titled her head in my direction. "I was just telling my council how you've returned just this minute."

"I will deal with you another time, cousin." My eyes slid over her, barely registering the woman who'd caused so much pain in my absence.

Pasha leapt onto the table and settled back on her haunches, releasing a ferocious growl in Neela's face. She wasn't going anywhere.

The well within me was far too empty and Neela's was nearly full. Something in me hungered to drink from that well, but I couldn't draw Neela's attention to the power of the gods. I only let myself take a sip. Just to know I could do it.

Neela didn't react to the infinitesimal siphoning.

"Thea?" A familiar voice reached me through the fog of my anger. I stared blankly at my grandmother's pale face, unable to fathom how she could support any of this. But there she sat, free of Neela's magic. Beside her sat Princess Svana, my aunt, the uncrowned queen of Vöstland. Traitor to me and my mother.

"You've returned." My grandmother's words fell on deaf ears. Clearly, she'd chosen a side and it wasn't the right one.

"You have much to answer for, young lady." One of the council elders reprimanded me like a naughty child.

I shot her a dark glare, binding her and the other elders to their chairs as well.

"Do not move and the burn will not harm you." My voice grated with the power of my Valkyrie. "I am the daughter of your queen and you will address me as such. In my absence you have allowed a usurper on my mother's throne. You will each pay dearly for your part in this."

Magic coiled in Neela's hand and I hit her hard in the chest with the burn. She shouted in fury and Pasha hissed. With her hands bound with the threat of the burn, Neela was helpless and at Pasha's mercy.

"Alithea Ahlstrom, you are acting like a spoiled child. Call off that cat of yours," another elder said, also free of Neela's magical influence. I would see them all burned as traitors.

"You left us to clean up your mess. The council has moved on.

The power of the gods has clearly chosen Neela." The elder sat calmly in her chair. "Guards!" she called. "Take the princess and throw her in with her useless mother."

"Your guards have joined their Queen Heir and have returned to the Citadel with their queen. Those who chose to fight us are all dead." My harsh voice bounced off the stone walls of the council chamber. I pinned them each with a hard stare, my eyes lingering on Neela. "I returned more than a week ago, right under your nose. In that time I've released dozens of your prisoners, raised an army and rescued my mother. You will pay for dearly your crimes, cousin. You will all pay for what you have done to my people."

I turned, leaving my stunned audience behind as Pasha leapt off the table to follow me. When the doors slammed behind me, Druan grabbed a spear from a wall display and wedged it through the door handles to hold the council inside. It wasn't necessary, I'd left them chained to their chairs with the burn binding their arms. It would fade … eventually.

"Thea, we have to get out of here," Vendela urged. "It's only a matter of moments before they regroup and come after us."

I nodded and slowly made my way back down the stairs littered with the bodies of the men and women who chose to fight against me. Anger seethed inside me at their betrayal. Putting one foot in front of the other, I allowed the storm of my rage to fill my mind and senses until I could see nothing else. I'd embraced the darkness that had hindered me before. Now it fueled my anger, making it writhe like a slick, scaly creature. I clutched it in my talons and refused to let go.

"Mother?" I shook my head to clear the fog from my mind, glancing around the sitting room and wondering how I got here.

"Alithea, my darling, you've returned." The frail queen broke into a fit of coughing where she lay on the settee in a stifling hot room. Servants flew around the room gathering blankets, food, watered wine, and hot tea while they waited for the palace surgeon to arrive.

My mother looked as though she were on death's door, but I couldn't make myself go to her.

"Don't strain yourself, Brenna." Astrid crouched beside her, grasping her sister's fragile hands. "Take whatever power you need from me, sister."

"I'm not sure I can." Brenna couldn't seem to take her eyes off me, like she thought I might disappear.

Vague memories of the last hours floated through my mind, but they felt like someone else's memories. Like I had just been a passenger, a witness of the events that freed my mother from her prison. A prison she'd endured because of me.

I thought I might collapse from the weight of my mother's stare, so full of love and forgiveness, I couldn't stand it. The shame that had plagued me since I returned was too much. Like a coward, I lurched from my chair and fled the room. I couldn't handle the way everyone looked to me in expectation, like their savior had finally arrived to fix everything when I didn't have a clue how to do it.

They'd all told me Mother wasn't strong enough to rule again, but I hadn't believed them. In some small corner of my mind I'd seen a future with Queen Brenna restored to her throne. A future where I might have to be the Queen Heir, but I wouldn't have to rule. But the frail woman in that room would never recover. That couldn't have been my mother.

I ran up the grand staircase of the Citadel, charging along hallways and around corners. Muscle memory took over as I burst through the glass doors to the grand terrace overlooking the Citadel park. I'd spent most of my childhood years playing in the park with the children of the noble houses, sent to become the young princesses' playmates.

Filled with tall trees and fragrant flowers, the park was a maze of pathways and fountains, a place of beauty no matter the season. A blanket of snow covered the ground now. In my memory the pathways were always clear of snow in the winter and bright flowers bloomed in shades of black, red, and purple—chrysanthemums, poinsettias, and winter cactus. The gurgling fountains of spring were replaced with the most spectacular ice sculptures. Fir trees covered in fairy lights lined the paths and the bare branches of the tallest trees swayed in the breeze.

All that was a distant memory now. Staring at the barren

garden below, I tried to comprehend what I saw. The trees were all gone. The stone pathways erased. No flowers. No winter wonderland. Blocks of dark, tilled soil sat empty nearest the terrace steps. Cows and goats bleated behind ramshackle pens. Chickens roamed freely around a coop constructed from bales of hay.

Men and women came and went. Nobility and servants alike trudged along the muddy trails to the tents in the distance. Some cared for the animals, others shoveled snow and manure from the muddy fields.

"Greenhouses," I murmured, my gaze settling on my sister's golden dreadlocks as she issued orders to those around her. Sylvi bent to shovel dried manure into a waiting cart.

Acrid smoke billowed from the mud chimneys behind the greenhouses. Rows and rows of them. During the years of the siege, they'd transformed the gardens into a thriving farm. The greenhouses were their source of food for the winter months while their spring fields lay fallow for the season. Fruit trees and vines made up a small orchard that would bloom in the coming months. Everyone worked, but Sylvi was clearly in charge. My sister had worked her fingers to the bone to keep our people fed. While I lived a life of solitude, serving drinks to humans and eating my fill of junk food and binging television shows. My freedom had been so important to me, but what had I done with it?

Pride filled me as I watched my sister pull a heaping cart to each of the greenhouses, shoveling peat into the fire pits keeping the greenhouses warm. The bottom half of her skirts were damp with mud, but she didn't seem to notice. Fiske followed her at a close trot, lighting the fires as she shoveled peat into the makeshift braziers. They looked as though they'd performed this task together a thousand times.

"She's a wonder, your sister." Druan stepped up beside me and placed a warm cloak around my shoulders. I hadn't even realized I was shivering. "She's also kind of mean." He chuckled fondly, watching Sylvi give a tongue lashing to a couple of young boys who were supposed to be working.

I had to tell her about Mother before someone else did.

Ignoring Druan, I clutched the cloak around me, flinching when a cold splash landed on my hand. I looked up, expecting to see rain.

Druan swiped a thumb across my cheek, wiping my tears away. I hadn't realized I was crying.

"Coming home to this must be a terrible shock." His voice was gentle and his eyes filled with concern. The low hum of his voice calmed me.

I watched a young girl following my sister around. I vaguely recognized her as Annika, my not-so-secret cousin. She'd grown into a beautiful girl in my absence. Annika was Astrid's daughter, but the Queen of the Citadel was required to be celibate, so she could never claim her daughter as her own.

"Knowing it's all your fault probably makes it a thousand times harder." Druan leaned against the terrace balustrade, his arms folded across his chest. "But after three years of playtime, you don't get the luxury of wallowing, Thea." His voice was still gentle, but I didn't like his words.

"Watch yourself, Druid." I shot him a warning glare. Everything he said was true, but he didn't have the right to say it to my face.

"I'm not, you know."

I gave him a blank look.

"Druid, I mean. I'm not even Berserker. Or Valkyrie, even though I've lived among you for the longest. I'm just Druan. A man with no ties to any one people." He crossed his ankles, staring at me. "What are you going to do to fix this, Princess?"

"I don't know." I swiped at the tears still trailing down my face.

"You'd better figure it out. And soon. Now's not the time to be emotional. Your people need you and you've neglected them long enough."

"I didn't know!" I took a step toward him, shoving him back against the terrace railing. He barely moved. "I left my people in capable hands. I left them with a strong queen, a formidable ruler of the Citadel, and my sister as Queen Heir. They didn't need me."

"Maybe. But that's not what happened." Druan shrugged. "Get over it."

"Get over it?" I slammed my hands against him again, hoping he'd fall right over the side to the ground below. But he was immovable, like a boulder. And stubborn as one. "Look at them!" I pointed down at the farmland that was once the most beautiful garden in all of Valsgard. "My people are slaving away just to feed themselves. Trapped in this mountain fortress for years just waiting for me to come save them? How do I just *get over* how I've utterly failed them?"

"The past doesn't matter, Princess." He shrugged his wide shoulders. "You can't change it so there's no use dwelling on it. But you can change their present and promise them a brighter future. You just need to step up. Do better. What do the humans say? Man up."

I snorted. "You definitely aren't from around here if you expect that to be some kind of pep talk."

Druan pushed away from the wall. "Then go be the strong woman I saw take charge today and every single day since she stepped foot in this realm. Not this sniveling little girl too afraid to face mommy. You took what you wanted right out from under Neela's nose and you rubbed her face in it. You can do this, Thea. You *are* doing it."

"I don't know what that was." I stared down at my hands. "It wasn't me." I shivered, afraid the shadows I felt whenever I called on my magic were responsible for what happened. And when there was no more light left within me, what would be left?

"Yes, it was. You let your righteous anger take precedence over your fear. Find that confidence again when you face your people."

"Face them?" Just the thought of addressing the very people I'd abandoned made me queasy.

"After what you did today, everyone will look to you for leadership. Even Queen Astrid. So you need to get out of your head and make a plan, because Neela will retaliate. Soon. You shocked her. You made a fool of her, and you took her most important prisoner—the source of the power she needs to hold her position. She's not going to let that slide, so the question is, what are you going to do to meet her head on?"

"I have no idea." I bit my lip. He was right, it was up to me to make the next move—quickly.

"Look at me, Thea." He turned me to face him, his hands on my shoulders. "You are not alone in this. No successful ruler has ever done the job entirely on their own. If you try to take on this burden all by yourself you will drown."

"Thank you." I laid my hand over his. He wasn't nice. He certainly wasn't impressed by my title, but he seemed to care about my people. I could respect that even if I didn't like him very much.

"For what?" The dark arc of his brow raised in question.

"For not being afraid to tell me exactly what I need to hear, no matter how much it makes me want to scratch your face off." I took a step back, needing some space between us before I completely fell apart and collapsed in his arms for a good cry.

"Thea?" Ben called from within the Citadel.

"Out here!" I took another step away from the tall, intimidating Druid with the Berserker eyes.

"Your mother is asking for you." Ben stepped onto the terrace, looking completely disoriented in this new world. Dressed in his human clothes and leather jacket, he seemed so out of place. Gone was the confident, cocky rogue who took home a new girl every night. In his place was a lost little boy I felt a visceral need to protect.

"I can't face her." I reached for him, needing the familiar reminder of my human life.

"She's a nice lady," Ben said, opening his arms to me and resting his chin on my head.

Druan snorted irritably. Either from Ben's understatement or from his familiarity, I wasn't sure which.

"You could have told me about all this ages ago, you know." Ben murmured into my hair. "I would have understood."

"The princess has bigger things on her mind than you, kid." Stiffly Druan stepped to my other side. "Make a decision and don't put it off." With that, he left us on the terrace alone.

"A bit of a jerk, that one." Ben scowled at Druan's retreating figure. "He probably just doesn't like me because I'm prettier than he is."

"I love you." I laughed and drew away from his hug, beckoning to him. "Come on, I want you to meet my sister. I have to tell her about Mother."

"I've met your mother. I found her and Astrid when I went looking for you. I think the queen likes me more than you. Especially right now. You're kind of up to your neck in trouble, aren't you?"

"Pretty much." I sighed, grateful my friend was here, though it was only a matter of time before his secret was out. If that happened, I wasn't sure what I could do to save him. I had to send him back home before he ended up on the executioner's block.

CHAPTER 21

The next morning I was determined to visit Mother. I couldn't avoid her any longer. But I couldn't seem to make myself enter her room.

"Thea, my darling. Don't linger in the hallway." The queen's voice sounded a little stronger than it had the day before, but not by much.

"Hello, Mother." I stared at the floor as I stepped into the doorway of her bed chamber.

"Come in, Thea. Let me see you."

I chanced a look at her. The queen's smile lit her pale face as her eyes rested on me.

"She's a little loopy," Astrid whispered. "The healers gave her something to ease the pain."

"She's so thin." My eyes brimmed with tears. I couldn't bear to see my once proud, strong mother reduced to such a state. Her slivery-white hair had fallen out in places, leaving patches of bald scalp. Horrified, I realized those chunks of hair were probably snatched out from the roots.

"She's eager to talk to you, darling. She doesn't blame you." Astrid squeezed my hand and left us.

"I should go and leave you two to get reacquainted." Ben leaned over the queen and placed a kiss on her forehead. I froze for a moment, afraid my mother would tear him to shreds for such liberties. But my mother giggled—actually giggled—and curled her thin fingers around his hand. "Please stay, Esben."

"Esben?" I frowned at my friend.

Ben shrugged. "She's been calling me that. I think she has me confused with someone else. But it seems to make her happy so they let me stay with her."

"Come now, I'm not broken or addled. Just a little bruised. Alithea, sit with me and let me look at you." She patted the mattress to her side.

I trembled as I sat beside my mother, taking her skeletal hand in mine. Emotions tumbled inside of me. Regret, shame, and an avalanche of fear threatened to smother me.

"Don't do that, Thea." My mother tried to use her stern, queenly voice, but it came out in a raspy cough. "Do not blame yourself for how things went with your cousin and my sister. No one—not even Sylvi or Morgana—could have seen that coming."

Hot tears spilled down my face as I lunged for the comfort of my mother's arms. "I'm so sorry, Mother. I was a coward." I buried my face against her shoulder, acutely aware of how easily I could break her brittle bones.

"Hush, my girl, you were no coward. You were brave. I was the one who refused to listen to your hesitations about the traditional betrothal. I forced you into it because I knew no other way. I was too afraid to be the queen who defied tradition so I ignored my daughter's deepest fears and I pushed you away." She leaned back to stare into my face. "Do you hear me, Thea? I pushed you so far into a corner you couldn't see another way out. This is *my* fault."

"It isn't. I should have returned ages ago."

"You know what I think?" Ben asked. "I know I'm just the third wheel here and I only know what I've managed to piece together, but I don't think this is anyone's fault. Something like this probably would have happened whether you left or not, Thea. This Neela chick sounds pretty scary so I'd say we should probably focus on getting rid of her and let this blame game die right here."

"We?" I managed a half-smile.

"Yes, we. You need all the help you can get, girl."

"Esben's right." The queen lifted her hand to cup his face. "Such a handsome face."

"Mother, you know I brought Ben back from the human realm, right?"

"Of course. And I should be mad." She turned toward him fondly. "It's much too dangerous for you to be here, but I'm just so happy to see you. How are your parents, dear? They were such wonderful people."

"I don't have parents, ma'am." Ben hung his head. "I grew up in foster care."

"Ben is an orphan, Mother," I explained.

"What? No." The queen shook her head. "That's impossible. What happened to Elizabeth and Thomas? They doted on you as a child."

"I... don't know." Ben shot me a pleading look. "I'm afraid I have no memory of my parents. I'm just Ben." He shrugged again, his shoulders hunching forward.

"You grew up alone? Among humans?" Mother's hand fluttered to her mouth as tears shone in her eyes. "I'm so sorry." A tear rolled down her face as she leaned close to him, looking into his eyes. "You are not just Ben. Your name is Esben."

"When I met Ben—er, Esben—he didn't know what he was." I squeezed her hand. "But you know him? Are you certain he's this boy you remember?"

"I would know my son's face anywhere, Thea."

My heart shuddered as I met Ben's confused gaze. "Mother... are you saying Ben is my ... brother?" That couldn't possibly be what she meant. Mother was dazed and tired.

"No darling, look at him. He's the spitting image of you. I'm saying he is your twin and you must protect him. He will always be in grave danger among our people, but even more so if others discover he is a prince of Valsgard."

"Prince?" Ben's face paled and his hands shook. "Twins? What's happening here, Thea? She's just confused, right?"

"I don't think so." I studied my mother's eyes. She might have suffered physically, but she was still the mother I respected. And she was dead serious about Ben.

"I had to give you up, my sweet boy. It was that or watch my husband carry out your execution. I couldn't bear to place that burden on him any more than I could bear seeing you harmed. I took you to the human realm myself. Just hours after giving birth. I left Thea with your Aunt Astrid—she's the only one who knew I gave birth to a foreworn Valkyrie boy. Yet even she believes I did my duty that night."

"You...execute your sons?" Ben's eyes filled with horror as he looked to me for confirmation. "I think Thea neglected to mention that little detail."

"Only those boys capable of shifting," I explained. "Like our girls, they are born in their Valkyrie form and shift to human within the first few days. Our law dictates they must be executed before they shift. It's supposed to be easier for the parents. I just ... couldn't bring myself to tell you such a horrible thing."

"Why must we die at birth?" His voice trembled and my heart

broke for him, wishing I could protect him from all of this. He didn't deserve to find out his life was rooted in such tragedy.

"Our history is stained with wars and atrocities committed by Valkyrie kings," the queen began. "Before the final battle, when the gods first made the Valkyries, we only gave birth to daughters—their fathers came from the other races. After the gods left their power to us, we began giving birth to sons too. During our darkest time, our realm was ruled by a council of Valkyrie men, drunk on the power of the gods coursing through their veins. They sought to make themselves gods over all the remaining realms." Her voice faded as she broke into a coughing fit.

I helped my mother sip her tea and picked up the thread of history I knew by heart. "Legend says the power of the gods manifests in foresworn Valkyries in a strange way. It's like they can't fully contain it and the more they use it, the more destructive they become. A thousand years ago, the women rose up against the men to put an end to their destructive rule. When the queens took their rightful place on the throne once more, the council enacted a law that dictated every male child born with the ability to shift must be executed on the day of his birth. Since that day, we have ruled as a matriarchal society. Over the last few centuries, the birthrate of foresworn Valkyrie males plummeted."

"So much that by the time you were born," the queen said, "I'd never even met a woman who had to order her son's death."

"We thought we'd bred them out," I continued. "The only males born now are grounded males without the ability to shift. Most have their own magic, but it is weaker than a female's magic. Most men serve as soldiers to the shield maidens. A Valkyrie soldier will do anything to protect the maiden he's dedicated his life to.

"So there are none like me, then?" Ben's face was desolate. "And if anyone finds out about me, I'm a dead man?"

"That's why you need to go back home," I said.

"No. We will protect him," the queen insisted. "I will not turn my back on my son again. I thought I left him to a loving family who would explain everything to him one day when he was old enough to understand. Instead, I discover I left him alone in a strange world to grow up without even knowing who and what he is. I will not send him back to that life."

"What do you say to that, brother?" I whispered, reaching for his free hand.

"Gaining a mother, a few aunts, and two sisters in one day—not to mention an evil cousin—and a nation of people who would want me dead if they found out about me...it's a lot to absorb. I understand the danger, but since arriving in this realm I feel more like me than ever before. I don't want to leave. This has been like finding out Santa and the Easter Bunny really exist."

"It makes total sense we're twins." I shook my head. "We're pretty much the same person."

"I'm just prettier than you," Ben quipped, making the queen laugh through her tears.

"What is a Santa?" Mother whispered, her eyes bright with happy tears.

"It's a human winter solstice thing." I waved my hand. "I swear Ben's more human than Valkyrie."

"That might save his life in the end. We have a lot on our plates right now, darlings, but it does your mother good to see you both together, finally. I'm just so, so sorry I was never there for you, Esben. I vow I will be from now on."

"You need to rest." Ben leaned in to kiss her cheek. "I want you nice and healthy again real soon. We need to get this woman a few cheeseburgers and a milkshake, Thea."

"We don't have those here."

"You just broke my heart. We're going to have to open a McDonald's franchise if you expect me to stay here."

I gave him a playful shove.

"One more question before we leave you to rest." Ben stood, tucking the blankets around our mother. "Who's the oldest?"

"Thea was born seven minutes before you." The queen gave him an indulgent smile.

"Yes! I've always wanted to be the bratty little brother."

"Well, you have certainly taken on that role with gusto. Get some sleep, Mother. We'll be back to check on you later." I gave her one last hug. I had a million questions for her, but she needed her rest.

"What have I always told you, Thea?" the queen said, almost as if reading my mind.

"Trust my instincts."

"We will talk of what comes next and we will figure it out. But … you know it's time you take up the mantle, sweetheart? There is no coming back for me. I will recover, but I will never rule again."

"I know," I whispered past the tightness in my throat. "There will be time to talk about that later. Rest now."

I shut the doors to the queen's chambers behind me.

"Twins, huh?" Ben shoved his hands in his pockets.

"Talk about earth-shattering revelations." I smiled. "Turns out I shared a womb with my best friend."

"Heck yeah, and my sister-bestie is going to be an amazing queen." He draped an arm across my shoulders. "Can I be a line item on your budget labeled 'mooch.'"

I shoved him playfully. "You've been that since the day I met you."

"Seriously, Thea, you've got this. You'll be a great ruler. We just need to work on your people skills so you can be more charming —like me."

I rolled my eyes at his narcissism, but in reality, he was right. "First, I have to figure out what to do with Neela." We walked side by side down the wide, empty hall.

"We'll deal with her." He paused, turning to face me. "I just need you to know one thing."

It wasn't like Ben to be so serious. "What?" I frowned up at him. He may be my twin, and I might be seven minutes older, but he was taller than me by several inches.

"I don't want your throne. Not even a little bit. It's way too much work and you know how I feel about work."

"We've been over this, Ben. You can't be allergic to work. But it's good to know where you stand."

"I'm serious. Given the history of my kind, I just need you to know I will never be like that. I've just been given the family I've always wanted. No way am I going to screw that up. So I'm a thousand percent in your corner—and nowhere near the line of succession. I don't want it. But I am here for you anytime, anyplace, and for any reason. I've got your back."

"Thanks, Ben. Now we just need to convince the rest of the people I abandoned that I'm not a hopeless cause. I think it's time we call a council meeting to discuss next steps. Care to join me in a battle of diplomacy?"

"Nope." Ben took a step away. "I am more than happy to leave the politics to the women. You know how I like smart, bossy women." He turned at the great staircase, heading down the first few steps.

"Where are you going?"

"To find the kitchens. If you expect me to stay here, someone's got to teach these people how to make cheeseburgers. After that, there's a hot dragon girl I need to talk to."

"Esben, that dragon girl can't talk."

"I know." He grinned. "But there are other ways of communicating."

"She's going to turn you into a charcoal briquet."

"She totally has a thing for me. Besides, we legendary mythical creatures have to stick together. Catch you later, sis." He winked and sauntered down the stairs.

"Be careful, Ben." I shook my head in wonder.

My brother would carve out a life here, making everyone fall in love with him. I had to protect him, to keep the realms from ever finding out who he was. That thought alone gave me the strength and motivation to fight for the throne I'd never wanted. As queen, I could shield him from harm. It was time to put on my big girl pants and take care of this mess. The sooner I sent Neela back to the Warder realm where she belonged, the sooner I could ensure my family's safety.

I turned the corner toward the healing ward. I wanted to check with them to see how Mother was really doing. Except, like always, my seer sister was ten steps ahead of me and everyone else.

"Sylvi," I called to her down the hall where she'd just stepped from the healer's quarters.

"Thea!" She gasped. You are two now." She charged toward me, the basket over her arm swinging as she ran. "And your aura is amber. What's happened?"

"Amber is for positive energy, isn't it? That's so unlike me."

"Don't crack jokes, this is important. What's changed since I saw you last?"

"You're not going to believe this, but I just came from visiting with Mother and—"

"She told you about Esben?" Sylvi was always quick to finish my sentences and I'd forgotten how annoying that trait was.

"You know he's ...?" I arched a brow at her, not sure we were talking about the same thing."

"He's your two." Her head bobbed as she nodded. "Mother told me about him last night."

"That's what you've been babbling about your whole life? Did you always know about Esben?"

"No, but the second I got a good look at his aura, I knew he was your two. But I couldn't see the specifics." She lifted an elegant shoulder and dropped it, like the specifics of our sibling relationship didn't matter.

I pulled her into an empty room that served as a hospital room for injured residents of the Citadel. I leaned in to whisper the news. "He's my *twin*."

Sylvi clapped her hands together. "Isn't it exciting." She beamed at me. "I can see it now. His aura is very similar to yours in many ways. But he's much more charming than you."

"So he tells me," I said dryly.

"Oh! Thea." Sylvi reached for my arm. "I just realized that young man is my brother too! I have a brother?" Her eyes widened as though the significance had just now hit her through the fog of her seer senses.

"We have to keep his identity a secret, Sylvi. You can't let it slip, no matter what."

"Why?" Sylvi frowned. "Oh, are you saying..." she paused a moment. "I see. Poor Mother, that's why she sent him away. Well, we will just have to protect him at any cost. No one's executing a brother of mine while I am heir to the Citadel."

As Astrid's heir, protecting the Valkyrie citizens fell to her. And once I ascended, Sylvi would become commander of my army and my right hand in ruling our people.

"I should have always known you were meant to be the protector."

"How could you when even I didn't know it at the time?"

"Ouch."

"What's wrong, sister? Did you stub your toe?" She glanced down at my feet.

"No." There was no sense in trying to explain to Sylvi that she'd just insulted my intelligence.

"Oh no, don't mind me, that's tomorrow." Sylvi waved her hand. "Watch out for furniture legs so you don't injure yourself."

"Got it." I nodded, following my sister from the room and back toward the staircase. "Um, Sylvi. I need to speak with you and Astrid and any other members of the council here. So … how do I make that happen?

"Leave that to me. Go freshen up and for heaven's sake, change out of those old training clothes. Remember who you are now. You need to dress as your station demands."

"You sound just like Mother."

"I'll take that as a compliment. Meet us in the Indigo Drawing Room in an hour."

"Thanks, Sylvi. I couldn't do this without you."

"I know." She smiled and swept down the staircase, her mind already on something else.

"That girl never sits still."

I turned at the familiar voice. Vendela leaned up against the banister, her eyes sweeping over me from head to toe. "She makes me tired just watching her."

"She was always the best one for this job, but I guess I'm the only one who will ever see it."

"She's perfect for the job she's got." Vendela shoved off the banister. "She's a born leader, but she's not a ruler."

"Aren't they the same thing?"

"No. Sylvi inspires people. They adore her. She's led the Citadel through more than two years of siege and her people would do anything for her. She has a mind for battle tactics and a talent to aid her in that regard. But she's not a ruler. She's an organizer. That's why the power chose you and not her. You don't need to walk into this meeting looking the part of the perfect courtly princess, eager to please. Leave that role to Sylvi. Your people need a queen, and a queen is a warrior with a backbone of steel and a mind of her own."

"Maybe in your kingdom, but in mine, I have to be both."

"You know precious little about the Berserker kingdom if you think they'd ever follow a queen of any sort." A sneer distorted Vendela's face. "Our men believe their women's strength lies in giving birth to strong Berserker sons and beautiful daughters. In Úlfaheim a queen is nothing but an incubator for the next generation. You are lucky to live in a strong matriarchal society where women are revered enough to rule on their own."

"That much I learned from living in the human world," I muttered.

"Let's go to your room. I'll help you prepare for this council meeting."

"What do you know of politics?" I followed her down the empty corridor to my rooms.

"Plenty." She held the door open for me and followed me inside, seating herself on the bed and lounging on her elbows. "My father is the King of Madmen and I'm his only legitimate heir."

"Your father is King Hagen?" I gaped in surprise.

The Berserker king was once a great ruler, but like so many of their kind, over time, his Berserker nature overpowered his human nature, leaving behind a feral beast of a man in a seat of power. Hagen had no interest in ruling but refused to give up his crown. His brother ruled as a sort of regent, but Hagen tied his hands on so many matters of State, the man had little power beyond attending the high council meetings and reporting back to his insane brother. I hadn't realized he even had a daughter.

"My uncle sent me away when I was twelve." Vendela shrugged. "My father was convinced I was trying to kill him by poisoning his food so I could take his throne. Not that my father's Jarls would allow a woman to inherit the throne."

"But if you're his only legitimate heir, you should inherit the throne."

"Spoken like a true Valkyrie. My uncle sent me away to save me from the Jarls who would only want to marry me off to some old nobleman."

"So you can rule, but they want you to be married first? That's not much different from our ways. A queen must have a husband to ensure a legitimate line."

"No. My husband would be king. My sons would continue my father's line. That's the only way I even matter to them."

"That's barbaric."

Vendela shrugged. "The Berserker clans have always been barbaric, misogynist brutes."

"So you're a princess?"

"Only sons can be named prince. Daughters of a king aren't titled. I am simply Lady Vendela. I don't even get to use my father's last name."

"It's the opposite here. Sons are second-class citizens. Good enough for the life of a soldier or even a general, but they rarely inherit their mother's fortunes or titles."

"Our people are opposite sides of the same coin," Vendela said.

"You'd think by now we'd have found some kind of middle ground where all our people could be equals. We're all the same. Nothing else matters."

"Maybe one of these days things will change for the better when the young rulers ascend and the old ones retire. You'll be the first to ascend. You can set the tone. And you're going to set it right now before we leave this room."

"I am?" My eyebrows shot up in surprise.

"It starts with what you wear to this meeting."

"My clothes can't matter that much."

"Your clothes speak for you before you have a chance to say anything. So what do you want your clothes to say?"

"Preferably, I'd like them to say, 'I'm not naked.'"

"You're impossible." Vendela slid off the bed and headed for my closet.

I didn't even know what was in there but I could guess.

"It looks like Sylvi and Astrid threw up in here." Vendela stuck her head back out. "You can't wear any of this frilly white stuff."

"Hold on a second, there might be something in here." I shifted my gaze to the trunk at the foot of my bed. I hadn't used this room in years, but my things should still be here. Whether any of it still fit was a different question. I opened the lid and gasped. A glint of gold caught the sunlight streaming in from the window.

Vendela's shadow loomed over me as she peered into the chest. "Now those will make a powerful statement."

CHAPTER 22

I approached the Indigo Drawing Room with dread. Even when I was just a young princess sitting in to observe Mother at work I detested these meetings. Now I was… I didn't even know what I was. Not a queen. Not merely a princess, but not really my former identity as Queen Heir either.

"Remember, you set the tone. Right here. Right now," Vendela reminded me.

"No pressure there." I heaved a sigh staring down at my outfit. My mother would kill me for arriving at a formal meeting in such casual dress, but it suited me more than the white frilly dresses stuffed in my closet.

Black suede leggings hugged my muscular legs with high black leather boots reaching past my knees, making me appear taller. A white blouse with wide sleeves cinched in at my waist behind a black bodice.

A scabbard hung at my waist with a golden axe at each hip. My father gave me the pair of priceless weapons when I became Queen Heir. For two years, he worked with me daily until I mastered the axe. And when he left to lead his soldiers on an expedition to the Southern Kingdoms—the one he never returned from —I practiced with Astrid until I left them behind the night of my First Ascension. I hadn't touched an axe in three years. But the council didn't need to know that. They just needed to be reminded that I was a warrior in every sense of the word.

Along with my black attire, I wore a floor-length black cloak designed to accommodate my wings. It was trimmed in white and black ermine—a symbol and a reminder of my royal status—and clasped at my throat was a white opal broach I'd received the day I was named Queen Heir. Perched on my head was the crown I was meant to wear after my betrothal to Fiske. It was a queen's crown set with white and black stones framing rows and rows of diamonds. To top it all off, my wings cascaded down my back, trailing along the floor like a feathered gown.

My outfit spoke volumes, proclaiming I was a strong warrior queen with a will none could break.

"Here goes nothing." I nodded to Vendela to open the door.

I was prepared for the stares. Prepared for the looks of disappointment and skepticism. I was not prepared for all the activity in the room. The Indigo Drawing Room used to be a place where the Queen of Valsgard and the Queen of the Citadel met with their councils to discuss matters of state in a formal setting. It was never a … kitchen.

"You're here!" Sylvi cried. "Come taste this plum jam. It's delicious. Elder Leda makes all our jams."

"Jam?" I stared blankly around the room. Gone were the fine furnishings, pushed aside to accommodate long tables at the center of the room. A roaring fire burned in the fireplace where my sister stirred a cauldron of bubbling fruit.

The three elders worked at makeshift kitchen stations set up on the tables. Each stood behind a simmering pot with low fires burning beneath the pots. Jars of food sat in the simmering water.

"It looks like a cannery in here," I muttered, feeling ridiculous in my crown and cloak.

"Everyone works day and night to feed the people of the Citadel," Astrid explained. "Even when the council meets we make use of the time."

"It's canning day," Sylvi said. "The kitchens haven't been able to handle the workload so we took over canning for next year."

"Next year?"

"We have to plan for the worst," Astrid said.

"So we shell peas, dice vegetables and pickle things while we talk," Sylvi continued.

"All right, clearly the crown was a bit much." I slipped out of my cloak and laid it on a console table against the wall, dropping my crown on top. "Give me something to pickle." I pushed up my sleeves.

Sylvi placed a pile of cucumbers in front of me.

"Slices or spears?" I thought about how easy it was in the human world to pop into the local supermarket for a jar of pickles. Talk about taking things for granted.

"Slices."

"Where have you been all this time, Thea?" Elder Ragna asked. She was a senior council member with only a few years left to serve before she retired, replaced by someone from my generation. That was the way it worked across the realms. As their power weakened with age, each ruler eventually passed the torch to the younger generations, trusting them to lead the Nine Realms forward into a new era.

"The human realm, Elder Ragna," I replied with a tone of respect.

"And why did you run away like a spoiled child who didn't get her way?" Elder Leda asked. Leda was Mother's favorite. If I could sway her, it would be a step in the right direction. Leda was a no-nonsense kind of woman. She liked simple things and straight answers. And she also adored me. At least she used to.

I was so weary of explaining myself, but they had a right to know. "I wasn't ready. I firmly believed I was the wrong choice as Queen Heir, but no one would listen. And I didn't want to marry Fiske or any other Chosen Son because it's a barbaric custom," I said bluntly as I cut cucumbers into thick slices. "I couldn't commit to marry a boy whose only goal in life was to please me. I find the concept abhorrent. To my knowledge, it has never been an actual law. I questioned—and still do—whether that particular tradition needed to be observed. Wouldn't you prefer a Queen Heir to follow her convictions and learn from her mistakes than a puppet going through the motions, dictated by tradition, only to end up on the throne completely unprepared?

"It is not for you—" Elder Sonje began.

"Please, Elder, allow me to finish?"

Sonje gave a curt nod for me to continue.

"In the months and weeks leading up to my betrothal ceremony, I asked all of mother's council to discuss the possibility of postponing my betrothal for a few years, yet you all dismissed me, calling me a spoiled child. This is my life—the only one I get. As a future queen of Valsgard and the High Council I realize there are many 'normal life' things I'll never have. But a husband is one decision I would like to make for myself and at a time of my choosing. Removing myself from the line of succession felt like my only recourse. I always intended to return once I'd given Sylvi a few years to establish her reign. I never dreamed anything like this could have happened in my absence. I ask the council to forgive the mistake of a confused girl who felt like she was drowning right in front of your eyes and no one bothered to throw her a lifeline."

"We all thought Sylvi would receive the blessing of the gods in your absence," Elder Vanya said as she shelled peas into a silver bowl in her lap. She'd taught my classes in diplomacy. She was a stern woman, but I had always respected her. "We cannot fault the child for believing the same."

"How do we know you won't run again?" Elder Sonje asked. She was the one who would take the most convincing. Sonje had always despised my streak of independence. And it didn't help matters that she was Fiske's mother.

"Because my mistakes almost killed my mother and left my people enslaved to a monster thirsty for power that has never belonged to her. I made a choice for myself and it affected thousands. I can't undo any of that, but I'd like the chance to fix it. I believe I can take back my mother's throne and avoid a war this realm can't hope to survive in its current state. But I need your blessing and support."

"Can you defeat her?" Astrid finally broke her silence. She was part of the council, but she wouldn't allow her convictions to cloud their judgment. I could count on her support … once the council stood behind me.

"I don't know. But I'm the only one who can try. I know I can break her Warder magic. I freed a few thousand of our soldiers and they willingly fought with me and followed me here. I faced Neela upon my arrival and brought my mother home, along with most of the palace guard."

"You survived this long because you had the element of surprise on your side," Sonje said. "Now that she knows you've returned, she will not allow such skirmishes to happen again."

"Which is why we need to send an envoy so I can speak with her."

"You need to remain behind Astrid's protection, child," Sonje insisted. "Let the Elders handle this."

"Handle this? What exactly have you *handled* in my absence? I mean no disrespect to the work you've all done here, protecting our people, but it's time to end this." I nearly sliced my finger open with my frenzied chopping.

"You are not ready." Elder Leda spoke softly.

"Maybe not yet, but when I faced Neela, I siphoned from her. Just enough to know I can, but not enough for her to notice. I can defeat her."

"Truly?" Ragna asked, a note of hope in her voice.

"It won't be easy, but I have something she doesn't."

"And what is that?" Sonje asked. The whole council watched me intently.

"A thirst for retribution. The power of the gods chose me once before. In my absence, it chose her. But I have returned and believe it is only a matter of time before the power shifts back to me. And when it does, there will be Hel to pay for what she has done."

"Very well," Sonje relented. "Give us one day to prepare and you may have your envoy.

CHAPTER 23

I marched through the grand hall with the council at my back. I felt like I'd earned their support over the last twenty-four hours—at least for now. But I needed a win today if I was going to keep it.

"You set the tone," Vendela murmured at my side.

"Don't freak her out," Druan said, matching his stride to mine.

"What are you doing here, Druan?"

"Protection. You can't walk out of here on an envoy to the usurper without protection."

I glanced over my shoulder to see Amara and Ben right behind me. I stopped in my tracks and turned to him. "And what do you think you're doing?" I glared at him. "Go back to your room." My voice was a whisper but I wanted to rage at him. Calling this kind of attention to himself could be fatal.

"No way I'm missing this. Besides, they all think I'm part of Dru's team now that Fiske has returned to his hidey-hole, playing farmer boy with sister Sylvi. No one knows, Thea. Relax."

I turned my glare on Druan instead.

"The kid's a skilled fighter," he reminded me. "He held his own in battle. We need all hands on deck today and he wants to be here. You might not like it, but the boy has a right to make his own decisions."

"You're right, I don't like it." But I couldn't tell Druan all the reasons it wasn't safe for Ben to leave the Citadel.

"I don't care. Don't worry about the kid, I'll keep him out of trouble, I promise. Do what you came here to do."

"I'm trusting you to keep him safe."

"On my honor, I will make sure he doesn't get in over his head."

I finally agreed. Hiding Ben in plain sight might work.

"Do you know what you're going to say?" Vendela asked as we set out again.

I nodded, staring through the front doors of the Citadel. "Pretty much."

"Pretty much? You need to do better," Vendela hissed as we walked through the massive doors.

"We're just testing the waters today. I want to see if she's willing to budge. If there's a possibility of peace instead of war."

Neela's envoy already waited for us on the opposite side of the bridge arching over the rough waters of the Queen's Bay. Neela stood alone at the center of the bridge. It was a show of power that she felt confident enough to meet with me one on one. It was meant to intimidate me. And it worked. Neela was a frightening sight to behold.

After my last meeting with Neela, I couldn't have picked her out of a crowd, so consumed with my rage over my mother's treatment at her hands. But I was fully present and focused now. Neela was tall and muscular, she outweighed me by at least thirty pounds. She was dressed as a warrior from the lowest pits of the Warder realm, looking like no queen I had ever seen, but she exuded regal authority, despite her well-worn clothes. I eyed the vast span of her red wings, the shade of her auburn hair. Three sets of wings—royal wings—just like mine. Except for the left side of her body, where the feathers were burned away. A gold mask covered that side of her face, and matching body armor covered her left shoulder down to her wrist, her hand hidden behind a black glove.

"What happened to her wings?" I asked.

"When she was thirteen, her father tried to set fire to them for sport. The entire left side of her body was burned." Druan's teeth made an audible click as the muscle in his jaw worked. "King Ulric is known for his brutality and it's no secret he has no use for a Valkyrie daughter. I'm told her mother spent most of her married life in a prison world of his making with her own daughter as her Warder. They must have escaped together."

"I'd like nothing more than to send them back where they came from." I meant it too, though I felt for the young girl who'd suffered under her father's brutal hand.

"Stay here," I instructed. "I have to meet her alone."

"Nice try." Druan argued.

"I can take care of myself, Dru." I narrowed my eyes at him. "But what I cannot do is appear weak in front of her now."

"At least take Pasha with you," he relented.

I nodded, leaving him and the other members of my envoy to cross the bridge on my own. Pasha followed close on my heels; a low growl rumbled in her chest to let me know she was with me.

I approached the usurper in the same gear I'd worn to meet with the council the day before, except this time I wore my pair of axes crossed over my back in a halter that made it easier to draw them when needed. Somehow my pristine wardrobe looked like I was trying too hard. But maybe that could work in my favor. I opened myself up to the power of the gods, seeking to fill my vessel. Carefully and so she wouldn't notice, I pulled a trickle of the power from Neela into myself. When she didn't' react, I pulled a little more until a steady stream flowed into me.

"Cousin." Neela spoke first, her tone clipped.

I nodded once in response.

"Back from your vacation in the human realm? And I see you've brought your little kitty cat too." She barely glanced at Pasha, but my little kitty cat didn't like to be ignored.

Pasha's hackles raised and she let out a ferocious growl, showing her teeth in all their toothy glory.

"We didn't come here to be mocked. You usurped my mother's throne and I've come to negotiate terms with you."

"So negotiate." Neela waved a gloved hand in my direction. I wondered if her hand had received the same treatment as her wings.

"I'm giving you a chance to bow out gracefully now that I've returned."

"Bow out?" Neela sneered. "Why would I do that?"

"The Valkyrie people recognize me as the rightful heir. It is time for you to step aside, Neela. Time you return to your own realm and reunite with your family."

"But you are my family, cousin." Neela forced a fake smile. "I think it's time we all get to know each other again. I'll even throw a ball to celebrate your return to my court."

"Surrender now. End this siege and release my people under the influence of your magic."

"I don't' know what you mean. They are all here of their own volition."

I snorted a very un-queen-like laugh at her ignorance. "You should know I can see magic, Neela. I can see every ugly thread of every bond that connects my people to you against their will. Do not play games with me."

Neela's fake smile withered from her face. "I have no need to surrender, Thea. I have the blessing of the gods. What do you have?"

"The rightful Queen Brenna, four elders of her council, Queen Astrid of the Citadel, and her heir all stand with me—without magic to bend their will. I also have my birthright and the blessing of the gods as well."

"You lost their blessing when you shirked your duty. It belongs to me now." Neela laid a hand on the sword at her hip.

Pasha hissed, flicking her tail in agitation at the perceived threat.

I smiled, sinking my fingers into Pasha's thick fur. Neela had just confirmed what I already suspected. She had no idea I was siphoning from her this very moment. It wouldn't be an easy fight, but I was confident I could best my cousin. I just didn't want it to come down to a war. "Surrender now and we can avoid bloodshed. The Valkyrie people have suffered enough. I am prepared to make you an offer."

"What kind of offer?" She tilted her head, eyes narrowed.

"When I ascend, I will honor you and your mother with a full pardon and award you each a royal title with lands and estates. You may return to your father's court if you choose, or you may live out your days in exile in the northern regions of Valsgard—under the careful eye of my guard, of course." It was a fair offer. One I didn't want to make, but I was willing to bet my life that freedom from her father was all Neela ever really wanted.

"That is quite an offer," Neela said, but her tone gave nothing away. Though I suspected she was tempted.

"Do you accept?"

"Would you?"

"I was born to rule this realm."

"I'll take that bit of entitlement as a no." Neela scoffed. "You may have been born to rule, but I'm the one who deserves it." She took a menacing step forward despite Pasha's warning hiss. "You lost your birthright when you walked away like an ungrateful fool. You neglected your people and I stepped in to save them." She slammed a fist against her chest. "Those who have resisted have brought their hardships upon themselves. With me as their queen, the Valkyries will flourish and they will support me when I reclaim this world for them, dissolving the other eight realms into a single kingdom under my rule."

"You're delusional if you think the other kingdoms will allow you that kind of power."

"When I am the only living vessel for the power of the gods, the other kingdoms will have no choice but to bend to my will."

So that was her plan for ascension. She might lose her Warder magic when she became queen, but if there was no one powerful enough to contest her claim to the throne, she wouldn't need it.

"One woman cannot hold that much power, Neela. There is a reason we have two queens and two heirs between Valsgard and the Citadel. With four strong vessels, we can contain the power we all need to survive. If you try to take it all, it will rip you apart and destroy our whole world. You cannot make yourself a god." The woman really was insane if that was her plan.

"And what makes you think you get to walk back in here after three years to pick up where you left off? A Queen Heir doesn't get a furlough, Thea. She does her duty for her people because she must."

Neela was partially right. Did I deserve the chance to prove to my people I could be trusted to care for them? To be their queen? Probably not, but I intended to fight for the chance to redeem myself. No matter what they thought of me, I couldn't leave them to Neela. If only to save them from this monster who would see them all under her control. It no longer mattered to me who was queen, as long as it wasn't my cousin.

I approached my enemy like she was a predator ready to spring. "You've executed thousands of my people because they refused to follow you. You've enslaved thousands more with your Warder magic. You think to rule through fear and intimidation, but these are not the actions of a benevolent ruler. A reign of terror like yours has an expiration date. The Valkyries will not abide a tyrant on the throne. Not while a true Queen Heir resides in the Citadel."

A fleeting look of uncertainty flashed across Neela's face. But her mother, Svana, came to her side, whispering something in her daughter's ear. Neela's eyes widened in alarm before she threw her head back and laughed.

"You expect me to surrender, allowing you to take my throne out from under me while you offer some country estate as a parting gift? Yet you stand there with a pack of wild bounty hunters at your back, and a few starving members of your mother's council? You think I would ever surrender to you when a man who shouldn't exist stands among you?"

My mouth went dry as fear crept up my spine.

"What would the council say if they knew a foresworn Valkyrie male stood among your loyal bounty hunters? Would they be so quick to support you then?"

Gasps sounded behind me and I froze. I couldn't openly support Ben, but I couldn't allow Neela to take him either.

"Guards, take the boy."

"No!" I lunged between Neela and Ben as a contingent of Valkyries swept down from the palace. Pasha drove Neela back from me, but the others were on Ben like carrion birds on roadkill.

"Leave my bounty hunters to me." I drew an axe from my halter just in time to clash with Neela's sword. "I will handle the male."

Bedlam erupted behind me as Druan and Vendela fought to save Ben from their clutches. He was as good as dead now that his secret was out. If Neela didn't kill him, my council would.

"If you haven't executed him yet, you clearly aren't going to," Neela hissed in my ear. "My mother and I will destroy the Ahlstrom dynasty. I'll keep your Valkyrie boyfriend safe for you, but you will never sit on my throne now, cousin."

Anger surged through me like a charging bull. Ever since my return, my magic seemed to respond with my temper, growing darker by the day. But I was beyond caring anymore. I embraced my rage, pulling it around me like a dark cloak. If Neela wanted to play rough, I was ready for the fight of my life.

Screaming like a feral beast, I kicked Neela in the stomach, sending her flying back against the bridge railing. A little more power behind my kick and she would have found herself at the bottom of the bay.

As she tried to stand, I pushed her back to the ground, my foot at her throat. Throwing my head back, I drew on my magic, surging around us like a cloud of dark smoke. Neela's magic responded, but she was no match for the burn. I lashed out at her with the burn, striking her like a red hot whip.

She screamed as her skin blistered with each strike. Pulling the darkness toward me, I siphoned from her, directing the power of the gods into me. I relished the feel of so much power surging inside me as I pulled on Neela's life force. The choice of the gods wouldn't matter if she was dead.

With a crack of her foot against my back, Neela broke free, grappling with me for control. Desperate, she pulled back, breaking my hold on her power.

"Enough." Druan charged between us as Vendela and her

kindred took up the fight with Neela, driving her back across the bridge. "Live to fight another day, Princess."

"I was winning." I shoved him, raking my talons across his face. "I could have ended this now."

"Not without the boy's death on your hands." Druan dragged me back toward the protection of the Citadel, forcing me to witness what I had missed. During my fight with Neela, her guards had swooped in to take Ben across the bay to the palace gates. Even now, he struggled against them as they dragged him toward the dungeon.

"Ben!" I screamed for him, but it was too late. I turned on the Druid, focusing my rage on him as the one responsible. "You promised." My talons ached to close around his throat. "You promised you would keep him safe!"

"How was I supposed to know the boy was a Valkyrie when you told me his father was a Berserker and his mother a human?" Druan and Amara closed in behind me, guiding me through the Citadel gates.

"How dare you stop me from destroying her!" I raged. "I am your Queen Heir!"

"You aren't my queen anything." Druan pushed me down on the grand staircase. "And if you don't get control of that temper, and the dark power raging behind those eyes, you never will be."

"She'll kill him," I whimpered.

"She'll make a spectacle of him first. That's her way. She'll use him as propaganda against you and your family. And that gives us time to rescue him. If I hadn't pulled you out of the fight, she would have gotten the upper hand and then she would have killed him right in front of you. This way we have time. He has a chance."

"I will kill you with my bare hands if she harms a hair on his head."

Druan rolled his eyes, the clear gray like storm clouds just waiting to unleash their fury on me. "Put your feelings for your little boyfriend aside and go do damage control with your council."

I leaped to my feet, yanking Druan toward me. "If he dies, I will end you."

Druan backed away, surprise and something akin to respect flashing in his eyes. "I see. We will bring him home, Thea. I promise."

But I wasn't sure I trusted in his promises where Ben was concerned.

CHAPTER 24

"How dare you bring that filthy man into the Citadel?" Elder Sonje raged at me. "After all we've done for you? After all the chances we've given you?"

I cringed as she and Leda descended upon me. "I-I didn't know." The lie lodged in my throat. I'd just thrown my brother under the bus when he needed me most.

The two Elders grabbed me behind my wing joints and dragged me up the stairs to the formal drawing room. With crimson walls and gilt-edged furnishings, it was a room built for intimidation and the Elders knew how to use it to their advantage.

"What are you doing?" Aunt Astrid dropped her shield and sword as she came in from the training grounds. "Unhand the princess this instant."

Leda and Sonje shoved me through the door, standing over me like executioners waiting for the final order.

"Thea?" Astrid came to crouch beside me. "They know about Ben?" Her eyes filled with worry.

"Of course we do," Elder Ragna barged into the room. "The whole Citadel will know by nightfall. Astrid what did you know of this?"

"I swear, I didn't know he was Valkyrie." I scrambled up to my feet, clutching Astrid's arm. "Ben didn't even know he was from this realm. Druan believed he must have been a Berserker. How were any of us supposed to know when we haven't seen a male of his kind in centuries?"

"The girl is right, Sonje," Elder Ragna interjected. "Though if she expects to be our queen one day, it would be prudent she learn to be careful who she trusts. The boy will die at Neela's hands. Problem solved." She moved to sit in one of chairs arranged in a circle at the center of the room.

"No. We have to save him." I followed Ragna, crouching at her side and begging with my eyes for her to listen. "He is innocent."

"Innocent? Child, do you remember your history lessons at all?" Leda stood over me, hands on her wide hips.

"Yes, but he's such a gentle soul. And he's the first in ages to be born. I can't imagine killing him simply because that's what our ancestors did. It was a different time."

"You thwart our traditions too much, Alithea Ahlstrom." Sonje's voice took on a menacing tone. "You are not ready to rule. I don't think you will ever be a queen we can trust."

"Your only other option is Neela. Would you prefer her to me?"

"At least she knows her duty where this vile creature is concerned. I don't agree with her methods, but she gets things done."

"Oh, shut up, Sonje," Vanya finally spoke up. "There is no way you would prefer serving under that half-breed to our Thea. She's just confused by this boy. None of us saw it either. We were all taken in by his charm."

"I'm not confused. He doesn't deserve to die. I will send him back to the human realm, but I will not let him die." My lies continued to stack up, but I was desperate to save my brother.

The door crashed open and my mother hobbled through, wearing her nightclothes. "Esben?" Her red-rimmed eyes bore right through me. "They have him?"

"Mother, please." I shot across the room to her side. "You need your rest. I will take care of him. I promise." I silently pleaded with her not to reveal Ben's true identity. The council would never support my claim to the throne if they knew of Brenna's crime.

"Your Majesty, you have been through too much. You're confused." Sonje fussed over the ailing queen. "You must rest and let us handle matters."

"I might be weak, but I am still your queen until my daughter ascends. And my mind is perfectly clear."

I led my mother to a gilded chair with red cushions the color of the walls. When the queen seated herself, it became her throne.

"Vanya." Mother beseeched the Elder historian. "The boy is important."

"Your Majesty, we cannot doom ourselves to repeat the mistakes of our ancestors. The histories are clear—foresworn Valkyrie males are dangerous. They've been responsible for every major catastrophe this world has ever known. Worse even than the gods themselves."

"Brenna, no," Astrid whispered.

"He is my *son.*" The queen's voice, weak as it was, captured the room.

"No, Mother. Please." A tear slipped down my cheek as I turned to the Elders. "She is confused."

"I have never been more clear-minded than I am right now." Brenna stared them down. "Vanya, the boy is Thea's twin."

"Twins?" Vanya's knees gave out as she sank down on the chair nearest her.

"Twins?" Ragna took a shaky breath, glancing at Vanya for confirmation of something I didn't understand.

"Thea was born first?" Vanya asked, a note of desperation in her voice.

"Seven minutes before Esben," Brenna confirmed.

"Who knew of this?" Ragna continued.

"Astrid was the only one who knew at the time of their birth, but she doesn't know the histories. Not the full story." Brenna gazed at her sister, her eyes bright with their intensity. "Esben was drawn to Thea in the human world and he followed her home. I've only just told them since her return. Sylvi knows too, of course. But none of them know what this truly means."

"Svana knew." I cast my eyes down, watching my hands as they twisted in my lap. There was no way the council would back me now that Mother had confessed her crime. "She told Neela."

"How could she have known, Brenna?" Vanya asked. "She was married to King Ulric years before the birth of your first child … children."

"It must mean my elder sister left spies among my court before she married the king. Spies who are still in her service and likely here among us in the Citadel."

"No." Astrid shook her head. "She knew."

"How could she know?" Brenna asked. "She was half a world away the night the twins were born."

"I-I told her," Astrid said in a rush. "It was years ago when the girls were little. During one of Svana's infrequent visits." Astrid wiped a hand across her brow, tapping her palm against her forehead. "I can't even remember how it came up. Just that Svana was different during that visit. She was happier, more settled in her life among the Warders since she had Neela."

"She already knew her daughter was a royal vessel." Brenna dragged in a ragged breath. "Do you think she was planning this even then?"

Astrid nodded. "She was so amiable and talkative. I just let it slip and she swore she would never tell a soul. I forgot all about it after."

"Isn't that sister's one talent?" Brenna arched a brow at Astrid. "We know she is weak but Svana still has magic and she speaks with a silver tongue."

"She talked me into trusting her and I betrayed my queen." Astrid's shoulders slumped and she bowed her head in supplication.

"No you didn't. Our sister did. You should be able to trust your own sister to keep your confidences."

"Her Majesty is right," Sonje said. "And so is Princess Thea. We must rescue her brother immediately."

"Wait." I glanced around the room. "I'm missing something. Not two minutes ago you were applauding Neela for sending him to the executioner's block. What changed?"

"He is your *twin*," Mother said. "That changes everything."

"How?" I slipped into one of the vacant chairs and massaged my temples. The pounding in my head left me nauseated.

"Not all of our history is widely known," Leda explained. "In fact, only the reigning queen and her council have access to our most disturbing histories."

"Someone fill me in. Now. This is my twin we are talking about. I may not have known him long, but I love him and I will not allow him to die because I failed to protect him."

Leda sat beside me, gently laying a hand over mine that still moved restlessly in my lap. "Male Valkyries who are born with the ability to shift have never been able to control their power. The first Valkyries were all female. We don't believe the gods intended them to ever bear children, but they did and something went wrong with our male children. In many cases these male Valkyries are a result of a Valkyrie mother and a Berserker father. The Berserker madness and the Valkyrie power do not mix well in males. It is one of the biggest reasons we do not get along well with the Berserker realm. The only time in history when a Valkyrie male has ... beaten the odds, for lack of a better term, is when he is born the younger twin of a female Valkyrie. She tempers him and gives him the balance he needs to control his power. And in return, he amplifies her power."

"Thea, darling." Mother leaned forward, a glimmer of her old strength showing. "Don't you see? This is how you will defeat her. But you must have Esben at your side. He cannot die. If you can harness the strength your brother gives you, you can end this."

"I have studied the histories all my life. The true histories and not the watered down versions we teach our youth. The reign of terror was a brutal time in our history. The Valkyrie kings and their councils were mad with power. But can you tell me how the reign of terror ended, Thea?" She turned to me, sounding just like the teacher who taught me history as a young Queen Heir.

"Queen Birta defeated the last Valkyrie king."

"She did, but it took her and her twin brother Prince Dagur to do it," Leda said gently.

"She had a twin?" I turned incredulous eyes on my teacher. "How is this not taught?"

"It was decided long before us that any mention of such male Valkyries be expunged from our history," Mother explained. "But I knew. I knew the moment I saw my baby boy's kind eyes that he would be like Prince Dagur."

Thea." Vanya leaned forward and took my hands. "You've

changed. Your time away was good for you. I believe now that on some level, your twin must have called to you from the human realm, and that is why you felt such an urgency to leave us. And you've brought him home. I can see the newfound strength shining in your eyes. You will save not only us, but all of the Nine Realms. You and your brother."

"You think Ben and I will have this power? That he will amplify my power?"

"You already have it, darling." Mother laid a hand on my shoulder. "You've had more focus and determination than I've ever seen in you since your return. And Esben has no thirst for power of his own."

"But, but, that's because I'm determined to fix the mess I caused and Ben's just lazy."

Mother laughed, her eyes dancing with love. "All that matters is that you are together now and you are loyal to each other. He adores you, Thea. My council *will* protect him now that they know you have the power to temper him. But others will not understand. He will always be in danger. That is why I sent him to the human realm. It was the only way he would ever survive long enough to learn to protect himself."

"He still doesn't know how to do that." I laughed and some of the tension left my shoulders.

"I imagine you left your Esben with one of our Valkyrie families in the human realm?" Vanya said. "Do they know he has returned?"

"They died," Brenna whispered. "Ages ago. I can only imagine Svana sent someone to kill my child and the parents I chose to raise him. Esben has been on his own all his life."

"When I first met him, he thought he was an angel of death," I said. "I didn't trust him at first, but I couldn't shake him."

"He was drawn to your twin bond. He needed you, Thea."

"He did a good job on his own," I admitted. "His worst quality is his ability to worm his way into your heart until you can't live without him. It's really annoying. But I won't let my brother die for crimes he hasn't even committed."

"Of course not," Sonje said. "The boy must be protected, if for no other reason than his very existence as your twin will give us the most powerful queen we've known in an age. And a powerful queen begets powerful Queen Heirs. I have spies among Neela's court. I will find out what's happening." She stood to leave but paused, looking down at me. "You were right to protect him, Thea. Even against us. You will make a good queen. Someday."

I wished I could have those words on video to commemorate the one time Sonje almost apologized to me, or anyone for that matter.

"Your Majesty, please let us take you back to your rooms," Ragna said. "We will do everything we can to save your Esben, but you must take care of yourself."

"Very well." The queen nodded, accepting Ragna's help.

"I'm so sorry, Mother."

"It's not your fault, darling. My elder sister and I have been rivals since Mother and her council chose me as Queen Heir. She's waited more than twenty years to enact her revenge."

Ragna and Leda helped the queen to her feet, supporting her slight frame between them.

"Revenge for what?" I stood to open the door for her.

"For being born more powerful than she." Brenna gave a rueful smile. "If not for me, she might have been Mother's heir and her life would have been very different. She's never forgiven Mother for marrying her off to the Warder King. And now she's using her daughter to fight for the life she thinks she deserved."

"Why did Grandmother arrange her marriage to such a barbaric king?"

"She didn't know just how treacherous King Ulric is. She believed Svana needed a firm hand and a great deal of distance to temper her ambitions. I think if Mother really knew what kind of man he was, she would never have accepted his offer for Svana' hand. Once the marriage was done, there was no undoing it, as much as Svana begged in those first few years. After a while, she stopped writing and we believed she'd found her place among the Warders."

"Rest, Mother. We will talk more later." I closed the door behind her.

"Let's discuss your next move, Thea." Leda patted the chair beside her.

I sighed as I complied, sitting gingerly. I'd always had the best relationship with Leda among all of Mother's council members. "I have to get Ben back. No matter what. But I also have to defeat Neela, preferably with the least amount of bloodshed, and ideally both of those things at the same time—very soon. The people have suffered enough for my mistakes."

"I think we can come up with a solution that accomplishes both," Leda said. "But I don't know if we can do it without bloodshed. You've already given Neela a chance to step aside and she's refused, which means she cannot be motivated to negotiate a surrender."

"I wish we could offer an exchange for Ben."

Leda shook her head. "The only exchange she would accept would be you or Brenna. Or maybe Svana if we could get our hands on her."

"Could we?" I sat up straight. "We need something Neela wants."

"How would you approach this hypothetical exchange?"

"I would use Svana to get her attention. Offer Neela her mother for Ben."

"But that won't solve our larger issue."

"I could add a stipulation to the exchange." I stood to pace the length of the room. "We offer Svana in exchange for Ben, and a challenge." I turned to face Leda, my voice rising. "I challenge her for the throne. One fight for the power of the gods. Just her against me and the winner takes the throne."

"How is the winner determined?" Leda asked.

"The one who drains her opponent of power wins. It doesn't need to be a battle to the death."

"That's a risky plan. Can you beat her? You will have to because we cannot trust her not to kill you."

"I wouldn't risk it if I didn't think I could. I have more motivation. The lives of everyone I love rest on my shoulders. I have to win."

"You need time to prepare for such a battle. I've seen her fight. You may be more powerful than Neela, but she's spent her life fighting her brothers for her father's attention. She might very well kill you with her bare hands and take your power that way."

"We can't do anything until we have leverage. We need Svana."

"We'll need Sonje's spies to find her."

"And my sister's bounty hunters. They will know what to do."

CHAPTER 25

"We have a window of opportunity—right now." Elder Sonje burst into my bedroom with Druan and his bounty hunters on her heels.

"What?" I kicked the covers off and sat straight up in bed, my hair a bird's nest on top of my head, complete with feathers. "What's happening? What time is it?" I rubbed my eyes in the dim light of dawn creeping through the windows.

"Wake up, Thea." Sonje snapped her fingers. "My spies tell me Svana spends her mornings in the west gardens, alone. We have a limited timeframe to pull this off."

"Okay. Yes, let's go." I flung my blankets back.

"We just need your permission, Princess." Druan leaned against the doorframe, looking as though he'd already been up for hours. Amara stood silently beside him, armed to the teeth. I could just see Vendela in the hall with a fourth bounty hunter I didn't recognize. Judging from his height and muscular frame he was Jötnar.

"I can be ready in a minute." I rushed to the trunk at the foot of my bed, tossing the lid back and rummaging through the contents for anything battleworthy that wouldn't make me look like I was trying too hard. "Vendela, help me find something I can wear to blend in."

Vendela peered into the trunk and shook her head. "I'm not sure you own anything normal." She plucked a silver tunic and a pair of black trousers from the tangle of fabric. "This could work for now."

"Out of the question." Sonje slammed the trunk lid.

"I guess you are too important." Vendela shrugged. "But we've got this." She patted my shoulder. And that was when I realized I was wearing a nightdress that looked like it belonged on a grandmother in her sick bed.

Cheeks flushed and avoiding Druan's gaze, I sank back onto the edge of my bed. "I want to help, Sonje." It killed me to let others risk their lives helping me fix my own mess. But that was the life of a queen. I would make the hard decisions, but I would never get my hands dirty.

"I will let your Mother know we've made our move." Sonje turned to leave. "You four, be safe." She gave Amara a nod of respect as she left my room.

"Wait. Vendela, before you all leave." I grabbed the letter I'd written last night. "Once you return with Svana, please see this gets to Neela as soon as possible." I handed Vendela the parchment with my official seal. It was my final grasp for a quick and dirty end to this mess. If this didn't work, it would mean all-out war.

"I will see to it." Vendela nodded, following Amara from the room.

"Nice gown, Princess." Druan winked. "We'll let you know how it goes after we do all the hard work."

"Ugh!" I threw my pillow at him. "Be careful, Druid, or I'll feed you to Pasha for breakfast." Pasha growled from her bed in the corner, as if in agreement.

"Nice ankles too." Druan grinned as he left the room.

I glanced down at my frilly white gown, wishing Druan hadn't caught me in bed, unprepared. I would give anything to have my old wardrobe of t-shirts and jeans back, but I'd left with just the clothes on my back and a few necessities.

"One of these days I'm going back to make a Target run for some decent clothes. If I have to rule, this queen is wearing jeans and leggings."

I fell back on my pillow with a sigh. The next few hours were going to be a nightmare because my entire plan hinged on gaining leverage over Neela. We needed this to work.

"You're still in bed?" Sylvi leaned against my doorframe. Druan hadn't even bothered to close the door on his way out.

"The sun's barely up, Sylvi. How are you already dressed and perfect?"

"I'm usually up before dawn." She stepped into my room, closing the door behind her. Her pale blue skirts whispered as she walked to my closet. "I'll help you dress, and we'll go sit with Mother until this is over. I won't rest easy until they're all back."

"Me either." I rolled out of bed, frowning at the fluffy white skirt my sister pulled from my closet. It was most definitely not one I remembered. "When things settle down again, we need to talk about my clothes."

"I know these aren't your tastes, sister. Most of these dresses are from my closet. We've only had time to make over a few of my old things for you. I'm afraid it's the best we've got."

"I appreciate all the work you do around here, Sylvi. You're amazing." I accepted the underthings my sister offered.

"I'm just so glad to have you back." Sylvi smiled. "It hasn't been the same since you left. For obvious reasons, but others as well.

You're the lifeblood of our home, Thea. You have been since you were born. More so now that you are two."

I turned at Sylvi's direction as she laced up the front of the pale green overskirt. "And this third you speak of? This is another important person?"

"Yes. You are three." Sylvi shoved the matching bodice over my head.

"Yes, but what does that mean?"

"It means you are three. You won't be complete or fulfilled without them. They are part of you. Sit." She pointed to the vanity chair in the corner of the room. "You can't go out looking like this." She picked up a silver-handled comb and worked it through my snarled hair.

"Is this *third* another secret sibling?"

"No, silly." Sylvi concentrated on the tangle of feathers in my hair. "Your third is your mate."

"*Mate*?" I rolled my eyes.

"I don't know if he will be your husband or your lover, but he will be important. You did the right thing, leaving as you did. Fiske was not your third. It will be important to keep the different parts of yourself close. Mother's council may insist you resume the betrothal with Fiske, but I don't think he's the right one for you. You may have to push back until they allow you to choose for yourself. I shall have to consult your aura and compare it with Fiske's to see how you align. Perhaps you are a better match now than you were before."

"Okay, then. That clears that up." I fumbled with the scattered contents of my seldom used vanity. "So who was the Jötnar with your bounty hunters?"

"I don't think they qualify as mine anymore," she chuckled softly as she brushed my hair. "I selected them carefully with you in mind. I think they will each be important to your reign. "The

Jötnar is Sloane, a long-time friend of Druan's. I believe they were in school together as boys. He stayed behind so Fiske could carry my message to you. I would have sent him as well, but your party would have been far too large to make a speedy return trip, especially with Esben. I studied their auras before they left and determined Sloane might fall to danger along the way due to his size. He was not very happy with me."

"He is a giant of a man, isn't he?" I'd only gotten a glimpse of him, but what I'd seen was enormous, but that was normal for the Jötnar clans.

"He's a very kind man, despite his ferocious appearance."

Sylvi smoothed my hair back in a simple twist and secured it with a few pins. "You'll do. Get your slippers on and let's go have breakfast with Mother. You too, Pasha," she called to the big cat snoring in the bed under the window.

When Sylvi wasn't looking, I shoved my feet into my sneakers and followed my sister down the hall to Mother's rooms, Pasha slinking along behind me with a great yawn and a swish of her tail. If only I could see things as clearly as my sister, to have Sylvi's confidence that all would go as it should.

"Knock-knock," Sylvi called as she pushed through the chamber door.

"My girls." Mother beamed at us from her place on the settee before the fireplace. Under a pile of furs, she almost looked healthy again. Her cheeks had regained some color and her eyes were bright and clear of the dark circles. Even her short hair was beginning to fill in.

"You're looking wonderful, Mother." Sylvi moved to a chair opposite Mother when Pasha jumped up and settled herself on the settee beside the ailing queen.

"Oh Pasha, I've missed you too, sweet girl." Mother sank her hands into her soft fur.

"I'm feeling much better after some rest, good food, and a nice long soak in the hot springs. There's nothing like home and the love of family to speed up your recovery."

I knelt on the floor beside my mother, taking her cool hand in mine. "Take what you need from me, Mother. Please," I begged.

"No." Brenna squeezed my hand and then withdrew hers. "If you are going to battle Neela, you need to take in as much power as you can hold. You should be siphoning from Astrid and Sylvi. I would tell you to siphon from me, but I have nothing left to give. I only have enough to sustain my life for a while longer."

"When this is over, I will see you restored to your former self," I promised.

"This body is no longer a suitable vessel, darling." Brenna ran a loving hand over my hair. "That burden has fallen to you and you are more than ready to take up that mantle."

I bowed my head, pressing my forehead against my mother's knee. "I'm so sorry I've done this to you."

"We've been over this. It's not your fault. It's done and in the past." Mother tilted my chin up to meet her gaze. "As of this moment, we move forward."

I nodded. "I think I can beat her, but at the same time I'm afraid I'll only make everything worse."

"That means you're ready, daughter. Neela is too confident and cocky to worry."

"What if she's right?" I picked at my cuticles. "I don't deserve to be queen."

"Thea, darling, you were born to rule. And not because you are my daughter, but because our family has the strength to hold the power of the gods. We are vessels for our people to draw from. Without us, the people of the Nine Realms would wither and die."

"Wouldn't they be fine with Neela? I can't help but think the people probably don't care who leads them. I don't want to put our people through a war that won't really matter much to them in the end."

"That woman has killed hundreds, maybe even thousands of our people just because they don't agree with her." Sylvi's eyes sparkled with rage. "She has torn families apart and left our rural villages and towns to starve because she takes everything they have to feed her army. Her mercenaries have pillaged and plundered our realm. I don't care who she is; no one deserves or wants a queen like that. You will be so much better for our people, sister. You will lead us into a new age when you ascend."

"I don't feel worthy." I fussed with the laces of my bodice. "I'm just me." I shrugged, unable to articulate just how inferior I felt when faced with the role of queen over Nine Realms, all looking to me for peace and guidance. It was too much responsibility for one young woman.

"That is precisely why you will succeed, darling. You will never *feel* ready for this. But you *are* ready, Thea. More than ready to take the throne."

"Thank you, Mother." I felt a little of the weight on my shoulders lift.

"Now, let's talk about more pleasant things. Like that young man Sylvi has been kissing in the shadows."

"Mother!" Sylvi's face flushed pink. "I don't know where you get your information, but the queen and heir of the Citadel are celibate."

"Oh pish tosh, that rule has been broken a thousand times since it was made. Just ask Astrid. She's had plenty of lovers over the years."

"Mother!" Sylvi tried to hide her laughter. "What's gotten into you?"

"I am headed for retirement, my dears. My children are all here with me … once we get Esben back. My heart is light, and my daughters are finally old enough to talk about the fun stuff."

"What's his name, Sylvi?" I nudged my sister's knee.

"No one of consequence," she whispered. "He's not at all appropriate."

"Oh, Sylvi, is he dreamy?" I couldn't help but tease my prim and proper sister.

"Yes." She turned toward me, tears spilling from her eyes. "He is a good man, but it cannot be. I am Astrid's heir. I have responsibilities."

"Sylvi, I didn't mean to upset you." I moved to sit on the chair beside her.

"It's not that … I'm just … so ashamed."

"Whatever for, Sylvi?" Mother stood, dumping her furs on the floor and gathered Sylvi into her thin arms.

"I'm so sorry, Thea." Tears streamed down her cheeks and she buried her face in Mother's shoulder.

My heart stopped for a moment as it hit me. "It's Fiske, isn't it? You've fallen in love with him?" My heart broke for her and the boy who had thrown himself into doing his duty despite loving another.

Sylvi nodded, her face still hidden. "Please don't hate me, sister."

"Oh, you silly girl." I laid a hand on her back. "Fiske is a good man and you both deserve as much happiness as you can find together. No wonder he's avoided me since we returned to the Citadel. I've barely caught of a glimpse of him this whole time." And the times I had seen him, he was with Sylvi.

"You're not mad?" Sylvi sniffed as she slowly sat up.

"Of course not." I patted her arm, sharing a smile with Mother. "Please, take him. Go have marvelous, perfect, fat little babies with him."

“Thea, no! It isn’t at all proper.” Sylvi hiccupped. “He is the Chosen Son. For you.”

“And you know how I feel about that.”

“Listen to me, girls. I should have taught you this lesson long ago,” Mother returned to sit on the edge of her seat, reaching to grasp our hands tightly. “Do not spend your lives doing your duty and forget to live. As vessels, we must serve our people, but we also deserve to experience all the things life has to offer. Yes, we have roles to play and a nation to protect, but we get to be individuals too. Your father was my best friend in the world, and we loved each other in so many ways, but that is not the kind of love I want for my girls. Whenever you have a chance for true love, darlings, grab onto it and never let go.”

CHAPTER 26

"It is done, your Majesty." Sonje bowed her head. "Your sister Svana is in the Citadel dungeon."

"And the bounty hunters?" I asked.

"All have returned unscathed and supremely full of themselves." Sonje's mouth narrowed into a thin line.

"I must go to her." The queen rose on unsteady feet.

"No, Mother." Sylvi and I objected together.

"It's too dangerous," I added. "I know she is your sister, but right now, she is the enemy and we must be cautious."

"Svana is my sister. I may be able to talk some sense into her. I will take your bounty hunter with me. The pretty one. Druan, isn't it?"

"He's not my bounty hunter." I bristled. "And he's not … pretty. I will go with you myself."

"Thea, the council must discuss the next steps," Sonje said. "Now that we have leverage over Neela, we need to decide what to do with it before she has a chance to react. We can be sure she is already plotting."

"Let's meet in the indigo room in an hour. I will help Mother to the dungeon."

"I'm fine, darling. I've asked for a litter to carry me down. I know I don't have the strength to get there and back on my own. Go find a quiet corner to gather your thoughts before your meeting."

"Just ... be careful, Mother." It killed me to let her out of my sight. A primal need to protect the woman who gave birth to me rose up within me. The Mother help me, I would kill anyone who dared lay hands on her.

Back in my room, I changed from my princess attire into my own street clothes. Dark leggings, a white linen tunic, boots, and my leather jacket from the human realm. I was ready to meet with Mother's council.

"Don't look at me like that?" I returned Pasha's snort of disapproval. "This is the best I can do with the clothes I've got. Now come on, we don't want to be late."

Thoughts of who I might appoint to my own council in the near future filled my mind as I approached the indigo room. It was tradition for a newly ascended queen to keep her mother's council for the first few months, but she would be expected to build her council from her own generation, keeping at least one of her mother's advisors among them. That was a tradition I could get on board with. I would undoubtedly keep Leda as the senior elder, but I wasn't certain who I could rely on to fill the other positions. I didn't know enough of my own generation to make those choices yet.

"Ah, Thea, there you are." Sonje frowned at my clothes as I entered the room. "We must decide how to approach Neela with our demands."

"We wait." I took Mother's seat—the unofficial throne. Pasha sat back on her haunches beside me where she busied herself with licking her paws.

"Wait?" Vanya pursed her lips. "We will act now while we still have the upper hand."

"We will wait," I repeated, propping my ankle against my knee.

"Nonsense." Sonje crossed the room to the queen's desk. "We've drafted a notice to deliver to Neela. It just needs your signature."

"I believe my niece said we will be waiting to further engage with the usurper." Astrid spoke for the first time.

"You support this indecision?" Sonje turned on Astrid.

"I don't believe I indicated I was indecisive on the matter," I interjected. "I am very decisive. We will wait. I've sent Neela a message already. She will come to us."

"If it matters, I support the Queen Heir in this." Astrid sat gracefully in her chair beside mine. We were a pair of queens on our thrones, making sure everyone in this room knew it.

"She is not Queen Heir. She has never completed the First Ascension rites."

"Meaningless waffle," Leda said. "We are under siege, Sonje. Tradition and rites be damned. Princess Thea is our Queen Heir and Queen Astrid is our protector, while Brenna is recovering, Thea is the highest authority in this room . We will support her."

"Thank you, Leda." I appreciated the gesture of support, although I couldn't help but wonder if she was posturing for the senior elder position within my future council.

"Waiting will only make us look weak." Sonje huffed, reluctantly lowering herself onto the settee. "We are just giving her time to plan."

"This is a military matter," Astrid reminded her. "That is my wheelhouse, not yours. Thea is right. We've taken Svana right out from under Neela's nose. We don't need to send out the heralds to announce it. She will come to us."

"With an army of mercenaries at her back," Vanya muttered.

"I will speak with her when she arrives," I said. "Alone."

"I'm afraid we cannot allow that, Princess," Sonje protested. "You are not ready for such confrontation."

"You misunderstand, Sonje. I'm not asking for permission. You forget, I've been on my own these last three years. I am no longer the child you remember."

"Yes, serving men drinks while eking out a living is the same as fighting a strategic battle."

"And you forget how many bounty hunters I evaded during my time in the human realm. How long I survived with nothing more than my instincts and my Valkyrie guiding me. Three years without the power of the gods, and without my own magic. Could you survive even a day cut off from the magic your queens provide you?"

"That is enough, child."

"There is a reason tradition dictates a newly ascended queen chooses her own council from among her generation. I am starting to see the sense in that."

"You dare threaten my position?" The elder's eyes flashed with fury.

"I am ascending right before your eyes, Sonje. Wake up. I grow stronger every day. My mother will never sit on her throne again. Your days on this council are numbered."

"Of all the disrespectful—"

"Sit down, Sonje," Astrid said quietly. "Our Queen Heir has made her choice and we will support her. She knows best."

"She knows best? She is a child."

"She is a *woman* blessed by the gods and with the ancient lineage of a powerful dynasty flowing through her veins and the kind of magic you cannot hope to achieve in your wildest dreams. You've served two generations of Ahlstrom queens. You know the law will not allow you to serve a third."

Sonje fussed with her hands in her lap, clearly wanting to say more, but even she realized she'd overstepped. "My apologies, Queen Astrid. I was out of line. I'm sure we will all find that Thea is more than capable of leading us."

"Thank you," I interceded before Astrid could voice her disapproval of Sonje's half-hearted apology.

A knock sounded at the door and Leda rose to answer it. Sylvi stepped through the doorway, with the very large Sloane carrying the Queen.

"Mother?" I leapt from my seat. "You do not have to knock. You are the queen of this council."

"In name only." She let out a shaky breath.

"Please, sit, your Majesty. You don't look well." Sonje and Vanya moved from the settee to make her comfortable.

"I'm fine. Just a little tired."

"Here you are your Majesty," Sloane said in his deep voice, placing her gently on the settee.

"Thank you for your help, young man." Mother grasped his hand, twice the size of hers and offered him a weak smile.

The giant of a man blushed and backed out of the room as fast as he could.

Mother let Sylvi drape a blanket over her lap and prop her feet on the footstool, but that was all the fussing she could tolerate.

Insecurity bloomed inside my chest as I returned to my seat. The seat that belonged to the queen. I suddenly felt like a little girl playing dress up.

"Darling, you are leading us right now," the queen said, as if reading my mind. "I pass that seat of authority on to you."

Warring emotions welled up inside me and my throat tightened. I would give anything to see my mother strong and seated on her throne once again, but I also felt proud. Honored that she would trust me to carry on in her stead.

"How did it go with Svana?" Astrid asked.

"Not well. I believe we've seriously underestimated the horrors our sister and her daughter have experienced. Once our elder sister was wed, we wrote her off as queen of another realm, but it seems she's been little more than a prisoner since she failed to produce a Warder heir—a male, Warder heir."

"Neela is his most legitimate heir," Leda interjected. "She is strong and powerful with the blood of kings and queens in her ancestry."

"But she is female. And more Valkyrie than Warder," I said. I knew enough about the Warder culture to know they would never respect a queen who was so obviously Valkyrie—whether she could wield their magic or not.

"Svana and Neela have given everything they have to this coup of theirs," Brenna continued. "They are prepared to die before they will ever return to Vöstland. What awaits them there is far worse than death."

"Which means she will resort to every underhanded ploy to thwart Thea." Sonje shook her head as if they'd already lost.

"True, but we have something to use against them." I sat back against my throne, feeling a surge of confidence.

"And what is that? Pray tell." Sonje scoffed.

"I've suspected it before, but now we know their deepest fear. The very last thing they want is to return to the Warder realm. I say it's time we send them back where they came from."

Another knock sounded at the door. Louder this time.

"Enter," I called.

Vendela stepped inside, giving a quick nod to the queen and to me. "She is here."

"Is she alone?" I stood.

"It appears that way."

"Take me to her." I crossed the room. The women of my mother's council rose to follow.

"Be seated." Astrid's formal command sent them all back to their seats without a second thought.

"Be careful, daughter," Mother called as Pasha and I followed Vendela from the room.

"We will go with you," Druan said the moment I closed the door behind me. Sloane stood tall and silent beside him.

"If Neela is alone, I will not approach with a horde at my back." I accepted my golden axes gratefully from Vendela, strapping them onto my back with the harness she'd brought for me.

"Majesty, we will remain inside the gates if you need us," Sloane said in his gravelly voice, ignoring Druan's protests.

"At least don't go beyond the Citadel's protection," Druan insisted. "And take Pasha with you."

"I have to face her as an equal. As a queen." I crossed the grand hall to the front doors of the Citadel. I waved away the guards who leapt to open the heavy, tall doors for me. Today wasn't about posturing or making a grand entrance. This time I needed to be myself. I turned to Pasha, ever my shadow. "I'm sorry, girl, you can't come with me this time."

I swear the cat sneered at me, before she turned tail and retreated to Vendela's side.

"Promise me you'll be careful, Thea." Druan pulled me back, searching my face for some clue to what I had planned.

"Yes, Mother." I patted his handsome face as I stepped through the doors.

For the first time, I felt truly alone without even Pasha at my side. Maybe it was a mistake to leave her behind, but I had to do it this way. Holding my head high, I took the wide stone steps down to the bridge that led right to the palace on the other side of the Queen's Bay.

As I walked, Neela rode toward me on her chestnut warhorse. A strategic move to put me off-guard so she could tower over me.

"You have something that belongs to me," Neela called from her intimidating perch on top of her mount.

"And you have taken someone who is under my protection."

"Your council must be in irons if you're still in charge after bringing that filth into my realm."

"This realm belongs to its people and the queen who serves them." I made my way to the center of the bridge, stopping at its highest point when I was level with Neela. I refused to look up at my opponent.

"I suppose you want to negotiate a trade?" Neela's face twisted in disgust.

"Perhaps we can reach an agreement." I planted my feet wide and rested a hand on my axe handle.

"What did you have in mind?" She slid from the back of her horse to face me, her sword at her hip and her ever present golden armor in place to cover her childhood scars.

"You could release Esben and I could release your mother, but that doesn't solve our larger issues." I could feel Neela's anger pouring out of her, but I remained calm, controlling my emotions as I siphoned from her. Just a hint to judge her reaction. She still didn't seem to notice. I wanted nothing more than to rage at my cousin and demand news of my brother, but I knew I'd make more progress keeping my temper in check.

"I'm not here to back down to a coward who lets others make her decisions, sneaking like a thief in the night into my palace to take a poor defenseless woman prisoner."

"I sent my bounty hunters to seize Svana because I needed leverage. And she's neither poor nor defenseless." I continued to speak calmly, but all the while, I pulled at the power Neela guarded like a treasure clutched in her fist. She was strong, but she was also distracted and easily angered. I siphoned slowly as I spoke. "She will not be harmed so long as the same can be said for Esben."

"I've left orders to have him tortured daily." Neela's grimace twisted into a gleeful smile. "What have you done with my mother? Sent her to her childhood bedroom without dessert?"

"You know very well she's in the dungeon." I pulled ever so slightly at the power, taking a little more each time Neela's voice rose in anger. Soon the power flooded me and I wondered what it would take for her to realize what I was up to. This meeting was about more than offering our terms. The more I could place myself in proximity to my cousin, the faster I could fill the well within me.

"That's the difference between you and me," Neela said. "I won't hesitate to torture and maim the boy, but I know you won't retaliate against my mother. You don't have it in you to cross that line. Your fancy breeding won't allow it."

"You seriously underestimate my dedication to my 'breeding,'" I muttered. "And you underestimate me."

"You come here expecting to use all the negotiating tactics you've learned in princess school, but I won't play that strategic game with you. You've never suffered a day in your life and you're so far out of touch with reality, you have no idea what the people want."

"Wow, you don't know me at all, cousin," I laughed. "The first lesson in diplomacy is never to make assumptions about your opponent. Surely Aunt Svana taught you that much."

Neela shrugged. "Keep her. She's useless to me now."

"If that's the case, why bother to come here at all?"

"I wanted to hear your offer. Now that I have, I see I've wasted my time."

"I haven't made my offer yet, Neela. If you didn't give into your anger so easily, you might have noticed I said I *could* exchange your mother for Esben. But I won't."

"Then what is your offer, Princess? What do you possibly think you can give me that I will accept? Please, enlighten me with your entitlement."

"You're right, you know." I took a few steps forward, no longer fearful of this meeting. "I left. I turned my back on my heritage and my position. I had my reasons, but you couldn't possibly understand how difficult leaving was for me. And in my absence, you received the blessing of the gods, which I never anticipated. But nothing in life ever works out the way we expect, does it?" I dropped my hold on my weapon, relaxing my stance.

"You might have made a great queen, Neela. Of your own realm. But this is not your home. I'm afraid you're too much of a Warder for the Valkyries, and too much Valkyrie for the Warders. That's a tough place to be. I feel for you, I do. But not enough to let you continue hurting my people. I might not be the perfect Queen Heir, but I'm all they have and I will fight for them. I'd just rather it be a fight between the two of us than an all-out war. They've suffered enough. I won't ask them to lay down their lives."

"What are you saying, you want to fight me?" Neela laughed. "You wouldn't last five minutes against me. I wouldn't even need my power. I could just kill you and be done with it."

"Here is my offer. Listen carefully, Neela, I'm only going to say this once." I closed the distance between us to show I was unafraid. "End Esben's torture. Today. Your mother will be treated as a prisoner of war. She will not be harmed but she will continue to stay in her cell. I promise, I will treat your mother far better than you treated mine."

"The boy's execution has been set for the night of the next full moon," Neela taunted. "The people—your people—call for his blood to run through the streets."

"Then we will meet on the day of the full moon," I continued. "Esben will be unharmed, well-fed, and clean, as will your mother. This will be a fight between you and me. No stand-ins or seconds."

"You want a fight to the death? Fine." Neela reached for her sword. "Why wait for the trial? Let's be done with this now."

"No," I countered. "It will be a fight for the power. The winner drains her opponent, takes the throne and leaves the other to live out her days—however long they might be."

"Why wait?" Neela snarled. "We don't need to turn it into a ceremonial killing with all the fussy Valkyrie fanfare. Unless you crave a public death."

"Because you don't want to fight me right now, cousin. Not for the power of the gods." I folded my arms across my chest.

Neela snorted in disgust. "You're full of yourself if you think you can beat me."

"Full of the power," I said flatly. "I've been siphoning from you this whole time, or didn't you notice? If it's to be a fight for the power right this moment, I will win."

Neela's expression gave nothing away, but the flow of power between us trickled to a stop.

"Very well, what do I get when I win?"

"*If* you win, you get the throne and your mother back. I will return to the human realm with my family."

"And the boy will bleed."

It pained me to say it, but I had to agree, even if I would never allow it. "If he must."

"You're making this too easy." Neela let out an evil laugh, worthy of those kids' fairytale movies I was secretly obsessed with back in the human realm.

"I'll warn you again not to underestimate me." I let a hint of the power into my voice to give weight to my words.

"Your deal is naive and you will pay dearly for that mistake."

"You haven't asked what happens when you lose."

"*If* I lose." She jutted her chin at me as if the possibility were out of the question.

"If you lose, I take my mother's throne back. Esben will be released to my care and your mother will live out her days in exile."

"And what happens to me? Execution?" Neela rolled her eyes.

"No. The deal is we both walk away from this. One with the power of the gods and one forever powerless."

"Finish your terms, cousin."

"I take something you value—to be decided on the day of our battle—and send you back to your father."

"Leave it to you to come up with a plan where no one dies." Neela shook her head, but there was fear in her eyes. Just a momentary flash before it was gone. It seemed I was right. Neela feared returning to her father more than her own death.

"There are some things far worse than death, Neela. Do we have a deal?"

"I could just kill you right now and never think of you again."

"You need my power first."

Neela shrugged. "I could take that easily enough."

"Could you?" I arched a brow at her as I turned to leave.

"Fine! We have a deal." Neela snarled at my back.

"See you at the full moon, cousin." I crossed the bridge and ascended the stairs like a queen.

CHAPTER 27

"Faster," Druan demanded. "Neela won't go easy on you like I am."

"Easy?" I scrambled to match his unforgiving pace, lifting my axe blade in time to meet his sword. If he was going easy on me, I was a dead woman.

"Your form is good," Vendela observed from her perch on the terrace wall. "But your stamina is dreadful. Neela will cut you to ribbons before she takes your power."

"Thanks for the vote of confidence." I tried to ignore all the eyes watching me. Everyone from the garden workers to the court nobles working beside them stood by, watching my lessons with the bounty hunters. Even Pasha paced the training circle, casting judgment on my performance.

Everyone inside the Citadel had a vested interest in my looming battle against Neela. If I won, they would get their lives back. If I lost …

"I have to win," I muttered as I picked up my pace.

"Then don't get sloppy," Druan barked. "Watch your form. I've seen this woman fight. She is a master with a blade in her hand."

"So am I." I lunged after him, crashing my axe against the slash of his blade. I'd grown up with a weapon in my hand, learning to fight from my father and the Queen of the Citadel herself.

"You've had three years of inactivity to make you slow and useless."

"I had a job, you know. One of those things that pay you to work so you can eat and have a roof over your head. And I fought off every bounty hunter Neela sent after me."

"Is that what you call it?" Druan ducked my lead blade and slipped behind me, locking me against his chest with his dagger at my throat. "Because it looked more like you were running away when I caught up with you." His chest heaved in time with mine. But I wasn't out of tricks yet.

"Yeah, well, it took you how many months to catch me? I call that surviving and outsmarting my opponent." I rammed the blunt end of my other axe into his ribs and stepped back, ducking under his arm and away from his dagger.

"You have to do more than just survive now, Thea." Druan dropped his sword at his side and sheathed his dagger. "You have a nation to protect. You can't afford anything less than perfection."

"I know." The pressure building in my chest slammed against me like a charging stallion. "What I lack in speed, I'll make up for with my magic and my ability to siphon. That is where I will outshine Neela. She's had the power for a few years. I've had it my whole life."

"Well, you won't have it much longer if she kills you first." Vendela stepped up to take her turn with me in the makeshift sparring ring at the center of the terrace. "You'll need every tool in your arsenal." She glanced at Druan warily. "Even ones you might not be aware of yet."

I shook my head. "This will be a fight for the power. Not a sparring match. And we agreed it wasn't a fight to the death." I sipped from a waterskin Sloane offered me.

"If you believe that woman will let you live, you're more naive than I thought," Vendela said, crouching for her attack. "She will kill you the first chance she gets and then she'll sap the power from your still-warm corpse. To survive this fight, you've got to get angry. Tap into that rage fugue that allowed you to enter her home and take her most valuable prisoner right from under her nose."

"Dela, no." Druan leaned against the terrace wall, his expression grim.

But I knew she was right. It was naive of me to think Neela would play by the rules. Of course she would kill me at the first opportunity.

"Get angry, Thea." Vendela ignored Druan's warning and charged across the ring, brandishing her daggers. We grappled for control as she tried to push me out of the ring. I dug in my heels and wrapped my arms around her middle to thwart her attack. I didn't fight like a Berserker, but the training would be good.

"That's good, Princess," Sloane offered. "Use your smaller stature to latch on and then throw her off balance."

I tried to do just that, but Vendela wouldn't budge. The fight with Neela would take place in the skies, but I wasn't ready for that yet. After a little more practice with Vendela, Sloane and Druan, I would move on to Sylvi and her shield maidens. Maybe even Amara if she was willing. My training would come back to me. It had to.

"You have to be prepared to fight dirty." Vendela slipped out of my grasp, twisting until she had her arm around my throat. "This is not queen training. It's life or death. And not just yours." She threw me to the ground where she easily pinned me with each of her daggers, one at my throat the other at my side. "This is going to be the bloodiest battle of your life and you need to get that through your head."

I nodded, wishing people would stop telling me things I already knew. I was nervous enough. "I know she's the better fighter. I'm not stupid." I shrugged out of her grasp. "Let's go again." I stood and brushed myself off as I moved to the outer ring to face her again.

"Get mad this time, Thea." Vendela crouched, her white wolf and silver fox pacing behind her. Pasha eyed them warily from her place beside Sloane. Apparently, she adored the big man and the treats he slipped to her when I wasn't looking.

"If you can't find your anger with me, at least find it for Neela. She's the one who nearly killed your mother. If she wins this fight with you, you'll be dead and everyone you love will be next. She'll never let Astrid or Sylvi live once she gets her hands on them. And if that's not enough to get your blood up, Neela will take pleasure in killing Pasha as well."

I ran at Vendela in a crouch, clashing with her at the center of the ring, a scream of frustration bursting out of me. She was right. I had to get angry. Anger could drive me forward where fear would be my undoing. My Valkyrie rose within me. She was angry. Angry at the thought of any harm coming to Pasha.

"That's it, Thea," Druan called from somewhere over my shoulder as I swept Vendela's feet out from under her. When she hit the ground I pounced on her, wrestling with her as I tried to pin her to the ground the way she had me. The slick oily darkness of my magic seemed to feed on my anger, strengthening me as I flipped the Berserker woman on her back and finally took the upper hand.

"Is that all you've got?" Vendela growled, the odd flickering of her eyes the only indication that she'd merged with her kindred. She was so much stronger that way. But I still had the upper hand as I locked my arms around her, twisting her arms behind her. "Your rage is the key to winning this fight. Embrace the darkness inside you."

I went limp at Vendela's words, scrambling back on my heels. "What do you know about the darkness?" My voice came out softer than a whisper with all the prying eyes watching me.

"Vendela, it's none of our business." Druan stepped into the ring to stand between us.

"She deserves to know." Vendela stood, brushing the dust from her leathers. "You know as well as I, she needs this if she's going to win."

"Know what?" I demanded. I didn't like the look on Druan's face. "What is this thing tainting my magic?" If they knew, I would force it out of them.

"Not here." Druan relented, taking my arm and towing me back inside. I followed him through the hallways to the guest quarters where they were staying.

By the time we reached Druan's room, my nerves were spiraling out of control.

"Whatever you think is wrong with my magic, tell me now." I ran a hand through my hair, limp with sweat. Pasha nosed her way into the room with Sloane at her back.

"I will leave you, but the skýja wants to be with her mistress."

Pasha gave a worried snort and came to my side, rubbing her head against my hip. "It's okay girl," I whispered, waiting for Sloane to close the door behind him.

"When you first crossed the queen's chamber and the power of the gods returned to you, you said it felt wrong but you didn't say how." Druan leaned against the desk beside the bed. "Does it still feel that way?"

"Yes. It's so different from when I was younger. Tainted somehow." I shook my head, unable to stand still. "The more I call on the power of the gods, the more I lose the light. I'm terrified what will happen when the shadows overwhelm me."

"It's not tainted, Thea," Vendela said carefully. "Valkyries—particularly Valkyrie queens and their heirs—are unique creatures of this world. You are the vessels that hold—"

"I'm well aware of how the power works, Dela. What's wrong with it?"

"Nothing is wrong with the power of the gods. But your magic has changed now that you're of age. You left this realm when you were only sixteen."

"That shouldn't matter. Valkyrie royals develop their magic early. Very little changes in regard to our magic once we've come of age and I've had magic of some level or another since I was ten. I should be stronger now than I was when I left. In some ways I am, but in other ways, I feel blocked." I wandered restlessly across Druan's unnaturally tidy room.

"That's what makes you unique, Thea." Druan said. "Nearly every creature of the Nine Realms possesses some level of the power of the gods through you and your mother, but only when we come of age. I was seventeen before I felt the first stirrings of my Druid magic. Sameerah came to me when I was fourteen, but I was eighteen before we bonded in truth through my Berserker magic."

"You're not telling me anything I don't already know." I tightened my arms over my middle, hugging myself like that would somehow hold me together.

"When you crossed into Valsgard after your absence, it was like you came of age in that instant. So when your power returned to you, it … changed."

"And why would it do that?" I threw my arms up in the air. "Valkyries are born with magic. We come into this world in our natural forms and shift to human within a few days. We don't shift again until we gain control of our Valkyrie during puberty and then our magic comes to us in full. Age doesn't matter for Valkyries."

"You are more than Valkyrie," Vendela said gently. "The darkness you feel *tainting* your power feeds on your anger, yes?"

I nodded, not sure what she was getting at.

"The shadowy sensation you feel when you call on the power has a slickness to it, doesn't it?" Druan asked. "Like it might cover you and drown out the light."

"It's like oil. Thick and sticky. It feels like evil itself."

"You're describing Berserker Magic, Thea." Vendela crossed the room to my side, laying a gentle hand on my shoulder. "And it's not evil. It's just a different kind of magic than you're used to."

"Berserker magic? That doesn't make any sense." I laughed, thinking they were playing some kind of trick on me.

"It only makes sense if one of your parents was a Berserker," Druan said. "And since you're obviously Queen Brenna's daughter —I've seen the wings and talons—your natural father must have been a Berserker. A very powerful one."

"My father is Valkyrie. A Chosen Son." I scowled at them, searching their faces for a hint of a smile. But if it was a joke, it was a cruel one.

"The man who helped raise you and your sister is Valkyrie," Druan said. "But there is simply no way he could be your natural father."

"What are you saying? My mother—the Valkyrie Queen—had an affair with a Berserker, one of our greatest enemies?" I laughed at the absurdity of it all. "You think she wouldn't have told me if my father wasn't my father?" But there were a lot of things my mother had never old me.

"Then explain the darkness that has latched onto your power." Vendela guided me to sit on the bed before I stumbled to the floor.

"How do you know this?" My body trembled and my hands shook as I stared at Vendela. "How do you know about the darkness? Back in the sparring ring you told me to embrace the darkness. How did you know?"

"Because I have that darkness too." Vendela took my hand in hers. "Don't' be afraid of it, Thea. Shadows and light can work beautifully together. Some of the greatest, most beautiful paintings in all of the Nine Realms are a symphony of shadow and light, two sides in opposition that still work together to find beauty and harmony."

"It can't be true." My heart raced in my chest. "Mother would have told me by now. She can't have lied to me my whole life. Not about this."

"The queen has her reasons, I'm sure," Druan said. "But the day you walked into the palace and brought your mother home, you were in a Berserker rage. I knew you had Berserker magic then, and I knew you didn't understand it. I had hoped your mother would tell you at some point over the last days. It seems she hasn't found the strength for it yet."

"Wait, I can't be part Berserker. I don't have a kindred, and since I've returned there have been no signs of one showing up." They had to be wrong. A Berserker's magic didn't work without a kindred.

"What about Pasha?" Vendela asked. "She follows you everywhere. Even the day you rescued your mother, I don't think you were aware of it, but Pasha was with you every step of the way, from the steps of the Citadel, down to the dungeons, and into the council chambers, and back."

"Pasha's been with me since I was a child. My father gave her to me when I was twelve. She was just an orphaned kit. She didn't come to me the way kindreds do."

"Petra has been with me since I was twelve," Vendela said of her wolf kindred, "though we didn't bond until I came of age. I bonded with Aska years later. It seems Pasha has chosen you, but because of your absence, you've not yet fully bonded."

"But she's never shown any signs of being more than a skýja leopard. She's a rare breed of cat, but she doesn't speak to me the way Sameerah does with Druan."

"It took Petra years to speak to me in the way of the kindred. Aska was easier, though we bonded much later and she isn't as persnickety as Petra."

"Sam came to me when I was fourteen," Druan added. "But even after we bonded when I came of age, she didn't speak to me for several more years. It takes time to build trust and to learn how to speak to each other."

"This doesn't make any sense." Tears burned my eyes. If the father I'd always known wasn't my natural father, then who was? And how could Mother not tell me? It wasn't unusual for a Valkyrie Queen to have lovers outside her marriage to the consort chosen by her council. It was expected that if she couldn't find love there, she would seek it elsewhere—after she produced a Queen Heir.

"Unfortunately we don't have time for you to come to terms with the emotional side of all this." Vendela stood up, dragging me with her. "You can deal with all your feelings of betrayal later. Right now, you need to focus on defeating Neela. And to do that, you need every tool in your arsenal. I can teach you to use your Berserker magic, even without a kindred. But you have to embrace your Berserker half." Vendela met my gaze. "This is a good thing, Thea. It means you have a source of boundless strength and magic Neela will never see coming. It could be your only chance to beat her. Otherwise I would never have told you at such a terrible time."

"Is it true?" I barged into Mother's rooms to find her resting by the fireplace.

"What, darling?" The queen's already pale face whitened even further at my outburst.

"My father…Elias" I choked on the word. "The man I loved and looked up to my entire life … isn't my real father?" My voice trembled and my eyes grew bright with tears I refused to shed.

The queen closed her book and set it aside before she met my eyes. "How did you find out?"

"Apparently, I have Berserker magic." I paced in front of the fire, my blood buzzing in my veins like a nest of angry bees ready to swarm the room.

"I can see it in your eyes now." Mother shifted the blanket over her lap. "Nothing changes the fact that Elias was your father because he raised you and loved you as his own."

"Did you lie to him too? Did you make him believe I was his daughter?" The anger burned at my skin, like my Valkyrie wanted out, but this was different. For the moment, she was subdued and my other half seemed to be making an entrance.

"Of course he knew." The queen spoke softly. "And he didn't love you any less for it."

"Did he know my father was a Berserker?" I stood stiffly, my hands balled into fists.

"Elias knew and respected your natural father. They were friends a lifetime ago. I won't have you disrespect your heritage,

Alithea. Come. Sit and I will tell you about the man who would be so proud of you if he could be here to see the woman you've become."

It broke something inside me to hear my mother speak of another man as my father. To speak with such love in her voice.

"Please sit with me." The queen urged me again, patting the settee beside her. "I always intended to tell you when I thought you were ready to hear it. Since you freed me from my prison, I've been trying to work up the courage. I'd hoped this conversation would come after the Neela situation was resolved. I thought you had enough on your plate, darling. I didn't want to give you another burden to bear."

I sat on the straight-backed chair opposite the settee, too angry to sit beside my mother. "Who is he?" I asked through gritted teeth.

Mother looked down at her hands in her lap before she met my gaze. "Hagen is your natural father."

I shot up from my seat. "King Hagen? The madman who holds the Berserker throne? That Hagen? The one they call the King of Madmen?"

"Please sit, Thea."

I returned to my seat, trembling with new fear for my brother who didn't yet know how much his life was in danger if anyone ever found out he was Hagen's son. Especially the insane king himself.

"Hagen wasn't always the madman he is now," the queen began. "With the strongest of the Berserkers, over time, their magic can drive them into madness. When I met Hagen more than twenty years ago, he was a beloved king and the first to sit on his throne and contemplate an alliance with Valsgard. But even then, he struggled with bouts of madness known only to those closest to him."

"I can't believe this." I hunched over, bracing my arms against my knees. "I expected you to tell me I was the crazy one for thinking even for a second that Father wasn't my father."

"I am sorry that you found out this way. Truly. But I won't apologize for loving Hagen."

"How did you even meet him?"

"I visited Úlfaheim to meet with the king to discuss our potential alliance. While I was there, we fell in love." The queen shrugged. "It was the first and only time I've ever known that kind of love. I shared a deep regard with my husband, but ours was always a relationship of respect and a mutual desire to put our people first. Elias was my best friend and I will always love him, but what I shared with Hagen was the kind of love I hope my daughters will find some day. He challenged me in a way no man has ever dared. We loathed each other at first." A smile tugged at the corners of her mouth.

"Hagen and I traveled with my council to meet with some of his supporters in another city. On the way a group who opposed our strengthening alliance attacked us. I was grievously injured and separated from my council. Hagen found me and cared for my injuries. I couldn't fly so we traveled many days back to the palace. It was an adventure I'll never forget. I spent many months among the Berserkers, and it was the best time of my life. But I had duties of my own to consider and I had to leave Hagen behind. Weeks after I returned, I learned I was pregnant. I never had the chance to tell Hagen. It wasn't something I could send in a message."

"So you never told him about us?" I asked. "He doesn't know about Ben?"

"The madness took him in the months after I left. The Hagen I knew lost the battle with his magic. That man is gone now. Not long after, they started calling him the King of Madmen, praising his decision to refuse the alliance we'd worked so hard to achieve.

It broke my heart to lose him that way, but I couldn't tell him about either of his children."

I clutched my hands into fists, trying to quell my anger and the urge to lash out at Mother for falling in love with the wrong man. I didn't know how to respond to her confessions. And I didn't know how I felt about Hagen.

"Blessed Mother Sigrún, that means Vendela is my half-sister." Shock rolled through me at first, followed by some emotion akin to happiness. I liked the feisty Berserker woman. I would be proud to call her sister.

"The Hagen I knew adored his only child. In his right mind, he would have fought for her to succeed him."

"Instead she had to be sent away because he believed she was trying to poison him." I felt sorry for the little girl who had lost her father to madness before she ever had a chance to fight for her place in his court.

"His mind was broken," Mother said softly. "He tried to have Vendela killed, though she doesn't know that. I helped her uncle get her out of the palace and provided a safe haven for her here. I hoped one day I could help her take the throne her father would have wanted her to have."

"And what about Sylvi?" I could barely get the question out. My eyes still burned with tears, but somehow knowing my beloved sister was only my half-sister broke my heart.

"She is Elias' child."

I swiped at the tears falling freely now.

"Oh my darling, no. Don't cry, I can't bear it." Mother came to my side and tried to comfort me, but I couldn't bear her touch just now. She seemed to understand and sat in the chair beside me. "That doesn't mean Sylvi is any less your sister now than she was two minutes ago. She adores you, Thea."

"That will change when she finds out my father is the King of Madmen." A strangled sob nearly choked me as I let my tears fall.

"I know you are angry with me, but you will never speak of your father by that awful name ever again. And you don't know your sister at all if you think she will care one bit about any of this."

"I'm sorry. I'm just ... shocked and sad and ... a million other things I don't even know how to express right now." I sobbed into my hands, trying to keep the tears from falling and my heart from breaking.

"Your heritage is hitting you all at once." Mother reached toward me again and this time I let her. "When you came for me in the dungeons, I was delirious. It wasn't until just a few days ago when Sylvi mentioned how strangely angry you were that day that I realized your Berserker magic was coming to you as it would have when you came of age. I was a coward for not speaking to you about it immediately."

"Oh, Mother." I squeezed her hand. "If there is one thing you have never been, it's a coward." I wiped the tears from my face and took a deep breath. The anger began to subside and I felt a little more like myself.

"You're a natural." Mother smiled. "I've seen many adult Berserkers unable to manage their emotions half as well as you just did."

I let out a breath and looked at her doubtfully. "I don't even know what I'm doing."

"Just remember, it doesn't matter where you come from, darling. Your father's magic will only serve to strengthen you. Embrace it. Own it and be proud of it."

"That's easier said than done when our people hate the Berserkers. What are we going to do? The council will never tolerate a half-Berserker queen."

"I'm not sure they have much of a choice. It is clear that our next queen will either be you or Neela, both with fathers the council would never approve of under normal circumstances." Mother sat back in her chair and I noticed she was looking much better. Stronger and healthier, though I could sense the power within her was weak. "But maybe this will force our people to see a different way."

"Maybe you're right." I clutched Mother's hand, not ready to let go. "Unless they can unearth a stronger vessel somewhere else, they're going to end up with a less than desirable queen on the throne."

"You know, Hagen and I once dreamed of a world where all the people of the Nine Realms could come together as allies. That one day we would be one people and it wouldn't matter who the queen married as long as she was a chosen vessel. In some twisted way, I think that is what Neela is trying to do, but she's gone about it the wrong way."

"I wish you had talked to me about such things before I left." I saw my mother in a new light. I'd always thought of her as the staunch traditionalist, but there was so much more to her than I ever gave her credit for. "I've always believed that we foster too much separation between the kingdoms. That Valkyries, especially here Vahland Reach, are too isolated. They can't see past their traditions to consider another way."

"Our generation couldn't accomplish those first steps, but I believe yours can. I have great faith in you, Thea. You remind me so much of both your fathers—in all the best ways."

"I don't know what to do with all of this." I met my mother's gaze, trying to see past the traditional queen to the woman who once dreamed of the impossible. "But I do know I will need all the help I can get."

CHAPTER 28

"You aren't even trying." Druan stepped toward me with his hands out like he might strangle me.

I took a step back and Pasha growled in warning from her perch on the rocks. "Touch me and I will kick you where it hurts, Mr. Man."

"Then just do what I ask." He paced back across the old training grounds. Long abandoned, the ruins of the first Valkyrie queen's fortress stood among the cliffs above the Citadel where I could train in private.

"I'm trying, but you're not explaining what I am supposed to be doing." I kicked a loose stone at his back. The sun had set more than an hour ago, but they were all determined to make progress before calling it a day.

"You're afraid of the Berserker magic inside you. I can tell by the way you try to merge with Pasha. It doesn't respect you yet."

"That doesn't even make sense! It's magic, but you speak of it like it's a person I have to win over."

"It's not a person, Thea." Druan rolled his eyes and Vendela snickered from her seat on a nearby boulder. "Our magic lives within us as a natural part of us." He threw his hands out in frustration. "It's like the air in our lungs or the blood in our veins. The power of the gods fuels our ability to merge with our kindred. To use their strength and superior senses as our own. You're trying to use your Berserker magic the way you use your Valkyrie magic and it's not the same thing."

"How is it different?" I raked a hand through my hair, looking to Vendela for help.

"What? He's the best possible teacher for you. He knows what it is like to have two heritages with differing magic. Harnessing your Berserker magic will be different for you than it was for me."

"You're not just secretly entertained by this nonsense?"

"That's just an extra perk." Vendela laughed. "You two need to learn to communicate better if you expect to get anywhere."

"She's right." Druan stood with his hands on his hips, taking a deep breath, like he might be praying for patience.

"Explain it again." I dropped onto the boulder next to my half-sister who didn't know she was my half-sister yet. Part of me couldn't wait to tell her, but I was also afraid of how she might react.

"You describe your Berserker magic as this dark shadow trying to smother your Valkyrie magic. That makes you fear it. When you fear your Berserker half, the magic has no confidence in you—"

"That's where you lose me. How does the magic have thoughts if it's not sentient?"

Druan growled irritably. "It's not sentient, Thea. You are. Or at least you're supposed to be, but I'm not so sure about that right now."

"Enough with the jokes, Dru. Keep going. I think I might actually be following you after that last bit ... at least for the moment." I pulled my knees up to my chest and waited for him to stop glaring at me. "I promise, I'm paying attention. Carry on." I waved a hand at him.

"You are a vessel, which means you are the source of your own Berserker magic. You have to let that magic rise within you. Let it fill you and embrace it—even the darkest, scariest parts of that magic. When you shrink away from it, it retreats back inside you—inside the vessel. You have to trust it or you'll never break out of this vicious cycle. As long as you fear the shadows, we aren't going to get anywhere.

"You get that it feels like the shadows are going to suffocate me, right? Like I can't breathe."

"That's your fear talking. Berserker magic cannot smother, you, your Valkyrie, Pasha, or the power of the gods because its origin is rooted in all those things. You are the thing that gives it life. You need to embrace both the shadow and the light. At the same time."

"I swear, that's what I've been doing." I shrugged, completely mystified.

"No, you're not. It's like you're sacrificing one for the other and that won't work," Vendela chimed in.

"But I thought the light is my Valkyrie magic and the dark is my Berserker magic." I closed my eyes, trying to get it all straight in my mind.

"No." Druan sighed. "The light and the darkness represents your magic. Alithea Ahlstrom's magic. It's neither one nor the other, but both. I know it's confusing when you're used to having one type of magic."

"But you literally just said they're not different."

"Let me try that again." He sank down onto one of the crumbling boulders. "Druid magic and Berserker magic come to me in the same way through my own personal magic. But there are differences in what I do with that magic. Things that are either innately Berserker or Druid."

"Okay, I'm with you now." I nodded for him to continue. "I like examples."

"I had to learn to command both as a single unit to perform the different kinds of actions. You will need to do the same."

"Okay." I nodded again. "So I need to stop thinking of my magic as two separate things and start viewing them as a single source of power?"

"Exactly." Druan's shoulders slumped like he'd done the impossible.

I took a breath and went for it. "But didn't you say I was trying to use the Berserker magic the same as the Valkyrie magic and I shouldn't because they aren't the same. I think you've lost me again." I leaned back against the boulder, looking up at the rising moon.

"Gods, give me patience with this woman," Druan muttered under his breath, kicking the boulder as he slid down to the ground. "Let's try a visual aid before we call it a day." Druan picked up a black rock, a white rock, a brown one, and a gray one.

"I'm not five years old, Dru." I rolled my eyes.

"Humor me," he said dryly. "The white rock is the power of the gods, representing your role as a vessel." He placed the larger rock at the center of the ring. "It is responsible for fueling all your magic. Like gasoline in a human automobile." He took a step away from the white rock before he continued.

"The black rock is your Berserker magic, over here with Pasha." He placed the rock at Pasha's feet. She snorted at him with a curled lip before he backed away. And the brown one is yours." He stuffed it into my hand. "Your Valkyrie magic you're most familiar with.

"Now the gray rock represents all of these things."

"A third kind of magic?" My head throbbed as I rubbed my temples.

"For the purposes of this visual aid, yes." Druan placed the gray rock in my empty palm. "You know the white rock. You've had it all your life. You know the brown rock just as well. Now you have this black rock creeping in, but it's not the enemy—"

"It's Pasha," Vendela interjected. "Think of the dark shadow of your Berserker magic as Pasha. She's a predator, but she is also your kindred. Do you trust her?"

"With my life," I said without hesitation, but I still wasn't so sure she was my kindred.

"Then trust her magic," Druan said, placing the black rock in my hand beside the brown one. "When you allow her magic to *merge* with yours, you get the gray rock." He pointed to the rock in my other hand. "It's not about trying to learn two different magics so much as learning to adapt yours to the magic Pasha brings you."

"And when they merge, the magic becomes both at the same time, making something new." I wrapped my hand around all three rocks, my gaze drifting to Pasha.

The white skýja leopard dipped her regal head for a brief moment.

Prowl.

The thought wasn't mine. "Prowl? What does that mean?" I couldn't tear my eyes from Pasha's.

"What?" Vendela straightened, her eyes widening in interest. "Did she speak to you?"

"I don't know what it means," I whispered, studying Pasha's fierce blue gaze.

"She is claiming you as part of her prowl," Druan said. "Leopards are normally solitary creatures, but when they accept others into their pack, they're called a prowl of leopards. She's accepted you; now you must accept her."

I bowed my head toward Pasha. *Prowl.* I let the thought resonate in my mind, not sure if she could hear me. "Again." I moved to the center of the sparring ring now drenched in moonlight. "Walk me through it again."

"Reach for your magic as you normally would, but wait for the shadow of your Berserker magic to join before you fully embrace it. Let the shadows and light merge within you and listen for Pasha's voice. Her instincts will guide you. You may not fully merge yet, it is too early for that, but you will form some kind of connection."

"Remember not to fear the shadows. It's just Pasha," Vendela added.

I nodded, turning to face my kindred. "I can't do this without you, Pash."

Calling on my magic was like breathing, but the slick, oily shadow I'd feared since my return soon followed. My instincts told me to shove the darkness aside and focus on the light of what was familiar, but I took a deep breath, holding Pasha's ice-blue gaze as I let the shadows wash over me.

This time I let the darkness twist and turn with the light, willing myself to not resist it.

Pasha let out a triumphant growl as I threw my head back and embraced the strange sensation of this new magic coursing through my veins. It wasn't unlike shifting into my Valkyrie form or embracing the burn. Strength flooded my arms and legs and I felt heavier rather than lighter. My vision blurred and then cleared, leaving the world painted in dark hues of black, white, and shades of gray and blue. My human eyes couldn't see well in the dark, but Pasha's eyes were suited for distinguishing fine detail in the dimmest of light.

I moved around the sparring ring with the graceful stride of a predator. Strength radiated through me and I felt … indestructible.

Like there wasn't anything I couldn't do with my kindred by my side.

"Am I still me?" My voice sounded rough, like sandpaper against wood.

"More or less," Vendela said. "You look like you, but also like a Berserker ready to fight. You can see it in the eyes and the way you move. Very feline. She's let you join her in a way. You aren't fully merged, but Pasha must trust you a great deal to come this far so fast."

"I've never seen even a partial merge this quickly," Druan whistled through his teeth as he studied my eyes. "I imagine Pasha has been waiting a very long time for this."

My heart sank at the knowledge I couldn't hide this.

Pasha hissed and the magic began to unravel.

"No, wait." I grasped for it, but the magic was harder to hold onto than I expected. A fog rolled through my mind and I was suddenly staring up at the trees.

"It's okay." Druan reached down toward me. "That was really good. We can try again tomorrow.

"How did I get on the ground?" I took his hand and pulled myself up.

"You kind of fainted for a second," Vendela offered in a cheery tone. "I think you offended your kindred with your thoughts."

"Can she still hear my thoughts?" I glanced at the proud leopard, realizing how my thoughts must have sounded to her.

"We don't literally hear each other's thoughts when we aren't merged," Vendela explained. "Between kindreds, it's more about reading each other's moods and coming to know them so well you can anticipate their next move."

"She's upset with me." I knew that much from growing up with Pasha. She refused to look at me whenever she was mad and right now she was looking straight up at the sky.

"What were you thinking right before you lost your hold on the magic?" Druan asked.

"I was thinking I can't hide this from my people, and I don't know how they will react when they realize the queen they've pinned all their hopes on is part Berserker."

Druan scowled down at me, folding his arms across his chest. "I'm with Pasha, you're being a jerk."

"What?" I glanced at Vendela to gauge her reaction. The normally easy-going young woman wore a frown much like Druan's.

"Why would you want to hide what you are? It's not a … dirty secret." Vendela turned her wolf-like eyes on me.

"Oh, Pasha, no." I sank to the ground in front of my dearest friend. "I didn't mean it like that. I'm not ashamed." I tried to get her to look at me but the big cat turned her back on me and I couldn't blame her. "I just meant our people won't understand at first. I only meant to hide it until I defeat Neela. Until that happens, no one can know about this."

"So what are we doing here, Thea?" Druan asked. "You want to learn to use Pasha's power to help you defeat Neela, so long as it isn't obvious you're part Berserker?"

"Yes, but also no." I stayed on the ground with Pasha. Her rejection broke something inside me. "I'm so, so sorry, girl. You know I could never be ashamed of you. I am proud to have you as my kindred and I want everyone to see just how wonderful you are. How much you mean to me. I just want to be careful how I reveal that."

The great cat snorted and resumed licking her paws.

Druan crossed the sparring ring and crouched beside me. "If you expect to use the Berserker magic inside you, you need to own it, Thea."

"I will." I turned to meet his gaze. "I'm so sorry if I offended either of you. I didn't mean it the way it sounded. My people hold a great deal of pride in their queen and they expect her to be the very best of what makes us Valkyrie. I will need to handle this … revelation delicately, when the time comes. But for now, you must understand we likely have spies within the Citadel. I can't have this getting back to Neela because Pasha is my secret weapon. She won't see this coming and I need it to remain that way."

"We understand that, don't we Dru?" Vendela marched up behind us.

"I suppose." Druan growled. He reached for Pasha, running a hand over her proud head. She leaned into him as he scratched behind her ears.

Something inside me went Berserk and I wanted to step between Druan and my kindred. Because there was no doubt in my mind now that Pasha was my kindred. *Prowl.* I sucked in a breath and clenched my eyes closed until the unreasonable rage passed. Pasha was part of me and she was angry with me. She had every right to be, but seeing her respond to Druan and not me hurt.

"That was good, Princess." Druan nodded. "You have very good control of your anger. That will serve you well."

"No," I gasped, clutching my chest as a bone-deep sorrow crashed into me. "Pasha?" My kindred's heart was breaking and I didn't know why.

A wave of loneliness hit me and I got it. She wanted me to know how sad she was when I was gone. "I'm sorry." Tears rolled down my cheeks and splashed on my hands. "I'll never leave you again. I promise."

Finally Pasha turned to me, a purr rumbling deep in her chest as she bumped her head against mine. I threw my arms around her and cried into her shoulder. I'd missed her so much before I knew what she was to me. I couldn't bear her thinking I'd abandoned her.

"I had to go, Pash. But I'm back now and I'll do better. I'll be better. For you and our people. I promise."

CHAPTER 29

"Dru?" I knocked on his door before walking in. "Do you have time for some train—" I stopped in the center of his room, staring at his bare back, streaked with faded lines from more lashes of a whip than I could count, but that wasn't what caught my attention. "What is that?"

"Nothing." He turned to face me, shrugging into a clean linen shirt.

"That's not nothing." I charged across the room, my legs reduced to jelly as I grabbed the hem of his shirt and pulled it up to reveal the tattoos across his back and shoulders.

"They're just Druid tattoos, Thea." He tried to twist away from me.

"Not this one." I traced the rough lines of scar tissue around the dark circular brand on his left shoulder. It was an indecipherable lump now, but I knew what it meant. Inky lines of a newer tattoo tried to erase the brand, but no amount of ink could conceal the initials bearing the seal of the Ahlstrom dynasty. Not from me.

"No." I shook my head, refusing to accept what my eyes saw plain as day in front of me. "No. Please, please, not you," I whispered. "Please." I sank onto the edge of his bed. "You were a Chosen Son?" My hands flew to cover my mouth, horrified by what this man had gone through in my name.

I understood now why he'd hated me so much in the beginning. I couldn't fathom why he didn't still hate me.

"I told you I lived among the Valkyries for a time." He reached for a belt from the chest at the foot of his bed, refusing to meet my eyes.

"You're a Druid royal. Your mother is the High Priestess and your aunt is Mother's best friend. Of course you were chosen. Why didn't you tell me?" I buried my face in my hands, too ashamed to look at him any longer.

"Because it doesn't matter, Thea. I left the fortress when I was seventeen; that was another life. I lived there for five years until the council decided I wasn't fit to be your consort."

"They marked you for me when you were only twelve years old?" I could hardly see through the veil of tears in my eyes, but I knew by his rigid posture he wasn't happy I'd found out.

"I received the brand when I was two years old." The muscle in his jaw worked furiously. "But I didn't join the other boys until I was twelve. My mother wouldn't hear of it before then. Later, when I was discarded as unfit, I returned to my father for a time, but that was a disaster. I tried living among my mother's people again, but that has never worked well either. I guess I am more at home among the Valkyries even if I'm not good enough for you."

"I'm so sorry." My soul ached for him and all the other boys whose lives were ruined for the sake of an archaic tradition. "I know those are empty words, but I'm so sorry that was done to you. You were just a baby and they branded you like cattle." My stomach heaved at the very thought of such abuse.

Druan lowered himself onto the bed beside me with a sigh. "For five years I learned everything about you. What you liked, what you didn't like. I learned how to be the proper mate to a powerful queen—and I hated every minute of it. I hated you with a passion and I did everything in my power to get kicked out, but that is a lot harder than it sounds. Most of the other boys adored you, but to me it always felt like…"

"Slavery?" I supplied. "Blessed Mother Sigrún, please know if it had ever been up to me, none of that would have happened to you or any of the other Chosen Sons." Tears splashed on my hands folded in my lap. "I'm so, so sorry." There was nothing more I could say. Nothing that would restore the lost years of his childhood. "You should know, my abhorrence for the tradition of the Chosen Sons is a big part of why I left. I couldn't condone such barbaric…"

"Stop, Thea." He took my hand. "It was not your doing. And to your credit, the old men teaching those boys how to anticipate your every need—your every desire—they have no idea who you really are. In here." He tapped my forehead. "If they did, they'd know all their work was in vain."

"Why were you sent away?"

"Well, that's a long story." He laughed. "But the gist of it is they believed I was too stubborn and willful. I don't know how it took them five years to figure that out."

I snorted at that. "The same could be said for me. Has been said, many times."

"They claimed I could never be subservient to a queen, but they never realized how much you would hate that. You are a queen who needs someone to challenge her. Someone unafraid to tell you when you're being a stubborn fool."

"Exactly." I wiped my tears away. "Try convincing a room full of stuffy old traditionalists of that."

"I gave you a hard time when we finally caught up to you. But now that I know you better, I have to admit, you were brave for leaving. For not marrying Fiske just because they said he was the one. I thought you were the spoiled, entitled girl I was raised to believe you were."

I turned to look at him and said the most honest thing I'd said in a long time. "I'm not sure I would have left if it were you."

"Yes, you would have." He swept the hair from my face. "I was there that night and you barely noticed me."

I titled my head to the side. "After you were sent away, you came back for the betrothal ceremony?"

"I was the one who escorted you that night, but you barely acknowledged me."

"That was you?" My jaw dropped, but for the life of me, I couldn't recall the face of the young man who had escorted me down the stairs. "I was scared out of my mind. A gargoyle could have been by my side and I wouldn't have noticed."

"I realize that now." Druan gave me a hesitant smile. "I hated you so much, Thea. But I didn't know you. Not the real you. I only knew the girl they painted you to be. The girl they wanted you to be."

"The girl I tried so hard not to be that I ran away from everything I knew just so I wouldn't become her." I studied my hands in my lap for a moment before I asked the one question I wasn't sure I wanted to know the answer to.

"How do you not hate me still?" I met his gaze, my lips trembling as his warm hand cupped my cheek. "Because you definitely should."

"Because you fought back. You fought for your freedom and

the freedom of every boy who was ever chosen to train to be your husband. And you won."

He leaned in, his lips pressing against mine, warm and firm for a moment as I responded to his gentle kiss. A low growl sounded deep in his throat as he crushed his mouth to mine in a bruising kiss.

"Thea," he murmured, breaking away to press his forehead to mine, his breath warm against my skin. "I can't do—"

"Don't you dare finish that sentence." I searched for his lips again, needing another taste. Something primal rose up within me and I recognized it as my Berserker half wanting to claim him as mine. Did he feel that way too? I let my hands move to his shoulders as our kiss deepened and he pulled me onto his lap. I felt the brand through his shirt, hot under my touch, wishing I could take all that old pain away from him.

"It doesn't matter." He pulled away, taking a breath to steady himself. "Not anymore. It's just a lump of ruined flesh. It doesn't mark me. I haven't let it have that kind of power over me in a very long time."

"I wish I could erase it." I searched his eyes, not sure what to make of this heat between us.

He took my hand, moving it away from the scars on his back. "Let's not dwell on the past. We know each other better now. No matter what happens next, now we both have a choice."

CHAPTER 30

"Very good, Thea," Sylvi praised my flight maneuvers. That was one thing I wasn't out of practice with. Battling Neela in the skies would give me an advantage. I knew I could outfly her, but I needed to beat her in close combat, not just evade her.

"You're not giving it your full strength yet." Druan's disappointment was evident even from his position on the ground.

I cast a glance at Sameerah, soaring alongside me. "I know, but I need to be careful when and how I reveal my other side. And now is not that time." My words were low, but I knew Druan would hear me through his link with Sam.

Sam gave me a baleful look, her gyrfalcon eyes rimmed in gold.

"I'm just being cautious." I flew back into the fray with my sister's shield maidens, each prepared and willing to give their all to help me prepare for a fight to the death with Neela. Because no matter what parameters we laid out before hand, that was what this was going to be. But I didn't need my Berserker magic to win this mock battle. I was always more warrior than princess.

Before I left Valsgard, I preferred to spend my days sparring and honing my battle skills. Back then I wanted nothing more than to follow in my father's footsteps and become the general of Mother's army. I'd always thought I got my ambition from Father. I probably did, but not from the father I'd known all my life.

"You've got this, Thea." Sylvi flew to my side, coaching my every move. My sister's white wings reflected the brilliant sunlight, casting a halo around her. "I just wish I could fight with you. Won't you even consider taking me as your second into battle?"

"Absolutely not." I blocked my opponent's weapon, my shield and axe like a natural extension of my body. "I know you're more than capable, but this fight is about limiting the loss of lives. It's between me and Neela."

I freed my opponent of her weapon and slammed into her shoulder, sending her spiraling toward the ground.

"But if she brought a second too, it would be more of a fair fight. You need someone to watch your back. There is too much on the line."

I have Pasha for that. But could I risk revealing my kindred to Mother's council? I feared what they might do to her to conceal my secret from the world. I didn't think for a second they would accept her ... or the part of me they would despise.

"If I die, I will take Neela with me. I need you to survive to pick up the pieces and carry on." I lowered my weapon as I dispatched the last of the shield maidens. One by one, I'd sent them crashing to the ground.

"Did it ever occur to you that I'm more than just your backup? I'm not a spare, Thea. I will rule the Citadel one day. It's done. I will never be Queen of Valsgard, so stop trying to make me into something I'm not. Like it or not, I am the warrior for our people. Not you."

Sylvi's wings snapped in close to her body and she shot toward the ground, issuing orders to her maidens to pack up and get back to work in the gardens.

"Sylvi. Wait, please," I called after her. She was right; I had to stop thinking of her as the sister I always protected. She needed to know I respected her much more than that.

"What?" Sylvi asked stiffly as I landed beside her.

"You are not my backup, Sylvi—you are my rock. And you are the heart of this place. I know you can stand with me and fight, but you belong here, in the Citadel, keeping our people safe. I need you to stay here with Astrid and I need you to do something else for me."

"What?" Sylvi asked again, though her tone was softer.

"While Neela is distracted with me, evacuate the Citadel. We can't continue to hide behind the safety of the Citadel and Astrid's protection. Guide our people across the Broken Isles to the Druid borderlands where they will be safe. I need to know that if I fail Neela will return to an empty city. I need to know you've positioned yourself to fight back even if I'm not here to fight with you. I don't want to die thinking you will all waste away behind these walls until there's nothing left to keep you going. Take Mother and Astrid and abandon Vahland Reach."

Sylvi gaped at me, shaking her head. "Thea, do you have any idea how much preparation goes into something like that? I'd need weeks to plan it, not days. The pathway through the Broken Isles is treacherous. It would take several days to move so many people to the borderlands."

"If I know my sister, you already have an emergency evacuation planned and you've just been waiting for a time to implement it when Neela and her soldiers weren't looking. That time is coming,

Sylvi. If I fail, Morgana will come to your aid. She will help you gather our people from the surrounding villages to take refuge among the Druids. Once you're all there, you will need to call a meeting of the High Council and demand they remove Neela from power, even if it means war."

Sylvi nodded. "I will care for our people, but sister, you will come back the victor. I have every confidence in you."

"Thank you, Sylvi." I watched my sister leave with her maidens.

"That was a pathetic performance up there." Druan sidled up behind me. His eyes still shone like a predator's, rimmed in gold like Sameerah's. I wondered what I looked like when merged with Pasha. We'd only managed a partial merge a few times. Pasha and I were still wary of the magic that connected us.

Pasha sat back on her haunches beside him, looking equally disappointed.

"It was just practice. I didn't need to … merge."

"But you both need the practice, Thea. You can't wait until you need her strength to try it."

"I know. I'm just scared, Dru." I stretched a hand toward Pasha, pleased to receive a head bump from her. We were getting better at reading each other through this tenuous bond. She understood I was only trying to protect her.

"What do you fear?" He stepped closer, his hand skimming along my arm in a quick touch that sent shivers through me.

"I'm so afraid for Pasha. The queen's council are my mother's people. Traditionalists. I won't have a council of my own choosing until I ascend. With Mother so weak and still recovering, it is my responsibility as the Queen Heir to act for her. So for the time being, her council is my council. If they find out about my heritage and what Pasha is to me, they will kill her." I leaned into Druan, my body trembling with anger and fear. "They will do whatever it takes to conceal my Berserker nature from all of Valsgard. If they can't have their ideal queen, then they will dress me up to look like the ideal queen they expect me to be."

"Even if that weakens you?" Druan guided me up to the terrace above the gardens and away from prying eyes, Pasha leading the way. "They would care that much that your natural father is a Berserker?"

"It's the Berserker madness they'll be concerned with. They will believe I will succumb to the madness and it will forever taint the Ahlstrom line and dilute the power of my heir, making any future daughters of mine lesser vessels who will beget lesser vessels and so on until there is no longer a queen strong enough to support all the Nine Realms."

"I suppose that is a valid concern, though the thinking behind it is rather backward." Druan pulled me into the circle of his arms as we hid among the shadows behind the stone pillars of the terrace.

"If anything, I think my Berserker half is what has made me a stronger vessel than Sylvi. But it will take time and a lot of patience to overcome generations of prejudice." I was too ashamed to admit I'd once held some of those same prejudices. But that was before I experienced my Berserker magic for myself.

"I understand your concerns for Pasha." Druan released me and leaned against a stone pillar. "But you have to understand she is so much more than the animal she appears to be. All kindreds are special. Their magic protects them. Your council may wish to eliminate her, but she will prove harder to kill than they might expect."

"They will have to go through me to get to her." I leaned into Druan, letting my cheek press against his heart. I smiled when his arms enveloped me again.

"And me, as well as any other Berserker and kindred among your people. I can't imagine you are the only Valkyrie with

Berserker heritage. Others have surely had to hide their nature before you."

"The magic is nothing like I thought," I admitted. The anger and rage that accompanied my Berserker magic didn't come from a place of madness or even from the beast that was my kindred. It was a righteous kind of rage that took more self-control to manage than any Valkyrie could imagine.

"Having Pasha as my kindred is an honor. I know that now. And being able to borrow her strength and passion, letting my kindred's instincts merge with my Valkyrie's, is an incredible, beautiful thing, and I've only just begun to explore this side of my nature."

"And it will only serve to make you more powerful in a way Neela will never expect." Druan pulled away. "But we have to practice." He held out his hand in invitation. "And we aren't going to find that kind of privacy here."

I hesitated to take his hand. I wanted to trust him with everything. I would need his guidance in the coming days and weeks. My Berserker magic was only just beginning to manifest as it should have when I came of age. My time in the human realm delayed this part of my magic. A part no Valkyrie could teach me.

"All right, let's go." I took his hand. "But I have something more to tell you." I cast a look around, searching for eavesdroppers. "I can't risk telling you here, though."

We left the terrace and crossed the gardens where the land began to rise in a rocky slope that led to the Armur Mountains at the back of the Citadel. The old training grounds sat high among the ruins of the first fortress that served the Valkyries after they survived the final battle.

Beyond the rocky terrain, the forest closed in around us and Sameerah gave an irreverent squawk as she landed on Druan's shoulder.

"Sorry, Sam. I know you don't like the palace but that's where I sleep." He stroked the gyrfalcon's soft gray feathers. "And no, I will not sleep in the forest with you. You can fly to my window anytime you want."

"She's beautiful." I admired his kindred and the special relationship they had. It seemed he spent more time arguing with the bird and letting her have her way than anything else.

"She has a big enough head already, so don't be liberal with your praise." His eyes darkened for a moment before hardening into the clear golden eyes of a raptor. I shivered at the sheer amount of strength that seemed to radiate from him and I wondered how his Druid magic worked with his Berserker nature. It was a strange combination of the powerful nurturing magic of the Druids with the brute strength of the hardened Berserkers. He must always feel at war with the two sides of his nature. I wondered if it would be like that for me too.

As we neared the old training grounds, I let my guard down. We were the only ones out here and I trusted Druan with my biggest secret of all. I had to.

"It will be good for us to practice here together without any distractions. Just the two of us."

I loved that he thought of us as a team. A we. There was too much on the line with Neela for me to dig too far into those feelings. But later. After. I definitely wanted to unpack those new emotions.

Druan paced to the center of the training ring we'd used the last time we were here. "The more you become comfortable merged with your kindred, I think you'll feel less concerned with what your council thinks about it."

"Honestly, I don't care what anyone thinks of me or my Berserker magic. I don't care if they whisper behind my back and call me a half-breed. Let them." I moved to stand in front of him. "I have bigger things to worry about. Like Pasha's safety for one, but also ... what my people will do to Mother when they find out she gave birth to King Hagen's Berserker twins—"

"King Hagen?" Druan's eyes widened, and he took a step back, Sameerah fading from his eyes. "Twins? How? What? *He's* your father?" A look of disgust drifted across his face and dread filled me.

"Oh no." I let a hand drift to cover my mouth. The mouth Druan had kissed not so long ago. "Please, no." I closed my eyes fighting back my revulsion. "Please don't tell me he's your father too?"

"No, no-no. Not that, thank the gods. It's just—that makes this a lot more complicated. You're Vendela's sister. Technically, you or even Ben—assuming he's your twin—could seize Hagen's throne, and Dela deserves better than that."

"She is his only legitimate heir. She should be queen. And I certainly don't want a third throne when I really don't even want one. Between trying to rule the Valkyries and eventually ascending as High Queen of the Nine Realms, I've got quite enough on my plate already."

"If you don't want it, why are you fighting so hard to take your throne back from Neela?" Druan sank to the ground, pulling me down with him.

"I'm the only one who can do it. I may not feel equal to the task. It might be the last thing I really want for myself. But it's not all about me and what I want. It's about serving my people. All of them. I owe it to our world to fix my mess and step up, whether I want to or not." Pasha nudged my shoulder as she lowered herself to the ground in front of me, letting her head fall into my lap. I was pretty sure that meant I was fully forgiven for hurting her feelings.

"Esben?" Druan pulled a knee up toward his chest, resting his elbow against it. His long dark hair fell down his back, the top half twisted back in his usual braids. "I knew that kid was more trouble than he was worth. It will be dangerous for him if he even survives Neela's prison."

My eyes snapped up from my lap to meet his gaze. "He isn't like the legends say. He doesn't have the ambition or the drive to reach for power." I studied Druan's face for clues to what he was thinking, but he wasn't one to wear his thoughts on his face.

"The boy just wants a family."

"Yes." I let out a relieved breath. "That is the only thing Ben has ever wanted. Now that he has a mother and sisters, I don't think he would ever risk anything to jeopardize that."

"I can better understand your desire to hide this secret." He dropped his gaze to the ground. "You want to protect Pasha, but you also have to think about Ben."

"And what my people will do to my family for concealing this secret for nearly twenty years. They could execute my entire family for treason if I don't handle this revelation with the utmost care." I scooted closer to his side, placing one hand on his arm while I let the other sink into Pasha's soft white fur.

"If I can get through this battle without revealing my Berserker nature then I will do it, to protect my family and Pasha."

Protect. Pasha stood and growled deep in her chest. I could almost feel the vibration of it in my own.

"There it is." Druan laid his hand on top of mine, his eyes full of wonder. "Thank you for being honest with me and for trusting me with your secrets. I can respect that. And it seems Pasha can too."

Fight. Pasha nudged her forehead against mine. *Win.*

I leaned toward her, meeting her fierce blue gaze. "Pride." I pressed my forehead to hers. "I'm proud to call you my kindred, Pash. Kindred, prowl, and family. I need you in my corner if we're going to make it through this." Pasha's deep, satisfied purr was response enough.

"Just promise me one thing, Thea." Druan pulled me back up to my feet, tugging me toward him.

"What?" I took in a sharp breath at the golden glint in his eye that reminded me he was much more than just a man, that a predator's nature lurked within him.

"If it comes down to defeating Neela or dying, do not hesitate to call on your Berserker magic, merge with Pasha and kill that woman. Whatever happens after, I give you my word, I will not let anything happen to you or your family. But you have to survive." He pulled me close, burying his face against my neck. "I can't have been branded for you for nothing." His whisper was warm against my ear, sending a shiver through me.

"It's a deal." I leaned back to brush the rough stubble of his jaw with my fingertips.

"Your eyes are blue." Druan smiled, sweeping the hair away from my face.

"My eyes are green." I frowned.

"Not when you've merged with your kindred." Druan scratched Pasha behind her ears, and I felt a whisper of the touch myself. "And you've held onto it all this time we've been talking."

"We did it, Pash." I held my hand out and Pasha nuzzled it with her velvety nose. "Thank you for trusting me, girl."

"You need to run with your kindred. It will be good for you both." Druan pulled away from me and gave me a gentle push toward the forest. "Sameerah and I will watch over you both and make sure no one sees you." The musical quality of his voice wrapped around me like a soft blanket.

"Let's go, Pasha." I took off up the trail into the mountains, my kindred quickly charging ahead. Merged with the skýja leopard, I was faster and stronger than I'd ever been. My claws and talons were sharp as steel. I leaped across the rocky terrain, following Pasha's lead. Still, I couldn't keep up with her.

As my Valkyrie form burst out of me and my wings unfurled, I leaped into the air with a flap of my wings. Pasha roared her approval, running faster into the mountains beyond the cover of the forest. I followed her, staying low to the ground, testing my new feline reflexes. Every movement felt more fluid and graceful as my muscles bent and flexed. Pasha's strength flooded my body and I felt like I could conquer anything. Neela didn't stand a chance.

CHAPTER 31

"You agreed to what?" Princess Morgana gave me a dark look. Her golden Druid face paint stood out against her tawny skin. The day of Ben's execution and my battle with Neela had arrived and Morgana and our co-army had gathered in the fertile valley just beyond the Ivory Forest in Vahland Reach.

"It's going to be a single fight between us, winner takes the power of the gods, Ben, and the throne."

"She won't stop until she kills you." Morgana's face paled and her eyes filled with worry.

"That's why I plan to win." I straightened my shoulders, pulling my cloak around me for warmth.

"So you're just going to let her walk away after you defeat her?"

"Of course not. I have a plan for that. And I'll need your help, but first, I have a battle to win.

"Neela's arrived." Druan stepped into the tent.

"I'll be with the army," Morgana said. "The moment she falls, her soldiers might retaliate. We will be ready to respond."

"Her army is made up of mercenaries and slaves," Druan said. "They scatter to the winds when Neela loses this battle."

"Then may the winds be with you, my sister." Morgana gave a formal bow before she left me alone in the tent with Druan.

"I'm freaking out." I turned to face him. "Why did I think I could do this?"

Pasha poked her head through the tent flaps, hissing at Druan like it was his fault her kindred was upset.

"Stop, Thea." He grabbed my arms, running his palms down to my wrists and back. "You are prepared for this."

"I'm just … I'm just me." My shoulders slumped and I dropped my head so I didn't have to see the confidence radiating in his eyes. "I'm the girl who runs when things get too hard."

"No. You are Alithea Viktory Skuld Ahlstrom—She who is becoming—the rightful Queen Heir of Valsgard, future ruler of the High Council of the Nine Realms and a Berserker Warrior. You were born for this fight."

"If I puke on your nice boots, I'm really sorry." I stepped closer and Druan wrapped his arms around me, chuckling.

"I will never understand your sense of humor." I could hear the smile in his voice.

"Alithea the Queen Heir is ready to die for her people, but … Thea the girl who likes funky human boots and soft t-shirts, is so not ready to die before she gets to know what this is." I gazed up at him.

Druan tipped my head back and kissed me, his lips soft and full against mine at first before urgency won over. My arms snaked around his neck and he kissed me deeper, like he never wanted to let me go. But I couldn't lose my head over a handsome warrior now. I broke away, pressing my forehead against his.

"I don't know what this is either, Thea," he whispered, "but I do know one thing." He pressed his lips against mine. "I was branded for you and it made me hate you for a long time. For stealing my choice from me."

I gasped at the words he used. I'd said those same words to Mother so many times. All my resistance to the Chosen Sons came down to the choice I wanted to make for myself. That Druan understood that so well without needing me to explain meant the world to me.

"If given the opportunity now, I would choose you." His lips softened into a teasing smile. "The woman who is becoming. The one who will understand like no other what it's like to live stuck between two kingdoms, belonging to both and neither at the same time. The one who tries my patience and leaves me guessing." He uttered a few Druid words of magic I didn't understand, but the melody of his voice made my heart race nonetheless.

"What was that?" I whispered, hesitant to leave the comfort of his embrace.

"A prayer for courage and protection for the coming battle."

"Thank you. I need all the help I can get."

"It was a prayer for myself, Thea." He grinned and rubbed his nose against mine, his full mouth twisted into a mischievous grin. "I am positive you will win, but I am also positive you will take risks that will make me want to strangle your pretty neck." I adored this teasing, not-so-serious side of him and I wanted more. So much more.

"You say that like you think you know me." I teased him back.

"I know you. And I know you have more courage than you know what to do with. You think you're the girl who runs away when things get too hard, but you're not. You're the woman who stands and fights for what she believes in, even when you stand alone."

All the breath rushed out of me at his words. "Courage seems to have failed me now." I wanted so much to stay right here in this tent with Druan and let Neela have it all, but the queen in me could never allow that.

"You need to win this battle. I'd like to spend a lot more time kissing that smart mouth of yours." His eyes danced with humor and something I wasn't yet ready to put a name to.

"Part of you must still hate me," I blurted. This was not at all what I needed to focus on minutes before the battle of my life.

Druan smiled that infuriating, arrogant smile of his. "You grew on me. Kind of like a fungus. Pasha helps; I can see her in your eyes now. She settles your wild spirit." He chuckled softly. "You should know that is normally supposed to work the other way."

"Thank you." I wrapped my arms around his waist and kissed his cheek.

"For what?"

"For the distraction." I stepped away and ducked through the tent flaps to meet my enemy.

"Make sure you come back to me, Thea," Druan called after me.

"I will." I smiled, making my way down to the battlefield with Pasha at my side.

We like him?

I glanced down at my kindred. That was the most she'd ever said to me.

"Yes, I think we like him very much."

"Welcome." Morgana stood at the center of the grassy field just beyond the palace gates. "We have gathered today for a battle between potential queens." Her voice resonated across the gathered crowd, amplified by her Druid magic.

I stood alone on the edge of the field, wishing Pasha was by my side, but she would come to me after the fight began. I'd left her with Vendela and Druan, out of sight with the other kindred.

I had expected Neela's council of elders and likely some of the nobles to come observe the battle, but I hadn't expected it to turn into an arena fight. It seemed as if Neela had compelled the whole of Vahland Reach to attend. The atmosphere was charged with celebration and anticipation of the violence to come.

Together with Morgana's troops, a sea of Druids and Valkyries had gathered to witness the demise of a queen. It remained to be seen which way it would go.

It gave me a sense of peace to know even now, Sylvi and Astrid were preparing those inside the Citadel for evacuation. It was their only chance to put the hard years of siege behind them.

Not all present here today fell under the sway of Neela's magic. I noted the bonds, some like streaks of blood, others like cold shadows tying most of the citizens and villagers to their Warder queen. I also noticed the lack of bonds among the nobles.

I even saw money changing hands as wealthy onlookers placed bets on the outcome. If I rose as the victor today, I would have a long road ahead to deal with their disloyalty. Perhaps it would be time to replace the heads of the noble houses with those of my own generation, allowing them to ascend with me. If I survived the next few hours … or minutes.

"This is to be a fight for the power of the gods," Morgana continued. "She who drains her opponent of power will rise as the strongest vessel, queen of Valkyries and of the High Council of the Nine Realms. It will *not* be a fight to the death. Queen Brenhilde's council, as well as Neela's, have agreed to recognize the winner—whomever she may be. The loser will be exiled, and the extent of her punishment to be determined by the victor. The prisoner, Svana or Esben, will be freed when their queen wins."

I gasped at the sight of my brother entering the clearing with one of Neela's men. He was beaten and bruised with no trace of the mischievous prankster my twin had always been. His condition was a sharp reminder of what was on the line today.

Svana stood behind me with Vanya, perfectly healthy and well cared for as agreed.

The crowd cheered as Neela made her way to the makeshift arena from her tent. Already in her Valkyrie form, her dark auburn hair fell in a curtain to blend with her blood-red wings trailing behind her. Her coloring was shocking in its beauty, marred only by the burns that destroyed one side of her left wing. The scars of her face and arms were concealed behind the golden armor she never seemed to be without.

She was a warrior fit for battle. Her lithe form moved like a predator. With a sword at her hip and a golden shield glimmering in the sunlight, Neela walked like a legend of the old Valkyries. The first generation warriors who saved all of Valsgard from ruin. For a moment, I could almost see the situation from Neela's point of view. If she hadn't used her Warder magic to enslave my people, I could easily bow out of this race for the throne. But I could not trust her to do what was best for the people of the Nine Realms. She'd shown she was capable of only ruthlessness.

As Neela neared, she passed by Esben, kicking him in the back and sending him sprawling to the ground in a bruised and bloodied heap.

"That is how we treat the forsworn sons of Valkyries. Evil creatures to the core. This one should never have lived to see his first shift." She kicked him again and Ben coughed, blood spurting from his lips as he curled in on himself.

"You were supposed to care for him as I cared for your mother," I said through clenched teeth.

"I'm pretty sure we fed him." Neela shrugged, her dark eyes boring into mine.

"Do you both agree to the terms as I have outlined them?" Morgana moved between us, demanding our attention.

But I couldn't take my eyes from my brother's face. Anger welled within me and I embraced it, letting it flood my body and bolster my strength. Pasha danced along the edges of my awareness, but I didn't let her in. It wasn't time. I hoped it wouldn't be necessary. Instead, I embraced my Valkyrie as the change swept through me, my back splitting open to reveal my wings.

"Yes, Princess Morgana, I agree to the terms." I gave a nod to my ally.

"Fine, agreed," Neela said, folding her arms over her chest.

Like Neela, I wore protective armor over my chest and arms. But where Neela came armed with a sword and shield, I carried my golden axes. They once belonged to my father, Elias, and I hoped they would protect me today. My wings fanned out behind me, a cascade of fine feathers of black and silver ending in silvery white tips. Elders Vanya and Lena approached me to dress my wings in supple leather armor that would protect me in flight without weighing me down like my battle armor would.

"Let's get on with it then," Neela said.

"Take your places on opposite ends of the arena," Morgana instructed.

Turning my back on Neela, I moved to the outer edge of the field, the heaviness of my wings dragging behind me. I took my stance and waited.

Morgana held her hands to the sky. "Let the true queen prevail."

As her hands dropped and she moved out of the way, I charged across the field toward my opponent, all trace of my earlier fear gone as I leaped into the air and brought my axe down on Neela, crashing into her shield before she'd managed to get off the ground.

"Is that all you've got?" Neela's laughter was swallowed up by the cheers and boos from the crowd below.

"I'm just getting started." I brought my second axe up in a sweeping arc, catching her arm and drawing first blood.

Neela shrieked in outrage more than hurt as our vast wings beat against the air and we gained height.

All around, Valkyries took to the skies, circling us for a better view, but I ignored the biting remarks and even the cheers. It was just me and Neela now.

The thick oily darkness I now recognized as my Berserker magic rose within me, wrapping around my Valkyrie Magic. This time it didn't feel like it wanted to smother me so much as protect me. I recognized Pasha's magic waiting in the shadows, eager to pounce, but I wasn't ready to merge with my kindred. Not yet. With a powerful swipe of my talons, I raked across Neela's face, tearing at the mask she hid behind. The golden half mask tumbled to the ground, revealing the ruin of her face beneath.

Neela gave a satisfying shriek of indignation as she tore after me. I sank into a dive, streaking ahead of her as her blasphemous cursing echoed behind me. She was volatile and quick to anger. I could use that against her.

"Fight me, Alithea, you coward!"

Ignoring her, I searched for the bonds only I could see. Streaks of blood and shadow followed Neela through the skies. Repulsive puppet strings she used to manipulate those who had refused to follow her. I dropped below her and slowed my pace, allowing her to pull ahead as I embraced the burn of my magic, letting it fill me.

"What are you playing at, Princess?" Neela pulled up short, hovering in the air above me.

With a victorious grin, I studied the strands of her magic, whispering a plea for guidance as I gathered the streaks of blood and shadow in my arms, letting the burn ignite them. Raking my talons through layers of blood and smoky shadow, I hacked away at her magic, watching strand after strand disappear in red and black vaporous clouds. Blood and grime sprayed my face and coated my hands until only the thick cords of the strongest and oldest of her bonds remained.

"What are you doing?" Neela's eyes widened and she made a dive for me the moment she realized the bonds were breaking all around her.

"Caring for my people." I raised my axe to block Neela's sword and maneuvered behind her, crashing into her weaker left side.

Neela floundered for a moment, buying me enough time to sever the old bonds with a slash of the burn.

"How dare you!" Neela slammed into me.

The crowd fell utterly silent below as I grappled with Neela in the air and we began to fall toward the ground.

"She's freed us." The shouts of the Valkyries in the air reached my ears. The same women who had cursed my name and shouted jeers at me only moments ago were now crying out my name.

"Pull up, your Majesty!"

"Don't let her drag you to the ground, Princess!"

"You have the advantage in the sky! Her left wing is weak."

With a kick to her chest, I broke away from Neela and soared higher to circle her, looking for my next move.

Neela's magic illuminated her aura in a bright glow of light as she worked quickly to reform the bonds I'd just broken, but my sisters in the sky evaded her.

"Fly, sisters!" I shouted after them. "Don't let her ensnare you again."

Just as quickly as I'd severed Neela's magic, freeing dozens of those milling in the crowd below, she'd recaptured them.

"You really can see magic." Neela taunted. "Go ahead, break the bonds if you wish. It's only a matter of time before I enslave your people again and again."

Rage seemed to vibrate from Neela's body as I circled below her, severing new bonds as quickly as she could make them. Below, I caught sight of Druan and Vendela helping those I'd freed flee the arena. It bolstered my confidence to know some would make it.

"Enough!" Neela dropped down to face me. "Fight me and be done with it." She charged me and I fell into a rhythm of defensive battle, letting her come at me only to evade her or clash weapons with her and retreat.

She was furious.

But I was baiting her.

Every time she came at me, my hold on her strengthened as I pulled on the power, siphoning from her. That trickle turned into a stream and like before, she still hadn't noticed what I was doing.

"If you think to tire me with your boring attack and retreat maneuvers, we're going to be here all day." Neela shook her head. "I will still kill you come nightfall."

Ignoring her taunts, I pulled on the power, calling it to me. Every single person across all of Valsgard needed the power of the gods to fuel their own magic. It belonged to everyone and it was the vessel's responsibility to hold it for them. Not just to make herself more powerful, but to hold what was left of our world together so we would all have a future the gods would have stolen from us were it not for my ancestor who received the Allfather's blessing during his final moments.

Neela would use the power to manipulate and destroy, but I would die before I allowed her to succeed. For most of my life the power of the gods flowed through me. Rarely had I siphoned deliberately, and never to this extent. But I knew how to call the power to me. To let it collect within me for others to use. I would bet everything I had that Neela didn't know how to siphon with purpose.

Now that I had a hold on Neela, I let the floodgates open, taking as much as I could hold.

The blood rushed from Neela's face as she crashed into me, her sword swinging wildly, grazing my armored wing.

And then she fell, spiraling toward the ground.

I rushed after her, seeing a quick end at last.

Neela floundered, unable to get her wings righted before she crashed into the ground close to the Druid army where Morgana and Elder Vanya waited with the prisoners. A look of terror flashed across Neela's face as I landed beside her. She knew she was going to lose on an epic scale now that I'd nearly drained her of the power.

"Yield." I demanded, triumph flooding my body as my people roared their approval and those loyal to Neela tried to slink away into the crowd.

"Never." Neela stood and nodded to her mother, and the two came to some unspoken agreement.

In the next moment, Svana collapsed. Dead.

"What did you do?" I gaped at the still figure of my aunt. She'd sacrificed her life and her power for her daughter without a moment's hesitation. I could see strength returning to Neela.

The crowd screamed in indignation and I heard the distant roar of my kindred, begging for the merge.

Horrified, I backed away, losing my grip on Neela's power. I nearly had the win within my grasp, but with Svana' sacrifice, whatever power she'd held transferred to her daughter, bringing us right back where we started. Except now, I was the exhausted one.

"Some things are worth a sacrifice." Neela charged toward me, brandishing her sword. I could see the strength of her mother's life force flashing in her eyes.

I faltered, raising my axe to shield her blow. The impact vibrated through me, sending me slamming into the ground. Svana had never been a strong vessel, but taking on her mother's life force had given Neela a burst of strength I couldn't match.

With a powerful kick, Neela sent my axe sailing across the dirt arena. I scrambled back to my feet. As I aimed to strike back with my remaining axe, Neela's shield came crashing down on my head.

I kicked out, sweeping Neela's feet out from under her. We grappled on the ground and I cried out when her blade bit into my thigh. I was no match for Neela now. I needed to put some distance between us until the power surge subsided and we were more on even footing again.

Taking to the skies, I outmaneuvered my enemy, trying to regroup as I soared up into the clouds. Blood gushed from my thigh and I felt my strength slipping.

I needed Pasha's strength.

It would change my life forever, putting my Berserker heritage on display, but I didn't hesitate.

Now. Pasha roared from her place beside Druan. *The red one must die.*

I reached for my kindred, merging with her in an instant. Strength and rage flooded my senses and I let out a roar that sounded foreign coming from my throat.

Gathering my wings close, I fell through the air, crashing into Neela. Sinking my talons into her, I grabbed on, flinging her with my impossible strength. Her body went limp and she lost control, her arms and wings flailing out.

Our eyes met and she saw my secret immediately. "You." She gasped as warring emotions played across her face. From triumph to fear and everything in between.

"She's a Berserker half-breed." Neela shouted to my sisters still trying to keep watch over me.

"Lies." They refused to believe it, but I could hear the hesitation in their voices.

"The red one must die." The voice that came out of me was rough and the words felt unnatural on my tongue. I gave myself over to the anger and the shadows of my Berserker magic and charged my enemy.

My axe sank into Neela's shoulder, cutting through muscle and bone.

She shrieked, twisting away from me for an instant before dropping onto my back and smashing her knee into my left wing, right behind the joint I'd only recently dislocated. Something snapped and scorching heat blazed along my wing.

I cried out as I struggled in the air, my wing useless as I plummeted toward the ground.

CHAPTER 32

I woke in darkness, my body on fire, every part of me crying out in agony.

"She's awake," someone whispered.

"Thea, darling, don't move."

"Mother?" The word left my lips sounding garbled. Pain exploded in my jaw. I tried to move, but my face stuck to the grimy stone floor.

"You're severely injured, try not to move."

"What happened?" The last thing I remembered was tumbling toward the ground.

"You fell from a great height after Neela broke your wing. If you could manage to shift, it should help with the pain."

"Shift." I closed my eyes, covering my face with my hands.

If Mother suggested I shift with a broken wing then it was bad. I would probably never fly again.

"Where are we?"

"The dungeons. Esben is here too."

"Ben?" I cried, tears burning my eyes.

"I'm here, Thea." His voice was ragged and raw.

"I'm sorry." I failed. The only question now was why I wasn't dead yet and how Neela had gotten her hands on Mother.

"There is to be a trial in a few days. We will likely be executed in a very public way."

"Mother." Hot tears ran down my face. "How are you here?" She was supposed to be with Astrid and Sylvi, evacuating with our people while Neela was distracted with me.

"I couldn't leave. I am still queen and I will not abandon this city until succession is secured. Though your sister put up a good fight before she finally agreed to leave."

"They had spies inside the Citadel, didn't they?"

Mother nodded. "They came for me as soon as the others left. I surrendered, knowing they would cast me into the dungeon with Esben." Mother scooted closer to me to peer through the bars between our cells.

"It isn't over yet, darling. We have time to make a plan."

"My body is broken. I can't even move. What can I possibly do but roll over and die?" With Sylvi and Astrid safely seeking allies outside our borders, there was nothing left to do. War would come for my people. But it was over for me and those of my family under Neela's thumb.

"It's not over till the fat lady sings," my mother said.

I snorted at that. "You've been listening to Ben."

"She's right, Thea. We need a plan," a new voice joined the discussion.

"Grandmother?" I tried to sit up, but my limbs didn't want to cooperate. I lay on my stomach, scrambling across the floor on my elbows to reach the bars of the cell beside me. "What are you doing here? I thought you were part of Neela's council."

"I was. But I made a plea for your life, begging Neela to send healers so you wouldn't be in pain. My estranged granddaughter took that as a betrayal and sent me to join you. But that was one of her many, many mistakes." Agertha reached through the bars to grasp my hand. "All is not lost, darling girl. I'm just sorry I wasn't there when you returned."

"She is your granddaughter too," I murmured.

"That was not why I stayed with her, Thea. I love all of my grandchildren, but I have never condoned Neela's actions. I stayed because I feared this day would come. It's been years since I've deliberately siphoned the power. When my daughter became queen, my time passed and I no longer needed to serve as a vessel. Fortunately for me, Brenna was strong enough to take the power she needed to rule, but also left me enough to live out my days in comfort. Not every former queen has been so lucky. But Neela discredited me. I may be old and past my usefulness, but I am still a royal vessel of the gods and I have regained strength in the many years since I survived the transfer of power that made my daughter queen."

Agertha grasped my hand tightly. "In a moment, I am going to pass what surplus of power I have collected from her over the past few years to you and I don't want to hear a protest. It will leave me very weak for a time, but I will recover. The surge will force your change and my healing magic will take care of your most serious injuries. I can't give you much, but I can at least give you a fighting chance. From what Ben has told us, you were winning before she and Svana resorted to their cheating schemes."

"No, Grandmother." I tried to pull my hand away, but I was too weak. "I can't imagine it will be enough to change our fate. Save your strength for whatever comes next for you. She might not execute you."

"Hush, my girl. I've made up my mind and you're our best chance of survival. You are by far the strongest of the Ahlstrom Dynasty."

"You can't mean that when we're sitting in our own dungeon and another of our family has the throne. She is strong, Grandmother. Much stronger than I."

"I would gladly give my life for you the way Svana did for Neela, but if I am to heal you in the process, I need to survive the ordeal. And as I am rather fond of living, I'll save a drop or two for myself. And before you protest, this isn't just for you. This is for our people. All of them. You must defeat her before it is too late and you can't do that with broken bones. You have the magic your natural father gave you. Use it and do not fear it." Agertha gripped my hand, hers burning hot against my chilled skin.

"Please don't. You might not survive, Grandmother." Tears rolled down my face and my shoulders shook with sobs. "What if I can't control it once the transfer begins? What if I drain you?"

"I think you are strong enough where it counts to stop. That kind of strength comes from your head and your heart. And if the worst does happen, I'll always be with you, my girl. Either way, you will go and be the queen our people deserve."

Ben cleared his throat. "Can we pause the sentimental boohoos for a quick second?" He raised his hand like he had a question in class. "It's sweet and all, but totally unnecessary." I could just make out the smirk on his face. He was up to something.

As Grandmother's hand loosened around mine, I snatched it away. "What have you done?"

"You say that like I've committed a felony." Ben sounded affronted, which meant he'd definitely been up to something.

Likely something that would get him killed before this was all over.

I stared at my brother in the cell across from mine. He was too relaxed for our dire situation.

"Because you are always up to something." I winced at the pain that radiated from my broken wing down the side of my body. I must have landed on that side because everything was broken, from my shattered wrist down to my ankle. No part of my body responded to my attempts to move off of the filthy, cold stone floor.

"Settle down, Alithea," Mother whispered. "You're going to hurt yourself further."

"I believe Esben has something to add?" Grandmother watched him through the bars of her cell, a wry smile on her face.

"You know being a guest of Neela's was no picnic." Ben rubbed his bruised jaw, his chains rattling against the floor. "She's enjoyed visiting me down here multiple times a day. I think she's got crush on me and has a funny way of showing it. But I don't think she's put it together yet that we're actually cousins and that's super gross. She can be a bit dim."

"This one definitely gets his sense of humor from me," Grandmother said with a chuckle.

"And that girl gets her jollies kicking a defenseless man's rear end. You have no idea the things she did, chaining me to the wall like a dog only to carve up my body with her knife. I have scars that aren't even the sexy kind."

"Why do you sound positively delighted about your experiences with her?" I wanted to carve bits out of Neela's hide for what she'd done to Ben, but at the same time I wanted to shake him so he'd get to the point already.

Ben stretched out, leaning his back up against the damp brick wall. "Let's just say Grams and I had the same idea." He raised his arms over his head, wincing at the pull of the chains on his wrists. "Great minds think alike, and all that." He gave our grandmother a wink.

"What do you mean?" I frowned at him in confusion.

"Jeez, you Valkyrie women are kinda thick sometimes. You cling to your traditions so hard, you can't see the light of day at the end of your noses. You treat me like pretty wallpaper. Nice to look at but no substance."

"Esben, don't say such things." Mother sounded shocked. "You know how much you mean to us."

"Of course I know, Mom. How could you not adore me? But I swear every human man needs to take a trip here just once to experience what it must be like for human women among the patriarchy. Your poor men have to work three times as hard to get anywhere in this society."

"Get to the point, Esben," I growled.

"Fine, ruin my fun, sister. "It's just you've all forgotten one very simple detail. I. Am. A. Valkyrie. Royal. Same as Thea. Same as Neela. If I wanted, I could throw my hat into this seriously messed up arena and try to take the throne for myself. But I am way too lazy to put forth that much effort. I'm more of the flit behind the scenes, espionage kind of guy."

"Spit it out, Ben. What have you been up to?" I still couldn't fathom what he thought he could do to help this situation.

"Like I said, Neela visited me often and for long periods of time." He shrugged. "And if I am a prince of this realm, brother to its next queen, that makes me a vessel too."

I gasped along with Mother and Grandmother. How could we have all neglected to see it?

"I'm so stupid." I pressed my burning forehead against the cool stone floor. We were all so used to men not having access to the power, I missed what was right in front of me.

"Yeah, it turns out I can siphon just as well as the rest of you. It kind of comes naturally. I didn't know what it was at first. I felt stronger, faster, and it was like I could feel the blood rushing in my veins. Heady stuff, this power of the gods."

Mother and Grandmother exchanged looks of horror, but I knew my brother had more self-control than any other Valkyrie this side of the bridge.

"Relax, don't get your hair in a twist. I'm not power hungry, but I can see how some of my kind might have let it go to their heads in the past. But they must have lived in a world where they already had everything except the respect of their female counterparts, and that likely festered within them all their lives. And then there's someone like me who only ever wanted to belong to a family. If I have that, I don't need or want this power."

My heart broke for him and all the years we'd been separated while he'd lived alone. Ben was my twin, and I would fight anyone who tried to take him from me again. "You've been siphoning from Neela all this time? How did you learn?" I grew up learning how to draw in the power and give it to others, passing it to whomever needed it the most with a cautious hand. But it was a difficult task to pass the power to another vessel. Particularly when one was more powerful than the other.

"Like I said, it's been instinct. It took some time, but I figured it out as I learned more about what a vessel is. In fact, I've been accidentally siphoning since I stepped foot in Valsgard weeks ago. I'm probably just as strong as you and Neela at this point. But in true Valkyrie form, you've all underestimated the handsome man in the room."

"Do you realize what it means to pass a significant amount of the power to another vessel?" I asked softly, sharing a look with Grandmother. "You seriously think I'm going to let you make that kind of sacrifice?"

"Absolutely not," Mother echoed my concerns.

"I can pass the power to you, Thea. I trust you not to kill me in the process. Let me play my part."

"The histories do claim a twin brother of a female can bring her balance and amplify her power," Grandmother said. "He might just manage it."

"I can do this, Thea. Take whatever you need from me. I'm perfectly happy just being a Valkyrie. I don't need magical abilities or power I don't even know what to do with. And I certainly don't need a throne to warm my bum."

I gripped the bars of my cell, hope surging in my chest. "I could kiss you, Esben Ahlstrom."

"No thanks, I have a mad crush on a dragon. But if you'd like to repay me, get me the hell out of here, please."

"You and Grandmother may have saved us all."

"Come dear, let's get you healed." Grandmother stretched her arm through the bars to take my hand again. "Your vessel will draw from me during healing and I need you to let it."

I grasped her cool hand with hesitation. "Ben, that whole 'you temper me' thing, let's try putting that to the test here. Don't let me kill her."

"I won't let you. I kind of like the idea of having a trouble-making old grandma to hang out with."

"Who are you calling old?" Grandmother shot him a glare. "I'll have you know this old lady still has her fair share of lovers coming to call."

"Ew, Gram, I didn't need to know that."

"Well, now that you do, see that you don't drain me of my life force. There are several gentleman who wouldn't be very happy with you for it."

"Mother, you are too much." Brenna chuckled softly.

"We've got this, Grandma." Ben scooted as close to the front of his cell as he could with the chains attached to his wrists and ankles. "It's okay if I call you Grandma, isn't it?"

"Handsome grandson of mine, you may call me whatever pleases you." She squeezed my hand, a twinkle in her eye. "And thank you for bringing him home, Thea. It does this *old* heart so much good to know him."

"Mine too," I whispered, terrified of what I was about to do. What if I killed her? I'd never be able to live with myself.

"Brace yourself, Thea. My healing magic does not have a delicate touch for broken bones and we cannot alert the guards with your screams. You must remain quiet." Without warning, Agertha's hand blazed hot as the power of the gods began to pass from her to me, seeking refuge within the nearest vessel.

My back arched as Grandmother's magic shot through me, healing the worst of my injuries like liquid fire burning away all traces of infection from a festered wound.

I choked back a scream as my broken wing snapped back into place and the shattered bones of my jaw and wrist shifted and fused. Darkness clouded my vision and I bit the inside of my cheek to keep from crying out as her magic scoured my body. Blood filled my mouth for a moment, but then that too healed.

As the pain receded, the power flowed into me, strengthening and restoring me. She'd taken much from Neela, and likely Svana too, over time. But I wanted more. Needed more. It was my nature to fill the vessel within. But a nagging thought in the back of my mind told me to stop. I just couldn't remember why.

"Thea, let go." Esben said softly. "You've taken enough."

But it wasn't enough. Not nearly enough to match myself against Neela and win. It would take so much more.

"Release her," Ben commanded, his voice harsh and veiled in shadows that reached into me, severing the connection between me and Grandmother.

With a gasp, I lurched away, realizing what I'd almost done. What Ben had stopped me from doing.

Grandmother's limp form slumped forward and I sat up, scrambling to slip my arms through the bars of my cell. "Gram?" I grasped her hand, warm to the touch. She stirred weakly, and her eyes opened to slits.

"See. I knew you could do it." She let out a sigh and her eyes closed with a mischievous smile on her face.

"Is she okay?" I sobbed, trying to find a pulse in her wrist.

"She's fine," Mother said from her cell. "She's only passed out. She will sleep a long time while she recovers."

Her faint pulse throbbed beneath my fingers and I let out a breath, laying my cheek against the bars of my cell. "I will make you proud, Grandmother." I pressed a kiss against my fingertips and laid it against my grandmother's round cheek.

Sitting back, I wiped the tears from my face, feeling stronger and clearheaded. "One down." Maybe we would find a way through this after all.

"Wait." I sat up straight, my head finally clear from the fog of pain. "Neela hasn't bonded us with her Warder magic. Why has she put us in the dungeon cells and not in a world of her making?"

"We haven't figured that out yet," Mother said.

"I don't really understand what her Warder magic can do," Ben said, "though I've seen how she enslaves her freaky little mind puppets."

"In Vöstland, the royal Warders and their nobility are prison wardens. They take in prisoners from all over the Nine Realms. Except their prisons don't consist of walls and bars like this one. When a prisoner falls under their control, the Warder *is* the prison. The Warder can enslave lesser prisoners like you've seen Neela do, but he can also cast criminals and even those who have personally wronged him into another realm. One of his making. And what the Warders dream up to persecute their prisoners can be far worse than death."

"And you say 'he' because female Warders don't have the same power?" Ben asked hopefully.

"Warder women aren't normally allowed to wield such power over men," I explained. "Only their children." My face twisted in disgust. "They use their magic to teach their children as well as to punish them. Some women who have a talent for it are allowed to act as Warden over the female prisoners. I'm told they are even more vicious than the men."

"But as a royal Valkyrie, I wonder if maybe Neela lacks the full talent of a Warder?" Mother asked.

"More likely, she's never been taught how to construct a prison world," I said. "She's the only legitimate child of a king with a dozen bastard sons who will fight for the right to be his successor. No Warder would want Neela capable of competing for the throne."

"The poor child has only known rejection. No wonder she's become such a monster." Mother's grim look plainly showed she wished she'd been more involved in her niece's life.

"I've watched her closely since my arrival in this dump," Ben said softly. "I know when she's full of bluster and when she's hanging on by a thread. Her fight with Thea left her exhausted. Both times."

"I almost drained her." I nodded, following Ben's reasoning. "Once I passed out, she siphoned from me when I was at my weakest, but it seems to be a difficult thing for her to do. Like she never properly learned how to siphon with purpose. Between that and the battle, she is weak."

"Too weak to cast us into one of her prison worlds," Mother added.

"And she thinks she's already won." Ben said.

"True," Mother nodded. "Neela believes Thea is broken beyond the hope of recovery. She likely has no idea what Mother has done or that she has healing magic. She wouldn't have thrown her in here with us otherwise."

"If you three didn't catch on to my siphoning, then Neela has no idea," Ben said.

"And she wouldn't know Ben is your brother, much less your twin," Mother's voice grew excited.

"Or what twins in our situation are capable of," I caught on to her excitement. "If she believes she has already defeated us, and she is weak, why bother binding any of us with her magic when we are so broken already?"

"Oh, our enemy has made many grave mistakes today." I could hear the smile in Mother's voice.

"Neela likes to celebrate." Ben's chains scraped across the floor as he moved. "The girl likes her wine. She's not thinking about winning. She's thinking about celebrating her victory before it's fully within her grasp."

I climbed to my feet, inspecting my lingering injuries. My wing had healed, but it was stiff and ached with a deep soreness that would probably stay with me for the rest of my life. I still wondered if I would ever fly again.

Pasha? I called to my kindred, but feared she was too far away for us to merge. Reaching for my magic, I was pleased to find both sides responding, though I couldn't sense Pasha yet.

"I feel stronger, but I don't know if it will be enough."

"Then let's give you my power." Ben stood, moving closer so it would be easier for me to siphon from him.

"Not yet." Mother said in a cautious tone. "Thea needs to rest to regain her strength. Esben, you need the opposite. I can sense your well is full. You have done well, but it has kept you strong despite your injuries. Avoid sleep and food for the next day. It will weaken you and allow Thea to absorb your power more naturally by leaving the weaker body to seek the stronger vessel."

"And then what?" I asked.

"Then we wait for the right moment to strike when she least suspects it. The next time you face Neela, you will be stronger than her."

CHAPTER 33

I wasn't surprised when Neela's guard showed up that first night to give me some of the same treatment they had offered Ben. They'd returned several times since then.

"Stand up, coward." One of Neela's pretend Warders tried to drag me to my feet.

I cradled my wing, hoping the guards wouldn't notice it was no longer broken. Ben had given me his belt to make a sling and I'd used the filth and grime from the floor to paint bruises where my previous injuries were. I shifted back to my Valkyrie form as soon as I regained the strength to manage the change.

"No please, not my wing." I winced and cowered in the corner of my cell like a defeated weakling protecting my most vulnerable parts. It wasn't purely an act. I was terrified they would reinjure my wing and Grandmother would be too weak to use her healing magic again.

But I was no weakling. I began siphoning from my brother early this morning after the guards left us. Ben had been giving me his ration of water and bread and Mother split hers with me. Gram was still sleeping.

After the first attempt, we decided it was best to do it slowly throughout the day in short bursts of siphoning to avoid getting caught by the frequent visits from the guard. Ben had taken on such a large portion of the power, it would take time to give the vast majority of it to me. Already I was stronger and eager for a fight. If given another opportunity to end this, I would not hesitate.

"It's not like you'll ever fly again." A foot slammed into my side and a fist struck my jaw.

I screamed, wishing I could fight back, but I needed Neela to continue believing she'd already won. That I was nothing more than the pampered, spoiled princess she thought me to be.

"Please don't hurt her," Mother begged.

"She's been through enough," Ben shouted.

"What happened to the old lady?" the head guard asked while his men enjoyed roughing me up even more. "She's been sleeping for two days."

"My mother is older than she seems. She is weary from the stress of recent events and needs her rest." Brenna's tears glistened in the lamplight. "Please, just leave us be."

It was over quickly. The guards left me in a puddle of my own blood, wearing satisfied smirks as they left to carry their latest report to their mistress.

"Please tell us what's happening?" Brenna begged, playing the part of a distraught mother to perfection. "What has that woman planned for my daughter?"

"Your new queen has scheduled your execution for tonight. But first, we feast." The men grunted their approval with flushed faces and wicked grins. I suspected they had started the celebration early. "Her Majesty wants the false queen and the foresworn boy paraded through the streets with the old queens leading the way with their weeping."

"She can't do this!" Brenna screamed as they left in a flurry of laughter. "We are royalty. We deserve better than this!"

Her mask fell the moment the door clanged shut behind them. "Okay, darlings, we have a few hours left to prepare." Mother turned to me with her serene queenly mask firmly in place. "Are you okay, Thea?"

I sat up, wiping the blood from my chin. "I'm fine. Do you think they bought my act?"

"I bought it," Ben said. "I thought they were going to kill you. Are you sure you're all right?" He scooted as close to the bars of his cell as his chains would allow.

"I'm much stronger than I look, thanks to you and Gram."

"Pretty darn good actress too."

"I could have taken Netflix by storm." I grinned in the darkness. Dragging my fingers through the blood on the floor, I dabbed streaks along my hairline and across my silvery white wingtips.

"What are you doing?" Mother asked.

"War paint," I murmured. "I have to make my injuries convincing."

When next I stepped from my cell and into the streets of Vahland Reach, I would look like a broken shell of my former self. All the while, I would wait for the perfect moment to make my move.

"The fat lip and swollen eye look does wonders for your complexion. And the dried blood effect is just fabulous. You almost look as pretty as I do."

"I'm afraid I got the good looks in this family," I snarked back, grateful for my brother's sense of humor.

"How did you two not know you were siblings the moment you met?" Brenna chuckled. "You're exactly alike and you remind me so much of your father … from before."

"I'd like to know more about him when we get out of this mess," Ben said.

"Me too," I added, and for the first time, I really meant it. If my mother once loved Hagen, then I wanted to know all about the man as she'd known him.

"The Hagen I knew would be so proud of you both," Brenna whispered. "Just as proud as I am."

"Enough chatter." Grandmother roused from her filthy pallet on the floor of her cell. "Have you two finished the transfer?" She yawned, her jaw creaking with the effort, but she looked better than she had last night. I could see the weariness lingering in her eyes, but my grandmother was pure grit and fire. She would recover from the transfer just as she had when Mother ascended.

"Not yet," Ben said. "But we should probably get a move on."

I nodded, moving to sit in the corner of my cell closest to him. "Make sure you keep enough for yourself," I reminded him. "I don't want you so weak you can't fight if it comes to it."

"Let's do this." He sat down just across from me in his cell and I closed my eyes to focus. It was a bit harder to siphon without direct contact, but I could do it.

"Stop me when you've had enough."

"Just do it already, Thea."

"Fine, I'm working up to it," I snapped back at him, secretly pleased to have a bratty little brother to bicker with.

Ben was open and ready for me as I reached for his stores of the power. It wouldn't take long to complete the transfer. Taking a deep breath, I pulled on the power, guiding it toward me. He was tired, and hungry, making me the prime vessel in the room. The power came easily this time, flowing into me like warm silk, filling the ancient well deep inside me.

During the time of the gods, the histories spoke of the three wells of Yggdrasil, the tree that once united the Nine Realms. The well of fate was where the Norns lived and watered the tree to sustain its life. The well of Hvergelmir was where the monster that gnawed the tree's roots resided. And Mimir's well was the source of wisdom. We believed when Yggdrasil was largely destroyed during the final battle, the first Valkyrie Queen—Mother Sigrún—became the well of Mimir and passed that responsibility on to all of her descendants.

But the wisdom of the well didn't come without a price. To this day, that was why a queen sacrificed any magic she might have been born with to become the absolute vessel, or the well from which all creatures of the Nine Realms drank. She took on the burden of sacrifice for them. And I would gladly step forward to do the same when my time to ascend came.

"That's enough, Thea." Ben tugged back from me, gently at first and more forcefully when I didn't immediately release him. I wanted more. The well within me wasn't yet full and I was close enough to my ascension that I was more aware of its emptiness than ever before. But I wouldn't drink my fill from Ben. Neela was my next and last target. The only vessel remaining other than my sister, Sylvi and Astrid who would keep the surplus of the power for me—the portion I couldn't contain on my own.

"Time to go," Neela's guard announced as the dungeon doors creaked open and I released my hold on Esben. The power surged within me and I wasn't certain I could hide it. As Queen Heir I had taken on a large portion of the power, as was natural for any vessel, but I'd never held this much. Glancing at Mother, I couldn't fathom how she had always made it look so easy when already I felt on the verge of exploding with the force of it.

Neela's false Warders stood ready with several sets of irons for each of us.

I winced when the shackles clicked around my wrists and ankles. A tether dragged behind me.

"Don't think about flying off and saving yourself." The guard yanked cruelly on my leash, causing me to stagger.

"I couldn't if I wanted to," I whispered, my lower lip trembling for effect.

Another soldier bound Mother's wrists. "No need for the tether. I no longer possess the strength or the will to shift."

I wasn't sure if that was true or not, but after this was over, I would make sure Mother regained her strength. Grandmother too. With Ben's help, I would ascend without harming any of my family. There was enough power of the gods to sustain us all.

"March." The guards led Brenna out first, followed by a weary Agertha and then me, with Ben bringing up the rear. I faltered, leaving the soldiers no choice but to push and shove me along. I had to make this look good. For the sake of all my people I had to put on the show of a lifetime.

Once outside in the palace courtyard, I cringed in the sunlight. Crowds of people stood by to watch our procession through the city streets. Villagers were brought in from the surrounding countryside, pulled away from their daily lives to witness Neela's victory. Most stood silent. Some wept for their fallen queen and what it would mean for their families. These were my people, and despite Neela's magical chains, they somehow still found the loyalty in their hearts to shed tears for me and my family.

"Majesties." Some whispered, bowing their heads as we passed.

"Blessed Mother Sigrún, give them strength," others prayed.

"You pray for a fallen queen and her heir? The one who abandoned you?" Neela's mocking voice sounded behind me.

I turned to find my enemy perched atop a gilded throne borne up by four of her pretend Warders. She sat in her battle leathers, one leg draped over the armrest of her throne, a golden goblet in one hand and a whip in the other.

"Your prayers fall on deaf ears." Neela cracked her whip, landing a blow on my shoulder.

"March." She sipped from her goblet. "Make your way to the executioner's block."

My shoulder throbbed as I turned forward, taking a few steps along the main road through the city. I was the defeated, bloodied, useless Queen Heir and Neela was poised to exploit that throughout her evening of revelry that would end in the executions of me and my family.

"This isn't what we agreed on, Neela," I rasped.

"We agreed the victor got to choose her opponent's punishment. I've decided your crimes against our people were heinous acts of treason, punishable by the death of your entire dynasty." Neela cracked her whip again, causing me to jump into action.

"You should include yourself as part of the Ahlstrom Dynasty, cousin." I wouldn't call her attention to Sylvi or Astrid. Surely by now she was aware that the Citadel was empty and Astrid and Sylvi wouldn't let her get away with this. If I didn't survive the next hours, I hoped Sylvi would have the strength to hold our world together until a new Queen Heir came to ascend in my place. Either way, Neela couldn't be allowed to remain in power.

I walked, taking strength from my people as they whispered encouraging words, while others shouted jeers and taunts of hate. The overwhelming response from the crowd nearly brought me to my knees, not because some said awful things about me and my family, but because the vast majority had opened themselves up to me to take their small shares of the power back, hoping it might give me the edge I needed over Neela.

I took what they offered gratefully, though the balance of power had already shifted in my favor. The power of the gods now recognized me as the rightful queen, but Neela was so focused on celebrating that she didn't see it, confirming my suspicions that she didn't know how to siphon on her own. I wondered if Svana had done it for her all along.

I slowly made my way along the streets to the city center, following Mother and Grandmother, walking side-by-side clasping hands. I lost sight of Ben behind Neela, but I could hear the gasps from the crowd when they realized he was the evil man Neela had saved them from.

As we neared the gardens at the city center, my shoulders fell at the condition of the once beautiful park. Fountains lay empty and shrubs and vines had overgrown the pathways, but the center of the park was a field of wildflowers, beautiful in its own way.

"Move!" Neela's whip lashed against my back. Stripes streaked my arms and legs, but I hardly felt them over the rage welling inside me. Pasha was near. I could feel my kindred pacing restlessly, eager to strike.

As the procession entered the clearing, Mother and Grandmother followed my lead, looking exhausted and defeated from their time in the dungeons. Theirs wasn't entirely an act though. I felt stronger than ever, itching for a fight. I clenched my fists at my sides, searching the procession for signs of Ben. He staggered forward, his back striped from the Warder's whip, but he wore a look of grim determination.

A raised dais waited for me, Brenna, and Agertha. Three crude thrones stood at the center where Neela's false Warders bound our shackles, forcing us to sit for the crowd and await our mockery of a trial. They shoved Ben to his knees beside me, clasping an iron collar around his throat and securing him to the dais like some kind of animal. The executioner's block rested at the center of the dais, a blatant reminder of what awaited us.

I let them confine me with the simple chains. Chains I would burn when it pleased me. Hanging my head, I waited for Neela's next move, vowing it would be her last.

"You abandoned your duty, leaving behind an inept sister to take your place. For nearly three years, you evaded my bounty hunters, only to return, sneaking into the realm like a coward to hide behind the walls of the Citadel. And to make matters worse, you didn't return alone. You brought your filthy *male* foresworn with you, concealing him behind a web of lies his idiot mother created when she allowed him to live. What do you have to say for yourself, Alithea?" Neela's slaves hefted her throne onto the dais directly across from me. A servant came forward to refill her goblet.

"I do not answer to you." I lifted my chin in defiance.

"You will stand trial, all of you." Neela's gaze drifted from one royal to the next. "My people will understand the depths to which you have fallen. To suffer a male Valkyrie such as Esben to live is the worst sort of treason. His kind are an abomination and you've allowed him to infiltrate our world."

"Wow, she *really* doesn't like me," Ben muttered under his breath. "Maybe I was wrong about that crush."

"We do not answer to a usurper," Brenna said, sounding every bit the queen she was. She didn't need the power of the gods to make her one, she was a queen down to the very fiber of her being.

"My mother is right; we owe you nothing. But I will answer your question for my people," I said calmly, gazing around the city square at the crowds surrounding us. "They deserve to know the truth. Esben is not just any man born to the true Valkyrie nature. He is my twin."

Murmurs spread through the crowd. The legends and myths of the male Valkyries ranged from nightmarish to fantastic, but most feared the very mention of a man with Esben's abilities.

Neela threw her head back and laughed. "Oh, come on, Thea. You're not even making this hard for me if you're just going to tell the truth. The boy is clearly your twin, and neither of you are the progeny of Queen Brenna and her Consort Elias."

The murmuring of the crowd grew louder.

"Wait, did she just say I look like you?" Ben snorted a laugh. "Clearly, I am the better-looking twin."

I shot my brother a glare, begging him to be serious for once.

"Just look at them." Neela turned to the crowd. "With their dark hair and eyes, the sharp noses and caustic wit, they look nothing like their golden-haired mother. Nor do they resemble the plain-featured Elias either. If we could drag Sylvi from her hiding place, you would see the striking resemblance between Princess Sylvanna and Brenna. While Thea looks nothing like either of her supposed parents.

"My sources tell me Brenna gave birth to this mongrel first, and then our little princess Thea came seven minutes later. But who was their father?" Neela drank deeply from her wine goblet, enjoying her victory.

"And even worse, Brenna failed to do as all Valkyrie mothers before her have done. She failed to have her foresworn son executed at birth. Instead, she secreted him off to the human realm to live peacefully. And now Alithea has brought him back with her."

The crowd erupted in shouts of disapproval and that was when I understood what Neela was up to. She'd known all along that

Ben was my twin. Of course Svana would have told her everything she knew of Ben. But now Neela wanted to force the queen to admit who our father was.

"It doesn't matter." I spoke before Mother could. "I'm not here to hide the fact that Esben is my twin brother. Look at us. Yes, he is taller than me and if you ask him, he's prettier than me."

"Darn right." Ben followed my lead.

I shrugged, relieved to hear some scattered laughter throughout the crowd.

"If you knew us, you'd see that we're pretty much the same person. I can't give you more evidence than that. He is my twin, but what most of you don't know is that a twin such as Esben poses no harm to anyone. I was born first. Esben came seven minutes later. That is an important detail Neela got wrong. It is the nature of our twin bond that allows us to balance each other. As the older twin, I temper his ambition and as the younger, he amplifies my power, making me a stronger queen and a more powerful vessel to serve all the people of the Nine Realms. More powerful than any vessel in recent history," I added. The people craved the strongest possible vessel. It was necessary to ensure our survival.

"There is no need for Esben to stand trial here. He has done nothing wrong. And there is absolutely no danger that he could ever become the kind of nightmare we've all learned about the foresworn Valkyrie kings of the reign of terror. If given the opportunity, we can provide evidence and historical precedence where a foresworn Valkyrie male who is the *younger* twin of a female is not capable of overpowering her. Esben is no danger to anyone." I lifted my chin and raised my voice. "The only thing my brother has ever desired is to know his family and I will not allow that to be taken from him."

"Yet, if you should be convicted and executed, this twin magic you claim to have would be broken and Esben no longer 'balanced,' and therefore a dire threat." A victorious grin spread across Neela's face, causing the lines of scar tissue peeking around her mask to crease into a grotesque smile. "As long as you are on trial, so is your twin."

Neela leaned forward. "All you have proven here today is that you are not the child of the former queen and her husband. The husband chosen by her mother's council to father Brenna's Queen Heir. As you are not Elias' child, you have no legal claim to the throne. As the bastard child of some unknown lover of Brenna's, neither you nor Esben fall into the line of succession."

"If legitimacy and the law were the only things that mattered, then legal succession would fall to my sister, Sylvi in my absence. Not you." I would not take Neela's bait. "The council chooses who will father the Queen Heir in order to produce the strongest possible vessel. It is a tradition, not a law. Trust me, I've made this argument many times. At the end of the day, it's the power of the gods that chooses the Queen Heir. The power chose me when I was twelve years old. And it has chosen me again."

Neela knew King Consort Elias was not my natural father and she believed that revelation would be the final nail in my coffin. Still, it wouldn't take much to turn the crowd against me and she knew it.

"And now we have come full circle. Everyone here knows I am the more powerful vessel." I lifted my chin in defiance. "Whomever sired me is of little importance."

Neela sat back against her absurd golden throne. "Maybe you have a point about the legality of it all." She gave an exaggerated sigh. "But I am a contender for the throne of Valsgard. The crown falls to the one who proves to be the strongest vessel but I don't believe that has been fully determined yet. Unless." Neela grinned with a triumphant sneer. "You're suggesting a *half-breed,* such as myself, isn't fit to sit on the throne of the Valkyries."

I smiled at my cousin. Clearly, she'd done her homework. "It doesn't matter who our fathers are, Neela. Only our mothers. You know very well my mother is Queen Brenhilde of Valsgard. My heritage trumps yours. Princess Svana was a weakling. You took her life force and it still wasn't enough."

"I defeated you." Neela's eyes flashed in the fading sunlight.

"You broke my wing and knocked me out of the sky and then you siphoned from me while I was incapacitated. You did not honor the terms of our battle. We agreed the fight was to be for the power, yet here I sit, just as strong as I was before you decided to cheat your way to the crown." It was time to make my final move. I searched the crowd for a pair of ice-blue eyes.

Pasha.

Kindred. Pasha sat quietly at the edge of the crowd between Druan and Vendela. Druan gave me a nod as I called on my Berserker magic, embracing the dark shadows of my kindred's predator.

"I grow weary of this game." Neela drank deeply of her wine. "You and I both know the people will not stand behind you when they know the full extent of your parentage. And I prefer to move on to the celebratory part of the evening. Alithea Ahlstrom, you and your brother, Esben Ahlstrom, are the children of the former queen Brenhilde Ahlstrom and Hagen, the King of Madmen." She paused for the crowd's response, and they didn't disappoint with their gasps of outrage and betrayal. Some already called for my head. But Neela wasn't done with her gloating yet.

"While Esben may be your magically faultless twin," she continued with a note of sarcasm. "The fact remains that he is a foresworn Valkyrie sired by a Berserker, and we all know how dangerous that combination can be. He cannot and will not be allowed to live. Nor will our people abide a Berserker half-breed such as yourself on the throne. Particularly one who has harbored a filthy male. I sentence Alithea and Esben Ahlstrom, as well as their mother and grandmother to death by beheading to be carried out this very moment. From this day forward, I shall be known as Queen Neela of Valsgard—she who overcomes—High Queen of the Nine Realms."

CHAPTER 34

"I'm sorry, Neela." I called on both sides of my magic, letting it fill me. "But after today, no one will ever call you queen again.

I lowered my eyes to the shackles binding me. Not that they could hold me now. I'd merely humored Neela by allowing her the illusion that she'd won.

I could feel the subtle shift now. My Berserker side was in control for the moment. I imagined my eyes were ice blue like Pasha's, but the burn was also still mine. It made sense now. How both sides of my magic were two distinct things, but at the same time they weren't separate things at all.

"And how do you propose to accomplish such a feat?" Neela taunted. "Or have you forgotten I still have you all in irons and your people are no longer with you. Listen to their jeers, cousin." She lifted her goblet, urging the crowd on.

"Execute her!"

"Filthy half-breed!"

"Kill them all!"

"You mean these irons?" I lifted my hands with a smile, the chains of my restraints rattling as I moved. "No, I haven't forgotten, though I do agree with you on one point. I grow weary of all this ceremony."

"Shall we get on with the executions then? I do enjoy a good feast and beheading."

"There will be no beheading tonight." I reached for the shadow of my Berserker magic. Pulling on Pasha's strength, I severed the remaining bonds that held my people under Neela's thrall. I didn't even need to gather the tendrils of shadow and blood now. Nor did I need my talons.

The crowd's cries died down and stunned faces stared back at me.

"My people," I called out. "You have my deepest apologies for what you have been through but you are no longer bound by the usurper's magic. She will never control you again."

"What are you babbling about?" Neela laughed, sipping from her goblet.

"I am sorry, cousin, but I believe your celebration is a bit premature."

"Guards!" Neela snapped her fingers, but no one responded.

I turned my focus back on my people. "It is true, my natural father is King Hagen. I am both Valkyrie, elder twin of Esben, a vessel of the gods, Berserker, and your Queen Heir." I gazed across the sea of uncertain faces, looking for one in particular. I found her staring back with a predator's eyes, one trembling hand clutching Druan's arm. Vendela. My half-sister. I bowed my head toward her, hoping the shock of such a revelation wouldn't bring an end to our friendship.

And then she nodded in return, a small smile tugging at her mouth.

My eyes drifted to Pasha, sitting beside her.

Come, kindred, let them see you and I are nothing to fear.

Pasha came bounding up to the dais, her presence a familiar one among my mother's court. She sat back on her haunches at my side, her eyes taking them all in, willing them to see her as they always had.

Friend. Protector. Prowl. Her intentions came to me more as whispers of thought than mere words

"Enough!" Neela slammed her fist down on the arm of her throne and stood, drawing a dagger from her hip.

Pasha let out a roar and sank into a crouch before she leapt across the dais, pushing Neela back down on her throne with a hiss, showing her sharp teeth.

Neela sat down hard, her eyes wide and frightened as Pasha stood over her, not letting her move.

"As I was saying. I am the same Princess Alithea I have always been, and your well-being is my greatest concern. It was the reason I left in the first place. I thought you would fare better under my sister's rule. She would be an amazing, loving, and loyal queen, but I realize now she is not the queen you need. I am."

With a careful sweep of my burning magic, the shackles binding me and my family blazed in golden light for a moment before they crumbled to the ground in a pile of ash.

"What is this? A final show of power?" Neela forced an unconvincing, deep, throaty laugh. "You've lost, Thea. It's done." A burst of magical bonds formed around Neela, weaving like a spider's web around her.

I swept them aside like smoke, but Neela couldn't see magic the way I could.

"Guards, take her to the block." Neela waved a lazy hand, yet, still no one responded. Not even her pretend-Warders. The few she had gathered around her wore confused faces, as if they no longer knew what freedom felt like. I hadn't just freed my people—I'd freed Neela's too.

"That is the difference between you and me, cousin. I inspire loyalty because I endeavor to put their needs ahead of my own." I stood, the power of my kindred turning my voice into a rasp. "You rely on your Warder magic to force your will upon others and when that magic is stripped away, as I have just done, you are left alone and with nothing."

My mother's guards moved to surround Neela.

"Seize her," Neela shouted, throwing her goblet to the ground. "I will not have it." She moved to reassert her bonds. "Obey your mistress."

I threw up my hand, burning my cousin's magic away with my own. "Truly, you might have had the potential to become a powerful vessel with the right training, but you don't know how to siphon, and you lack the ability to sense the balance of power among other vessels. Not on your own, and with your mother gone, you don't see how dire your situation has become, cousin."

"Take her to the block!" Neela demanded again, but Pasha took a swipe at her and she tumbled back against her throne.

"There is an important lesson to be learned here, Neela." I took a step closer, letting my taloned fingers trail through Pasha's fur as I moved to stand with my kindred. "Never celebrate the end of the war before you've actually won the final battle."

I lunged for Neela, my movements graceful and feline as I tackled her to the ground. My perfectly healed wings fanned out behind me as I gripped Neela's throat with my razor-sharp talons. "You are finished here, cousin. It is over."

Neela screamed in outrage, grappling against my hold on her, but I had the upper hand now and she was no match for my

Berserker strength. Pulling on the power of the gods, I siphoned from Neela, drawing on the source of her power and leaving her with just enough to keep her alive.

I gasped from the sheer strength of so much power coursing through me. I almost couldn't contain it. Like the finest wine, the infinite power I held was intoxicating, but I didn't need it—not even half of what I held. My people needed it, but I would keep it safe for them until Neela was no longer a threat.

"Guards." I shuddered, taking a steadying breath as I released my hold on her and she collapsed like a broken doll. "Take the usurper and restrain her. She will stand trial immediately."

Neela's dark eyes flashed with fury as my loyal men shackled her to the chair where I had sat only moments before.

I watched in satisfaction as Neela sagged against the rough wooden seat, too weak to put up a fight.

"She and her brother will destroy you and your way of life," Neela's voice rasped like sandpaper in her throat as the growing crowd of onlookers converged around the dais. "If you allow her to win, you will live to regret it."

"My people have the right to deny me the throne," I reminded the crowd of confused citizens, commoners and nobility alike. "I will deal with the usurper who has treated you poorly in my absence. I will honor the deal I made with Neela. She will not pay for her crimes with her life, but she will pay dearly. After that, it is up to the people to decide if I am capable of ruling them. While I may be the strongest vessel for the power of the gods, if my people do not want me, I will step aside for another."

"She lies! Look at her. How her eyes change and she moves like a predator. She isn't the Valkyrie queen you deserve. She is a Berserker."

"Half-Berserker, yes." I turned to my people. "I will not hide what I am. I am not ashamed of it, though I would have liked to reveal that information in my own way. I am the daughter of Queen Brenna and King Hagen, a fact I have only recently discovered myself. But that is an issue for another day." I paused, turning my focus back on Neela.

"We agreed to handle this battle between the two of us, sparing my people the burden of a war they shouldn't have to fight. It was to be a battle for the power alone. You decided to cheat, using brute strength to injure me and take my power while I was unconscious. Yet, I have won the battle for power and it is my right as the victor to sentence you for your crimes against my people."

"Bring on the executioner and be done with it." Neela stared at me with empty eyes; all the fight seemed to have gone out of her now that she knew she'd lost.

"An executioner won't be necessary. We agreed this was not a fight to the death."

"Then what's it to be?"

"Princess Morgana, could you assist me, please?" I called for my best friend to come forward.

"Princess Alithea." Morgan approached, dipping her head in a nod to her fellow royal. "How can I be of assistance?"

"Can you use your Druid magic so Neela will feel no physical pain?"

"I can." Morgana gave me a puzzled look. "Though I don't know why you would spare her any pain."

"This punishment will hurt her far more than mere physical pain." I nodded to my guards to take Neela in hand. I paced around the dais, searching the crowd for Druan. He appeared as though he could read my mind.

"Perhaps my queen has need of her weapons?" He gave a courtly bow and handed me my pair of golden axes.

"Thank you, Druan." My hands shook as I took the weapons in hand.

"Princess Neela, daughter of King Ulric of Vöstland, " I began in a clear voice. "You have been found guilty of usurping a throne of the Nine Realms. A throne that was never yours to inherit." I stopped my pacing for a moment. "If that were your only crime, I could find it in my heart to forgive you. But you put my people in bondage, and they have suffered greatly under your rule. That is unforgivable."

I turned to face her, letting the rage of my Berserker nature take hold of me. I would need it to do what I was about to do. "From this day forward, you are no longer of the Nine Realms. I banish you to the human realm. You will leave immediately under escort of my bounty hunters and you will never return."

Neela snorted. "Is that the best you can do? That's not even a punishment. I'll just come back."

I ignored her, waiting for Morgana's nod. I had to do this, but it would be painful enough for Neela in the months and years to come. I didn't want her to feel it until it was over.

As she taunted me, I moved behind her, quickly raising my axe. The first cut was swift and clean. Neela's blood-red wing fell to the dais as she still hurled obscenities at me for my weakness.

Her voice died in her throat as I made the second cut, the crowd as silent as the void between the worlds.

Neela's ruined wing fell to join the other in a heap of red feathers. Blood rushed down her back from fresh wounds she couldn't feel. Her mouth opened in a silent scream and she couldn't seem to find her breath.

As her Valkyrie features faded, and she took her human form, Neela found her voice. "No!" She shrieked and sank to the ground, gathering her wings to her chest. "No." She sobbed, her blood pooling around her.

"I have clipped your wings, separating you from your Valkyrie forever." My voice trembled with anger and regret that it had come to this. "You will never call upon your Valkyrie again. You will never fly again. You will never perform a Valkyrie's sacred duty again. And you will no longer have the ability to siphon the power of the gods because you are no longer a strong enough vessel. From now on you will be exactly what you've proven yourself to be through and through. A Warder. You have no family here." I turned my back on my cousin as she wailed for the loss of the most precious thing to any Valkyrie.

"You should have killed me." Neela's voice grated with raw, exposed hatred. "You profess to be a benevolent Queen Heir. A just and kind woman, raised by the great Queen Brenhilde." Neela hissed as tears rolled down her cheeks. "You are nothing. Nothing!"

"I don't profess to be any such thing, Neela." I hurt for her. Hated that I had to do such a cruel thing to another Valkyrie. But my mother always taught me if I had to punish someone like Neela, I must make it clear to my people that they should expect nothing less than ruthless justice for their crimes. "I am just a woman, like any other, trying to do the best she can for her people. That's all any of us can ever do."

"You will pay for this." Neela sobbed. "I will make you pay." Spit flew from her mouth to mingle with her tears.

"I truly regret what could have been, cousin. As the child of Princess Svana and King Ulric, no one expected you could ever be a true Valkyrie royal—a contender for the throne. Your mother hid that from us. Hid you from your Valkyrie family. You should have grown up in the Citadel with me and Sylvi. You should have been our family. For that, I am sorry. Things might have been very different for both of us. Instead you were raised in a prison world ruled by a cruel man who never respected your Valkyrie nature. He mistreated you, abused you. Scarred you. And most importantly, he was never a father to you. I may have never known my own father, but I was raised by a man who loved me as his own. He would have loved you too."

"You can't do this, Alithea," Neela cried.

"It is done." I paced to the edge of the dais, Pasha at my side. "My bounty hunters will ensure you are safely delivered to the human realm. You will mourn the loss of your wings, but I urge you to find a new path. I could have sent you back to the father you hate, but losing your Valkyrie is punishment enough. You will leave the Nine Realms and your magic behind. You are young. Carve out a human life for yourself and find happiness wherever you can. It will just not be among my people."

"No!" Neela fought the guards as they picked her up from the dais, but her strength was gone.

"Take her away." I returned my attention to my people. "There will be no celebration tonight—"

"Your Majesty, may I address the people?" Ben asked.

Surprised, I nodded. "Of course." I held my hand out for my twin.

"I will be quick." He grasped my hand and cleared his throat as he prepared to address the crowd. "Until a few weeks ago, I didn't know what I was. I grew up in the human realm, separated from my family." He glanced back at me and I squeezed his hand to encourage him. "I've since learned my mother gave me the best chance of life she could. She believed she'd left me with loving parents who would tell me everything I needed to know. But they died when I was still a baby. I grew up alone, believing I was the only one of my kind. Then I met my sister. My best friend. She never meant to bring me here, but the night she returned to Valsgard, I followed her, not realizing how I might strike terror in the hearts of my fellow Valkyries." Ben hung his head. "That still doesn't seem real. I'm just me." He cleared his throat again. "The only thing I ever wanted was a family. Now I have a mother, an aunt, and sisters. A twin sister I would do anything for. She's the best person I know. I would never betray her. I don't know how any of this works, but I renounce whatever *royal* title or position or … whatever privilege I may have as the son of a Valkyrie queen. I don't want it. I don't want power. I relinquished what power I had to my sister and I don't want it back. I just want my family. That's all I will ever need. Please … don't fear me. I am not my ancestors. I know nothing of their deeds. I'm just Ben. I … guess that's all I needed to say." He stepped back to stand beside our mother, looking like a lost little boy.

I watched the crowd as he spoke. They already loved him. Somehow my brother had managed to steal their hearts with one speech.

"Please return to your homes," I announced. "You are free of Neela's influence once and for all. In the coming days and weeks we will rebuild our city and our villages. I promise, no one will go hungry. No one will be left out in the cold. We are Valkyries, and we take care of our own. The question of who will rule us … we'll figure it out togeth—"

"Queen Alithea has saved us!" A single triumphant cry rang out among the silent nobles and citizens of Valsgard. Then the deafening roar of their cheers swept over me, bringing me to my knees before my people as they chanted, "Queen Alithea. She Who is Becoming!"

CHAPTER 35

I stared around the council table at the familiar faces. No longer confined to the Citadel, my family and I had reclaimed the palace as our home. It took a few days for them to return, but once Neela was no longer a threat, I sent messengers to catch up with Sylvi and Astrid, calling them home for good.

All citizens who had lived within the Citadel for nearly three years were allowed to stay there until they could reclaim their homes or make arrangements to rebuild. When I opened the palace coffers, I found Neela had stockpiled a fortune for herself. I doled out a portion of that money to help my people rebuild their lives—not only within Vahland Reach but anywhere in Valsgard they wished to go.

"Your coronation is in three days, Thea; you must choose your council," Elder Vanya reminded me again. "We have precious little time to dither over details with the high council convening in a few months."

"We aren't going to discuss my council until the matter of my marriage is put to rest once and for all. I will not marry Fiske or remain betrothed to him. I will not marry anyone simply to ascend. I curse the tradition of the Chosen Sons to the mists of Hel, Vanya. This council's obsession with tradition is what got us into this mess to begin with."

"But the people must know who will stand at your side," Elder Leda interjected. "Perhaps you will name a proper intended?"

"Why do I need a man beside me to prove I am a good queen?"

"It isn't about the man, darling," Mother finally spoke. She didn't like to express her opinions, preferring to let me assert my authority as the imminent queen of our people. "It's about your heir. The people need to know your reign is secured now and with legitimacy for the next generation. It's not about the marriage at all. It's about the security a strong union represents, and our people need security now more than ever. The Chosen Sons have been recalled. If you are amenable, we would like to choose another more to your liking."

I leaned back against my chair—still not used to sitting where Mother had sat since before I was born. I glanced down at my kindred, resting on her haunches beside me. "I could be amenable to that," I murmured, to the complete surprise of the entire council.

"Has the girl finally found some sense?" Sonje studied my face for a moment. "Or is she up to something?"

"Hear her out," Mother insisted.

"I will agree to marry from among the Chosen Sons, on two conditions. First, I get to choose him. And second, I will choose from among every male who was ever selected to wear the brand. Not only from those who completed their ridiculous 'how to please Thea' training. If a man was determined to be good enough to wear the brand, then he should be eligible for the role of my future husband."

"I think we can—" Elder Vanya began but I stopped her.

"Wait, I have three conditions. The third is that the man I choose must also choose me back. I will not marry a man who does not want me in return."

"I think we can agree to those terms," Mother said. "Just don't come up with a fourth or fifth condition. You're cut off, Thea darling."

"I find that an agreeable compromise," Leda said to the accompaniment of several more murmurs of agreement.

"And while we're at it, I propose we amend the laws to allow any future Queen of the Citadel the right to marry should she choose. I see no need to continue the archaic notion that the ruler of the Citadel must be celibate. None have adhered to that law in centuries."

"One thing at a time, my girl." Mother chuckled. "You must have your official coronation before you can amend the law, though I give my wholehearted approval. Your suggestion is something I should have done for my sister years ago. It is difficult for the older generations to lift their heads from the mire of tradition and see the possibilities that lie ahead. That is why we recognize our Queen Heir when it becomes clear she is ready to ascend. You have your eyes set on a bright future the older generations can't even fathom. I pray I live many more years to see where you will take us."

I shared a hopeful smile with my mother. My official coronation hadn't happened yet, but the transfer of power had, and I hadn't killed anyone. Thanks to Ben's assistance, I now carried a heavy load, but one I could bear. Astrid, Sylvi, Mother and Grandmother all carried a small portion of the power to lighten my load. Ben refused all but the smallest bit of the power of the gods for himself. He didn't want to get used to the feeling it gave him.,

"As Queen Brenna stated, Alithea cannot amend the law as of yet," Leda called my attention back to the meeting. "However, I think we can all agree on the sense of our Queen Heir's plan to choose an acceptable consort. Let's move on to the question of her council. The law states the ascending queen should choose her council from among her own generation while keeping at least one member of her mother's council. For the sake of recent events, we've all agreed to speed up the usual timeline for Alithea to select her council. The people of Valsgard need stability now more than ever."

"That is a tradition I am happy to keep." I smiled, eager to make my official appointments. I'd agonized over my choices since resuming the palace.

"Must we discuss the difference between a law and a tradition ... again?" Vanya asked.

I ignored her. "Mother, please ask my council to join us." I sat up a little straighter, feeling excited about my role as future queen for the first time ever.

"Of course, your Majesty." She beamed a proud smile at me before opening the double doors and inviting those outside to come in. Most of them didn't know it yet, but all their lives were about to change. Hopefully they would think it was for the better.

Gasps echoed around the room as eight people joined us. Five women and three men. It was unheard of for a man to sit on a Valkyrie queen's council. But it wasn't illegal. I'd checked.

"She's out of her mind," Sonje muttered under her breath and I gave her a sharp look.

"Please save your comments for later," I instructed Mother's council as I stood to welcome mine. "Thank you all for joining us. I promise this won't take long." I couldn't contain my excitement.

"Your Majesty," Astrid said. "I thought I knew what this was about but ..." She gestured at her daughter, Annika.

"Nika." I rose to stand opposite my young cousin. "I have something very important I'd like to ask you."

"Yes, your Majesty. I would be pleased to help in any way I can." Nika bowed, her voice strong and clear. The girl was never intimidated. She was perfect.

"I'd like to ask you to serve on my council as a junior elder."

"You want me to be an elder?" Nika's eyes widened in surprise as she leaned forward, whispering, "You do know I'm only ten, Thea?"

"Of course. But you won't always be ten. You're an important person in my book and I'd like you to sit on my council and learn. Observe for now, and as you feel comfortable voicing your opinions, we will listen and respect your input."

The girl's eyes shone bright with tears. She knew she was Astrid's daughter, but this was the closest she'd ever come to getting the recognition she deserved. "It would be my greatest honor, your Majesty." Nika gave a formal bow.

"Aunt Astrid." I turned to the current Queen of the Citadel. I value your wisdom and would be honored if you would join my council."

"It is my honor to serve." Astrid nodded, draping an arm around her daughter. "Thank you, niece. This means more to me than you can imagine." She pulled Annika closer.

I stepped to the next woman. "Grandmother Agertha, you have served in the past as our dutiful and beloved queen, but I would ask you to serve once more as an elder on my council." I took her hand in mine, pleased to see the spark of mischief in her eyes. She was still recovering, but it would take a lot more than a usurper to bring my grandmother down.

"Thank you, Granddaughter. I would be delighted to serve." She gave a regal nod of her head.

"Sylvi." I moved on to the next woman. "One day you will be my right hand as Queen of the Citadel. But I can't do this without you. Will you serve as my right hand on my council?"

"Of course, Sister." Sylvi dipped into a perfect curtsy. "It would be my honor to serve my queen."

"Fiske." I approached the first man of the group. "I am supposed to choose my council from my peers. Those of my own age. In my absence, I'm afraid I no longer know the young women and men of our court. And I trust only a handful. You are one of them. You risked everything to find me in the human realm. For that I can never repay you. Will you serve on my council?"

"Yes, your Majesty." His chest puffed up and he seemed overcome with emotion and pride. I leaned in closer so he could hear my next words clearly. "I release you from our betrothal, but as one of my council, you have my permission to marry my sister if you can ever work up the nerve to ask her." I didn't wait for his response as I moved on, but I didn't miss the looks of joy that passed between my sister and Fiske.

"Ben." I grinned as I approached my brother, taking his hands in mine.

"You must be completely crackers if you want me here, Thea. I don't know anything about serving a queen."

"Which is precisely why I want you on my council. You keep me grounded, Esben Ahlstrom. I know you said you want to be a lazy mooch, but I need you, brother."

"You never have to ask, Thea. I am always here. Even if it's just to remind you you're not fancy."

I pulled him into a crushing hug. "Thank you," I murmured. "Thank you for making me stop that night I almost left you on the side of the road."

"You did try to ditch me the next morning, if I remember correctly."

"But you caught up with me and it changed my life, for the better." I hugged him again. "I love you."

"Love you too, sis."

My next choice would likely cause more of a stir than the others. "Amara." I approached the dragon, nodding my head in respect. "Your people are wise and greatly respected. You choose to live solitary lives rather than uniting as a single tribe. It would make me so proud if you would call my people your chosen tribe and join my council. I value your ancient wisdom more than you could know."

Amara's nostrils flared as she struggled to suppress her emotion. I realized a moment too late that her hands were moving.

Ben leaned in to whisper. "She says the honor would be all hers."

"The sign language lessons are going well, I take it?" I glanced between Ben and the silent dragon.

"She's a quick study, my girl." Ben elbowed Amara and a shy smile spread across her startlingly beautiful features.

Amara made a few more gestures with her hands.

"She asks if you will learn?"

"We all will. To better benefit from your council." I leaned in closer to add, "And so Ben doesn't get any ideas about creative translating."

Amara snorted and a quick stream of fire escaped her as she laughed.

I ducked to avoid it, laughing with the dragon. "Well that's not something you see every day."

My gaze shifted to Druan's, standing quietly beside Pasha, who had joined him the moment he arrived with Sameerah on his shoulder.

"Traitor," I murmured to Pasha with a chuckle. "Druan. I have a very important question to ask you. Will you sit at my left side and call Vahland Reach your home?" The position normally went to a senior elder, but I had no qualms about deviating from tradition. I wanted Sylvi and Druan by my side as I ruled over the high council of the Nine Realms. It was the highest position any man had ever held in Valsgard and he wasn't even Valkyrie. But it was my decision and I could think of no one else I wanted beside me.

"If it pleases the council, I would be honored, your Majesty." Druan bowed formally as I returned to my seat.

"You have chosen five women and three men to serve as your council of elders, your Majesty," Leda said, and though I could hear the hurt in her tone, she added, "I believe you have chosen well. Mostly." She eyed Amara and Druan. "It is unprecedented for a queen to ask a child, a dragon, a Druid and two male Valkyries, but I think we can all agree we should get used to the unprecedented where our queen is concerned."

"I have room for one more, Leda." I smiled at the woman who taught me everything I knew about governing the Nine Realms. "I do not shirk all traditions. Just the ones that don't make sense to me. I would be honored if you would serve as my senior Elder and advisor."

"Thank you, my Queen." Leda's eyes filled with tears. "Though you may be the death of me, child, I shall die a proud woman to have served two of our strongest queens."

"Shall we make room for our new Elders?" Brenna stood from her place at the table. All but Leda joined her, moving to the seats along the wall. They would still serve in the coming months, but eventually they would all retire.

"Join me." I said, my voice betraying my emotion as Sylvi sat to my right and Druan to my left. The others took their seats. Even young Annika pulled her chair up, looking so proud she might burst.

"We have much to discuss, but first, I have one more ally to speak with." I crossed the room and opened the doors to find Vendela sitting alone. "Please join us for a moment, Dela."

Vendela walked into the room looking like a deer caught in headlights. "Don't worry, I've already appointed my council." I returned to my seat at the head of the table.

Vendela's shoulders relaxed. "Good. For a moment I thought you'd lost your mind." Her eyes widened in alarm. "I apologize, your Majesty. That was out of line and too familiar."

"Nonsense, Vendela. You are my half-sister. I trust you with my life. By all accounts, you should be seated on this council as well."

A few startled gasps rang out among the senior Elders. By now everyone knew I was the daughter of Brenna and King Hagen and naturally that meant Vendela was my half-sister.

"What's so surprising?" I rolled my eyes. "The whole of Valsgard knows by now."

"It's just a shock to hear you speak of it so openly, dear," Mother explained. "We will get used to your … brutal honesty. Just give us time."

"I thought about asking Vendela to join my council. In truth, I would like nothing more. But in the end, I believe she has a very different path before her. One I support."

"What are you saying, Thea?" Vendela asked.

"You do not have a place among my advisors because one day you will sit opposite me on the high council as the Berserker Queen. It is time you return home, Vendela. You are our father's rightful heir and you can trust that we will support your endeavor to claim that right and bring an end to the chaotic rule of King Hagen.

Pasha and I paced the hall in front of Druan's door, trying to work up the courage to knock.

Coward. Pasha studied me with her piercing blue eyes.

"You betcha, I am." I let out a breath and placed my hands on my hips.

Prowl. Pasha brushed my hand with her velvet-soft nose, a deep purr rumbling in her chest.

"You think so?" I scratched behind her ears. "I think so too."

"I can hear you pacing a hole in the floor. Come in, your Majesty." Druan held the door open for me. "You're making Sameerah nervous."

"I see she's finally found her way into the palace." I stepped through the doorway, my heartbeat thudding loud in my ears. Sameerah sat on a perch by the open window, sunning herself in the afternoon light.

"She isn't happy about it." Druan cleared a chair of random bits of clothing and feathers and offered it to me. I perched on the edge of the seat, wondering if I could find the words I came here to say.

"She won't like palace life." Druan pulled me back to the conversation.

"Who?" I placed a hand on Pasha's back, both to calm my nerves and to draw strength from my kindred.

"Sameerah. I was just saying I will have to find a cottage somewhere nearby, perhaps on the palace grounds. The city is too loud for Sam and she finds the palace stifling. Truth be told, I do too." Druan folded a shirt and placed it in a bag I hadn't noticed on the floor next to his bed.

"You're leaving?" My heart sank, dreading what he might say next.

"Don't worry, Princess, I'm not going far." The teasing lilt in his voice returned and I relaxed. "My kindred isn't happy and I must do something about it. Pasha was raised in the palace, so it is home to her, but Sameerah needs open skies and fewer walls."

"I'm not a princess anymore," I reminded him.

"And you aren't officially a queen yet either. Not until your coronation." He moved to stand in front of me. "But I think I will always call you princess. Just to irritate you." He winked and ran his fingertips across my cheek, grazing my skin with the lightest touch. "You will come visit me at my new home soon?"

Pasha bumped her head against my knee to urge me on.

"Stay," I blurted, gripping the armrests of my chair.

"I can serve your council just as easily if I live outside the palace walls or inside."

I nodded, my head bobbing like a cork on my shoulders. "I have to get married."

"I figured the betrothal to Fiske would likely have to stand." Druan's mouth thinned to a hard line as he stuffed his belongings into the bag.

"No. I broke the betrothal. The elder council has agreed to let me select from among the Chosen Sons."

"I see." His back stiffened as he turned away from me. "It is probably for the best. At least you get a choice now."

"I choose you." I pushed myself out of the chair to stand behind him. "I… if you'll have me." My voice came out in a breathless sigh. This was a disaster. I was about to ascend to the highest throne in all of the Nine Realms, but I had all the eloquence of a goat herder.

"I am no longer a Chosen Son." Druan refused to face me, but I found the strength to take another step toward him, pressing my hand against his back where the brand claimed he belonged to me. But I couldn't claim his heart with a brand. I had to put my heart on the line to see if he wanted this as much as I did.

"Doesn't matter," I whispered. "I had three conditions for agreeing to marry. First, I get to choose. Second, if I have to choose from among the Chosen Sons, I will pick from among all who wear my brand, not just those who completed their training. And third, whomever I desire as my husband must also have the freedom to choose or reject me as well."

Druan remained silent for a moment, his face still turned away.

"There is only one man I want to stand beside me. It's you, Druan. I choose you."

"Are you trying to propose to me, Alithea Ahlstrom? Because if you are, my answer is yes." He turned toward me, his eyes golden and smoldering with the power of his kindred. "We choose you, too." He pulled me into his arms, pressing his forehead against mine as he took a steadying breath. When he opened his eyes again, they were the clear gray of the man I loved. The one who challenged me to be better. The one who was unafraid to tell me what I needed to hear.

His full lips found mine and I sank into him, letting my arms slide around his neck, my fingers combing through his long brown hair. Pasha purred and rubbed her head against my side, trying to burrow between us. Sameerah shrieked her indignation ... or maybe it was a victory cry, I couldn't tell. I just knew the four of us were going to make for one strange royal family.

"Come with us and bring Sam. I have a surprise for her." I took his hand and guided him up to the queen's residence on the top floor of the palace. It was mine now. Mother had moved into the Citadel to spend more time with Astrid, helping her and Sylvi return the grounds to their former glory. Though they had decided to keep a portion of the farm should the Citadel ever needed to provide for the citizens of Vahland Reach again.

"Tell me if these rooms will make her more comfortable." I pushed through the double doors of the queen's suite and gave

Druan and Sam the grand tour. "Once we are married, we will have the whole suite to ourselves, but Sameerah might be more comfortable out here." I showed him to the wide terrace outside our suite. With open skies overhead and the privacy of a view overlooking the solitude of the Armur Mountains, she should find more freedom here.

"What do you think, Sameerah?" Druan moved to the center of the terrace where a tree grew from a large planter recessed into the floor. The gyrfalcon hopped from his shoulder to perch on a tree limb, squawking her begrudging approval.

"I think that was her happy noise, wasn't it?" I laughed.

"As happy as a gyrfalcon will ever get." Druan grabbed me around the waist and pulled me down onto the lounge where our kindred faded from our minds and it was just us and the peace we'd fought so hard for.

EPILOGUE

Three months later

"I still feel like a farce in all this finery." I fussed with the stiff high collar of my dark silvery gown. The winged crown on my head was a heavy reminder that I was Queen of Valsgard now and needed to act like it.

"You look beautiful," Sylvi said, as if that should make up for how uncomfortable the too-tight gown made me in the unbearably warm carriage.

"I'm with Thea. I could do without all the finery." Druan tugged at his collar.

"Two peas in a pod." Sylvi shook her head from her seat opposite us. "And that brother of ours is just as bad as you two."

"You always said I was three." I leaned into Druan, resting my hand in the crook of his arm.

"I miscalculated." Sylvi peeked out the window to find Pasha keeping pace with the carriage. "Clearly, you are four."

"I'm so much more than that, Sylvi." I thought of all the people who helped me reach this day. I couldn't have done it without my family and closest friends.

"Now I'm outnumbered," Sylvi said.

"You have Fiske and Leda to help keep us all properly proper."

On any given day since my coronation, I could be found running around the palace in yoga pants and tshirts, and sometimes jeans. As my wedding present, Ben and Druan had surprised me by making the most epic Target run of all time, traveling to the human realm to collect all my favorite things. I had enough comfortable human clothes to last a lifetime, along with a supply of gummy bears, and Diet Dr. Pepper. How they'd managed to bring it all back while navigating the bridge was beyond me. I made them swear never to take such a risk again.

"It's strange not having Mother or Astrid or even Leda with me on such an auspicious occasion. It's like flying solo for the first time all over again." Nerves swarmed inside me like a storm of angry bees. Today I would ascend to High Queen of the Nine Realms. In theory, I was as prepared as I could possibly be. In reality, I didn't think I was emotionally mature enough to get through this day without embarrassing myself.

"That's why we are here." Druan squeezed my hand. "You will never be alone in this, Thea."

As the carriage rolled to a stop, I took a deep breath. Sylvi and Druan exited first, standing on either side of the door. Druan took my hand as I attempted to navigate my exit from the small space wearing the contents of an entire fabric store. Grateful for my new husband's assistance, I managed to get my feet on the ground without incident. As I made my way along the cobblestone pathway through the forest, Sylvi arranged the massive train of my dress to flow behind me. I walked ahead of my council, my wings fanned out in all their glory. I gazed up at the tall trees creating a canopy over the ancient ruins of Asgard. A shiver ran down my spine at the thought of where I stood now. This was the hallowed ground of the gods. The same gods who found a way for their people to survive when all the prophecies foretold the demise of all at the final battle of Ragnarök. By ceding his power to the first Valkyrie queen, the Allfather gave us all a second chance, and a new world was born on the ashes of the old one.

It was now my duty to lead our people into a new era of ascension. I was the first of the new nine. The other young rulers would follow in the coming years.

And it all began, right here today. Though I had high hopes my new sister, Vendela would join me soon. But now it was time to meet the aging rulers who faced the twilight of their reign. Some, like my mother, approached their final years with dignity and grace, while others clung to their thrones with desperation, like my father. Today was for them. I would not speak until the end of the ceremony, yet they would have the chance to speak to me without fear of my response.

At the end of the path, I paused to take it all in. The forest floor was covered in a thousand shades of green moss, like the softest carpet under my feet. Castle ruins lay scattered around the ancient throne room and the crumbling walls of Asgard largely remained in haphazard sections encircling the forest. I could only imagine how spectacular the hall of the gods must have been once.

Eight thrones rose from the ground, built from the very ruins of Asgard millennia ago. Hundreds of queens and kings had sat on these thrones through the ages. At the opposite end of the throne room stood a raised dais for the High Queen's throne—said to have been built from the remains of the Allfather's throne. I made my way there now, walking along the aisle between the rows of thrones, four on each side. As I passed each ruler and their advisors standing behind them, they bowed, murmuring their greetings.

"Welcome, your Majesty," Queen Orlagh of the Druids—and my husband's aunt—was the first to speak above a whisper. "I bid you congratulations on your happy union with my nephew.

"Greetings." Queen Elva of the Jötnar gave a nod of respect. Small for a Jötnar, she still towered over the rest of us, but she had kind eyes that reflected a desire for me to succeed today.

"Child queen." King Ulric of the Warders had no kindness for me, though I expected none. "You have robbed me of a daughter. It is good that I have many sons, though they are all bastards unfit to carry my name. Perhaps I will just live forever and keep my throne."

I walked on, not acknowledging his grievances. There would be time for that later. My steps faltered as I approached my father, King Hagen. Mother was convinced he would send his brother in his stead as he normally did. Hagen had very little to do with matters of state within his realm.

"Your mother has robbed me of a son." My father turned red-rimmed eyes on me. "All the realms are talking about the son she kept from me." Spittle flew from his mouth as I passed. "The son who will ascend in my place!"

My eyes burned and my throat seized, but I refused to acknowledge his words. My unshed tears weren't because my father showed no interest in me. I knew the man my mother loved was no longer there, lost to the Berserker madness. My emotions were for the man I would never get to know.

I hardly heard the greetings of the kings and queens of the Southern Kingdoms. I just kept walking until there was nowhere left to go.

Standing before my throne, I took the final step, allowing Sylvi to arrange my train behind me. I took Druan's hand as I ascended the steps up to the dais and turned to face my subjects. Beside my throne sat the crown my mother once wore.

The crown I wore now was that of the Valkyrie queen. But today, I became much more. Removing my winged crown and setting it on the empty pedestal beside me, I lifted the High Queen's crown over my head. The simple band of silver and diamonds sparkled in the sunlight as I lowered it onto my head. Taking up my scepter, I sat, gazing at each of the rulers before me.

"I am Alithea Viktory Skuld Ahlstrom, Queen of the Valkyries, High Queen of the Nine Realms, and I have become."

I hope you have enjoyed Alithea's story, but we are just getting started. Vendela will begin her ascension in The Rejected Queen: Berserker" Ascension of the Nine Realms Book 2. **Visit your favorite retailer to purchase your copy**

But in the meantime, who's up for more Druan? The Chosen Sons is FREE and exclusive to Subscribers. Visit Melissaacraven.com to sign up and be among the first to read all about Druan's time among the Chosen Sons.

WHAT'S NEXT?

Ascension of the Nine Realms continues with Vendela as she returns to the human in realm in search of vital information that just might put her on the Berserker throne--that is if her people could ever accept a Rejected Queen.

(Familiar fan favorites will return to help Vendela on her journey--including a very quiet dragon and her not-so quiet Valkyrie love interest.)

Order your copy from your favorite retailer

The Rejected Queen is the second book in a brand new series by award winning author, Melissa A. Craven. Fans of her Queens of the Fae series will fall in love with this new world deeply rooted in Norse Mythology as you've never seen before! Don't miss the opportunity to dive into this reimagining of Asgard in a post-Ragnarok world where the gods are all gone and the Berserkers are led by the King of Madmen.

ALSO BY MELISSA

Visit Books2Read.com to see all of Melissa's books

Ascension of the Nine Realms

The Chosen Sons (Prequel)

The Reluctant Queen (Valkyrie: Book 1)

The Rejected Queen (Berserker: Book 2)

The Rebel Queen (Druid: Book 3)

The Ruthless Queen (Warder: Book 4)

Immortals of Indriell Series:

Emerge (Book 1) | **Edge (Book 0)** | **Judgment** (Book 2) | **Scholar** (Illustrated Character Journal) | **Catalyst** (Short Story) | **Volunteer** (Short Story) | **Captive** (Book 3) | **Assignment**: Novella | **Heir** (Book 4) | **Betrayal** (Book 5) | **Runaway** (Book 6) | **Proving** (Book 7)

Queens of the Fae Series:

Fae's Dilemma (Prequel Novella) | **Fae's Deception** (Book 1) | **Fae's Defiance** (Book 2) | **Fae's Destruction** (Book 3) | **Fae's Prisoner** (Book 4) | **Fae's Power** (Book 5) | **Fae's Promise** (Book 6) | **Fae's Rebellion** (Book 7) | **Fae's Refuge** (Book 8) | **Fae's Return** (Book 9) | **Fae's Enemy** (Book 10) | **Fae's Envoy** (Book 11) | **Fae's End** (Book 12)

ABOUT THE AUTHOR

Melissa A. Craven (the "A" stands for Ann—in case you were wondering) writes across the spectrum in a variety of Fantasy sub-genres with crossover appeal to audiences of all ages. She believes in stories that make you think and she loves twisty plots, and playing with foreshadowing, leaving clues and hints for the careful reader. She draws inspiration from her background in architecture and interior design to help her with the small details in world building and scene settings.

Come join the fun at **Fantasy Book Warriors on Facebook** to connect with me and other readers. We talk about books, fangirl over favorite new reads and get up to all sorts of shenanigans.

I appreciate your help in spreading the word about the Ascension of the Nine Realms series—including telling a friend! Reviews help readers find great books and if you loved The Reluctant Queen, head on over to your favorite retailer, Goodreads or BookBub to leave a quick review.

- facebook.com/MelissaACravenAuthor
- instagram.com/melissaacraven
- bookbub.com/authors/melissa-a-craven
- amazon.com/Melissa-A-Craven/e/B00VSPF86W
- tiktok.com/@ataleoftwoauthors?

A FREE BOOK FROM MELISSA

A competition he doesn't want to win
A miserable fortress far away from home
A Princess he despises

Selected at the age of two to compete for the hand of the Queen Heir of Valsgard, Druan's life has never been his own.

Among dozens of boys vying for the honor to become the future consort to a spoiled princess, he alone secretly despises the girl who stole his choices from him.

But with a headmaster convinced Druan will be the last one standing, and a system designed to force him not to lose, how can he evade the life he doesn't want among a matriarchal society that will see him as nothing more than a means to strengthen the line of succession?

Sign up at melissaacraven.com to get your FREE copy!

www.ingramcontent.com/pod-product-compliance
Lightning Source LLC
Chambersburg PA
CBHW020247030826
48979CB00030B/2641/J

* 9 7 8 1 9 7 0 0 5 2 2 3 7 *